TROMPE L'OEIL

Trompe L'Oeil
A novel
Is published by
Shiptree Publications - Honolulu, Hawaii 96822 USA

McKay; Gardner
Trompe L'Oeil: A novel
Shiptree Publications, ©2015
ISBN:978-0-692-20740-6

First Edition published October 2015
Printed in the United States of America

TROMPE L'OEIL

A novel

Gardner McKay

Shiptree Publications / Hawaii ©2015

Other works by Gardner McKay

Memoir
Journey Without a Map

Novels
Toyer: A Novel of Suspense
The Kinsman

Novella
Ten, Bloomsbury Square

Short Stories
"The Fortunes of Schlomo Khabout"
"One Summer in Charente"
"Into the Rose Garden"
"In Another Lifetime"

Stage Plays
Toyer
Sea Marks
Masters of the Sea
Untold Damage
In Order of Appearance

Teleplays
Untold Damage
Sea Marks

Near the snow, near the sun, in the highest fields
See how these names are fêted by the waving grass,
And by the streamers of white cloud,
And whispers of wind in the listening sky;
The names of those who in their lives fought for life,
Who wore at their hearts the fire's centre.
Born of the sun they travelled a short while towards
the sun
And left the vivid air signed with their honour.

Sir Stephen Spender

I have been so great a lover

Rupert Brooke

Preface

Chapter 1
Salve de Dios: Canary Islands, May 5, 2001

Chapter 2
The First Journal
New York City: John Jay Street,

Chapter 3
New York City: 72 John Jay Street

Chapter 4
Salve de Dios: Canary Islands May 6, 2001

Chapter 5
The Second Journal
New York City: John Jay Street

Chapter 6
Canary Islands: Salve De Dios, May 7, 2001

Chapter 7
The Third Journal
Flight One: New York - Paris

Acknowledgement

About the Author

Preface

꩜

First, you should know that a trompe l'oeil is a deception in art, specifically in painting, when an object is rendered so truly that you reach your hand out to touch it. Or a scene you might be seduced into entering. But a trompe l'oeil is only a trick of the eye.

What follows is a love story. It is the story of an artist who is quite mad, who refuses to accept that the woman he loves has been killed, an artist who has the power to do something about it. So it is a love story with miracles.

The artist's name is Simon Lister. Have you heard of him? Not long ago he was the most important painter in the world ...

CHAPTER 1

Salve de Dios: Canary Islands–May 5, 2001

༄ঌ

He hasn't spoken since I got off the steamer this afternoon. To me, to anyone. Now it's early evening. He's sitting in his good chair in the front room, staring out the open window toward the sun. It is low, an inch above the Atlantic, glinting furiously.

It's a house like any other on this island—small, three or four rooms enclosed in whitewashed stone, board shutters painted a hard boat green. I haven't seen a house here that isn't painted white with dark green shutters. Everything on this island seems to be made of stone. Outside the front door is a stone courtyard sheltered from the wind, an iron gate to hold in a dog, but I've seen no dog.

I'll wait, I don't mind. I've been waiting for a year. The woman tells me he knows I'm here. The woman, his cook, beckoned me into the house. She told him I was here. I saw him nod: he didn't speak, didn't turn his head. She didn't ask my name.

Eventually, I sit on a wooden chair leaning against the wall of the kitchen, watching her cook tomatoes and potatoes. She is wizened, not tall, with a long, man's face. She speaks to me in a loud choppy voice, as if she were angry at me. It is as if she had not spoken to an outsider for years. I don't understand what she says.

Through the doorway I can see the back of his head. Out the window, the horizon beyond. The sea is high today, a strong blue-green with some chop to it. I saw three boats wallowing in at Teguise while I was walking up here. They were pitching badly, foaming along, but I could see they had managed to catch fish and were rolling home, flags blowing.

From the kitchen I can see into his room. Not a large room, it seems to have just been painted with thick, white paint—deep cuts through its stone walls for windows, two doors painted the same tough, dark green as the shutters. A bureau, a dining table, three chairs, all plain, all without paint, all cut from the same wood—ash— maybe from Spain. Few trees grow here, mostly olive and scrubs. The chairs have woven string seats of hemp, except the fourth chair, the good one he's sitting in. That one has arms and a cushion. No pictures on the walls, not a framed photograph in sight. A man has aged in this room, I can feel his aging from the years of his exile. He still looks good. The remarkable head-bone, too large? Hair mostly gone, the clever eyes that someone once wrote "stared at you far too long." They're hardly seen now, defined by oriental hoods, webs of lines.

He wears Spanish shoes, canvas with rope soles, a white shapeless linen tunic and trousers. I am barely able to recognize him from a photograph I brought with me. In it, he is wearing a dinner jacket at a gala ball, standing halfway down a shining staircase. There is a beauti- fully gowned, dark-haired woman on his arm—Angelique, his wife.

Salvo De Dios is a Spanish Island maybe a hundred miles west of Africa, twenty-five miles long, pocked with a hundred craters of dead volcanoes. I have come here overnight on the steamer, *Ave Maria*, out of Cadiz, on its weekly tour of the islands, bringing mail and passengers, wine, lumber, cheese. There is still no airport here.

This is the terminus he must have brought her to years ago. This might have been the house they found when they came here.

The woman wakes me. I have dozed off, still seated on the wooden chair leaning against the kitchen wall. I smell cooking fish and wine and maybe garlic. She points. I move to the doorway to the other room waiting to be noticed.

Here I am, a man standing in a plain room—stone walls painted white, lit by the sun setting across the ocean. I have never been here before. I am facing a man I have been aware of most of my life. The sun is so bright behind him, I cannot see his features, only a black silhouette. He takes a sip of his drink. The sun through his glass is fool's gold.

His voice has rusted, but it is friendly, low, unused. Maybe this is the first time he has spoken today. He is still looking away, out the window.

"Rum's not as strong as it could be. You need to drink twice as much."

He's speaking to me about rum. I wet my lips, I want some.

"If you don't like the rum here you must bring whiskey or French Marc from the mainland. This rum is up from Grand Canaria, honey rum, you can drink from the bottom. It's so sweet you must crush a lime in it, if you have a lime. I can't grow 'em here, I've tried, they won't take a hold. It's this volcanic soil. It's like gravel. This lime's from Tenerife. Go ask the woman for a block of ice if you require it, but she'll have to walk down the road to get it."

He doesn't wait for my answer. Maybe he's trying to make me feel at ease but it's not working. I'm as nervous as I was when I walked in the door two hours ago.

"The word for ice is *hielo*."

He pushes himself up and goes to the window; there is no pane of glass in the opening and there never was. You close the shutters to keep the weather out. The sun is setting flamboyantly. The ocean has joined it. He swirls the rum in the thick tumbler. Its glass has gone white from use. He tips the tumbler toward the sun, toasts it, *"Gracias, por un otro dia."* He's thanking it for another day. He seems to be taking a private moment with the sun. He drinks, then he says, staring the sun down, "Fuck you, Señor." He sits in his chair.

I haven't moved from the doorway. I'd kill for a drink of that rum. The woman bends close to him. He listens, nods. She carries a chair from the wall and puts it at the table. She sets another place. A large spoon, fork and knife clatter onto the table, another heavy glass, another white napkin. There will be two for dinner tonight. She beckons me. I am to sit down to supper with him. Finally, he pours three or four ounces of *Ron Miel* rum into my tumbler. He nods. I reach forward and pick it up. At last. I sip then drink. It is unlike any drink I've ever tasted. It is perfect, full, strong, and somehow beneficial.

"The woman is cooking *mero*. She tells me there's enough for two. She must like you."

How could anyone tell? He sips. I finish my drink. He nods to the bottle. I pour myself another few ounces.

I am standing in front of him.

"Smell it? I love that smell! That's a fish you don't know. You can catch it over there, right off Punto Negro, even on windy days, and if the woman can get it, she'll cook it for me once-a-week the same way, a recipe from the 1600's, with the garlic we grow here, cut into slices and spread over it. Green olive oil from the few local groves. It's an old recipe. *Mero's* tough as an old catfish. There's something to it. It doesn't melt in your mouth. Nothing ought to melt in your mouth except butter. But she can't always get *mero*. She brought *tomates* and *cebollas* today—that's three plants that do well here, besides cactus and potatoes and grapes. They get their growing done at night, when the land stores water. Volcanic soil. Grainy. So. We'll have tomatoes, potatoes, onions with olive oil. Everything you'll eat here comes from near this house, land or sea. And a bottle of wine that's rich as port from the Benedictine Monastery up the road."

I am still standing in front of him holding my glass. The room is filled with cooking, its crude smells, elegant, experienced odors, powerful arrangements of aged recipes, fiery smells coming from the other room, the hot room. He changes chairs and sits at the table.

"Sit," he says.

I do.

The woman enters carrying an oval china platter, the *mero* split wide-open like a book, cooked honey brown, dark garlic and small leaves clinging to it. The fish is ringed with potatoes wrinkled as prunes, crystallized flecks of sea salt on them and tiny tomatoes blackened by olive oil. I didn't realize I was hungry. She brings a lantern over and puts it on the table.

She speaks to me loudly. Everything she says is too loud, as if we were standing upwind. It is all she can do.

"I can't understand what she's saying," I say.

"No one can. They speak a wild Spanish here, it sounds like they're chopping wood doesn't it? She's probably telling you that she grows these potatoes and tomatoes herself."

He presents her to me, *"La Señora Natti."* She glares at me and smiles, she has dog teeth.

"Gracias, Señora," I half rise and nod.

"You're well brought up," he says to me. But he hasn't asked my name or introduced himself. I can understand why it is of no interest to him. We take up our silver; slowly he begins eating. He savors the tastes prolonging the small ecstasy.

The wine from the Monastery is good, I feel it surge through me with the rum, it is thick and black, there is a fiery cat's eye in it, a ruby ghost. I am too excited to eat, I watch him. He eats with his head down, using his fork and his fingers, like a child.

Somebody has finally found him.

He doesn't ask me why I came looking for him, or what I intend to do with what I know. Or how I was able to do it when no one else could. Maybe he's tired, maybe he's through caring. He has accepted my presence. He might even respect what I've done, who knows? He must realize how difficult it was for me, but he doesn't seem to care how I did it. I'm not sure why he has chosen to trust me. But the honor doesn't escape me.

He breaks the silence. He asks where I am staying. I tell him the family name of a house on the road, half a mile down the hill, between his house and the water. He pours me another glass of wine. I eat. The fish is succulent.

Out the window, the island is black now, the sea is gone. There are no lights on the north end of Salve de Dios. He says it is because there is no electricity. We eat well. The food is gone, all of it. Our plates are clean. When the woman has cleared the table and closed the door to the kitchen, when we have finished the bottle of *Ron Miel* rum and the wine, he asks without surprise how I did it.

"It took a while," I say. He stares at me too long.

I tell him about the sketch book that he left behind at the Eisenstein Institute after his escape. Does he remember a sketch book?

He shakes his head. His breakdown had been complete, severe.

I describe it—a black book, four by six inches, full of pencil sketches—the only work of his that still remains. For years it has been in the permanent collection of the Whitney. No one ever understood them. One small sketch especially fascinated me, an abstraction. I kept coming back to it. Then I knew. By chance I discovered that it was a sketch of a chain of islands—map of the Canaries.

For the first time, he smiles. His teeth are gray.

"You were guessing."

"No I wasn't."

"The hell you weren't."

I bring out a photocopy the size of a post card. He smooths it out on the table under the lantern. "It's true," he says. He is amazed.

10

"I never knew we were coming here."

I ask him if anyone here realizes who he is.

"No one. They've never known that. They were suspicious of something about me for years. There was gossip. The Spanish need mystery and they can be a grueling people. Anyhow, I contribute to the Benedictine Monastery here."

He nods to the north and taps the empty bottle with his fork. "There's no one else left to give a damn, not around here. About who I was or wasn't." Then, each word pronounced, still surprised, he adds, "Some on the island actually thought I killed her."

"Her?"

"Savoia," he says quickly. "That was the name she wanted me to call her. It was her middle name."

The silence nags me again. After a while, he asks if I would want to look at one of his journals. He asks it very simply, as if I might refuse. Would I like to take a journal book back to my room tonight and try to read it before I fall asleep? It might amuse me, he says, smiling grayly. Oh, yes. I catch my breath, I never imagined the existence of diaries.

"Yes."

He strikes a match on the stone floor and lights a lamp and leads me into a small room off the kitchen. Under a table is a metal trunk with square corners, two latches. The trunk is black. Wherever the paint has chipped away, the metal is rusted. On the lid is painted "S. LASKER" with a fat brush in white paint. Rust has stuck the lid shut. With a table knife he pries it open. A waft of stale air fills the space around us. Inside are several journals of different sizes and shapes, each labeled, inscribed in ink—months and years. Each is tied shut with a random piece of string. They are all similar, cheaply bound books of various colors, surrounded by small black nuggets of volcanic gravel which, he explains, absorb moisture.

"Choose one," he says.

I do. I choose the earliest, written the month he escaped from the Eisenstein Psychiatric Institute. I lift it out. It is the thickest of the lot, maybe a hundred pages.

"I haven't looked at these since I wrote 'em," he explains.

The book is worn. I untie the string. The paper binding is shot and it opens stiffly, releasing a pleasant staleness. Glancing inside, I can see the handwriting is fine, small, an artist's hand, the words written quickly, maybe in various degrees of emotion—fear, happiness, pain. The words are slightly smeared. The pages might once have been damp and the book closed a long time ago. At the top of the first page is written "72 John Jay Street," the address of the rooming house on the lower East side of Manhattan where he hid for two-and-a-half weeks in a fifth floor room.

I carry it back to my room down the hill, down the unpaved road in the dark, hurrying. I slip on the volcanic gravel. I undress and crawl into bed. My bed is too small but I don't mind; it is chilly tonight and I will ask for a blanket tomorrow. I light two candles.

Chapter 2

The First Journal
New York City: 72 John Jay Street

ఞఞ

In the morning a rooster wakes me. The candles have long since burned away. I smell the mustiness of the journal. My hands are curled around it like a chimpanzee's. I re-read it before I get out of bed, waiting for the sun to enter my window and warm my room. Through his words I feel the pain of his affliction.

December 25, 1963

The lean-boned black kid was spellbinding last night riding the subway, the BMT—a flautist blowing the Shepherd's Baïlèro from Songs of the Auvergne through his silver flute, his wide, hollow notes, wavering breath-long notes, just a quaver, leaning against the subway doors, swaying, twisting his knees against the jerk of the tracks. God, what womanly tones! Their sweetness puts me above the city as the roaring train yanked us along below the East River, its black silt all around us. He put me in the fields above the lowlands. His balanced breath held the final note as we pulled into Canal Street and jolted. He nearly fell. My stop. Moved to tears, I couldn't move. I caught the flautist's eyes, mean mugger's eyes. He saw my tears, smiled a filthy smile, winked a dreadful wink. It was contempt, the bastard, he'd seen what he had done to me, tricked me with his skill. For a couple of seconds I couldn't stand. I grabbed for the door, stuffed a bill into his leather cup, just a bill, a five, a one, a fifty. I didn't look, I hope it was a twenty, he was that good. I always pay. I smelled his stink even in that wee-wee train. But oh what a way he earns his living! That's what I'd like to be doing; playing flute on trains. Not a bad life, a good living maybe. Why not? Someone is bound to spot me, not a talent scout. I must not travel on these subways at night, pretty soon a passenger will figure out it's me sitting beside him, Simon Lister.

I cry easily now. If certain people lean too close to me I get light-headed. I shake. I can't stop. If they talk too loud, too close, if I see people arguing, I shake, too. I even faint. I float. I'm trying not to shake, to stay calm, not to let people see me cry. Also, I shouldn't move my head too quickly or turn around fast. I fall down so naturally. I'm not talking yet. Mutus dysfunction, psychosomatic speech loss, like a super-stammer. No problem, I'll be alright. Won't I? ...

So begins the story of Simon Lister's last days as they were known before his infamous disappearance, following his escape from the Eisenstein Institute. He left no clue behind to indicate that he was ever at the rooming house on John Jay Street, or who he was. The most influential painter of his time, of any time, by then a wanted felon.

His landlady at that time, Mrs. Connors, claimed she remembered him when I found her in a nursing home some thirty years later. All she could tell me was that he paid his rent in advance and was very generous. Dr. Ellie Smilowitz, the attractive therapist who had treated him at the Eisenstein, told reporters that her patient was unable to speak, that he was psychosomatically mute. When she was told his real name, she was astonished. But she was not astonished to learn that he had just committed what the newspapers called, "The Art Crime of the Century," the day after his escape. One reporter wrote that she seemed to smile at the thought.

I love the way he writes. His style! He writes in painter's descriptions, reminding me of Van Gogh's letters to his brother Theo, when he had gone so exquisitely insane that he could paint those wondrous images. Simon and Van Gogh shared that madness. All that was ever known of the doomed, Dutch artist is contained in his letters to Theo. When Simon wrote this journal he was already on his way to becoming one of the great enigmas of our time. But I will let him tell you his story in his own words.

... I know I haven't come to this neighborhood by mistake. I'm sure of that. Was I drawn here, the Neverland south of Little Italy, and Chinatown? I've come here to pause, to find out what's right, to see if I exist.

My room, not wide. I pace it off. Seven by ten. Top floor front, sixty-two steps above John Jay Street. My window looks down across the street, a loud room daytimes. Intimate, deafening. Everything I have is close here. I like the scale. There's a breed of plant that can flourish in mortuaries and rooms like mine. A George Orwell plant, an aspidistra maybe. A veneered armoire with its miniature bent hangers. Mummy yellow walls, stains long established. A double bed, slung like a hammock from a leaning headboard, grainy chalk-white sheets, barracks blanket, a pillow filled with foam rubber popcorn. When it's squeezed, dust, the breath of sad heads, rises. A forty-watt bulb hangs inside an amber-yellow shade strung from the middle of the ceiling. Another light, a twenty-five watt bulb, sticks out over the sink. My room is small. The sink, the bureau, the veneered armoire, the bed. There is only the bed with its leaning headboard. Van Gogh's last room. That's where I'm writing this journal, on the bed, by the sink. The light's close to the bed. Everything is close to the bed.

It's okay that I live like a rodent in this grotto, not forever. It's got the same rising drafts that my vast East Village loft had, but here sourceless, trans-alpine winds blow with bad will along the floor, across the ceiling under the door, through the window, maybe even through the walls, every morning. There's no defense, it chills me deeply. I shudder in my blanket. I shouldn't have ridden on the subway last night. Any cop with a jolt of caffeine in him could have seen something was wrong with me and detained me long enough to find out what it was and who I am. Any alert cop.

Last year, when I burned all my paintings in my studio loft, I stood them together against the open windows and opened the skylights so that the smoke would be drawn up and out into the blend. Several large fire extinguishers, unused, were found standing around the black rubble like so many short blackened firemen. They asked me about them. The work I burned was my final sixteen months of painting on a linear, day-night, day-night schedule without hours or dates. No one had seen my work except a person I brought up there many times from the neighborhood, a waitress with a coffee pot who didn't know who I was but said that she found my Christlike looks haunting. She could not describe my pictures. When she finally came forward in utter secrecy, named in the newspapers as a friend of the painter, she used the words "wild" and "irresistible" to describe my paintings. She swore there was nothing between us except sympathy and she was left speechless when she was told that I was the most important painter alive, a recluse who has almost never let himself be photographed.

I left two small paintings, not mine, unburned, and hanging at the opposite end of my studio. Brilliant, sparking scenes, painted in a forgotten Krakow, alive in its final spring or summer. An eerie foreboding era, densely painted by Eli Mandel, an artist who never amounted to anything because his career was closed down at the age of nineteen in Treblinka. A gassed Jew, Eli Mandel's future had always haunted me. His future works were incinerated with his body. He inspired me. His unpainted works, the unknown longevity of his career. He would be middle-aged now. He makes me ashamed. Should you in incinerate paintings, or should you incinerate artists? I chose to incinerate my paintings. I'm sure that Anasor realizes what I did. Anasor of the Anasor Art Galleries. He discovered my hidden wall safe, disguised as a speaker. When a safe cracker cracked the combination, he found it empty. I'd left several enticing markers for packets of hundreds of thousand dollar bills to be found among the debris. Not one of the investigators estimated the amount that the safe had held. That night I stuffed my fortune in paper money in plastic bags and buried them in Central Park, not far from the Zoo. I know exactly where.

Anasor tried to have me picked up. An all points bulletin was issued for me, a warrant for suspected arson, and minor damage to the building. Without recognizing the good in the two small surviving paintings Anasor gave them to Angelica who passed them back to him to see what he could sell them for. After he examined them, of course, he found Eli Mendel's work to be strong, intriguing, but having never heard of the artist, a man of no reputation (there being no body of work that he knew of) the paintings were of no interest to Anasor, and worth only face value. Isolated greatness cannot be recognized, so no matter how great a painting is, there's no room for its survival in the art gallery world with only a name signed in a cursive, childlike scrawl But Anasor had bigger plans. For two years he and Angelica had been going through the ordeal of assembling all my work from museums and collections around the world, for a complete retrospective show at the Whitney Museum in the fall ...

December 26, 1963

Here I am, this morning, in deep seclusion, making my head out of coffee and a Kaiser roll, sweet butter, and last night's flute music. Outside my window, would that be the sky? Didn't I see that gray bag of light yesterday? Yesterday, I gave my warm scarf away by mistake! Horrible! Jesus, I didn't mean to, it was in the carton of my paperback books for Mrs. Connors, Landlady of Doubt. I keep giving my possessions away, whatever's admired, mostly to Mrs. Connors to keep her at a distance. Yes, maybe so. Mrs. Connors acts sullen around me. She's sure I've done something, that I've come from a bad source, "on the lam" as she would probably say. She suspects armed robbery in New Jersey. Or maybe a more personal crime, strangling a woman. She'd prefer that. She never looks at me. I found my mattress turned when I got back. She imagines suspicions. She'll never ask me. Maybe she needs me to be on the lam. Everything is maybe.

I pack what I brought. I pack every morning because I like to keep my hands working. It is my project. I own a luxe Italian bag, soft, a rich person's valise—a gift from Angelique. But I am a rich person. When I fill it, I close it, then I shave or read, then I open it and dump its contents on the bed. I refold my shirts and pants and underwear and put them back into the dresser drawers. In all, it takes me an hour. I don't use the top drawer of the dresser. I keep that drawer turned upside down and slide it out when I want to use it as a desk. Maybe I pack more than once a morning. It depends. It doesn't seem to get to me. It doesn't make me "nervous and upset."

I'm looking out at a cat in a window across the street. I'm waiting for him to turn around and look at me. If he looks at me I'll ride the subway again tonight. His decision. I wait. He does. That decides it: I'll ride the BMT tonight, look for my dark flautist.

The subway station is 186 paces—out the front door, left on John Jay Street, around the corner and down Henry Street. Or 220 paces—right to the corner and up Canal Street. Most nights I kneel by my bed and pray. Why not? I haven't done it since I was six or eight. It's diverting to look for the good in your life. The wind howling along the floor chills my feet and my bed feels better than it should. I ball up with my feet under my ass. I thank God or the responsible party that I am not in pain. At least I have that. Pain is an extended family. The sort of pain where suicide looks like two weeks in the country, that's the sort of pain I fear—the intractable pain of never coming back, where you say, "I want to get out of here!" I can use a little pain. There are so many nearby in pain.

I have an amazing history and a blank future. This room is my present tense. If I'm discovered here, I will get taken away. Arrested. It is all very formal. They will be polite. I didn't kill anyone. But once in jail, after a week or two, I will die. I'm trying to hang on now by writing down everything that happens on the advice of my therapist. A cure for my psychosis as a receptacle of the confusion swirling around me.

December 27, 1963

This morning the Croatian housekeeper, Astrida, bumptious, rock-solid, brings me coffee so dark it stains the cup and made me brush my teeth again. I point to my wrist, she holds up eight fingers: eight o'clock. Mrs. Connors has told me Astrida is not meant to bring me food. It is certainly not included in the weekly rent I pay. And no visitors. She believes she's being nice to me, but she no longer can, she's lost the ability. She wants to know more about me. So I give her things. Protection money. I pretend that I'm not well acquainted with money and give her fifty dollar advances for a week of coffees, which Astrida brings up on a cafeteria tray with a glass of orange colored fluid, air-dried white toast, margarine, kippers, herrings or sardines or sausage. Astrida has no English. Up she comes, seventy-two steps from the kitchen below street level, wide-faced, voluptuous, smiling vivaciously—a cheery pantomime. "Hot today hot hot hot!" By hot she means that although we can still see our breaths in my room, there's a fighting sun out there behind the shades and we'll probably live through the morning. It's a long climb up from the kitchen, but she's happy to be in America and out of Croatia. She knows I can't speak her language anyway. Then there's the crying business, my sudden bursts, my breakdowns, which she saw yesterday and I hope never sees again. I try not to let anyone see that. I don't want to lose the rest of my marbles—my little bag feels almost empty. I don't want her to tell Mrs. Connors and then get sent to Bellevue, et cetera. My fingerprints are on record, an old vagrancy bust—sleeping in the park.

The old guy on the ground floor caught me sneaking past his room this afternoon. His door flew open. His hair announced him as Gallic with miracle roots. Mrs. Connors told him I can't speak and to keep an eye on me. I wrote my name on my pad. He told me his name as if he were talking to a dog, hitting the "eece" on Maurice. He's not a "Morris." What a beautiful eyesore Maureece is. A stocky man, blunt, his mane dyed black with deep Stradivarius reds. Nose like a Macaw, squirrel-tail eyebrows. Map-like stains on his forehead, from what? Lips of an aged cherub. Maybe he'll allow me to draw his head.

"What is it you do, sir?" He wants to know details, he doesn't want hallway chitchat from me. Not Maurice. Accuracy. He's defending the halls of his rooming house against me and my sort, worried by my presence in the building.

"I noticed you like to keep irregular hours, sir." His quote unquote sir is New York standard suspicion. He probably knows the step of everyone who walks past his door, who enters and leaves the building but he doesn't know mine. I'm new here, I'm quiet, I wear tennis shoes. He can't hear me pass. He only senses me passing. It worries him.

"What is it you do, sir?"

I can't remember the last time anyone's asked me what I "do."

Do? People have always known. It's new, it feels free not know-ing, like not having a country. I write the word ARTIST on my pocket pad. To Maurice, it is the definition of a bum. He glances up, dubious. If I'm an artist. why am I mute? He doubts everything, wonders if anything's true about me. His sour New York instincts are right. He craves specifics. He wonders if my name is really "Jonathan Boot." it isn't of course, I wrote that on my pad for Mrs. Connors when I paid three weeks' rent in ad-vance.

Maurice needs to know my plans. I write, WHEN I KNOW I'LL TELL YOU. Big, in block letters. Maurice doesn't smile.

"Why are you growing a beard?" he asks.

I write, "WARMTH." Maurice doesn't like that either.

December 28, 1963

For some reason, Maurice thinks I am able to speak but don't want to. He's trying to nail down something about me to tell Mrs. Connors. I can't see what else he's got to do. He doesn't work; he's Chairman of The House, probably gets a break on the rent. I truly wish I could speak.

New York's problems exhaust me. Being a New Yorker is tough work. I don't walk too well. Can't stand straight. Need to lie down, sit. Tremble more than I'd like to at certain sounds. Certain voices. Voices up from the street, up the stairs from the rooms below me. Not hanging on well here. Nothing to do.

Can't talk, can't read, don't want to draw. No radio. Being discovered here is a matter of days. The old guy downstairs doesn't know it but he's on the verge. Wait'll he finds out about the reward. This time it wouldn't mean the Eisenstein, it would mean the criminal courts, the system, incarceration without bail. I've got to get away from him. But moving now would be a huge risk. If I only knew one woman who could take me in, even a whore. A whore with a heart of gold. They must exist. Better than incarceration.

Last night I killed Maurice in my dream. Just did him in with a pillow. This morning he startled me. He cut me off as I came back in from the delicatessen with my baguette and Swiss cheese and led me into his ground-floor room. Quite a room—the original living room, maybe the best room in the house. A plaster rococo tit jutting down from the high ceiling, waiting for its long-gone chandelier to return to its nipple. In 1880 this house must have belonged to an upper-middle class family. My room was probably the groom's. Taped newspaper clippings hang from the painted-over mantel of Maurice's blocked-up fireplace. Clippings still newsworthy to Maurice. I see two aged, musty television sets, one standing on the other. He is hoping to live until baseball season next spring, still months away.

While he is interrogating me, sitting with his back to me. He's pretty arrogant, talking to his walls instead of to me. I write answers to his questions and pass them over his shoulder while he watches morning conversations on television talk shows, apparently, better conversations than I could provide. Comments on personal health made by personalities. Absurd professional people like those who once stood in front of me at the art gallery holding their drinks, telling me about themselves, how they "did it their way," making me tingle with embarrassment for them. I befriend Maurice to nullify him. There are so many ways to kill him.

On the line of clippings I see it taped to his mantelpiece, the famous headline: ART TRAGEDY OF THE CENTURY. There it is. I can read my name, "Simon Lister." Here's a personality for you, Maurice, siting right behind you. A real tragedian. He'll be delighted to tell you what he eats for breakfast.

The back of his neck is inches away. I can easily kill him. I have strong hands. A simple smothering with a pillow. Hardly knowing what I'm doing and without Maurice seeing me do it, I flatten his morning newspaper out on the table behind him, and on a nearly blank Con Edison ad, I draw a quick sketch of the room. I was carrying a 2B pencil in my pocket. I can't stop my hands from drawing. It takes three or four minutes. I draw the three walls, they meet at the center panel, a triptych. One wall in precise detail, the other two in a psycho-organic style that just happens sometimes, the window nearly centered, asymmetrical. The bones and planes of his room held together by fluid muscle lines. Maurice's vast head of hair in the foreground entranced by the bobbing television heads in my center panel. Maurice turns around during the commercials. He assumes I've been reading his *Daily News*. He sees my sketch. He looks twice. He stares up at me, hiding his surprise by looking angry. "Christ," he said as I leave his room. "You can't speak, that's why you're an artist, am I right?" he asks.

I write on my pad, "No. I'm an artist, that's why I'm poor." It's nonsense but I'm worried. Maurice smiles. His idea of a smile is not to frown. The commercials are over, he turns away. Now I am "Rembrandt"—Maurice's new name for me. But even if I am Rembrandt, that doesn't clear me of crime. I've done something wrong, I'm a fugitive from a felony—maybe murder, robbery, a terrorist bombing, a drug cartel, a chain gang? An outcast. Clever man, maybe, but he wouldn't say that. But it seems to worry him more this morning. Maurice, too, is an outcast, but not from crime. A more sophisticated outcast, an innocent. He's lost. He's lived downstairs too many years, it seems to me, thirty years, no less. He's proud of that, refers to it as if his stagnation meant stability. I write, "When I was a very young boy ..."

"How young?" he interrupts.

"Twenty-three years old. I exhibited at the Grande Palais in Paris. I hung a huge painting of a storm in my eye ball, nine-feet wide. Bold for a first-time exhibitor, that reminded one critic of Turner. I wrote Maurice that Turner was influenced by Rembrandt so that his calling me Rembrandt is not a bad compliment for a compliment. Was that dangerous writing him that? It was involuntary. I couldn't not.

He nods diplomatically, meaning "It's okay, Boot, we all need to exaggerate." He didn't believe me.

It was gracious. His grasp had long since exceeded his reach. He's at a stage in his man's life when it's late to cling, late to discover old beliefs, late to develop new ones. So, it was gracious of him. I should not tell him any more details even though they're true about my life, even though he wouldn't believe me anyway. But it's not going to work out between Maurice and me. When I get my speech back, I feel I'm going to be telling him about the ART TRAGEDY OF THE CENTURY headline taped over his mantel. I know I'm going to tell him that it was me who burned a millions of dollars of paintings. My paintings.

I've got to get out of here.

December 29, 1963

This morning I woke up as usual I make my head out of coffee that Astrida brings me. Indigo black. Also a plate of sardines in olive oil, lemon, cheese, white toast, no butter. She retreats out my door. Astride Astrida? I think not. Not yet.

I decided that I was going outdoors for a long walk. I put on my favorite shirt, brick colored with black-to-red threads, and I tied my thick, black, silk tie—my last, my only tie. My good warm coat is gray with mottled taupe wool and covers my ankles and most of my shoes. I put on my black Astrakhan hat and a scarf across my mouth and nose, hiding my new beard. As I passed Maurice's room, his door opened. He said I looked like a 1917 Cossack cavalryman and asked me in, but for once, I refused. It was to be my first daytime walk since I moved down here almost a week ago. I kept the scarf across my face and went outside. My breath warmed my nose but wet my mouth. I walked east, my destination—the East River, to walk as far as I could, to watch a tugboat pass by towing a barge. The bright air. In the street, the horns and sirens and brakes made me dizzy. I was dreaming. It has been a year since I've walked loose anywhere in the city. The scarf was a disguise but no one in this neighborhood would imagine that Simon Lister would be walking down the market outlet streets in public. I never reached the East River. My walk ended early.

There was the regular, lunatic, midwinter carnival of victims out there waiting for me. Sets of jubilant-eyed street minstrels guided by voices no one else can hear, young and old, uncaring whether the ship sinks, rattling pots and pans. Beggars beset beggars. They demand money. "No," I write on my pad and hold it out again and again. On the way past Wing's Market, I pass pairs of crew-cutted, mega-macho gays wearing Marine Corps mustaches and linesmen's boots. Stronger than anyone. Further on I pass dying old people, mostly bent, creeping out in the safe hours of after-noon, never sure if they'll get back home in time to die. A jovial black man in a scrap coat dangling like seaweed fronted a board painted: "Help me raise $1,000,000,000.50 for research into wain." He spells wine "wain." A busted wino and his joke. I contribute fifty-cents for "lab costs."

Six or eight blocks from John Jay Street, my legs lose their spring, their ability to walk straight. Then into a café, its only name, an outdoor sign: "The Soup Kitchen." The excitement of soup from a simpler time. Steaming scents, immediate comfort, but I barely sit down on a small wooden chair, when I discover the origin of the name—a photograph of its original brick storefront façade, circa 1930, showing a line of despondent men, now long dead, standing out front, some holding pannikins. Inside, on the exposed brick wall near the counter, hangs an assortment of blackened soup ladles, made of aluminum or magnesium. The menu has traveled far from the boiling water bean soup of the 1930's soup lines. More exotic than its history, it now reads: Lobster Bisque, Crab Bisque Alvarez, Provençal Fish Soup with Rouille, and so on. I order Potage a L'Oignion. A moment later I am served a stiff square of white cheese floating above a spoonful of curiously florid hot water cluttered with uncooked pieces of onion. I realize that The Soup Kitchen means "chic," not what the poster says it means. I glanced around at the diners—trendy.

At Mott and Elizabeth Streets a matronly woman leaning against a brick wall stares at me directly and quietly requests, half-a-dollar, no more. Specifically fifty-cents. I give it to her. She reminds me of my mother. Further down Elizabeth Street a bullet-eyed man, maybe a fallen computer executive wearing safari mufti too summery for the freezing afternoon, presses a piece of paper on me: "God Says Please Don't Go To Hell!" One of my parting memories of the Almighty was that He never said "please," that He had no use for courtesy. Do what I say or go to Hell. And I wasn't sure if Hell would be any different than Elizabeth Street. I don't pay. I need to take this walk. My suspected madness and the street madness are no match. I feels saner, my only fear is that one of these explorers from another galaxy will point at me and shriek, "Simon Lister! It's you!" ask for my autograph, then blow the whistle on me and collect the fifty-thousand dollar reward posted by Anasor's Gallery.

Suddenly, the shock of seeing someone I recognize catches me. I knew him. Not his name. This is not uptown. This man is walking toward me. In this part of the city the odds of running into someone I know are small. I'm trapped. For a millisecond. Instinctively, I fall against the brick façade of a hardware store and hold my hat out.

This guy, his name was Mathews, nails me with eye contact. I give him beggar's eyes. He stares back at me. I can't breathe. I'm caught. I crank my head once, push my hat out, blocking his way. With effort Mathews reaches into his pants pocket, then drops some coins into my hat, then moves his eyes past me with city ease. He seems to have recognized me, but doesn't know me. I have to lie down. Four blocks from the river, I come across a tiny, pie-shaped park less than a block long, with plaques hung at either end:

CAPT. PADEWICZ PARK

DEDICATED TO THE PEOPLE OF MANHATTAN

BY THE NEW YORK CITY POLICE DEPARTMENT

I need a place to sit before I fall. There is an empty bench. I walk across the park, I believe I can reach it, the light is dimming in my head, almost out. I reach my chosen bench and drop onto it, rolling my head back in an arc and see dead branches swinging overhead and morphing into glass chips—a pallid kaleidoscope. I open my eyes. On the nearest bench is a homeless man.

At the far end end of the park I see a woman seated on one of the three benches, bundled up in drab woolens, legs wide, her dress forming a hammock between her thighs, low heels planted, toes out. She is tossing pebbles at the pigeons near her. Unusual. Mrs. Capt. Padewicz? It is too cold for recreation, too brittle. My first impression is that she is too pretty to be sitting the way she is sitting and doing what she is doing, too pretty for the neighborhood. I look again at her face; she is not pretty. She is unusual looking, probably fascinating, maybe even glamorous. I close my eyes. When I open them, she is still there, looking toward me. I'm gripped by mindless awe. To me, without staring at her, she seems to have true beauty. I can't say what color her eyes are, but what difference does it make? I feel my throat relax, it begins to untie itself. A minute passes, I feel it open. I watch her. Then I realize I have to speak to her. That I can speak to her. Without trying to make a sound, I feel the possibility of speech returning to me. Words, sentences, talk—the boulder has rolled away from my throat.

She'd been staring straight ahead. She seemed dazed. I have not intercepted her stare. I hold my breath. I will cross the short distance between us and sit by her. I lower my head and put my hands on both sides of the bench, but when I look up, she has gone.

Capt. Padewicz? Who are you? Where are you? Are you buried under the park? Does your widow come here when the leaves bud on the trees? Did you purchase this soiled strip of Manhattan with profits from drug busts and then, in penance, endow it to fête your memory while living out your days on South Bay, Long Island, a power boat docked outside your house? Anyhow, Capt. Padewicz has a park and I don't. Heavily-veined blacktop, three benches, three elm trees, a small crop of grass that has managed to hoist itself above the urine-rich soil to sing the Captain's name. The park is encrusted by the slightest frame of charcoal-black ice. Is that the Captain himself, sleeping over there, stretched out under the financial section on a park bench?

December 30, 1963

Maurice continues to inspect me whenever I come in. He reminds me of a dog with failed eyes. He spends all his time down there forted up on the ground floor in his room, not wanting to believe in anything except baseball and chess. God, I envy him that. I wish something that simple would do it for me. I wish I needed less of life. His wife walked out on him by dying twenty years ago, and his existence has been hung out to dry ever since, along with those newspaper clippings he tapes on his walls. His life is clear to him and, yes, his grasp exceeds his reach by the length of his hand. He saw my picture blink by him on the TV screen today. He didn't know it. He tells me it was some guy on the TV looked something like me.

"You got some imagination," I scribble.

"It was a flash picture," he says, "with a be-oo-tiful woman."

I know the one—I'm in a dinner jacket smiling, clean-shaven. That picture was taken when I used to smile. Now there's no more smile and no more dinner jacket. And regardless of her elegance and breeding, Angelique stole like a whore. She looked like a Greek movie star or an Italian opera diva—she got both comments. She was the society post-debutante who had me committed to the Eisenstein because I half-heartedly stabbed her in our kitchen. She was the one who signed releases for the gallery paintings to be exhibited at the Whitney Museum. She's from Charleston. The paintings would have made her rich—well, richer.

No, Maurice won't connect me to her or the festivities or with the man in the flash photograph. That man was Simon Lister and I'm Rembrandt Van Rijn. Poor Maurice, he's much too old for this game. It'd be too much for his palsied health if I told him that I am Simon Lister.

Would he drop a dime on me? Yes. He'd sell me for a few bucks, he doesn't even know about the reward. He asked to see my wristwatch today, the last emblem of my marriage. A gift from Angelique. Legally, she's still my wife. A misted gold chronograph, dimmed, gold-faced, with four dials, one that offers planetary data I'd never asked it for. An impressive machine created for someone who not only wants to know the time, but where it came from. "This is not a watch" he said in admiration, "this is an appliance."

Did he tie it to my life of crime? Did he recognize it from that picture of me in Newsweek, no longer on his wall, that I'd slipped under a newspaper.

I gave Maurice my watch today. He handed the watch back to me, the old chess player's light rising in his dead eyes. Then he said: "Tell me, Rembrandt, tell me something." I interrupted him and told him to take the watch. It was his. Maurice was stunned and stared at me, then put his hand out and clasped it to his wrist, admiring it from several angles. What else? I'm running out of vigorish. Take the watch Maurice, I don't want to do the other thing. Please don't find out too much.

December 31, 1963

Did I hear humming? I believe a woman has moved into the room next door to me, Room 14. There is one other room besides mine on the top floor. We share a toilet and a bathtub. Since I've been a tenant here, ten days, I've only seen one old man climb the steps up from the street to the other room. So a woman, if that is what she is, is not what I've come to expect living on the top floor of this rooming house on John Jay Street. And in my sleep I dreamed I heard her solid heels clacking down the stairs. I listen for her through the thin wall between us. If she's there, she's being very quiet. Did I imagine her? Still, at night, I sense a woman lying beside me, asleep alongside my bed. This morning, in my sleep, I'm sure I heard humming, a woman's humming and later, the sounds of solid heels clacking down the stairs. If she's there at all I want her to be there. I believe it's true, but I can't knock on her door. This morning when I got my feet to the floor and went out into the hall and into the bathroom to piss, it smelled like a florist shop.

Downstairs in the hall I tap on Maurice's door. Maurice is wearing flannel pajamas that have not been washed recently. He is already talking.

"Why couldn't I catch a good Jewish disease, like Bernstein's? Parkinson? It's like a country club I couldn't get in."

Maurice has Parkinson's, it's the first I've heard of it. He shakes his head. "Sorry," I write on my pad.

"So whaddaya?" He shrugs, fate has dealt him a pair of treys. I hold up my pad. "Did a woman move in upstairs?"

"Yeah a very hoity-toity spiff."

"Pretty?"

"You got that right, Rembrandt. She's a beaut." He enjoys calling me Rembrandt.

"You met her?"

"Mrs. Connors met her. She calls her 'too delicious German'." He raises his grandee's nose. "No, Rembrandt, I didn't dare speak. She walked right by me like I don't exist."

January 1, 1964

Last night, I heard her humming a French tune, then, this morning, her heels clacking down the stairs. I got to the split in the door in time to see the top of her head bobbing out of sight down the staircase. I looked out the window but she kept close to the house-fronts below me. The bathroom smelled of flowers again. I stayed in bed most of the day.

January 2, 1964

This morning I had my first sexual thought since I left the Eisenstein. My first independent, unassisted, how shall I put it, Hardon. The semen felt sweet, dappling my belly, it reassured me. I let it dry. I stayed in bed again with the ceiling and the walls. When I got hungry, it was dark, so I went out and had meatballs and spaghetti. This is a preview of death, like standing in line to die.

January 3, 1964

The woman who hums, who sleeps beside me with only the thin wall between us, makes me think of the woman in the park. This morning I thought about her before I woke up. I hadn't realized the strength of my feelings when I'd gone to sleep, but in the night something must have happened in my subconscious. This morning her beauty terrified me, it seemed uncontainable.

My property line runs through my head, it lays just behind my eyes, no human has trespassed it, certainly not Angelique. Only my painting has ever crossed that line. Has someone now crossed it? A stranger? At first it seemed inconceivable to me that a careful man, especially an artist, especially me, could feel this strongly about a woman before he'd spoken with her. It's crazy. But so am I. And why is speech essential to love? Why is knowing someone's data essential to loving someone? I can study a leaf in my palm and love it. Learn everything I need to know about nature from it. Why do I need to have a conversation with a woman I might love? Couldn't we hum melodies to each other? Dolphins do that. The longer I lie in bed the more reasonable the idea of wordless love becomes. Talk? There's a ritual for you. Do I need to take piano lessons to marvel over the music of Satie, Mahler, Beethoven, Ravel, Rachmaninoff? Or may I do it intuitively? Isn't a woman a bouquet of decisions already made? And isn't it up to a man to untangle her decisions? A careful man, me, can tell what he needs to know about a woman from watching her sit on a park bench, her legs wide, throwing stones at pigeons. Underhand. But she was gone. I had let her go.

In ten minutes, I'm out of bed downstairs, outside, bundled up, walking toward Capt. Padewicz Park. I know she'll return to that brittle strip of dirt. A drab day and colder than the day before. Walking through the living curios, I'm able to make it over to the park still early but without knowing the time and I sit where I'd sat yesterday until the noon whistle, without a break. By then the cold breaks me and I go into the Soup Kitchen for chili and coffee and sit in a corner, in sight of the park, while I nurse heat back into my legs and feet.

Over the next three hours I take short breaks and walk back and forth from the park to the café. By mid-afternoon I'm sitting in place on my bench, glazed, when she appears. I act as if I've just gotten there. She walks along behind me, sits where she sat yesterday, serious-faced, and takes a box of Crackerjacks from her purse, eats a few morsels then tosses a handful toward one of the elm trees nearby. In a thick flutter two pigeons dropped from a branch and she picks up her first piece of gravel and tosses it at them. I have to speak to her. I have to. I love this woman. I've been forming sentences all morning trying to imagine speaking them and now try to say them quietly, as though we've already been talking and have simply been interrupted. I get up and cross the walkway between us and sit down beside her. She regards me fearlessly, without a word, wondering why I've chosen to sit beside her. Close, I could see she possesses true country beauty—her mouth formed to smile had small lines where her lips close, her eyes have a child's brilliance but are unoccupied. When I don't speak to her, with an invisible shrug she turned back to continue feeding and stoning her pigeons. I suck in my breath and without rehearsing, blurted out, "You'll only stun them that way. If you want to kill pigeons, you throw overhand not underhand."

"It works!" I speak! I'm elated, I wanted to shout, "I'm talking!" I knew I could. "She's given me back my speech!" She's been spoken to in public parks before and continued to stare straight ahead.

"I am not trying to kill them," she says, her country cheeks sanguine. Her voice is light with maybe a foreign mark, prim, sure, bright. I don't think she would have bothered to answer me if I hadn't criticized her actions. Strands of yellow hair have been tucked into her drab woven babushka, other strands are left out dangling, some to her nose, as if she hadn't looked in the mirror before she came out.

"Well, are you feeding them or stoning them?" What poise. My first words. I'm smiling, happy to be hearing my own voice speaking sentences once again after so many silent weeks.

"I'm keeping them away from my Crackerjacks," she said with a chiseled edge in her voice. She is doing a good job, too. Her victims were loitering fatly, pumping their necks in confusion, chuckling among themselves. "Wur-erble werble. What's it gonna be, lady? Wur-erble wur-erble. Crackerjacks or rocks? Crackerjacks or rocks? Wurble wurble."

Watching her profile, her brow, her cheeks, her chin, her wrist and hand, was the highlight of these past few months; there was no beauty at the Institute. "How can they eat if they can't concentrate?" I tried to make her smile. "Pigeons have bird brains, genetically." She doesn't smile.

"I am not feeding them."

This is a woman who brings Crackerjacks to pigeons, then stones them for trying to eat. She glares at me with a bright flash in her eyes. Now what color are they?

"I am feeding him." She pointed across me to the base of one of the four elms. There he stood, a distance away, double-breasted little fellow, Mr. Squirrel, posed ornamentally beside his own elm, looking rich by any standards, the proud owner of a tree, chewing gum, taking them both in with his wet, black, know-it-all eyes. Waiting quizzically but in no hurry. Here is a woman who prefers to feed a squirrel over pigeons.

"I'd have thought this park too small to accommodate squirrels." I am now talking almost without hesitation, a slight glottal block telling me to go slow, making me measure my words elegantly, enjoy my sentences. The pleasing sound of my own voice again.

"There's only one. But you'd think so, wouldn't you?" A lovely sound to her voice, sympathy, a trace of tension, a delicate accent.

She watches the busy street. "I wonder what brought him here."

"Taxi. I saw him get out of one." At last she half-smiles, lips closed. She cared. Now she threw a handful to the pigeons. Maybe she is surprised that I have any knowledge of the spending habits of certain species.

Suddenly, Mr. Squirrel cracked from the tension of watching good food wasted on dumb birds, and in a fit of jealousy he sprints into the flock cackling, waving his black fingers, hopping mad, screeching. He scatters them, sends them aloft, fat-flapping overhead to nearby limbs. Frightened, she ducks her head into me, intuitively grabs my lapels tightly for a moment then recoils, embarrassed.

"I'm sorry, please." She seemed to be trying not to cry. She wakes a long dead element in me, an element I haven't heard from for a long time—spirit. Clearly, she's not stable, something's gone wrong with her. I know very well the signs of barely hanging on. If she wants to tell anyone about it, I'm the one, let her tell me. She dropped her hold on my coat and looked right at my eyes, her eyes sharp, bright navy blue, she looked at me as if we were related and have just met again after years. I was awed by her look.

"My name is Jonathan."

"Anna."

I give my other name, Boot, but she wouldn't give hers or even answer me when I asked her to tell me hers.

"What's wrong?" I asked gravely. Something is, I know. She doesn't answer, looks away, then, after a while, begins in a whisper, her eyes looking everywhere but into mine.

This is Anna's story: The week before, a married man she'd been having an affair with off and on for a year, died on her sofa during a pre-dinner cocktail, after he'd stopped by from his office to take her out to their favorite clandestine restaurant, a man she'd been wondering about—if she wanted him to leave his wife, whether he wanted to, if she would marry him? Now he's dead. All speculation is off. The coroner couldn't have been kinder, nor could the police have been more discreet and, yes, his doubly-abandoned wife had been told about Anna. I couldn't believe I was hearing these words and had no idea where to put them but while she was talking in a low voice, I had to lean forward to hear, and came dangerously close to telling her that I thought I loved her. If I had, I knew that just as the pigeons had flown away so would she.

Still in a mixed state of confusion, Anna stayed home from work the next few days, called in sick, and then, out of the blue, a telephone call had come from one of her father's neighbors in Grand Haven, Michigan, telling her that her father, whom she hadn't seen for twenty-years, had suddenly died. A horrible death. An accident on the job, crushed behind a truck on the loading dock just ten weeks before his retirement party, an inglorious finish. The neighbor who called her said her father had spoken about her all the time, carried her picture, was aware of her job and her telephone number. Anna wondered why he hadn't ever called her? Now she would never know. So, everyone was dying. She tried to go back to work, she needed to be with people but she kept breaking down. She asked for a stress leave and got the key to a cabin in the Adirondacks from a friend, and drove up there to be alone. She had requested three days, but would take a week, whether they liked it or not. Only Faery, her confidant, would come with her. Faery, a calm gray cat with a slight limp who'd weathered storms alongside Anna, who'd absorbed her outpourings; griefs, joys. For ten years he had filled an exact place in her life that had not been covered by anyone else, no one and nothing, and had slept with her a hundred times more nights than any man. Anna brought her skis, delicatessen food—cream cheese, smoked salmon, herring, Milano salami, baguettes, Camembert, Stilton, red Bordeaux, packets of soup, frozen dinners—a box of LP's from Beethoven and Mahler to Bossa Nova, a sack of books she'd been meaning to get around to reading for years, Dawn Powell, Beryl Markham, Flannery O'Connor, Jean Rhys. Her women. What a week. She would rebuild, she told me, and that seemed to be an ideal way.

As I listened, I felt myself aching at the impossible thought of having been invited by her on such a rebuilding excursion, into the woods in a snowy cabin for a week with her, the warmth of a fireplace burning pine logs, and that nurturing her would nurture me as well. Save my life, actually.

The snow started falling the first night. She built a fire and dozed in front of it, Faery purring in his sleep in front of the burning logs warming the cabin. It snowed through the night. When she woke early the next morning, it had stopped snowing, Faery had moved onto the foot of the bed, still sleeping deeply, she petted him two or three times, Faery chirred, half-asleep, and they both dozed off again.

When Anna woke again the snow had stopped, it hid half the windows but there were bright patches of sun glistening. It was noon, the world was hushed, white. She felt a savage hunger for breakfast, her first appetite in days, a good sign. Faery was asleep, he'd moved up beside her, to be close to her face and peacefully sleeping, or he seemed to be. But he was dead.

She fled the cabin, left her books and skis, everything behind her except Faery. She barely survived her escape from the cabin through the drifts. She had no memory of her drive down from the mountains, driving with Faery wrapped in a blanket on the seat beside her.

She is through crying. She's repeated the details one by one to me, dry-faced, staring straight ahead, stone-cold. I try to console her but I couldn't. What would I say? There are lines in The Rubaiyat that would sooth her but I couldn't think of them. I could only tell her of her good fortune, that she had those three friends for as long a time as she did and that it is over now. She can hardly ask more than that. Rubbish. She didn't answer. A married lover, an absent father and a cat. I should cry and kiss her, make her weep, which is what I felt like doing. But I didn't. I have northern European bearing. Stoic. Bullshit. She catches me with an indelible look, I see tears at last, not a gush, just an admission. She has moved back into her face. Maybe she is thinking, "Thank you for listening." The working of her tears transforms her face from pain into beauty. Her mouth quavers; it was never meant to be solemn. I barely lean my face toward her. She senses that I am about to kiss her and looks down, turns away. I feel thick-faced. I stand as if to complete my gesture.

"Will you be here tomorrow, Jonathan?"

"Yes." I'm startled that she asked, of course I'll be here tomorrow,

I'll be here forever.

"Same time, same bench?"

"Same time, same bench."

I have what I want, more. Something to say. "Do you know what it is?" I hold my wrist out as if she were deaf. "The time?"

She looks at her watch. "Three-fifty."

I stood, half-bow and strolled away. I could have touched her shoulder, maybe even brushed the few strands of hair that marked her brow, or even shaken her hand. Europeans like that. Should I have asked for her telephone number? Her address? Asked her name again?

At the rim of the park, the far street corner, I turn to wave. The bench is empty, she's gone. Okay. But she has been there. And she'll be there tomorrow. So will I; a note signed by Death will not intervene. Why does she need to rely on me? Why did she talk so openly to me, a stranger, scouring the details of her past month? I have an open face. Once a girl waking up beside me called me Christ. A newspaper, lacking a photograph of me described me as resembling Robert Louis Stevenson. But I have a beard now. Anyway, there have been no photographs. None exist, a blessing now that I am a fugitive.

I can't fully realize how this woman, Anna, has made me speak. She's been through hell. She's beautiful, she's sexual, strong, weak, broken, sensitive, lean, fine-boned. I don't know how tall she is. She's got everything. She's even having a breakdown like me. Whatever the reasons that she spoke to me, or that I spoke to her, she's the only person I've been able to talk to. We behaved like a pair of mental patients in search of a sanitarium out there in the park today. I'll find out why tomorrow. But my time is definitely a wastin'.

I'm living here without motive on the run, and time is running out. Now I see what's going on. She's gone home and she regrets telling me too much. She won't be there tomorrow. I'll never see here again.

Walking away, mumbling along to myself, I felt the words stop coming. Closer to John Jay Street, I feel my throat grip and close, I feel my speech going. Before I enter the rooming house, my words leave me. When Maurice catches me in the front hallway, I feel my throat clamp tight shut. I sweep past him, nodding like a busy priest. I want to feel other feelings that I am afraid to think about right now.

January 4, 1964

Late in the night, I heard her voice. The voice of the woman in the room next door to mine. Sometime in the night or early this morning. It was black and the city was quiet. Below in the street, I could hear someone whistling. But I wasn't dreaming, I definitely heard her voice next door. She was moving around, humming to herself, a French love song, a wine-stained little melody, "Vous Qui Passez Sans Me Voir." It was a small reedy voice, sad but not tragic. Sweet. She hummed bright notes at the end of each song, so that her songs didn't leave sadly. Then something toppled over and broke, maybe a glass, and after that there was no more humming. But her light stayed on all night, as if she might have been afraid of the dark. The wall between our rooms is thin. There is a crack in the plaster along the ceiling, and if my room is dark, I can see when the light is on.

I might have fallen asleep after that. In my dream I saw myself step outside my room into the hallway to listen at her door, ready to knock. The hallway is always dark, day and night. The bulb is burnt out. I stood in the dark listening in the hallway above the stairs. Instead of boiled onions coming up the stairs, I smelled small white flowers. I heard her doorknob turn. I couldn't see anything, of course. I stepped back. The door opened and closed. I heard a key turn in the lock. I struck a match. It was a woman. She was turned away from me facing her door. In the matchlight, I could see she was wearing a dark green dress, rather tight at the waist and on the hips. She stood still. Finally I was about to meet the woman who claws the toilet paper off the roll, who leaves the bathroom smelling like a florist shop, the woman who hums French songs, whose heels strike the stairs. Then I remembered I was asleep.

"Don't be afraid of me," I say, "this is only a dream." She doesn't even turn around.

"I know it's a dream," she answers. "You dream about me every night."

At that instant the match burns my finger and goes out. "Ai!" The hallway is black. In the dark I hear her voice.

"What happens next?" she says, intrigued.

I'm shocked. "I don't know." But I do know. My dream continues: The match goes out. In the dark she slips past me, goes downstairs, I cannot stop her. I return to my room and wait for her. After a long time, I hear her heels on the stairs then in the hallway, then a quiet knock. I open my door. She comes into my room carrying a bottle of champagne wrapped in a scarf. She asks if I have glasses. In my sink, I try to wash the toothpaste stains off of two thick-bottomed tumblers, but I cannot. I open the champagne and we sit on my bed and drink it.

That's what always happens in my dream. But she had never spoken and I'm still standing in the hallway facing her in the dark. I cannot see her. The second match burns out. I can hear her breathing She says, "May I go downstairs now?"

"Anna?"

"How do you know my name?"

"We met in the park."

I strike a third match. She turns to face me. It's her.

"What are you doing here, Anna?"

"I'm in your dream," she says, "I have to be here."

She turns away from me. The match is out. The hallway is black. I hear her voice.

"I had trouble finding you, Jonathan," she says.

"I bet you did, I answer."

I reach for her arm but she's gone, I hear her heels clacking down the stairs. I go back to my room to wait for her, close my door. In my room I begin to feel that I might have truly found Anna again, even though I know this is my dream, it's just possible that she's really living in the room next to me with only the plaster wall between our beds. I feel a chill. Or has she vanished down the stairs again, this time for good? I wait. In my dream, when I go back into my room I always turn the lightbulb off and light a candle stuck on a café saucer. Then I wait for her. After what seems to be an hour I hear a quiet knock on the door. I open it. Anna. She comes in carrying a chilled bottle of Champagne wrapped in an Hermés scarf. I pop the cork, I try to wash the white stains off the two thick glasses, we sit side by side on my bed and drink. The bottle on the floor at our feet. Just to talk, I ask her what she is planning to do with the rest of her life. She tells me I asked her that once before in the park. "I told you, I'm flying to Paris." I ask her when. "Soon. Air France."

I watch my hand move, it touches her barely, just between her knees. She crosses her legs. I take my hand away.

"Do you want to make love to me?"

"Yes," I say.

"Then you need to fall asleep. When you do I'll come back to your room."

I'm already in my dream in my room. I swallow my champagne. Anna stays seated on the bed. She tells me to lie with my head on her thighs and doze off. It's easy, I'm already dizzy from the wine. Later, after I've fallen asleep, she blows the candle out. In this dream's sleep, I dream again. I see my dark room, I can barely make us out as we are—Anna seated on the bed, me lying with my head on her lap. I can see myself open my eyes and look up at her. I reach up with both hands and I bring her face down to mine. We kiss. I can no longer see her face. We kiss again. She says, "Do you want to make love to me?"

"Yes, but isn't the dream over?"

"No," she says.

Her breasts, she is naked. Her thighs, her back, her buttocks. She is around me, her limbs, her extremities everywhere, she has no center, she is all motion. I cannot see her, my fingertips are everything. I hear her sighs, her breaths, her sobs. Her smell, her scents, she is sopping oozing, she cannot have enough of me, or I of her, there is nothing else to have in the world, she will not leave me alone, she cannot stop, there is no air in the room. I am falling through blackness. Through the frightened mattress, the dirt under the pavement, the graves under the city, out into a black void, the nearest planets.

I wake up then, still in my dream, alone on the bed. It is still night in the black room without walls, I am thirsty. I reach for the bottle under the bed; it is dry.

"Anna," I whisper. "I love you, Anna."

I am alone. The dream ends there. I open my eyes. I am awake. Day. Outside it is becoming light. Yelling joins me from the street, horns. I am no longer dreaming, my dreams are quiet matters. There is a weak knock on the door.

"Who is it?"

Silence.

"Is someone there?"

No one speaks.

I stand and go to the door and open it. The hallway is dark as always.

Anna. She looks as she did yesterday in the park. Taller. She is gaunt, her child's eyes bright her hair is wild. She is wearing the deep green dress, green as the sea, the color of old ponds. Her color. She is holding a bottle in a bright scarf. She seems exhausted.

"I had trouble finding you," she says.

"I bet you did," I say.

"Are you alone?" she asks.

I turn around and look behind me. I am alone in my room.

"Yes. Alone," I says, "Why don't you come in?"

CHAPTER 3

New York City: 72 John Jay Street

ৡৈ

January 5, 1964

I woke up lying on my stomach, dried sperm sticking me to the sheet. Astrida will love that. Sexual dreams, making love to Anna who lived in the room next door. I remember making love to her then falling into black. I woke up not knowing whether she'd be there or not? I had all morning to kill. Until 3:00 p.m. I jumped out of bed when I heard knocking on the door, but it was only Astrida with my tray, my English breakfast—fried kippered herring a hard boiled egg in a cup, cold dry toast and of course, my pot of hot black truth serum.

About noon I went out into the hall, knocked on the door to the room next door, the only other room on the top floor. Nobody answered, of course. I pushed the door open, the bed was made, the room was empty, there was no sign of life. I returned to my room, closed the door, pulled the shade down.

I realized that last night I didn't sleep. I realized that her visit was not a simple dream, that she was standing in my room.

I was trying to slip out of the house early to meet Anna when Maurice snared me. Doesn't he have a life? He knows. He senses something about me and it's driving him crazy. Did I want a piece of fish? I did, I was starving, but not his. It was two-thirty on his mantel clock. He was wearing his hat, a fedora.

He offered me a piece of cod. I wrote on my pad that I couldn't eat and put my hand on my upset stomach. He loves my afflictions. All afflictions in general. On the table under his plate of fish was the *New York Times* open to page four: SIMON LISTER REWARDS TOTAL $100,000. Tokyo Gallery Ueda matches Anasor's.

What was that? Was that a coincidence? If so, not a good one. I've never seen him with the *New York Times*, only the *Daily News*. He read the article aloud to me. The added reward from the Japanese Gallery that had always tried to get me to fly over and appear at an opening. Big money. He read every word. It reminded me of my orientation interview at the Eisenstein. I don't know what he's doing, but he's making it hard for himself to stay alive.

"Sit down, sit, wait a while." Hatted, Maurice has been glancing covertly at me from under his squirrel brow. His face is blank, his pulse has doubled. He forks fish and eggplant into his mouth, he reads too loudly from the newspaper.

"Listen to this, Rembrandt. Sunday's enta-tainment section." Upside down, I can read my name in the headline. This is what it's about. The furor hasn't died down. I understand that, it's an unsolved mystery. A bedtime story.

Maurice sits with his plate of food at the table he uses for everything, faces me, begins reading aloud: "Unless you've spent your holidays in Tierra del Fuego, I needn't tell you that when Simon Lister walked out of the Whitney Museum and then Anasor Gallery twelve days ago Tuesday, he disappeared into thin air. Leaving behind him in a veil of oily black smoke and burning canvas, the rubble of what may be this century's greatest art. It is a tragedy of incalculable magnitude and adds one more facet to the already complex prism of this enigmatic man, Lister, about whom surprisingly little is known. The question is, why couldn't it have been prevented? Six months earlier he did, after all, destroy his own studio by setting fire to ..."

I wave at him to a halt. "Who wrote this garbage?" I write.

"William Byron Mallory. He's English" he adds as if it matter.

"Why are you reading it?"

"Maybe you can tell me, Rembrandt."

I get up, go to the door.

"Wait a while, wait a while. Let me read on a bit."

He pitches a massive bite of boiled cod and eggplant into his mouth, sharing with me the processing action that takes place within. He talks, reads, chews.

Tell me what it means when it says here ..." His doctor at the Eisenstein did not act surprised when she was told of his actions.

She said he had 'mutus dysfunction.' Is that like not being able to speak?"

I feel naked, dry. What does he know? I shrug. My thoughts are that this is a wordy article and that I have never killed a man but that I could.

Maurice snaps the paper shut. "So what do you think of that, Rembrandt?" He doesn't wait for me to answer. "Did you ever meet this fellow Lister?"

What does Maurice know? "Yes, Inspector, I met him once," I write. I stop when I feel a rush in my bowels, another pale tremor. I'm sure it can be seen but Maurice's head is under the table looking for his knife on the carpet. I write, "Why do we need the British to tell us about our own artists?" My unconscious forms a longish answer and I begin to write it slowly. Maurice surfaces and puts his hand over my pad.

"What's you're real name, Rembrandt?"

"Jonathan Boot," I write. "What's yours?"

Maurice squints at me. "Prove it."

Mrs. Connors, God bless her, knocks on his door. "Three o'clock!"

Maurice looks at the golden watch I had given him, the watch of many dials, the talisman.

"Two minutes 'til," he says. "We got our show at three."

Maurice has nothing more to say. He goes to the door. Mrs. Connors has gone down to her basement apartment. He holds the door open for me. Squints up as he passes.

"Until tomorrow, Rembrandt Van Rijn."

Maurice and I are only a matter of time. Tick tick tick. fifty-thousand dollars. He's not quite ready. He keeps to himself. He's not going to tell the landlady. He'd have to split it. Fear makes me stronger now. I'm ready to make my move. Rub out Maurice and run. Out of this house this city. I jog practice laps around the block midnights, when it's not too cold. Test my endurance. I've been taking the subway back and forth under the river, round-trips to Brooklyn, looking for my brave flautist. But I've got to go. Getting out doesn't mean moving to Elmira, New York.

Maurice said he wanted company, but that was a lie. He had an

X-ray look in his eyes, some species of a smile. He keeps it taped on his mantelpiece, THE ART CRIME OF THE CENTURY. My royal ass. No one has figured out how I did it.

Over and over in my mind I smother him. Sometimes it seems easy, sometimes impossible. There has to be no blood. No agony. The act itself, the struggle on the floor. Mrs. Connors below listening.

It sickens me. He already has his country club disease—Parkinson's. How far away can he be? At his age? But once it's done, I'll give up going to the park looking for her. I'll be even more of a fugitive than I am now. Astrida will describe me accurately. Someone will collect the reward. He knows something, but not enough, not yet. Please, Maurice.

Anna isn't there. I wait two hours and I am too nervous to sit still any longer, I leave a note under a stone on the bench. 'Back soon, Jonathan.' I walk to the East River and watch the shipping, tugs chugging past, and out to sea on the tide.

Is she sick? Where is she being sick? Has she moved? Vanished? Aren't the laws of love meant to be simple? You meet someone, you fall in love, you feel pain? Of course, I went to the park today, why not, it's a good thing for me to go. I don't know anything about her but I have dozens of feelings forcing themselves together. Can I love her without her knowing it? She'll be at the park tomorrow, Won't she?

I'll go back to the park tomorrow at three. I'll bring her white flowers from the flower market on Canal Street. With a pocketful of coins I'll pay off the pageant of jesters lining the way, wait for her in the park, feed the pigeons, eat the fake soup at the trendy café, wait for her, and if she doesn't come, if she doesn't come …

This is where the Journal ends.

CHAPTER 4

Salve de Dios: Canary Islands: May 6, 2001

๛

It is past midnight, 1a.m. The room glows dimly, I have lit two candles side-by-side. The crucifix above the bed looks down on me begging for pity. But I pity Simon, his tortured soul. His loneliness. His fears. He was so brilliant.

By candlelight, the fine pen marks of his journal have made me drowsy. I blow the candles out. In the morning I will set off up the hill. Will he give me the next journal? Will he talk to me?

It is morning. The journal is in my hands. I must have fallen asleep hugging it. Protecting it? A rooster wakes me crowing just outside my window, and close to my head. Roosters always sound like they are having emergencies. It's been years since I heard a rooster crowing in the morning. Or been woken by a church bell in a village. What purity. Where have I been since then? Maybe Sunday, if I'm here, the wind will carry the sound of a bell and wake me.

He has taped an envelope inside the back cover of the journal. I open it carefully. The tape has dried and hardened. It is a neatly folded clipping dated Sunday, December 30, 1963. New York Times:

> To trace Simon Lister's life, one must look at his origins as a misunderstood youth, a Navy veteran (four years on submarines), then, in the years following his remarkable development under the sponsorship of Martin Anasor. He was a misfit who painted as if an external force were passing through him, an artist who demanded fulfillment of every mystery from his art and yet managed to hide the keys to his kingdom from the others. He certainly asked no compromise.
>
> I have three theories on Simon Lister's fate. The first involves revenge: Lister quite simply might

have met with foul play. I personally feel this has not been the case, but his crime against art has so enraged the culturati that any one of a cadre of insiders might have caused his demise, directly or indirectly. The love of his art being of such a passionate nature, that feeling continues to run high and will do so without abatement for some time to come. If this country recognized its icons as national treasures, as is the custom in Japan, I would say, without question, that Simon Lister would be an American national treasure.

Theory number two: Faced with what he faced from justice he could easily have taken his own life, I would certainly deplore this, but it would not be inconsistent with the nature of his crime. He has, the cognoscenti tell me, been institutionalized for stress on and off for three years. If he was disturbed enough to destroy every one of his priceless paintings, I theorize he might have been disturbed enough to take his own life along with them. A psychiatrist I've spoken with, Dr Jerry Segram, concurs that this is a consistent pattern. But thankfully, no body has been found, so far.

My third theory and one that many of us in the art world hope is the truth, is that Lister is simply hiding out, either with friends or alone, licking his wounds, recovering, looking forward to a sensible return to the art world—the world he had stood on its ear. A world that would applaud his sincere and humbled return. Of course, he must pay for his crime, that's only fair. Remember, art is a billion dollar industry. Needless to say, he will face severe criminal charges already brought against him by the Anasor Gallery as well as other galleries, museums, and collectors across the country and around the world. These are grave charges, and no one would be surprised if he were made to serve a lengthy sentence in prison for the destruction of their property. Although some value will be reimbursed by insurance companies, it will only be money. The full impact of the loss of each painting cannot be over-estimated.

But whether or not he likes it, Mr. Lister is owned by us, the public he has mesmerized. And one hopes that the $50,000 reward posted by his mentor, Anasor, and now the $50,000 added by Anasor's sister gallery in Tokyo, Ueda, will yield the man himself, safe and sound, contrite, willing to take his punishment and to make amends and begin painting where he left off.

I'll walk up to his house hoping he'll give me another Journal, hoping he'll talk to me. Even if he doesn't, I already have enough to sell an exclusive article. I came here to get his story, with or without his permission. I thought it would make a great article with photos. But if this first journal is any example, if the others are half as good, it will make an amazing book. These journals are my main chance, of course. My future. His lost voice rings on every page. His voice in his house. If he lets me read all the journals, if he answers my questions, it is the sort of book publisher's dream about—his journals and my narrative to fill in the gaps.

The Whitney fire was the engraved mark that defined his life's work, and he turned away. He rejected all of his creations on that day. His life. Others can kill various parts of their lives, parts of the thing they love, and then run away, but no one can erase his life completely. It is still there, waiting, behind him. When Simon Lister disappeared, he left nothing but ashes behind him. Nothing tangible, just the power of his memory and the vast crime of loss. It was sine qua non. He had been, after all, magnificent.

It is too early to go to his house. I wrap the journal in newspaper and slip it into my bag. There are no road signs, no cars, people point the way. The day is sharp, clear, beautiful, but there are clouds. I walk down a bumpy road to a stone hut at the water's edge, teetering above the rocks where four tables and a few more chairs wobble. The coffee is strong, a black spank, and there is fried calamari being offered today, normally not my breakfast food, and a species of bread. No butter or cheese. It is a deprived island. I nibble. I am too excited to concentrate. Sheltered from the wind, I sit at the wobbly table and write notes from his journal. When I have finished, without breakfast, I walk up to his house. Will there be a second journal waiting for me?

It is about nine when I get there. His mattress has been hung out the window, airing. What will I say to him? Will I be able to ask him a question? The woman, Señora Natti, is alone. From the doorway I smell fresh bread, coffee and something else, a less familiar smell.

"Esta señor acqui?" I ask her.

"No, no" she says, *"momentito."* He will be back soon.

She indicates the vast plan of volcanic rock edging down into the sea. *"Senta senta,"* she points to a wooden chair in the courtyard.

"Café?"

"Si, si," I say, *"Gracias, Señora Natti."* I sit. She brings a tray. The coffee is strong, the bread is all crust. The clouds have covered the sun, there is a chill. I sip and wait.

I hear him enter the house from the ocean side. I listen as the woman explains my presence. He must have nodded because I don't hear him answer. I'm sure he expected me. In a few minutes he comes to the door and beckons me inside. I enter his room, the small main room. A frying pan sits on the table. In it is rice, fragments of chicken and seafood, a type of sausage, peppers. *paella.* He's been swimming, dripping water from the back door across the stone floor to his bedroom.

"It's a good island for sleeping," he says. "You like the coffee?"

"Yes I do." I unwrap the journal and put it on the table.

"Imperia Coffee from Venezuela." He nods to the pot. *"Natti, un otra taza para el señor."* She enters with a demi-cup and saucer as if she's been waiting for a cue. She picks up the crumpled newspaper and takes it away. There are cubes of sugar on the table. No milk.

"You get to read it?"

"I did."

"I never have."

"It was wonderful." I want to add, "beautiful, fascinating."

"Anything you want to ask me?"

"Yes. There's so much. Do you mind if I ask you about 'the art crime of the century'?"

"Not at all. But I wish you wouldn't call it that."

"What then?"

"Just call it, 'the fire.'"

"Okay, can I ask you how you started the fire?"

"Sure, why not? What are you doing for supper?"

"Nothing."

"Come back and I'll tell you all about it."

I spend the day walking. I've brought rubber-soled shoes but they're no match for the razor-sharp volcanic edges, the black rocks, lava finger-stones, shards. It is not a pretty island, but walking it is exhilarating, the wind, the clarity, the starkness. There are no trees; the green plants grows niggardly in rows tended by leather-skinned women who wear black bonnets. At the north end of the island, just off shore, there is a wreck of a tanker, half-submerged. In the distance is the Monastery. It is quite old, made of great blocks of volcanic stone, crude yet elegant. Its design Romanesque, imitating the vague splendor of a cathedral. Maybe it was begun centuries ago with a dormitory and the abbot's lodge. Then the church was added, then a belvedere, a cloister, a walled cemetery beyond. The buttresses that have been added have all been in keeping. There are men in brown robes with ropes around their waists pulling up greens and putting them in baskets, others tilling earth, robed men walking. In a stone shed down the hill a boat is being built, formed wood stands around it, iron rods waiting to be heated on the open fire. I must ask him about visiting there before I leave.

By evening, I am hungry. I have found the winery and bought two bottles of black, syrupy wine. I wait outside as before, sitting on the chair out of the wind. I have a two-day-old Spanish newspaper that holds my interests.

Tonight is chicken stuffed with garlic. The chickens come from the mainland but are raised here. "The island chickens are not robust," Simon tells me, "they're made of ashes." It's Wednesday so we have English gin. "You can have it with lemon squash if you like."

I do, and it is quite good with a crude domino of sugar crushed at the bottom. After we finish supper, he goes to the window. I am afraid to take notes, afraid to cut into the gift he's giving, afraid it will all crash down. I am ready to answer the question he hasn't asked: What am I doing here? Why do I want to know about him. I sense he wants to tell me. Is he tired of silence?

I know Simon Lister stories, everyone does. My mother actually saw some of his paintings. I have come here, after all, and it has taken me a year. He was the Amelia Earhart of painting with Robin Hood thrown in. Rumors that had been hammered into truth—that his mother had put him onstage when he was five, in Illinois, to paint blindfolded; that he was a savant powered by the sun and that he had extra sensors to receive its energy. And years later, how Anasor had found Simon, in his twenties, painting bricks on a cement wall for his landlady. On 14th Street, in the hot sun. A trompe l'oeil, with a skill that was startling. And Anasor had seen right away that Simon knew what he was painting, what painting was about. So important in this field of high-stakes art speculation. Simon had a magazine cover face. The distinctive indentations behind his eyes, so clearly visible in a pit viper, but unusual in a man's head. They gave him a breath of danger. The elongated head would stand up to anyone's scrutiny, that glinty-eyed, bemused expression, the healthy mass of fine hair. He belonged in Art. You trusted Simon Lister, like seeing your captain walk through the cabin before the flight. Anasor gave him his card, told him he could exhibit at his gallery anytime. Simon had refused. He wasn't ready. He also refused to be photographed. Anasor assumed he was a wanted felon. But no, it was simply the imprint on film Simon was afraid of. He felt the suck of it, the diffusion. Who knew where a photograph went and for what purpose? No, to him the photograph was the lowest form of expressionism.

Simon knew he was different. It was clear in everything he painted. Of course, he was different. He'd scoured himself and found something deeper, a primary force. Anasor didn't get it, but what he called Simon's *madness* lay in his ability to convey external power, and the fact that he was only an instrument in the creation of his paintings. That Simon was helpless, he had always known. From the beginning, he tried to act normal, but he'd always been what he was. He had been called *different* for years and as an adolescent he'd been called *mad,* and he had learned that in the world of art and even in nature, madness settles in naturally. It belongs, it consorts, it looks okay on the walls.

I knew all this before I came to Salve de Dios.

After supper, after gin and wine, Simon begins speaking, still staring away from me at the window. Now a bottle of dark Ron Miel, still half-full stands on the wide stone sill, the whitewashed walls plastered, crude, the night out the window, moonlit. I have to remember everything. He speaks so softly I can barely hear him.

"First I want to tell you something you might or might not know. Before I came to New York, when I was in my late teens, I'd been in submarines. It was a perfect escape, running away to join the navy, to be clothed and fed, although the clothes on subs were blue and the eggs green, I kept signing up again and again. Going deep. My personality profile fit that. Everyone else on board was in denial.

"Anasor gave me my start. He sponsored me. At that time, the world of painting that surrounded him was directionless, derivative and it still is. The art in art just wasn't there. Art was mocking art. What passed for art was ideas, what passed for originality was devices. What passed for new was homage to the past, Dada without the anger, Impressionism without the need. It was all design. But what did I know? I'd never studied. He saw my way was different and he was happy to sell it."

"Anasor realized right away that I was different. He drew up a contract and gave me a rent-free loft in the West Village, living expenses and materials included, and absolute privacy, even from him, until I felt ready to show him my work. It was worth it. In the first six months Anasor didn't know what to think. He wasn't sure what he had done. He left telephone messages for me at his studio, then sent messengers. I didn't answer. Anasor began to wonder about his investment. Who was this Simon Lister he had invented? He tried to stay away, but he had growing fears that he might have done something to disable me rather than to help me. After eighteen-months of silence from the huge West Village loft, Anasor cracked.

"He invited himself down and gave me a date. He was the king, I was his jester, so I agreed. I put him off for a week, then another. Finally, he just showed up late one summer afternoon, wearing a summer suit a Panama hat. I sat in a corner between windows with a glass of whiskey and a cigarette—an unfiltered Gitane. Anasor moved toward the middle of the loft standing in front of a painting. There was only one finished painting to see. It was huge. It was the first of my canvases that he had ever seen—a grassy hillside in the early evening, when it is night on the land but day in the sky. I waited, looking away, glass in hand, cigarette between my lips. A defining moment, as we used to say. Anasor was standing six feet in front of the painting. He'd put his glass on the floor, and was fanning himself with a folding fan he carried in summer."

Simon plays the scene from memory acting both parts, Simon's the more innocent of the two voices.

"What's going on here, Simon?"

"I don't know, Mr. Anasor, why don't you tell me?"

"Do I see underpainting?"

"Do you?"

"Simon, tell me what you've done here."

"What do you see?"

"I'd never seen Anasor hesitate," Simon explains. "I'd always seen him as direct, sure rude, certain and always right."

Anasor stepped forward touched the canvas lightly, stepped backwards.

"Well, I'm not sure I see anything but a a field and a house over there."

"I see them, too," I told him. "But not always."

"Not always?"

"Not always the same way."

"Then it happened. Quickly. He was overwhelmed. He felt faint. He got a jittery, troubled feeling. He'd finally stopped talking and the painting took him. It reached a corner of him he didn't know was there, sickened him at first, then elated him, then dropped him hard. It had touched something in him he'd forgotten, and for the first time in his life, Anasor found himself weeping in front of a painting. He wept! Privately, to be sure, but he wept. I saw him weep. This painting, *The Field,* was plain, yet, he told me later, there was nothing he'd ever seen painted that was fiercer.

"It knows so much more than it's showing," he said. "How can this be? It breaks the already broken rules of realism, but it breaks them by returning to the rules. The brushstrokes are superb, coiling, fine. Your detail is extremely exact. It beckons me in. The illusion of space is old stuff, but once it gets you in to the field, it does something that hasn't ever been done by a painting before, that I know of. Trompe l'oeils have traditionally been painted by tricksters, dull magicians, who discover pigeons in little velvet sacks."

In *The Field* Anasor saw lost time; it recalled his childhood—early years living in Europe that he had long before obliterated, being hidden from the Nazis by relatives long gone. And then an incident of betrayal that he had always denied to himself.

"I know about *The Lake,*" I interrupted.

Simon turns to me and asks "How?"

"My mother had an experience she talked about all her life. It was in front of *The Lake* at the Chicago Art Institute. She was pregnant with me."

"I think *The Lake* was the last one I burned. But that was much later."

When he saw *The Field* at my loft that afternoon. Anasor was impressed with his own judgment.

"It's extraordinary how right my instincts are!" he said when he'd recovered. I laughed and told him he knew everyone in the city better than he knew himself and maybe that was about to change. He said he loved me for telling him that. God knows, I was the only one who talked to him that way. But he didn't change. What he saw in the painting affected him deeply but it didn't change him. He was incapable of change. But he did manage to tell me this.

"Simon, you have now been painting in your loft for one-and-a-half-years. It is time to show."

"Anasor had suspected for a long time a tidal movement among his buyers, what they secretly wanted—paintings they could respond to emotionally. Radical notion! The culturatti had long ago announced, 'If you get it, it ain't art.' But his art buyers were a shy lot and could never admit that where painting was concerned, invoking their feelings was more interesting than using their intellects. They did intellect all day. What they needed was more viscera in their lives.

"One by one, his clients began to realize this much—home late from the charity balls alone in their sitting rooms, their dinner jackets askew, stretching their toes in black silk socks, their feet resting on Noguchi coffee tables, glasses-in-hand, facing their new acquisitions across the room—a painted flag in a white frame, lit by its personal, square-focused, Denhoff Quartzlicht lens—they realized the million-dollar Jasper Johns did nothing to bring them comfort. Did not move them. Did not amuse them. Did not intrigue them. It bored them outright. They didn't want to get it; they wanted to feel it. Oh, my, how they hated it! Only late at night, alone, could they bring themselves to admit this in silence, as secret as their extra-marital affairs, their wives never to know.

"Anasor was dying to show them my work. These huge paintings of mine were classical, never imagined, surreal, vacant without seeming to be, sexy, strange, embarrassing, depressing, uplifting, filling, deeply touching, completely unsettling. Horizonless. And above all, simple, simple, simple. But he knew. For years his clients had collected truly disgraceful paintings with snotty titles like, *Light 22*. They, of course, had only needed a few supporting words to ease their gamble. But now they wanted more. Not only financial investments but emotional investments. He had once told them that hating the art they bought was okay. It was normal; not essential to like it, but it might help. That they never 'bought a painting, they acquired investments.'

"That was the point. You could bring it up, your latest acquisition, talk about it anywhere you dined. How could you discuss buying a peed-on five-story parking structure in Hell's Kitchen? And certainly your dinner guests don't want to hear about your pork-belly futures. Investing is not a pretty business even in art. 'I paid eighty thou for that little hummer; think it'll double? Think it'll go anywhere?'

Now they could love their paintings, permission had been granted. The paintings did not pass through their minds before their checkbooks; they passed through their viscera. And so, even before my first exhibition, Anasor gave what I did a name. He christened it 'Visceralism,' and I became a 'Visceralist.' I painted the paintings that went right to your viscera, your guts. Suddenly, I had my own school of painting. Without knowing it, I had originated an art movement. Anasor was delighted, I was not. Things were getting out of hand.

"Astoundingly, the name caught on. But who was this Simon Lister? The name sounded vaguely mittel-European but I wasn't mittel-European. My past was non-existent, my paintings were large, seemingly bland nearly blank descriptions of the simplest elements—house, tree, moon, hill. Where were the people? Fairly realistic, too, another mark against me. Oh, the critics were slavering. Their guns were loaded and ready. Still, no one expected it to be any more than just another superfluous, hyperthyroid opening at The Anasor Gallery.

"It became a continental divide. That first evening just after six, a guest with a glass of wine, who'd been standing in front of a painting of a house, began to sob. She could not stop and no one could console her. It happened again in front of another painting, someone fell over. Then someone passed out, fainted dead away in front of *The Trees*. No one knew what to do. This was getting strange. Anasor thought that his reaction had been isolated. Then about six-thirty, a man who'd been staring at *The Valley* had a heart attack. The fire department came. The party broke up; the guests were sent home. The man died in the ambulance on the way to the hospital. Anasor knew then that he had in terms of a godsend, but he didn't know what it was, and he certainly hadn't anticipated anything like this. He'd hung sixteen large canvases, each dramatically overpriced, and he sold each one of them that evening. He closed the gallery while he figured out what to do.

"The next day signs were posted in sixteen languages. Then there was another death. A week after the opening, another man suffered a heart attack. As he was lying on the floor in front of my painting of two houses in the moonlight, he described a wonderful conversation he'd had with a man he'd murdered 20 years before. When someone asked him who the victim had been, he said, 'My father!' He didn't recover. Anasor hushed it up; no one ever knew about it. Soon there were warnings posted at showings of my work—NO PACEMAKERS, NO CHRONIC HEART CONDITIONS, NO HIGH BLOOD PRESSURE. It became a litany. After that no one died, but some still fainted.

"He used it. As a public service he contacted all the art critics and cautioned them to advise their readers on how to look at a Simon Lister painting. The critics took it seriously. Readers were told to stand or sit in front of a painting with their eyes closed until they felt stable, ready to open them. When they did, they were not to stare at the painting directly, but to find a spot somewhere on the canvas, off to one side, and continue to the other side and let the painting happen to them. The danger lay in focusing. They must not, under any circumstances, focus too long. Those who did agreed that they felt as if they had lost contact with their world and were tumbling forward into the painting. That in itself wasn't harmful. It was that they became most vulnerable and that the most deeply set fears or longings harbored in their minds, whoever they loved hated or feared at that moment, would come to life within the painting. The Anasor Gallery had definitely become the place to go.

"Another thing went wrong that night. Late that evening certain guests who had left the gallery gathered at Anasor's apartment for a small after-party. Angelique discovered me asleep on the floor of the library, my head on a Bargello footstool. She told me later that she tip-toed out, having suddenly fallen in love. She was Society, I was not. After a brief courtship, we were married and moved to 63rd Street and Madison, and although she left me alone to paint in my West Village loft, she never grew to understand my paintings. She was never able to enter them. All she was able to enter were the books at the accountant's office.

"I soon became an inconvenience for the leading hostesses. On the one hand, I was at the top of the A-list, the guest of the hour, New York's Guest. On the other I was rude, irritating, insulting. I had mossy teeth, the lead oil paint I used had eaten my cuticles, and I only spoke the truth. Quietly, but still.

"My paintings became deeper, more sensuous, more harmful, even more excruciating than I had ever imagined they would. They were not abstract, not surreal, not real, they were simple, empty scenes, devoid of people. Or sometimes they were rendered in *sfumato*. None of them could be shown publicly until I was ready to show them, until I said so."

"Was that why you were committed?"

"Well, you may know I stabbed my wife—not seriously of course. That was a very famous thing to do, and then about the same time, I burned my studio loft and all my paintings in progress, and that wasn't considered normal either. Anasor was very upset so was Angelique. I'd been inconvenient. Now I'd become a threat."

"Did she commit you?"

"Angelique? My, my. Here was a woman who couldn't face herself for more than a moment, unless she was putting on makeup. Here was a woman who believed that by changing clothes she could change her life."

"Why did you marry her?"

"Let me count the reasons."

"Why did you stab her?"

"Why did I stab her? Why does anyone stab anyone?"

"To kill them?" He shakes his head. "To get her attention. I was sending her a message, as they used to say in that era. 'Stab' was their word. I threw the knife. She'd helped me to becoming a kitsch item at penthouse garden soirées where you dine with your head in bucolic centerpiece arrangements, your feet on carbonized grit, in air that would kill flowers by morning. It was odd that I'd ever submitted to that sort of marriage, but I was repressed, suppressed, and too busy to care. You might say she stole me. Charleston society. That could be an oxymoron.

"Anyway, my vision reeled. Suddenly, the contents of the kitchen were in motion, in a tumble-dryer, the alphabetical spices on the spice rack were mingling with the never-used copper pots. The blades, the blades seemed handiest. I swayed against the counter, I felt a knife handle tingling in my hand, I squeezed it, then thrust it toward her without hitting her.

"The next night during a discussion I will describe later, threw a kitchen knife at her. For everyone's peace of mind, it was then agreed that I was having a breakdown and that I should be put away. Angelique decided this; Anasor agreed. At the time, I felt it couldn't hurt. Anyway, she committed me to the Eisenstein. It was all taken care of at night, two cops and a judge, and not a lawyer in sight. The bribes had cost Anasor thousands. Not a peep from the press, and, whisk, I was gone. In the morning, the same bribed cops drove me there. Very few people knew what I looked like, so the secret exchange was complete. It was good to know the New York bribe/result system was still intact. My wife, with whom I hadn't ever discussed anything except keeping myself clean for guests and choosing presentable clothes, agreed with Anasor after visiting me there that I seemed calmer, relieved. A rhino would have been calm if he had been given the massive levels of tranquilizers that I was becoming addicted to.

"Without recognizing the value in one tiny surviving painting, Anasor let it go with me. I told him I needed it—a small, framed image nestled in a dark red leather box. As worthless as Judy Garland's ruby slippers at a church sale in Nairobi. Anasor had bigger plans. For a year, he and Angelique had been going through the ordeal of assembling all of my work from museums and collections around the world for a retrospective at the Whitney Museum in the fall."

"Why?"

"Anasor appreciated my product, his word, 'product,' but not its source. I was not of his world, the only world he understood. He thought I was a mongoloid savant. He wasn't sure what he had. He just told people I was ahead of my time."

"Weren't you?" I asked.

Simon shook his head. "I wouldn't give time that much credit. It's not as if time catches up and we'll be waiting for it with the goods. If someone's an inch ahead of their time they call him a genius, if he's a foot ahead they commit him to the Eisenstein Institute. Time's only a witness. A moron. Time's as dumb as a clock. It has no idea where it's going."

"There were rumors."

"Of course there were. But remember, madness looks fabulous walking the city streets, it matches the drapes, it's always been a cheerful part of the flow, the folksiness, a nice blend of desperation, hunger, rage and sex. Madness dresses well, dines at four-star restaurants, sleeps without socks in winter on subway gratings, hails cabs at the Plaza, cowers in alleys with handguns, bellows numbers on the floor of the New York Stock Exchange. Madness is that fucking city in all its colors. It may or may not speak English. But madness looks bloody awful at the Eisenstein, the institute set up to confront it, to highlight yours. The mad were us, the paying guests, the illuminati. We were set off against the eye-easy green walls, the waxy floors. The zoo keepers who wore the uniforms, oddly crisp, the norms, the therapists who want your strange brand of moodiness pumped up inside them, the horny medicos who squeeze syringes into your ass, the velvet-tongued male nurses who watch you in the blue-eyed dark, the tiny night persons who don't speak any known language, who come bearing armloads of sweet Thorazine candies, their petty footsteps hissing along corridors buffed and buffed and buffed, the eery smells of medico know-how, involuntary repetitions, clinging ugly faces, too calm against suicide's bland decor, the expanded steel mesh across our cages' windows. Because to have cured me of my madness would have been to dissolve me into the system, to rip me away from my art.

"Of course, to them, madness had been a vital part of my training. Why did it take them all these years to see it? Six months bolted in at the Eisenstein. Locked out of New York. When I close my eyes at night I go back there."

"How did you get out?"

"My daring moonlight escape? I'd been sleeping with my therapist, Doctor Ellie Smilowitz, who gave me street clothes—a tweed jacket and pants and a VISITOR badge. There were three locked doors to pass through. A desperate curfew had sounded, alerting prey not to venture in tall grass at night.

"My body shone silver-gray in the floodlit, courtyard white light, dead as moonlight. The tweeds Doctor Ellie had brought me fit pretty well but the shoes were as tight as nuts screwed over bolts. So I was limping pretty badly and it was too cold to go barefoot. She'd even brought me pocket money. She'd left her address in Queens for contact. She never knew who I was though, I'd been registered under another name. She knew I was someone else. That intrigued her.

"I'd been admitted for observation by my loving wife, the last person I wanted to see. Eisenstein is in a tough neighborhood. Ellie told me that four vigilante women had cornered a local rapist in an alley, held him down and raped him with an ebony dildo until he drifted away into an area he never fully returned from. So at 1:00 a.m., I entered that neighborhood, out into the dark, dry, chill-freezing night, cat-eyed vigilante women watching me. I spent the night in a diner, then at 8:00 a.m. took a taxi and slipped into the Whitney Museum, nodded toward the guard who nodded back. It was still early. The museum was closed. I passed the downstairs walls, felt the familiar chill of my favorite dead clowns—Jasper Johns, Liechtenstein, DeKooning, Rauschenberg, Pollock. Further on, I passed the other doubly-dead keeping my eyes down to avoid infection, feeling their soulless geometry, their mindless duality of post-realistic-nihilistic-minimalist ditties, blind to the current defeats. It hurts, believe me, to live through a time of low expectations.

"What was I talking about? I was trying to make a point. About my work, Anasor, Angelique, something … When I couldn't paint, my mind turned spiroid. I raved, spoke in screeds to Angelique or whoever was standing in my way, usually strangers in downtown cafeterias and parks. I formed editorials while I was standing against a building talking to someone I'd never seen before who looked receptive. I had no male friends, no one among the cognoscenti, the normal high-level opposites a darling artist consorts with when the price of his work is so absurdly high that sycophantism is natural. Nobody in the serious, chatty high-level artists' colony. I just enjoyed the dumbstruck downtown zingaroes, dry salvages I met at the Ola Cafeteria, who didn't know who the hell I was. Their conversation was far more useful to me than the governor's.

"No matter how I felt toward her that day, I savored Angelique dressing, disappearing into her clothes, and today, a rarity, I was able to watch her dress because I was apartment-bound, sick, in bed. It was an occasion, her getting dressed before I did, and in spite of our nearly two years together, it was a procedure I was tempted to abort, especially on our way out for the evening, at any moment, with an explicit sexual demand.

"'Want to take a whack at breaking my fever?'" I said, eyes cast out the window, up toward the wintry sky, feigning indifference. More in good humor than ardor. 'I can't. I'm latish already,' she said easily, stepping into her panties, modestly, mustn't inflame the patient, the sick dog. I could still grab her. Destroy all her good art work. I'd go raving on, she knew, until she could get into her dress and slip away. Gimme a rain check? She'd become used to my raving. Husbands raved, she'd been instructed, part of the bargain, no? She had married a man her friends had warned her not to marry. Her men friends had told her I was different, one ungallant swain had even confided to her that I was, hold on, 'an eccentric.' Her women friends told her I didn't work at a job and never would. But Francis Henry Beech, an art critic, a friend of her mother's she'd met in Charleston, had visited my West Village downtown studio with her, disguised as a banker, before my first exhibit, and wrote in *Art News* that Simon Lister was a wondrous painter who was to become a great painter. Proclaimed me The Next Great American Painter of the Decade, whatever that meant. He had written his prediction with renegade abandon, an immediate impression he'd formed based upon his single visit to the studio in my first year when only Anasor knew of me, and supported me, on the basis that I would not sell a painting until Anasor decided I was ready. Now Beech had glimpsed my work and proclaimed me 'great.' It had given Angelique a chill. Greatness. The thought of sleeping beside 'greatness,' being penetrated by 'greatness' pestered her. And so she had fallen in love with my eyes, their green-grayness overwhelmed her in candlelight, and those slim indentations behind each eye at my temples, like tiny mutated vents. They'd been there for life, I told her. She adored my lean profile, the high break in my lean nose, my lean height. As a boy I'd had a fine little head-bone, I looked then as I would look at seventy or eighty when I'd lost most of my hair, a wise brow, deep mysterious eyes, lit by a deep boredom that easily crossed over into anger. The result was a clear concerned look, sane and wise. But it was also the face of the man in the police drawing who'd run amok through my neighborhood killing for the wrong reason, the man they never catch, or if they do, the quiet neighbor everyone liked who'd always kept to himself. But that was then."

Simon stops talking. Then after a long moment, "Let's take a walk."

I go to him. It is the first time I have stood beside him. He is taller. We walk to Haria. There is a moon. We sit at a table in a room with three tables. A generator lights a bulb and refrigerates tapas and beer.

We are drinking rum as usual. A radio is playing music from Spain. I go to the bar and buy our drinks and bring them to our table. I sit.

"The night you escaped from the Eisenstein?"

"Yes."

"The next morning was the fire?"

"Yes. Do you want to hear about it?"

"Of course." I will remember, I tell myself, I will always remember.

"Anyhow, the entire second floor of the Whitney Museum was devoted to my work. Fifty-one of my paintings gathered by Anasor and Angelique. The gray-on-gray classic lettering curved above the archway: Simon Lister Exhibition—The World Retrospective. But of course they were no longer mine. They had risen in value, all well over the million mark. They came from galleries and private collections around the world, heavily insured. The cost of the shipping, astronomical. Of course, I no longer owned them, no successful artists does. The artist stands off to one side like an abandoned host while the master of ceremonies invites the brokers to take over. They barter your paintings like stocks calling out prices you could not imagine. Pity the artist who is bought cheaply and later when he's broke sees his work selling in a gallery for a millions. That wasn't to be the case with me.

"It was early on the morning after, just about eight, the exhibition was being set up, but work on it had not started for the day. The curator, Mr. Karoly, recognized me with a bow and let me enter. He allowed me to go to the second floor to be alone with my paintings, which I hadn't ever seen gathered. Again, no successful painter does.

"I stood in front of the first painting, a triptych. It was taller than I was. Then I opened my overcoat and shot a nearly invisible jet of fluid from a can hidden inside. I was squeezing liquid butane through a pin-hole spout onto the width of the painting just in front of me, I stopped for an instant to watch it run down the painting's face. *The*

Houses, it was called. Very simple. Very large.

"Now I was standing in front of a second painting, squeezing a lesser amount. Mr. Karoly surprised me. He passed through the gallery, eyes front, pretending not to disturb the artist viewing his paintings. Then I was in front of the third painting before the butane had even run down the face of the second painting. You see what I was doing? One at a time, I was anointing each of the fifty-one paintings with death fluid. My World Retrospective. My fifty-one paintings, how must I have felt, they will always be my paintings no matter who owned them or in what museum they were hung. Of course. They are shiny from streams of butane."

Simon drinks. Nods to me. We finish our drinks and walk back to the house in silence. He is not finished he refills our glasses. Between us we have drunk most of the two bottles of *Ron Miel* rum that I brought with me. I can see this is not easy for him. At the table he continues talking, turning away from me.

"Now I was standing in front of the first triptych, *The Houses*. I actually spoke to the painting. I was remembering its origins, so many decisions made painting it, then I said goodbye to it, apologized and, with my cigarette lighter, I ignited the shiny canal wetting the base of its frame. I was at the next painting. I stood by it an instant before I lit it, then I was at the next painting and I lit it. I lit each painting quickly now, learning how to burn paintings, one by one. I left Gallery One aflame, glowing behind me and entered Gallery Two. By the time the fifty-first was aflame, burning nicely, the original triptych was nearly gone. The effect was brilliant. Galleries One, Two, Three and the Jewison Room, were ablaze, the walls were not, nothing burned except the paintings, each a private pyre. The heart of each painting had effectively stopped beating.

"The aroma! For moments I stood on the stone bench in Gallery

Three breathing the air, my head nearly eight feet above the floor, watching each painting burn in its own colors, the impasto flaring widely, I turned slowly and slowly in the center of the room, I watched paintings burn their different fires. Orange paint burning with orange flame, blue with blue, black with black. Sweet-smelling country fire smoke. Molten paint dripped to the parquet oak floor, each wad burning itself out where it fell.

"Fire! Where was everybody? Two, three, four minutes have passed since the first flash of fire. Where were they? Was I the only one who cared? The triptych was gone. Its molten flaming paint dripped down the pale gray wall, now black inside its frames, black at the top, still silver along their bases, where flaming paint was flowing down, burning droplets to the floors. Extraordinary beauty! Those frames wouldn't burn.

"My face was warm. The smell of flamed paintings, my paintings, was exquisite. An elegant lunch-time fragrance emanating from the cuisine of a three-star restaurant. The steady burning canvas covered with a blending of my oil paints with cold-pressed linseed oil and beeswax, long dried. It was a blend I painted with, a recipe from the early Flemish School, once used on their paintings, the ones that survived today. The blend's base, litharge of lead, amber, heavy, earthy, poisonous, made it a deadly black smoke.

"Volcanic fissures smoldered where paintings were burning through to the wall behind them. So much paint spread on the canvas, so few people realize how much. Burning fragments dropped from all the paintings. Black smoke lifted from all sides to the high skylight, drifted back, and joined the new smoke coming up with nowhere to go, aimless smoke. The smell of their burning oil was exquisite. Quietly burning. This, now, what I was seeing, was the real Simon Lister Exhibition, the Worldwide Retrospective. The sound each painting made flaring, each at its own time, was startling at first then soothing. I turned to each as it reached its flash point. My pictures were thickly painted, they were good burners, burning across, burning quietly, hissing; *SSSSSSSssssssssssssssSSSSSSS*. Now I felt their warmth on my hands in the immense gallery.

"The triptych was smoking black without flame. Woodrow Parker was the first to call it priceless and it would now remain priceless forever. The network of bracing wires seen behind it against the wall gripped each silver and black frame, criss-crossed the walls, black with bursts of umber, cobalt, ochre. A glamorous wall, ready for a new exhibition. Would they show that to the public? The ghosts of each painting? Most of my paintings were burning low, two had gone out. I looked for my last painting, *The Harbor*, but could not find it. Then I remembered, it was still at the Museum of Modern Art. They had refused to loan it to the Whitney. A political decision, revenge for some slight. I needed to go there. At last I heard alarm bells, at last felt the cool rain shower spraying from above. It was time to go. Mrs. Inez, a docent, whizzed through Gallery Three without a sound, into the Jewison, trotting back and forth, mouth open, moaning or screaming, in silence, hysterically. I could hear such a clamor in my ears! Mr. Karoly re-appeared, aghast, mouth wide, pale, faint, confused, stumbled to the floor, then across, nothing to do. He was ill, he could not get up, he crawled out of danger, he lay curled on his side, twitching, weeping.

"Outside, I didn't feel the cold even though it was 30 degrees. There was sprinkler water in my hair, my coat was drenched, I left a wet beaver trail behind me on the pavement but I was heated by the fires in the New Wing. I passed cow-faced people on the street just beginning their day, people who do not imagine. I was trotting, I was on Madison Avenue, then in a cab, quick, to the Anasor Gallery, where a woman with the slightly deformed beauty of an heiress, whose mouth dropped when she saw me enter, recognized me, smiled 'Hello.' She was sitting behind the desk in the office, shocked to see me. Wasn't I supposed to be institutionalized? She dumbly escorted me through to the main showroom, I asked to be left alone to view my paintings. She smiled respectfully with manners gained from gallery insight, then fled to wake Anasor and whisper into the phone, 'Mr. Anasor, he's here!'

"In less than two minutes all seven of my paintings at the Anasor were burning. When I passed her on my way out to the street, she was still on the phone nodding. She saw me and smiled again, half stood, about to speak, just as she smelled the first black fingers of smoke, but I was gone. From half-a-block away I heard Anasor's fire alarm clanging behind me. I walked the six blocks to the Museum of Modern Art. I had just enough time. No one would guess, not yet, not until afterwards. It was early. I was privileged. Up to the third floor, past the guards without even looking at them, the Permanent Collection. There it was. Outside again, I hailed a taxi, I was running late."

He stops talking. His head slumps onto the chair back. In a moment, the first gentle snore. I am exhausted, alert, and very drunk. I presume he is, too. He is turned away from me mumbling in his sleep. He told me later this was the most he's spoken since he came here.

The next journal is on the table. As I leave, I take it. I slip it inside my shirt to protect it from the elements. The moon shows me the way down the hill, though I stumble on the loose gravel. The door to my room has been left open for me. When I undress, brush my teeth and wash in the pan of water on the bureau before getting into bed, I pull the blanket over me, and by the light of two candles, I begin to read.

The rooster wakes me. It is a bright morning, no wind. The journal is still in my hand. A pool of wax is all that remains of the two candles, guttered and burned away. The journal is open to page one. I begin reading.

CHAPTER 5

The Second Journal
New York City: John Jay Street

᪥

January 7, 1964

We woke early, Anna and I, at exactly the same instant but in different rooms. Somewhere across the blank city, its residents were not yet awake, not yet ready to push each other around. Lying there in bed I realized that she would never go back to the park, she knew too much. In our moments together, I should have interlaced my fingers into hers. Hers were pale blue with cold, mine calloused and neglected. She had watched me through tired child's eyes with what I now realize was a child's fear. I lay in bed and listened, suspicious of the truth. Jesus, there it was, the good clamor out there! Yes. Jackhammers busting concrete! Shouts, cries, air-brakes; busses, trucks, horns, subways, sirens, planes. What a great city, New York, the great city of the planet. It's the people living here who scare me.

I went back to sleep again. No dreams. I had to get up. The floor was cold. I put my socks on and my sweater. I had to get to Capt. Padewicz Park.

When I went out, Maurice, didn't stop me, but I felt him watching from his window. I felt his Spanish eyes searing my back. He knows, he knows, he knows. Why doesn't he say something? Will the police be waiting for me when I come back? Who else knows?

I got there at three, Anna's time to sit and feed the resident squirrel. Her beauty terrifies me; it seems uncontainable. I passed out.

Suddenly I dropped to my knees, passes out on the blacktop. My head hits it with a 'donk.' I lie under the lacework of dead limb-twigs overhead. They form windows for me, branches become beams, trunks become pillars. A few of the curious walkers slow down to appraise me, then a man almost too old to care stops.

"What's with you, Chief?"

My first spoken words to a stranger, laid down like a bet.

"You doing drugs?"

"No, forget it, I'm okay."

"You drunk?"

"I fell over, okay?"

"Beats getting shot." The man chuckles, he is a lifer.

"I'm okay down here I swear to God."

"You gonna be okay, Chief." It is not a question.

"Yeah, yeah, go, I'm telling you, thanks, go, I fall over all the time. I take medication."

"Okay, Chief."

The man turns and walks away. I lie on the blacktop another minute, enjoying his rights, being a chief, looking up at the lacework of tree limbs turning above me.

"She's not coming. I'll never see her again."

Two black athletes sit down on the bench opposite to better observe me. They're impatient, running late for a half-court game. They are taking interest in me, my yield. Hyenas passing by, glaring at the disabled wildebeest.

But I'm lying there, comfortable, waiting for her, hearing her last words, seeing her delayed, dead-eyed stare.

"You've killed yourself," I tell her quietly. "Don't kill yourself. Kill me."

The blacks are fascinated. It speaks. This can't be ignored, here's a talking white man who needs them. The shorter one, a carnival figurine in peppy clothes, idles over, stops comfortably above me, the casual pose of the point guard. He grins intimately, extends his hand.

"Lem'me hep you up, my man."

"I'm okay thanks."

"I be worried you catch cole, lem'me hep you up."

"No. Thanks."

"Soo-soo. Well ten bucks ought to take care your bill."

"What bill?"

"'The my-expenses-walkin'-over-an-walkin'-away-from-you' bill."

"It's in the mail."

"Uh-uh. Life's a bitch, my frind."

The taller one has joined us. He walks as if he were crossing a bed.

"Do I owe your friend?"

"Ax him why don' you? He don' confide in me."

The taller one squats, I sense anger, his dark heat.

"You're telling me twenty bucks covers your expenses?"

"Ought to do it."

Behind them, at the edge of the park, I spot a man in a blue overcoat looking my way, a policeman. I push myself up on an elbow nearly touching the taller man's nicely rounded nose with mine. They have not seen the cop.

"Take a shit in your hat," I whisper to them. "And be sure to eat it while it's still warm."

I walk away. Their arias follow me, "Ooooeee! Whitey! Ooooeee! Whitey!"

Approaching John Jay Street, I know something's wrong. There are no police but Maurice's door is open and there is no Maurice. Mrs. Connors comes out and gives me the news: he's gone to St. Vincent's Hospital. She tells me. He's gone before, she says, he'll be back. Her implication is that he's faking it. I see her denial. Mrs. Connors is always looking up at me, wisps of red hair, bright cheeks. I never liked her but now I do.

Maurice is faking, taking his annual holiday, the old fool. But it's serious, I can see that she senses danger; she's been crying. Suddenly, I see it: she loves Maurice. The magpie and the crow, a fable out of Aesop.

I went upstairs and lay down for a while. Very depressed. Anna's gone. It was a blue evening when I dressed and walked the mile across town to visit Maurice on the second floor in a ward of 14 beds of St. Vincent's Hospital.

Maurice lies half-asleep in the peed-on necropolis of Ward Four. I'm stunned. In one day Maurice has deteriorated, his skull resembles an icon, an historic figure. A pale scrim from the next world hangs between us. Death. I see it even before I pull a chair up to the bed and sits down close to him, breathing his baby smells. The loyal homburg is perched on the bed by his side, as if for luck. I've never seen him out of his homburg. Now his head is tightly wrapped in a pink skull bandage, he resembles a fossilizing bird I once discovered in the desert. His eyebrows, now in need of fierce brushing, resemble sleeping gray squirrels. I sit a long time, Maurice's great beezer stuffed with cotton wads reminds me of the keel of a shipwrecked sloop. The sere face wakes gently, catches me half-dozing, his failed eyes have gained a yellow tint. When he speaks it is as if he were speaking from another room. He tries to put on a bored mask, maybe to put me at ease. The trick, I suppose, is to pretend you don't realize that you are in the presence of death. But you do.

"Rembrandt," he whispers.

"Goodbye," I write and holds the pad in front of his face and regret it immediately.

"Goodbye? I look that bad?"

"No. Goodbye, I'm leaving the city," I write.

Maurice raises his eyes. "Where to?"

"I want to get to Paris."

"That's nothing, I want to get to John Jay Street!" He waves my pad aside and squints at me.

"Come on, Rembrandt. Would it kill you to smile when you come to visit?"

"Like you?" I write.

"Schmuck. No, not like me. O-o-ooh, my head hurts. I'm the patient. Who are you? Tell me something, anything I don't know."

"I think I betrayed you," I write.

"I think you did, too." His eyelids flicker and close.

"And myself," I write.

Maurice opens his eyes. "What is betrayal?" he asks. "You who are a beautiful artist. What do you know about betrayal?" Immediately drowsy, bored before he finishes speaking. "Betrayal against yourself is a bargain. Real betrayal lies elsewhere my friend." He waves his arm to indicate that Ward Four is his kingdom, the great gold watch shines from his sparrow thin wrist. "If I don't wear your watch night and day believe me, my new friend in the next bed'll steal it." He turns his great keel nose toward the next bed. "I could get mugged riding the gurney to the toilet. Don't talk to me about betrayal. Bullshit!" he sighs. He smiles. "You remind me of the time I found the answer to the mystery of life on this planet."

Maurice's mind has overtaken his body. He takes slow, gentle breaths. "I was twelve, summer had come to Queens. I was sent out of the house with a spade to remove a stack of dogshit someone's dog had left on the pavement in front of the building. You know Queens?" He goes on, "I didn't clean it up. I became transfixed by it, I reveled in it. Understand? I couldn't take my eyes off of it. Five minutes. This is everything, I thought, right here in front of me."

I wait for Maurice to reach his point, if he has one. Maurice moves thoughts like chess pieces.

"That's it." He gives a hoarse outcry, "That's what it is! The secret of life! I never changed my opinion since." He lies back, exhausted.

"But you're a chess player," I write. "A lover of baseball." I try to think what else. "You're supposed to solve everything when you're old, then you die."

Maurice's head shudders quickly, rejecting that notion. With a jolt he continues.

"I had it all figured out when I was only 12."

Suddenly I see it. Jesus, he's actually leaving. He doesn't want to know any more about the world than he has to know. "It's possible, Maurice, really, I swear to you." I think he's fallen asleep, bored by my presence.

"Never heard of it," Maurice says, opening his eyes abruptly, glaring yellowly at me, only a very rich man could enjoy such a fabulous disease. He takes a slow breath: "Don't look for anything you can't find."

I shudder. "Don't die. Not now." I hold his arm, it is like a baby's arm. Maurice stirs, then a small tremor passes through him. He glares at me again.

"I was dreaming."

I wait for his breath.

"Look for something you can't find and I can guarantee you un-happiness."

I think, "That's me." His vision is filming over.

I see myself loading up a Pharaoh's Sun Ship with memorabilia to keep him company on his death voyage to the Sun. It appears that Maurice's mummification ceremony has already begun.

I write, "You know, right?"

Maurice cuts a smile out from memory. "It did cross my mind."

Pause.

"Why didn't you turn me in for the reward?"

Maurice reaches out, tries to grip my arm. He touches my hand instead. "You did good, Simon."

" Fifty thousand dollars?"

"I'm proletariat. Where would I spend Fifty grand? Seriously. I like you, Simon. You're a jerk, but I like you."

"How long did you know?"

"I knew a while. I'll be honest, I wasn't sure. But when I put the newspaper on the table and you took it, I knew." He half-smiles, looks at me with reproach. A surge of strength passes through him. "No one is called 'Jonathan Boot.' But I figured Simon Lister to be older." He dozes.

"I want to tell you something." I write. "I've brushed the cosmos. I never told that to anyone."

But he won't open his eyes. A nurse walks through the room, she could be a lineman with the NFL.

"Six-thirty. Everyone out!"

Visitors obey. Stand by other beds. There are flowers left on bed tables. Clean pajamas folded. I don't stand. The nurse comes over to Maurice's bed. She has determined that his visit be terminated.

"Time to go!" she says.

"I know," Maurice says in his sleep.

I scribble on my pad, "Read this to him. Please." I hand it to her. She tears the page off the pad.

"I'll give it to him tomorrow. He's asleep."

I still don't stand. I shake my head, grip Maurice's arm. The nurse senses trouble.

"Okay!" she says. She pushes Maurice's shoulder gently waking him. His eyes go from the nurse to the paper to my face. The nurse reads, badly, from the paper, word by word but with accidental clarity.

"I want to tell you something, Maurice. I brushed the cosmos I never told that to anyone."

"I figured." Maurice whispers.

The nurse doesn't understand, but she continues to read: "Years ago, I discovered a strength; I didn't know where it came from. I was connected to the cosmos."

Maurice whispers. "Put in a word for me."

The nurse has become strangely involved, intrigued. She realizes this may be a letter of goodbye. She reads: "So can you, Maurice. It's perfection."

I write and hand her the pad.

"Have you ever felt part of anything more than a house, a church, a school, a city? A country? Part of a cosmos?"

"A little late, my friend. But I thank you for the effort."

"It's possible," I mouth. I want Maurice to cart this information away with him.

"Thank you for telling me that," he whispers, "It could happen."

I want him to take this with him wherever he is going. I write: "I hate to go." I stand up.

"Hey, I hate to go, too."

I take his hand.

"We're getting in the World Series this year. The Yankees. Believe me I'm sorry." He tries to laugh.

The nurse seems dangerously close to showing emotion.

"Next time," I write. I walk down the row of beds without saying goodbye.

January 8, 1964

Astrida came, brought me coffee and toast, no fish no margarine today. I knew. She was crying. She told me that Maurice had died in the night. I had hardly slept. All night I saw Anna lying beside me, dead. Sleep overcame everything. Finally in that grave void I joined them. Forgive me, Anna, for not saving you. Have you killed yourself? Is that what you were telling me? Your married lover, your father, your cat, were you next? Forgive me, Anna, for not saving you. I was never able to save myself, how could I save you?

Anna. My desire for you blurs. Am I supposed to be alone? My arms, spare parts? Do I deserve any more than I have? I am alive, one up on Maurice, is that enough? He's dead, but alive he had nothing—marks to stand on, a door to breathe behind. Do I abandon myself to someone I hardly know? Imagining your heat? Inventing your wit? How do I know? Am I supposed to die never having poured you your breakfast coffee? Never having felt my ears deafened between your thighs? You are the woman in Paris. My imagined Paris. When I was painting, I was never longing. The painting took everything I had.

January 9, 1964

She's alive. She came to my room last night. She's going to Paris. She said it. She said Friday. She said it, I heard her. Paris. It's very possible.

Maurice's service is tomorrow down the street. He left his things to Mrs. Connors. Maurice is dead. She behaves like a widow. There's a black wreath on the street door. She told me she'll move into his room. A bit late.

Anna's alive. Am I supposed to follow her to Paris? Paris or Elmira, I don't care, but should I risk it?

January 10, 1964

I watched the striped gray cat sitting in its window across the street. A lush tub of a cat, it sits there every morning tucked up under itself. It never looks down at the street the way any normal cat would do. It never watches the pigeons drop their shadows down the face of the building then land with them, on them, in the street. No, this cat sits there with its back to the world, staring into its own apartment. I decided to stare at the cat until I was able to make it stare at me. Until it faced me. I willed it. If it did, then I would go to Paris. I stared and stared. The cat never turned its head. Then after maybe an hour its eyes appeared to me through the back of its head. It wasn't doing anything. It was staring at me. But it was me who was staring through the back of the cat's head into its eyes. Chrome yellow. They stared at me through its own head. So I was going to Paris, the Paris of my imagination.

I've got to do all this just right. First, I need a passport photo and another passport. Next, I'm going to need a steady hand. I'll need to buy a photo, retouch ink, krim acid, acetone, a sable brush. Choose the brush carefully. If I'm such a great artist, I certainly ought to be able to change a three to an eight. And a T to a K. There's one Air France flight daily. Flight One. I know. I paid a shoe salesman to call for me. I haven't eaten since Maurice died. Not hungry. I guess he never tipped Mrs. Connors off about me. Now I need to exercise, I need to get out, I need to be with strangers, breathe air, get stamina. Ride the subway tonight after midnight over to Brooklyn, every night, until next Friday. Nobody I know rides the subway to Brooklyn. Whoever's looking for me rides in limos. Can I survive on John Jay Street until Friday? She'll be on that flight. Flight One.

January 11, 1964

Busy all day. Passport photos, passport forging. Three days.

January 12, 1964

I am "Samuel Lasker!" I finished my passport early this morning on my upside-down bureau drawer under my new 100-watt light bulb. Mister Lasker is a bearded gentleman whose profession is searching for rare books, I'm not sure why. But I am an art forger, a credit to my profession.

The daily Air France flight to Paris. The shoe salesman called and made a reservation for a Samuel Lasker, rare book collector. I'll need to get to the airport early Thursday. I've got to do it all just right. My flight could begin and end at the Air France ticket counter with some varnished ticket agent saying, "Kindly follow me, sir," in French.

Paris'll be colder. Paris is cold even when it's hot, but if it's cold winter here it'll be a colder winter in Paris. I gave Mrs. Connors my other scarf by mistake. Damn! I just left it out in the hall yesterday morning in front of my door with a few newspapers. Wool scarves are a couple of bucks on the street by the subway station but I'm pretty sure mine was cashmere and it kept my neck hot.

January 13, 1964

Stayed in all day. Rode subway late. She was here again last night. We made love. Does what happened last week surpass that? No, it is part of it. By whatever power was in me, I know that last night when I saw Anna, I was not dreaming. Is it a suggestion I have created beyond the canvas? That I may have been created by myself. Myself and Anna. It had not been a dream. And so this morning I realized that last night was not a dream within a dream. This was new. My ability to see was strengthening. Outside, the day had become loud. I went out for food, a Greek counter-top lunch. I knew I would see her. Back in my room, I threw Angelique's soft Italian bag on the bed and began to fill it. I had an empty carton that Mrs. Connors gave me. It was marked NOXZEMA.

January 14, 1964

Stayed in all day. Late subway ride.

January 15, 1964

I bought an infantry pack shovel at Army Navy 28th Street. Carried it under my coat. I rode the subway to Central Park Zoo. Dug up $$. OK.

January 16, 1964

My Central Park deposit, buried for a year by the zoo. It was still there last night at 1:00 a.m. sealed in its plastic box. Angelique never knew. No one knew. Hundreds of bills: glaring William McKinley five-hundred dollar bills, up through the bundles of five-thousand dollar bills and one ten-thousand dollar bill, with the portrait of a scowling Salmon P. Chase. It smells so good, the money, damp, woody, smoky. Government fresh paint, crisp when I buried it, and the year underground has given it an irresistible aroma of rainy day, attic goodness.

The money is my only commission from my years, from the fifty-one Whitney Museum paintings, the seven Anasor paintings, the lone Museum of Modern Art painting. From all those millions, some say a billion, this is my final cut.

Stayed in all day. Packed. Late subway Brooklyn. Flautist on train. Incredible luck. I gave him a hundred. Tomorrow, Paris!

January 17, 1964

As I leave the rooming house, I carry the Noxzema carton and my leather bag, down to the ground floor. On the hall table where the mail sits, there is a brown paper bag bound with a rubber band. My name is on it. There is a note inside from Mrs. Connors, something small, gravid in tissue paper. "Dear Mr. Boot, Maurice wanted you to have this. Mrs. Connors."

My wristwatch My misted gold chronograph, an embarrassment from a bygone era. He had not wanted to take it with him on his death trip toward the Sun.

The second journal ends here.

CHAPTER 6

Salve De Dios: Canary Islands, May 7, 2001

It is early. I go down the hill for coffee and oysters and to write out my notes until nine, then walk up to Simon's house. Señora Natti comes to the door. I hand her the second journal, more or less surrender it. I can see Simon behind her eating his breakfast. He calls out, she goes to him. She relays a message to me, *"Venga a las seis,"* she says, *"para comida."* (Come back at six o'clock.)

During the day I walk the island again. I find a store in Haria not far away that sells wine and rum, and I buy both, as well as Condal cigars made in Palma.

Supper is garlic soup followed by grilled sardines, served on the oval, white platter sprinkled with coarse salt. Tomatoes, potatoes, and roasted grapes circle the fish. There is a plate with fennel and bread. Afterwards, Señora Natti clears the table. I offer Simon a cigar. He accepts. I don't mind drinking again. I'm beginning to enjoy it. The wind comes up. The moon rises. He hands me the next journal.

"Do you want to talk?" he asks.

I nod, surprised. "What about the leather box?"

He holds his hands a foot apart. "It was really very small. Angelique had it made in Florence. Deep red with gold embossings. It carried an oil painting not much larger than an 8 by 10 photograph. Framed."

"Was it yours?"

"Yes, the only one left in the world."

"A *trompe l'oeil?*"

Simon nods.

"What was the subject?"

"An adobe house and a palm tree in a desert at night with a half moon. I rarely opened the box to look at it, but when I did, I entered the house and stood inside it. Literally. She would be sitting there at the table or coming downstairs. We would talk."

"Do you understand?"

"You went inside the house?" I ask, amazed.

"Yes,"

We let silence trail off. We sip and puff on our cigars. The smoke passes quickly through the always-open window. The connection between cigars, rum, time, and the meal we have just finished is perfect.

"Why didn't you …?"

"Burn it?"

"With the others."

"I believed in it."

He gets up and goes into the bathroom. I hear him urinate. When he comes back he sits in the more comfortable wooden chair by the window.

"What did you mean you 'dug up money at the zoo?'"

"That was the money Anasor owed me, money I'd squirreled away, my cut of our 50-50 that he probably would have stolen because Angelique had proved me incompetent. So what I did was …"

He interrupts himself.

"Did you know that six months before the Whitney fire I'd burned my paintings in my studio?"

"Yes. A week before your wife committed you."

"I had no way to keep any money I'd earned, but once in a while I'd get a check and cash it, so after the fire at my loft, they discovered a wall safe that I'd concealed, disguised as a speaker. It was locked, and when Anasor's safecracker broke the combination, he found some enticing packets of hundred dollar bills I'd left, bound by paper bands marked $10,000—enough to satisfy him. Not one of the investigators could estimate what amount that the safe had held.

Anasor guessed there was more. But it was missing and so was I. He tried to have me picked up. An all-points bulletin was issued for me, a warrant for a suspected arsonist. I had to do something with the money, so that night I stuffed it into several large plastic bags. I went to Central Park and dug a deep hole and buried it not far from the zoo. The spot formed a simple triangle between the Seal House and the statue of Marshall Foche. I'm sure Anasor realized I'd taken my money and run, but he could never put out that complaint against me. He knew it was two or three million dollars, but he couldn't say anything to the police because it wasn't his money."

CHAPTER 7

The Third Journal
Flight One: New York - Paris

ᵍ⌒ᵍ

January 17, 1964

… I'm sitting in JFK Airport, just renamed to honor our fallen king. The snow hasn't stopped falling since midnight. It lands without hope. It lies in gray stacks of gelato muffling the tires of the taxis, the propellers of the planes. I've been here since dawn listening to announcements, Flight One being delayed again and again. I walk the distance to the ramp to see the waiting plane. I am overwhelmed. She is silver. Lines of blue and red, a Super Constellation. She is monstrous, a hunched silver tube powered by four, many-bladed propellers. Sweepers stand on her wings sweeping lush piles of wet snow to the ground. The day is already dark.

One more announcement, a dusky-voiced French woman with a seductive accent is whispering, "Air France Flight One: New York-Paris-Rome-Cairo, will be delayed two hours. Please excuse the delay. Runway conditions have not improved."

So many motionless passengers weary of not flying. I am not at home here. I am a receptacle, my vortex swirls. I look for Anna, her lean height, her brisk walk. I am no longer sure if she is alive. When she came to me last night it was not a dream. I understand that now. I understand now that she was not with me in tangible form, even though we touched, she was not with me in any form that I had ever known.

When we met in Capt. Padewicz Park, if I had been able to feel the weight of her despair that I now see was beyond despair, I might have helped. The death of her married lover, a sudden shock, the death of Faery, a deeper trauma, but the death of her father such a long way off, after so many years of silence, inflicted untold damage. A deep despair caused by her unresolved mourning. She may have taken her own life. She may have come to me last night post mortem.

I look for her. I stand up, stooped, but tall anyway. I wear my black Cossack hat, my fireproof wool overcoat that smells of wet sheep. I seem too weary, like a warrior returning from a revolution he has lost. I am wearing metal spectacles. I have grown a small, fine beard. I walk back down the dreadful white corridors as far as the check-in counters looking at shapes. So many people don't resemble her. Airport lighting is a preview of euthanasia.

Last night, my illusion of her was real. For years I have felt impulses stronger than I could gather in my mind, illusions from out there. I have never tried to explain them, even at the Eisenstein. I told my handlers I was simply tired of seeing too much. This is the most important thing about Anna's visit. She was real to me regardless of what has become of her.

What if she is not on Flight One? Why go to France? By now the French will have warrants for my arrest. My crimes against French museums and collectors are less grave than those against the American collectors, but vengeance is vengeance. I have destroyed their investments. They were no longer my paintings. They were no longer paintings at all. They had become dark, blue chip stocks, liquid assets, futures. Anything but my paintings.

It is nearly noon. No Anna. Oh, the day wears on, my mock passport melting my shirt pocket. My excellent lettering, the number I have invented that may well turn out to be the number of some other wanted felon.

Air France Flight One: New York-Paris-Rome-Cairo will be delayed. Runway conditions have not improved. But they have asked for the passports of all departing passengers. My hands are trembling. Why not? My passport number looks good, but my new name, "Samuel Lasker?" I've got to find a passport agent who does not read the art page of the *Times*, who might make a wild guess. Also: someone who does not watch the magazine shows either, the ones that go on and on about me. I must find this person. Then I must slide my passport nicely to her along the counter. Keep my gloves on because my palms are wet with worry.

Rehearsal: "How long are you going to stay in Paris, Mr. Lasker?" I will scribble: "Two weeks." The customs control officer, a woman in her early thirties will be attractive, maybe sensuous. She will smile and nod, examine my picture approvingly, look up and say, "I prefer you without your beard, Mr. Lasker." She will recross her legs, tightening her nether regions. She will flick blank pages. Obviously, I haven't traveled much, a shut-in, but her mind is clearly not on it, pause. "Reason for your visit, please?" I write, "Vacation." Thud-stamp, thud-stamp. My mock passport gets an 'A.' It is slid back. She has long fingers, with fine crotches in between each. "Bon voyage, Mr. Lasker." her eyes add, "Perhaps some other time, under some other regime?"

I mouth, "Thank you."

I have passed my exam. Fat chance. My funny passport. The customs officer will be the one over there on the left, a tired man. He will glance at my forgery, laugh "Ho, ho, ho," then hold it up for the others to see. "Nice try, Mr. Lister. Come with me. Let's discuss my reward money. Ho ho ho."

I wake. I must have been dozing. It is now early afternoon. The note from Mrs. Connors must have fallen out of my coat pocket. Poor Maurice. I cannot imagine those eyebrows dead.

"Air France Flight One is now scheduled to leave at 4:45 p.m. Boarding will begin in one hour at Gate 4. Please have your passports ready …"

A ragged cheer goes up around the airport. The snow has stopped. A small line has formed. I scan the three customs officers, each at their rostrums. I will place my bet, my bet to choose my own bedtime for the next few years. I stand, take my place in line, passport alive in my hand. I place my stack of chips on the customs agent to my right, the youngest one, partly because she's Chinese, partly because she's stamping quickly. I like her style. I feels my bet is safe. If it isn't, I stay in New York, go to trial, plead *nolo contendere*, lose, then, to pay for my act of art-tracide, I'm trotted off to Federal prison for the rest of my life, which will take less than a month to ebb out of me behind bars.

I'm about to step forward when the line splits in two. A perfect family, perfectly matched—scarves, luggage, coats, shoes—sails ahead of me with the insolent skill that privilege entitles them to. The blended man introduces himself too clearly to the Chinese

customs officer in a language known as "Connecticut." I'm sig-
naled to another line.

"Passport please?"

Helpfully, I open it to the photo of the harried man named Samuel Lasker and slide it to her. She watches my gloved hands. Of
course, they are trembling.

"What is your destination, Mr. Lasker?"

To a world away from this barking place, anywhere with Anna. I
write, "Paris."

"Business or pleasure?"

"Death of my father," I scribble. Then add, "Pleasure."

Not funny, the Spider Lady loves her father.

"Paris is having its worst winter in twenty years," she says.

So am I. I write, "I am a chef, it is always summer inside the
kitchen, Madame." I slide the note across the counter.

"Precisely," she says. But something has gone wrong. She studies
the photograph again. Why? Is she studying the number? Has
some flaw caught her eye? She glances up at me, then down,
opens a fat paperback volume made up entirely of six-digit numbers Millions of errant passports. She scans the columns for
number B 593850. Or is she looking for the original, B 593350?
She flushes slightly. The book is closed and set aside. She looks up
directly at me.

"Would you step to one side, please, someone will tell you where
to go."

My stomach hits my boots. God, it's happened. I can't move.

"Please stand over there, sir."

The world tilts another ten degrees. I shrug and pantomime.

"Stand where?"

"Just over there."

Others are watching. The tall unkempt man has been caught doing something distasteful.

"That officer will tell you where to go. Next, please."

That officer is without opinion and walks me to a room with
glass on three sides. I sit on the chair that isn't near the steel and

rubber desk, naval gray. I wait. Flight One leaves in fifty-five minutes. I wait. I am back in the submarine on my first dive.

What is happening? I wait. I can imagine my passport illustrating the cover of a coffee table book, *Celebrated Forgeries*. I stand, I sit. My world spills onto the floor around my boots. I see dots of paint. Cerulean, amber, white. My soft Italian bag carrying shirts and the small, unsigned Lister painting boxed in leather. My Noxzema carton tied shut, carrying five pounds of fresh treasury bills, who knows how many? I sit. Two minutes pass. Who is this woman, Our Lady of the Passports? What does she know? Is she out to make her reputation on my behalf? I could make a dash for it now but I would only get as far as the exit gates. I bring out my journal, my pen.

I am deformed, did I mention that? A slight stoop. Just enough, therefore misunderstood, but just enough to need art to interpret the world for me, through my misshapen lenses. I could never have joined the club. There was no air in the clubhouse, too much good talk among the members. I made no friendships, either. I needed to separate myself. Am I being punished for that? Because it was helpful never to monitor what was being exhibited around me, to be unaware of fashions, ground rules, prices. To make a clean entry into the millennium of fine art and so, be distinctly apart from its membership …

Six minutes have passed.

There is no light on these winter afternoons. It is dark at three o'clock. It is windless; the heavy snow brings calm. There are no flights, the planes are hushed, still. I have always feared I will drown in still, icy water.

"Mr. Lasker?"

Two men have entered the room, a U.S Customs officer who wears a uniform trimmed with the gold of an Aztec high priest. and a younger man in a suit and neatly tied neck-tie. A civilian.

"Is this him?" the U.S Customs officer asks.

The younger man has an overcoat slung over his arm. I barely move, I am ragged, nervous.

"Is this him?" the officer asks again of the man in the dark suit. I turn away, ready to vomit. The younger man says nothing.

"Would you please stand up, sir?" the officer asks. I obey.

"Are you Simon Lister?"

I write, "No." I hold my pad up. I appear to be outraged. My pen drops to the floor but I don't reach for it. I recognize the man in civilian clothes. It is Mathews, the man who passed me on Elizabeth Street last week when I suddenly transformed into a beggar. Mathews!

"Do you understand the question?"

I'm able to scribble, "I am Samuel Lasker."

Mathews is looking at me. What for? Of course he knows who I am. Who else could I be? I remember that Angelique invited him to our wedding reception three years ago, that he and I faced each other at close range, armed only with a pair of champagne glasses, while my new bride stood close by, smiling broadly.

Seconds go by.

In his silence, Mathews makes them pass more slowly. He is about to speak; he will say, "Yes, this is him. Hi, Simon. Golly, I've been reading all these nasty stories about you." He will tell anyone who will listen everything he knows about Simon Lister. How once in Chicago, at the Art Institute, even he himself collapsed onto the marble floor in front of *The Field*. Mathews told the doctor that within the painting he had seen his father again. He remembered seeing snow on his father's shoulders, and how he talked with him about things he had never been able to talk with him about while his father was alive. A month later, Anasor received a small box addressed to me—twenty-five ounces of caviar with an note signed, "Your humble servant, Peter Mathews."

I'm on my feet. I raise my face to Mathews. Another second goes by. Now Mathews can see my eyes. Through my eyes, he sees my vortex—the complete horror, the gravity, the ravages, the pain. Of course, he knows that it was Angelique who had me institutionalized. He must know that there was something dreadfully wrong with her doing that. And maybe he knows that there would be something dreadfully wrong with saying "Hi, Simon" at this moment. Mathews may even sense that if he speaks my name aloud now, I will soon die of accelerated depression in a federal penitentiary.

Seconds go by, ten, fifteen, too many. It is almost too late. Mathews has gone pale. I can see the pores closing on his face. His eyes are wet. He tilts his head as if to avert a blow and turns away from me. He snaps his head around to face the customs officer, he has become agitated. His voice is sharp, dry.

"Of course not!" he says, "What on earth made you think this gentleman is Simon Lister? I know Simon Lister. This is not him, this is someone else." Then to me, patronizingly, "Please excuse us sir, I am Peter Mathews, art restorer. I just happen to be out here servicing the Calder sculpture. And you are?"

He picks up my pen and hands it to me. I write on my pad, "Samuel Lasker."

"A pleasure, Mr. Lasker."

I stuff the pad back in my coat pocket.

The customs officer steps forward. "I must apologize to you, Mr. Lasker. Of course, you are free to go. Here is your passport. There's still time to make your flight. Have a good trip."

He extends a hand to me I look down. It's not alright. Mathews says nothing more. They turn and go.

I am alone. The cubicle is hushed. I reach for the soft Italian bag with the dark leather box that holds my painting, the Noxzema carton with its bundles of bills. I walk quickly to the gate. I watch for Anna, she might still appear, running to catch the plane, late.

She is not among the passengers. I'm exhausted by fear. I wait until the other passengers have boarded. Then, without wanting to go but unable to stay, holding the umbrella I have just been handed, keeping my head down, I cross the slushed tarmac from the terminal to the great Constellation. I step toward the plane, up the metal steps of the ramp. The intoxicating effect of my final exhibition—each brilliant painting burning to its own end. The vision comes to me again and again, it comforts me, I carry it with me onto the plane, the greatest art exhibition ever seen by only one witness.

I walk the aisle scanning the faces. I find my seat, 21 A, sit without hope. I will never see her again. The flight is half full; many passengers gave up and went home. I have three seats to myself. A wondrous looking air hostess in a deep-water blue uniform swings down the aisle counting passengers. She spots me wedged against the window, clenching my carton.

"Is your seat belt fastened?"

It certainly isn't. Of course it isn't. I look up at her and smile.

"Your seat belt. Just reach over there to your right, you'll get it, now clip the two ends, see?" She reaches far out across me, glibly clips me closed. Her womanly style might or might not be her own, it might be Air France's.

She smells of Fifth Avenue perfume. She is pretty in a slightly battered way, a battered angel, an angel with many flight hours. Finished seat-belting me, she straightens and hurries away, left right left right, glancing left and right at the rows of seats. Everybody else knows about the seat belts. Her name is Kiwi. What does her half-smile mean? Do I amuse her?

In a moment, she is back. "Would you please put that box under your seat for takeoff?" She does it for me while I search for understanding from her. She breezes off again.

Sitting across the aisle from me, The Oldest Woman On Earth checks my seat belt with a glance and nods. She is a veteran. Basking in her oldness, she regards my face.

I watch Kiwi, follow her down the aisle, at eye level. Her tight skirt, gives confidence, gives her whatever is needed. For years her looks have been called angelic, a first impression, but angelic faces, in my life, have never concealed angelic ways. Her blue uniform, what blue is that? Delft blue. Darker than Anna's eyes? No.

Kiwi makes an announcement, gets everyone to look at her. As if crashing on land weren't wintry enough, we may go down in the North Atlantic, she says. If so, we will need to put on a yellow vest to die in. She models the correct way to wear it. The passengers watch as she slips into a life vest, blows into a tube, sucks imaginary oxygen from above. With a ballet dancer's gesture she points out exits, suggesting the women remove their high heels before jumping into the mountainous seas of the North Atlantic. I love her performance, applaud quietly. I believe every gesture she makes. While I'm thinking of my demise, one wing engine revs up, screams, squeals, whines. The propeller blades disappear into speed, spitting wet snow against the oval perspex windows. First one, then another, then another, until all four engines are roaring bursts of fire. I feel rivets jangling. I see no reason to go to Paris, no reason to stay in America. I don't see a reason to die. Without Anna, I would never be on Flight One. And now without her, I am on Flight One.

The Oldest Woman On Earth turns to me, reaches a fragile hand across the aisle, "Would you mind if I hold your hand, sir?" she says. "Taking off excites my heart so."

I welcome her mean little grip; she doesn't know how well it calms me.

The Constellation taxis toward the runway, turns into the wind, waits. The Vulcan God-of-Fire engines rage. They are angry; flames spew from their gorges as the huge plane barrels down the runway at fullest power, following a string of beads a mile long. Almost airborne, I lean my head back, taking the weight of the mach thrust. The engines claw the air for enough ground speed to lift them, and with a final lunge, the wheels leave the ground. Out the oval window in the gray afternoon—the last I will ever see of JFK Airport, of New York, of America.

As the wheels are sucked into the plane's belly, The Oldest Woman On Earth says, "Thank you," and leans toward me. "I have always wanted to spend this life taking-off. I always feel more alive then than at any other time. Don't you?"

"Yes," I say. I, too, want to be suspended in this perfect rush for the rest of my life. Delicately, she extricates her hand from mine —things shouldn't go any further. I feel the rejection.

For seventeen hours no one will be able to touch me. There are no felonies up there, I am safe for the night. But a wave of illness combs through me as I remember—I'll never find Anna.

Kiwi tells me that in three hours they will land in Newfoundland for fuel, I will stay aboard. I feel safer in the hunched tube than I have felt at any time since I left the Eisenstein. But when we land at Orly in Paris, I must answer for myself, for whatever happens. It is no longer my life; I have lost control over my destiny.

Kiwi brings me a miniature bottle of Courvoisier without my

asking her. Later she tells me that I looked airsick when I came aboard. Drowning in the din of the plane now, it is hot, there is no air. Kiwi brings me two more tiny bottles of Cognac. Soon I'm asleep. All is well until Orly.

I stir, I see snow. "Have we landed? Is this Newfoundland?" The propellers drone out the oval window, a full moon glows on the silver wing. Waking up to the night sky, I am amazed.

Outside, it appears to be a stunning night. But how would anyone know? No one has ever been out there. No one has ever stepped out onto a verandah above the clouds talking with a friend, holding a drink, admiring the thin icy air. I stare for a long time.

My arm is touching someone. A scent, warmth. I turn away from the window, face the person on my left.

Anna!

The child's eyes. She is sitting in the seat beside me. I touch her face. Anna! She is pale, her eyes enlarged. Silent, full of ordeal, smiling, her lips flat across her teeth. She doesn't speak. I have stopped breathing. I cannot make sense of it. I am close to crying out. My heart is pounding. I cannot think. I pale. Suddenly, I pass out.

When I awaken, she isn't there. Was she ever? Yes. I didn't create her. I didn't put her in the seat beside me. She was dressed rather formally—dark blue jacket, skirt, white blouse, stripes on her shoulders. I steady myself by staring at the window. When I can, when I realize what I'm doing, I stare through it. There is nothing more to see through the oval window. My furious heartbeat has relaxed. I stand up, glance back and around. There are pools of light the length of the cabin, fine campfire smoke rising through each. There is the unending *SI-He-ISS* of the plane's night, and beneath it always, the choir of motor and wing music. I can see sleepers warped in fetal positions, others bent in slow conversation—readers, game players—cards, backgammon. Do any of the passengers know where they are? That the screaming wind one inch away from their envelope's skin is 50 degrees below zero? That there is no such thing as being hurled through the night sky, above the clouds, blowing fire? That they are living like verbs. It is impossible. I cannot imagine it, yet I'm no more terrified being propelled through the stratosphere than I am walking on a crowded sidewalk, watching my fellow men shove their way home without casting shadows.

Her formal outfit, a uniform. Anna is wearing a uniform. It is so obvious—she is one of the crew. She is an air hostess. Kiwi is wearing the same blue uniform. I walk the aisle to the silver galley. Kiwi is reading a magazine in a beam of light, sitting tightly on a foldout stool. I describe Anna. She tells me none of the air hostesses fit Anna's description.

I have nowhere to go. I watch her prepare dinners. The scent of cooking, food, French cuisine thousands of feet above the sea, copper pans, garlic presses, how bad can it be? Do I smell wine sauce? All the butters, oils, creams, wines, fats. Kiwi has a strange accent. Half English half New Zealand. Watching her stand and squat relaxes me.

"There's no French health food," Kiwi says, "no diet *beurre blanc*, no whole wheat-croissants. The French just don't care."

I nod in agreement. "They stay away from exercise machines. They lose their weight in bed making love. And their bodies are not their temples, I say. The bodies of their lovers are their temples."

Kiwi touches the back of my hand. She is standing in front of me. She is tall, unfinished.

Later, she serves dinner, which includes two mini-bottles of Bordeaux, as well as two more miniature Courvoisiers. After dinner I doze off.

Something wakes me, fingertips on my hand.

"Anna!"

This time I touch her face, squeeze her chin, her nose, she smiles. I'm not imagining her. She is alive; she looks stunning.

"Where were you?"

She smiles, tilts her head toward the front end of the plane, "Forward."

"How long have you been sitting here?"

"I don't know, not long."

"You knew that I was on the flight?"

"Of course."

"Did you see me being detained?"

"It was very exciting."

"Where the hell have you been? You made me crazy. Why didn't you stay?"

We are smiling without release.

"You fell asleep."

"I passed out! From shock. You left me lying here unconscious."

"I had to go up front."

"But I looked everywhere for you, Anna.

"Where were you?"

"I was busy."

"Doing what?"

"Working."

"On the wing?"

"Further forward."

"But you're a stewardess."

"I'm a navigator. I'm in the pilot's cabin."

"Of the plane, on this flight? You, Anna, are my navigator?"

"Well, yours and, of course, the others."

"What's our course?"

"I just went up to change it to avoid a low pressure ball we can't fly over."

"What's our course, Anna?" I am smiling.

"You don't believe me? Twenty questions. How sweet. Okay, I changed our course from 41 degrees to nearly 42 degrees magnetic."

Her child's eyes have studied the stars and know them.

"I do believe you. And I agree with your decision, forty-two degrees is a far better course."

"Why shouldn't I be a navigator?"

"No reason at all. Have you ever flown a plane?"

"I flew by the seat of my panties all over Europe. I flew a T-131 trainer Dublin–Paris–Berlin–Moscow zero visibility on instruments. I've done aerobatics. I've flown cargo. But Air France will never make me a pilot, that's for certain, not the French anyway."

I'm amazed that she's absolutely survived in a macho world as a feminine woman, girlish in the best sense.

"Was it tough, competing against men on a French airline?"

"I never thought of it as against men. What if it was you, working in a dress store surrounded by women, would you lose your manhood?"

"I guess I am by gender a man and a man can't stop being a man. A man can't be led into change against his will."

"And a woman can?"

"Historically, yes. Men by definition change women, they hunt women, women are the hunted. Men perform the male rites, do the manly things."

"I guess I'm a woman by gender."

"I guess you are. By the way, this is the greatest thing that's ever happened—you being the navigator."

"Yes. I wish you could have seen the meteor shower just now before you woke up."

"Anna, you look amazing. Are you recovering?"

"Kind of, I guess. Enough to come back to work. This is my first flight since … everything."

She looks away, her eyes sparkle wetly. I knows she is not completely cured. I say, "Why did you want me to come on this flight?"

"I wasn't a hundred percent sure that I'd mentioned it to you."

"You did, Anna, you came to my room."

"Maybe you thought I did."

"It's the same thing."

"What do you mean?"

"I mean that certain things are possible for me. Tell me something. Did you live on John Jay Street?"

"I lived there for two weeks on the top floor."

"The room next door to mine."

She nods. "I needed to be somewhere else, anywhere, someplace I could not be found. Did you live there a long time?"

"No."

"Did you ever come to my room?"

"Yes."

Anna looks around. A woman has bent down over her, asks when they're due to land in Gander. Her large breasts tumble forward.

"We'll land in about an hour," Anna tells her.

"Will we be allowed off the plane?," the woman asks.

I can see up between her breasts. They are truly well formed, tanned deep into their gorge. Her nipples are generous.

"Excuse me, *Madame*," I say, "you have marvelous breasts."

The woman is caught off-guard, but in an instant, is outraged. It is my ruthless admiration. Breasts are private matters, never discussed, especially if they are beautiful breasts. She throws her arm across them, harvesting them.

"I find that extremely vulgar, sir," she looks to Anna for support.

None comes. Anna is looking up between them.

"He's right." she says, raising her eyes to the woman's face, "I'm afraid they really are quite marvelous. And yes, you will be allowed to step off the plane at Gander."

The woman reels away. The captain must be told! I smile at Anna; we are connected.

"I can't stand women who do that," she says.

"I can. I just wish she'd take compliments better. She was sharing them with us."

Anna pauses for a moment. "Well, I wouldn't mind sharing, I mean I think about it sometimes."

"What?"

"Well, touching the pretty ones, I suppose. Why not?"

"What a coincidence, I have too. Have you never?"

She shakes her head. "Why did I tell you that? You make me say what I'm thinking."

"We artists have been exploring the nude female for thirty centuries. We're way ahead of you there."

Anna stands, straightens her skirt.

"I need to go. We'll be landing."

I look up at her, my need for her is obvious.

"I'm not leaving the plane. Once we start across the Atlantic we'll have a long time together."

Suddenly, she sits back down. A passenger has caught her eye. She whispers, "Do you see that man over there?"

I glance back, see a blond head. The man is staring out the window or he is asleep. Gold objects wreath his neck.

"He's been watching me." Anna whispers.

"Do you really think so?"

"Kiwi says he has a first class ticket and he came back here about the time I did."

"Maybe he likes being close to us poor people. Our customs fascinate him."

"She says, he's Parisian."

"Maybe he's looking for a girl back here."

"Well, yes. Me."

"We certainly have you in common."

She smiles.

"Don't go."

She goes. I'm terrified that I won't see her again.

I can't imagine anyone who needs a navigator more than I do. Tonight, when I woke and saw her eyes staring at me, it was for the first time. Capt. Padewicz Park counts for nothing. I barely saw her there. Her depression over her losses, my madness. But now I've seen her, I've touched her, for the first time. And I'm frightened. The fear of being arrested and extradited is nothing compared to this. I have met a woman who can engulf me, and I know I would gladly vanish there inside her. I couldn't have created her. Could I?

We are landing in Newfoundland. Refueling for the trans-Atlantic hop to Paris. The final leg. After Newfoundland I'll no longer be escaping, I'll be arriving. The packets of money will make me a citizen of the world ...

I snap off my light and wait for the landing. The wheels thump out of their sockets, the wing flaps are lowered, combing the wind. The Oldest Woman On Earth reaches her nutty hand across the aisle for me to hold. She is afraid of landings, too. We grip hands wordlessly.

I stay in my seat sleeping, waiting for a uniformed Canadian to come on board and inform me that I am wanted for routine questioning. I expect him to lead me from the plane to the terminal, which is nothing much more than a hangar, and handcuff me to a doorknob, and put me on the next flight to New York. But he doesn't.

It seems impossible, rising from Gander through the icy air, above the snow, our four propellers grinding through nothing, our engines screaming. But after an hour on the ground, New-foundland seems more dangerous than the sky. Barren snow-drifts, wild smoky breath rising from any man or machine that breathes. Why do I feel the presence of that blond Parisian five rows away? It's not because of Anna. Do I have something to do with him?

We have surmounted the impossible. The plane's wheels tuck into its body like a great buzzard's talons. The Oldest Woman On Earth releases my hand. She is sleepy. Everything is in place for the night. *Poong*, the soft bell signals, that we may release their seat belts. We may light up. *Poong*, a passenger somewhere needs a pillow. *Poong*, I need a drink. I've nothing in my pockets; in my lap, a journal with a few words, otherwise empty pages. Excited and uneasy, I have met my navigator. I know where I'm going. I don't know who's going with me. The succulent fumes of burning oil paintings fill my senses. My head reels as it would from a good cigar or Cognac fumes. The plane's length is dim, safe. Passengers tuck themselves in for this very long night. This very important night. The winter ocean seethes miles below.

I feel myself sliding toward a new country where I know no one. It is not my government, it is not my place to care. The joy of blindness. It is so easy to live in someone else's country, play at their ways of doing things, their unique problems not mine. Nothing will be expected of me. I cannot be patriotic. I'll be amused by their politics. Insane people should first consider moving to foreign soil where their detachment can bloom, their unique qualities be honored, their felonies ignored.

Kiwi stops her cart. I ask her for a Hennessy without ice. Anna has been gone too long setting our course. I go to the magazine rack. The recent assassination of JFK is everywhere. A good moment to emigrate. The toilet is vacant. The fixtures pristine. In the brisk, aquamarine flush, chemicals flash down the sucking hole. Miles below, the the North Atlantic, always turbulent in winter. The crowned manes of its wild horses, the helmeted sky.

She enters and re-enters my vision when I stare out into the black, I paint her face in oils on the oval Perspex window, scored by jiggling drops of rain. Who is Anna? Her face is wise, she isn't old, she's been through soul-scouring experiences and now I wonder how many years she's been night-flying back and forth across oceans, how many years she's walked these aisles looking for someone and instead of finding him, picked up a child's dropped teaspoon? How these wakeful nights have shaped her senses, numbed her expectations? The ingenious torment of her past. She seems over-qualified. She seems ready to be stopped.

I see her walking aft. She nods and whispers something as she passes. I wait a moment for her scent. I turn, watch her walk down the aisle, her legs trapped tautly in her skirt. She stops and leans over the blond passenger five rows behind me, then sits with him. After ten minutes she is back, leaning toward my face, her scent mildly exciting. I don't breathe until I can catch the sweet breeze of her arrival.

"May I join you?"

"Of course. My turn?"

She senses my unhappiness at her visit with the blond man, brings her face closer to mine. She sits in the aisle seat, an empty seat between us.

"You never told me what you do for a living?"

"I was an artist."

"Was?"

"My lease ran out."

"Jonathan."

"Don't call me that."

"Didn't you tell me your name was 'Jonathan Boot?'"

"Now it isn't."

"What shall I call you?"

"'Simon.'" But you must whisper it."

"Why?"

"Just to make me happy."

"Simon," she whispers. "'Jonathan' didn't suit you. What have you been up to since I left you?"

"Reading my entrails."

"Better yours than mine. What did they tell you?"

"That we're going to live in France and that you will bear my children."

She laughs lightly. She knows it is a joke to be considered. Only I mine the Greek mystics for humor.

My drunken subconscious. She must see how I feel about her. It is so obvious. Her importance frightens me. It is out of scale with rational progression.

"Who's the man back there?"

"The one I was talking to?" I barely nod. "Well, he wants to meet you."

Red alert. "Why?"

"Maybe because he seems to enjoy your company."

"He doesn't know my company."

"He thinks he does."

I inhale deeply trying to clear my head and maybe even produce a thought.

"He says your clothes fascinate him."

"He is easily fascinated."

"He asked me if you go out of your way to look crazy."

"Partly."

"Well, I told him no; I said you are an original."

"Which is why he wants to meet me?"

"His name is Eduard de Haen. His family is a famous wine family, but he says he has no interest in wine unless it's passing from a glass across his lips, and he leaves the smashing of grapes business to his uncles whom he never sees."

"Sounds like a solid sort."

"He says he rarely feels the urge to struggle in business."

"What does he do besides avoid struggling?"

"When he feels like it, he goes to his villa in the forest for as long as he needs."

"With his *copains* Polo and Mouche."

"*Et moi*. He invited me."

A stab of pain sharp as a knife.

"Why would you want to go?"

"I have ten days after Cairo and I'm thinking, God knows I could use the rest."

"You certainly wouldn't need to think down there."

"I could even drive there. I have a friend in Paris who loans me his car. It's not far, just above the Mediterranean. Eduard says there're never more than a dozen guests."

"Then they'll probably be able to memorize your name the very first week."

"O-o-h, Simon." She shakes her head. "*Tsk tsk tsk.*"

"Why would I be jealous? I would think he'd be more interested in the pilot than the navigator."

"I'm sure he thinks I'm an air hostess. Anyhow, I know that's how he looks, but that's how they all look, Parisian boys are different than French boys."

"I see."

"They never seem to like you quite as much as they like themselves. It's a cat quality."

"But why go?"

"I told you. He gives a nice impression."

"Aren't you tired of first impressions? I am. Tired of people you'll never see twice. Talk-talk cleverness."

"It will give me a rest and it sounds luxe."

Jealousy—the international trademark of the amateur. I have it. She's going. Why am I so disillusioned with her? We have nothing, we have no link. Why does she want this? How can she meet a person she doesn't have any feeling for and on a first impression join his way of life for a week? Doesn't she want to be around for a second impression before she makes up her mind? Maybe she could teach me freedom or maybe I could teach her stability. I have five pounds of stability in small packets in a Noxzema carton under my seat.

"He's really very nice, Simon, after all."

"He really is very Parisian, after all."

"What do you have against Parisians?"

"Nothing important, I just don't want to live with them. I want to live in a country that doesn't know the price of plutonium, maybe Italy."

"He does want to meet you, Simon. He says you have 'fugitif' written all over you."

"Do not call me 'Simon.'"

"Why?"

"Because 'Simon' will be extradited from France and sent to jail in America."

My seriousness impresses her.

"So call me 'Jonathan Boot.'"

"But it doesn't suit you."

"Believe me it does."

She smiles at me until I need to look away. In a few moments, she leads me back to the Frenchman.

The blond man half-stands, extends his hand. Anna stays close to me, her hip touching mine. It is late, dark. Only the three of us are awake.

"Baron Eduard de Haen this is Mr. Jonathan Boot."

Anna is taller than Eduard and Eduard is less impressive half-standing than seated. Meeting Eduard is like meeting a house cat, nothing really happens. Nothing is given away. He speaks in a dramatic whisper. It is a confiding voice, a good Paris accent, the kind that breaks nicely into English, the charming, back-of-the-throat *r*.

"The flight is agreeable for you, Mr. Boot?" He says 'Boot' as if it were a nickname. My beard is three weeks old, born in a park near John Jay Street—not even good enough on a dark plane. We sit, Anna between us.

"You must call me not Eduard. All my friends call me, 'Pitou.'"

He is perfect, his leonine head-full of blowsy hair set in a gale. His face is ornamented by giblet lips, and a strong chin. The dimberry, light-eyed look, a trace of snarl in the smile, a slice of cynicism, stealth in his charm—the classic Parisian. Intuitively, I know what's happening to me and this Parisian does, too. I'm being studied, recognized. Anna lights a cigarette with her ringless fingers. She smokes exquisitely, it is as close to undressing in public as possible. I refuse Pitou's invitation for a Cognac and excuse myself.

"I'll stay on for a minute or two, Jonathan," Anna says.

I walk to my seat wondering what comes next. I could be detained by French immigration at Orly and returned to New York. That would be the simplest way. The reward is a fortune in francs. I take up where I left off, staring toward the window at nothing. I can't think clearly knowing that Anna is exchanging ideas with the androgynous Parisian, who only works when he feels like it and never quite does.

It is ten minutes before she returns, flush with excitement, brightening cheeks, alive, intrigued. She whispers, "He is very excited. He says your name may not be 'Jonathan Boot' at all. He says you may be someone else and that you're incredible and your paintings are very famous. But he won't tell me who."

"I get that all the time, Anna." I say it routinely. But I am sinking into my stomach, the contents of my body in flux.

She goes on. She is delighted. "The most highly respected painter anywhere! Powerful and influential! Who on earth does he think you are?"

"Simon Lister."

"Maybe I should go back and talk to him again, are you embarrassed? You're face is very red."

"No, Anna. And it isn't me, I'm not him."

She stands. "I'll be right back."

She returns in two or three minutes. "I told him, of course, you're name isn't Simon Lister, but he's still excited."

"So are you."

She grips my arm, lowers her voice. "Maybe because you might still be him. Everyone flies with us. I mean Yves Montand is sleeping up in first class right now." She nods forward. "But I know you as one person and now maybe you're someone else, but I already liked that other person. He was a lost-and-found person like me."

She says everything so simply, with the same lightness. No impressive luggage labels to describe her. I crave to be open with her, tell her everything.

"What does he intend to do?"

"He says he can't wait to tell his friends in Paris. He owns an art gallery there."

I feel the trap spring. My head is spinning. Nice try. Is it going to be over so soon?

"Well, then he's got a problem because I'm not Simon Lister, I've been mistaken for him before." I can hardly say the words without stammering. Unbelievably, my hands start to shake; I clasp them on my lap.

Anna seems genuinely hurt. "You must be him. I think I can tell."

"Please Anna, don't. You don't even know what he looks like. This isn't Yves Montand. This is different from being a movie star. Simon Lister doesn't like having his picture taken. He's rarely been photographed."

"Pitou says he looks like you." Abruptly she giggles. She shifts to face me fully, sighs, uncrosses her legs.

"Listen, Anna, what he's saying is very serious."

"Why?"

"He didn't tell you?"

"He said Simon Lister had made *un grand betise* in New York."

"He did. A great beastliness as he says ..."

"Well, yes, something, it was terribly bad."

"Did he mention that there's a huge reward for Lister's arrest?"

"No. Did he kill someone?"

"Even worse. He robbed the rich. Did Pitou tell you he could be arrested at Orly? That they could send him back to New York in shackles?"

"He only said, it doesn't make any sense what he did."

"That's fair."

"He doesn't understand it."

"He's not supposed to. He may one day, but as a gallery owner, he may never."

"He says that Simon Lister burned the most valuable paintings in the world. He said that the paintings were no longer art but had transcended into icons of great power and value. That they had exceeded themselves a hundred times. He said it was the crime of the century against art."

"The greatest crime against art is art."

"But he said it was great art."

"Art is so dead, it needs a new name."

"I wonder why he did it?"

"Someone said Lister suffered a chemical imbalance from smelling too much toxic lead-based paint. Someone wrote in the *New York Post* that Lister suffered."

"Is that true?"

"My opinion? He probably saw he'd gone too far. His paintings had become dangerous and he burned them because it's funny to watch rich people lose their toys. The trick is to stop wondering about me."

"I don't think he wants to hurt you. Pitou's different. Different without being interesting. He did say you might have a slate loose."

"That's quaint."

"It's French." She giggles. "From the countryside."

"I hope I do have a slate loose."

"Is Simon Lister the richest painter in the world?"

"Is that what he told you?"

"She nods."

"Rich? The owners of his paintings were rich, they were like brokers who invested in his future."

"Every one of his paintings is gone?"

"I believe so."

"He also called him a genius."

"Would you like to know a genius?"

She nods, "Yes."

"Anna, if someone like Eduard de Haen can call Lister a genius, how can he be one? To recognize a genius you really need to be a genius. There is more to it than visible results."

"Do you believe that?"

"Yes, I think de Haen can appreciate what Lister created, but I don't think he can understand or imagine how or why."

"Then I think Pitou may only be a little clever," she says.

Her mind is clear, wise. I want to touch her with the tip of my tongue, anywhere, on her teeth, her neck, her lips, her hands, her eyes, her nose, anywhere. Her eyes are shining. She goes on.

"Yes, I definitely would like to know a genius."

"I think knowing a genius would be nothing but trouble."

"Do you really?"

"Yes. For one thing, they don't wash and they don't celebrate national holidays."

"Are you a genius?"

I shake my head.

Something about this genius business. It is vital to Anna, as if it'll take someone extraordinary to pull her up, away to someplace so deep and different and far that she might never want to escape, the way she's probably escaped so many times before, and I realize I want Anna to be this way, to be any way, to need me, whatever it takes, just as much as I want to wake up in the dark after having made love with her and to sit beside her while she sleeps, and light a candle and gently pull the sheet away and draw a simple pencil sketch of her until she senses what I'm doing, turns in her sleep, remembers, and reaches a hand out to me. Jesus I would love that!

"Pitou said Lister was far ahead of his time."

"Time is always there for us, Anna. No one gets ahead of time."

"I know what he means, though. It's exciting to be ahead."

"No, Anna, really. We're all standing in the same room and we are all asleep."

"I don't believe that."

"Okay, believe this. There once was a poet, Li Ho, who was way ahead of his time. His poetry was ignored during his short lifetime—the T'ang Dynasty, sometime around 805 A.D. He was ignored again a few years ago when Oxford scholars assembled a book of T'ang poets. But last year, Li Ho was discovered at last. His voice was unique, fresh, his style quite wonderful. Li Ho was radical, he spoke to us. His poems are beautiful, simple and strong, and romantic and short. See? He is new. But what is that to Li Ho, who was ahead of his time more than a thousand years ago?"

"Tell me something he wrote."

"I can't remember."

"Do you mind if I take a nap here?"

I smile. She stands over me and reaches a pillow and blanket from the overhead compartment. In a moment her legs disappear, wound in the blanket. She curls low against the pillow.

"I've got to get an hour's sleep."

"Are you going on to Rome after Paris?"

"Yes, and straight through to Cairo. I'm laying over a night, then flying back, so I'll be back in Paris in two days."

"How far have we gone?"

"We're almost halfway."

"Halfway." I look at my watch. The large gold chronograph. The dim face, the moon's phases. A watch for shut-ins. I can see the moon out the window and its reflection on the wing. That's the right time. When I look back she has closed her eyes. I stand, bend over her, whisper, "Have you stopped wondering?"

"About what?"

"Everything."

"For the night, yes."

"Goodnight, Anna."

I try not to kiss her. I want to tell her the truth. I must. I know I will. I slip out into the aisle. The sound of the plane sloughing through the freezing air has quieted down. I stand in the aisle stretching. The cabin is dark, long. There is no smoke, no one awake to play cards. The Oldest Woman On Earth is sleeping. It seems proper that during the landing in Paris I hold her hand again. Pitou appears to be asleep.

Pitou. I'm no good about cute names for grown-ups. I might wait an hour and visit him, sit beside him without waking him, and after a while, press my thumbs into his temples and crush his skull, killing him in five or ten seconds. Thank God I have my military background to fall back on.

Dinner has been digested. Liqueurs have been passed long ago. I have had wine, six Cognacs, not enough considering the conditions. The plane's racketing is noisy, my nostrils burn, the cabin's air has gotten dry from a weak mixture of oxygen, glycerine, and cigarettes. There is the scent of fuel, always.

Then with great respect for what the plane's night can give me—a few hours sanctuary—I squeeze past Anna's knees to my seat, and take my place for the night. I watch her. Of course, I won't sleep. If I did, I might wake up and find her gone, I know I need her. And if she doesn't already know who I am, when she wakes, I'll tell her.

I watch her sleeping, the child's eyes secret, her lips sealed, the compliant neck. I cannot sleep. Breathing is difficult; the soured air. I cannot think.

CHAPTER 8

Flight One: New York – Paris, January 17, 1964

୨‒ଚ

… Pitou. There is nothing left for me to do, I have to wait and see how he acts, what he does at Orly. I feel capable of anything, maybe Pitou should know this. It doesn't matter. I am ready to die, why not? But now there is Anna, what about her? I watch her sleeping. She is so opposite, so innocent so full. Is she beautiful? She has the look of an ex-Olympian, say, a sprinter from Scandinavia. Her beauty doesn't seem to concern her, she's moved into her face. It doesn't seem important but, yes, she is beautiful.

Her pale hand is asleep, curled open on the seat between us. There is a ring on a finger, a thin band. It wasn't there before, was it? She cannot be married. I cross over her legs, a lover slipping out of bed, she stirs, nothing more. I stand in the aisle. The dark plane is beautiful to me, *sissing* through the black. I have never been on a plane at night. The rows of seats, not one reading beam on, the curled people. Sleeping in public, so intimate, helpless. I don't see Pitou, he is not there. Has he gone to visit the captain? Will I have an escort waiting for me? Pitou is Parisian. He likes the game. He is possessive.

I walk the aisle to the silver galley. Kiwi is there. "Don't you ever sleep?" She doesn't hear me, she is reading an article on castles. I see her life; buying perfect shoes for an evening in New York; shopping for lettuce. Lying naked on a bed looking up at a well-dressed man. Holding a telephone at her side, crying. She asks nothing, she has no stake, she lives by seasons. She is amusing, but the type of man she loves never laughs. They give her a B+. Recently, she has been won by a church that sends her topics printed on colored paper, a religion that offers everything to all, including Kiwi. I will try to act normal with her. I have forgotten how to make small talk. Kiwi looks up prettily. She is heartbreakingly vulnerable.

"May I get you something?"

I shake my head. She looks helpless. She is angel faced. I hold nothing for her, she is comfortable with me. I fan my face with my hand. I have no chat in me. She uses a service smile that is quite wonderful. One day she will own a café.

"Are you feeling better now?"

"The air's fat isn't it?" I say.

"The night is shorter going this way. In just about an hour you'll begin to see the glow."

She catches my eye. Like a deer she can see if hunters are watching her. To her I am without hope, there is no equity in me, I will never buy her a house.

"Have you seen the passenger in row 21?" I ask. "The blond man?"

"M. de Haen. He stopped by about an hour ago. He's gone back up to first class."

We share a poor people's smile. Does that mean Pitou's work is done in 2nd class? Not a good sign. I've got to know his plans. *Buzz.* Kiwi picks up a phone set in a cabinet. She listens. "*D'accord,*" she says and hangs up.

Kiwi tells me that Anna has *un apprenti* who needs a question answered. She goes down the aisle to wake her. In less than a minute, Anna passes, arranging herself. She is calm, unhurried, gives me a tousled look. I melt.

"You have an apprentice," I say when she comes back to the seat. She is too vulnerable to have an apprentice.

"Yes, 'Claude.' I'm teaching him the ropes."

"I'd say that's pretty good." I say it stupidly. But I'm impressed.

"While I was forward, I kept thinking about what you said. I need to know what you meant."

"I still don't want to talk about it."

"Were you ahead of your time? Is that what you were telling me before?"

"Do you really want to know?"

"Of course."

"Do you have a minute?"

"I do."

"Yes, Anna, I've always been on a clock set a couple of years ahead of my time, but living in a time of low expectancy, that doesn't mean a hell of a lot. But I was also born on another calendar and that was quite accidental."

"What do you mean?"

I explain that I felt connected to the sun's magnetic field. "Were you institutionalized?"

I take a deep breath. I begin. I try not to stutter. "I wasn't going to tell you this on our first date, but I was. My wife committed me."

"Why?"

"For a couple of reasons. I threw a knife at her."

"You did? Why?"

"You never met her. You would have done the same. Anyhow, that was the reason she put on the application form. The real reason was that I burned my priceless paintings in my loft and she saw further loss of income unless I was restrained."

Was it horrible in that place?"

"I'd have a conversation with a new friend and the next day I'd see him curled up on the floor claiming he had a small monkey living inside his chest, and pleading for someone to cut it out of him and set him free. I knew I had touched the cosmos, but my wife and Anasor felt that that was something I needed to be cured of. I had been derailed. Their job was to put my wheels back on the tracks, so I could buy a house, a new car, breed, watch television with more regularity."

"What did you do all day?"

"I searched for my navigator, but no one stepped forward, no one wanted to probe into the core of my being.

"My correct gray room had a view onto a courtyard with a David Smith sculpture. If you want to heal anyone, I told my therapist, you don't want to show them a David Smith. You want to put a tarpaulin over that stack of rusting iron. You can't expect anyone to get well if cartoon junkyards represent wellness.

"My therapist, Doctor Ellie Smilowitz, was amused. She was quite a good memory from those gray ringing halls. Maybe stark landscapes provoke passion. She gave me an abrupt signal one gray, late-morning at the start of our session, yanking me down onto the bed, then covering my body with hers. A slim, boyish girl of thirty, she surprised me with her gymnastic approach. The code-of-conduct violated by her was massive and hazardous to her professional career. How could she ever hope to explain it? Never. She'd been hired to reassemble broken yolks like mine and place them back into their cracked shells. But her quivering long-nippled abandonment of all hospital rules made our dangerous liaison doubly wonderful, refreshingly unprofessional, and yet so right, as if to be healing. As if she could cure me of anything that was wrong with me with her pudendum. Who knows? It seemed after several weeks of our scrimmages to be the most therapeutic aspect of my stay at the Eisenstein Institute. Her jutting buttocks, her slight, ready breasts, her exaggerated nipples, always so handy and close to flash point, she was the only staff member who wore a skirted uniform that zipped, fell open and fell away. All other attendants wore slacks, male and female, and of course I wore the comic stripes of a cartoon lunatic, the loose pajamas, nothing more. How could I possibly be counted on to know whether it was good or bad for me? I was a patient."

Her deep-set blue eyes watch me calmly, they have become moist. I have always seen auras, felt them in my magnetic core. Anna has an aura.

"Are you married?" I touch her left hand.

"This ring?" She shakes her head, "No. It's part of my uniform."

"Were you ever?"

"Shall I ask Kiwi for a pot of tea?"

"I've told you about me. Tell me about you."

"I've done some very weak things, I suppose."

"I have too," I say.

"So you were married."

"Don't change the subject. You?"

"*Bon.* Yes. Twice. I began with Air France as a hostess. I always married my passengers, it seems. Why do I feel like telling you this?"

"Because I look like a rabbi."

"Because you look like Jesus, that's what Kiwi says."

She smiles. "I do wonder what you really look like under your fur. Anyway, the two times I was married I didn't even stop flying. We were forced apart which is meant to be tantalizing but knowing what my husbands were doing while I was gone, it was not. Coming home was only to interrupt our lives. I remember my marriages as part of a dreadful past. Are you going to visit Pitou?"

"He can cause me trouble."

"Why? Because of who he imagines you are?"

"Shall we have that pot of tea?"

"You are that person, aren't you?"

"I may be. I haven't made up my mind. Come back to Paris and visit me."

"No, I can't, I don't have a place to stay in Paris."

"I thought you lived there."

"New York. I have two roommates, at my age, I'm so ashamed. We share a kitchen like students. They go to singles bars. They ask permission to bring men home to dinner. It's a silly life, I can't believe it's mine."

"That's when I met you at Captain Padewicz Park. The afternoon it looked like it would snow."

"Yes, that filthy little park."

"You were hiding weren't you?"

"I had already gotten out. No one could find me, it was a scandal."

"John Jay Street. Top floor. Sixty-two steps up."

"You counted. Why did you live in that dreadful house?"

"I was running too. I'd hear you humming in the night. I never knew it was you. What was that tune, over and over again?"

"*Vous Qui Passe Sans Me Voir,* about a girl who walks past a man each evening without seeing him."

"Those were the days, songs like that."

"I was so sick, so very sick."

"Sometimes you'd be up all night. I'd see your light through a crack near the ceiling."

"I was drinking."

"What?"

"Champagne."

"That explains the occasional gunshot coming from your room."

My breathing. I open my mouth to calm my heartbeat. I can't resist touching her any longer, I put a hand over hers. She lets it stay. Her fingers are cool her grip on the armrest is desperate.

"I was not afraid of you in the park. I was weak and you were so strange."

"You were the one firing rocks at pigeons, not me."

"Let's not start with the pigeons again. I thought Fate had been playing tennis with my head, it was the least I could do."

"You promised me you'd come back the next day at three but you never came. Remember that? Why? You said three the next day."

I remember the hurt. I watch her face change, her eyes, until they show a sliver of concern.

"No, Anna, not Fate, do you think we just bumped into each other on our way to France?"

"I was surprised to see you. Were you?"

"No."

"I didn't tell you I'd be on this flight."

"Yes you did, Anna, you came into my room."

"Yes I did."

"Well, I'm trying to find out, aren't I? You made me crazy. I went to that park five afternoons. I had to see you, I worried about you, I've only had myself to worry about for months and months."

She tugs at her silk blouse, loosening it slightly.

We are finally in that hour of flying when clothes no longer fit. I catch a glimpse of her breast pressed out above her bra. Anxious tension. I want to loosen her brassiere, unclasp it, free her.

"I thought about you all those nights after I'd met you and here I was sleeping a few feet away from you. The morning after you came to my room, I went to yours and it was empty, you'd gone."

"What did you see in me?"

"A list? Your grace, calmness, beauty, modesty, clumsiness, innocence, curiosity, humor, lankiness, smoked-sun hair never quite in control, teary eyes looking into me, loose breasts, taut thighs, height size sadness. You seemed so caring. It's so rare in a beautiful woman."

"I'm not a beautiful woman. I think attractive."

"But you accept the rest?"

She smiles. Kiwi appears. Anna goes forward to the pilots' cabin. She leaves me staring out through the oval window into the black stratosphere. I can only love her in fragments. I don't know any more than that. Love suits me, I feel the bias of its expectancy. In ten minutes she sits beside me without a seat in between.

"All's well," she says professionally.

"How long?"

"Two more hours. I spoke to Pitou."

"Yes?"

"I think I will visit his villa. It is called Villa Roseau. There are too many rooms, he says, it goes on and on. He assures me I will be alone as much as I want."

Without warning we kiss. It is simple, straightforward, passion. I rest my hand without moving it on her thigh up under her skirt. She is bare-legged. We look at each other, startled by a burst of light. We are both beggars. Terrified, alone.

"Oh, God," she says. "Please, I don't want this."

She is talking about me as if I were infected.

I kiss her again.

My hand moves by itself. Syrupy, wet, hot, ripe. She jolts back in her seat once, twice, three times. Her thighs tighten, she slumps, sighs and drops her head to my shoulder.

"I feel something start to happen in me that I absolutely do not want to happen."

She touches my cheek, "You do intrigue me."

"The way helpless passengers do?"

"Yes. Please forgive me. Oh, God." She says it as if she had been bitten by a cobra. She has, of course.

"Every man I ever loved I met on a damn plane, usually at night."

"If we ever meet again, somehow, in France," I tell her, "it may be difficult with me."

"Even I know that," she says.

"I need to show you something. It's very important to me."

"Wait here."

I go forward and return with my soft Italian bag. Luckily, I was too late to check it through, so I put it in one of the bins overhead. Inside, wrapped in a scarf is the Florentine box, dark red leather, with a thin gold border stamped into its top. The box is not large, no more than twelve inches square. It is an elegant box, fit to hold a crown. I turn on the reading light and tip the box toward Anna, She leans in. A small key fits the lock. The inside is dark velvet, and there is a protective guard with a tab. I lift it away revealing a small painting in a gold frame depicting a desert night, sand, a moon, a palm tree, an adobe house, dark windows, a door. It might easily be dismissed as a child's painting. Yet there is a bright crumb of life to it.

Anna stares at the painting. She cannot take her eyes from it. She is trembling. She asks me to close the box. I see tears.

In a few minutes, she tells me what she saw: "At first it was a picture of a plain house at night, a children's moon above it. A small house, maybe stucco, not wood, four windows, no glass. There was a desert and a small palm tree, black moon shadows, little else. Then the painting changed slightly, as if a breeze had blown across it. A shadow moved, I saw that for sure. Then I saw movement behind one of the windows. I don't remember going through the door but suddenly I was inside the house. There was only the moonlight. There was only one room, with a narrow staircase along the far wall that led to a raised area at one end. I could see the desert out the window. The walls seemed to widen and disappear. A man lying on the floor face down. My married lover. Another man stood at the head of the stairs looking down. That's when I asked you to close the box. What in hell is that thing?"

"A trompe l'oeil."

"It's very dangerous."

"Yes, it is."

"It's yours isn't it? You're Simon Lister!"

"Of course."

Anna becomes radiant.

"Your new friend, Pitou, can cause me a great deal of trouble, Anna. In fact, he can kill me. If he turns me in at Orly and I am shipped to a trial in New York and then to Federal prison, I won't survive that, it is that simple."

"Is there a reward?"

"A hundred thousand dollars. I don't suppose he even cares about it."

"Well what does he care about?"

"I don't know yet. A game he intends to play? A painting? He'll get the reward whether he wants it or not, it's his. If anyone gets it, I want you to have it."

"I don't want any part of it. Are you insane?"

"Yes, I am."

There is more to the night, but not much. The plane drives on and on, the accumulation of fear, the man in first class who rides in second, the start of love, the possibility of death. The wing blinks in and out of the clouds, flames flash behind the propellers. There is a glow in the east. I pull the shade down over the window. Sleep, sleep. We have a few more minutes. Anna puts her head on my shoulder. Sleep. Last chance.

Thank God the Earth is round. Where would we be without sunrises? I can't imagine a better way to start a morning, a more sensible way. Dawn is the ultimate abstract painting. It can become anything.

I must have slept. Anna is gone when I wake up. In the sky beside me, it is deep gray, the horizon curves toward the continent in colorless light. Here and there passengers are waking up asking for coffee and croissants. The bell is going *'Poong poong poong.'*

I tell Anna that I must get rid of my beard. It is as soft as parsley and drops into the small sink as I shave. I feel ready. Afterward, in the silver galley. Kiwi is busy. The legendary odors, coffee, cigarette smoke, croissants.

"You have something in your ear," she says. She notices the shaving foam but not my shaved face, clean of beard. "Did you ever get together with Pitou?" She calls him 'Pitou,' a stab to my stomach.

"Pitou?" I ask.

She genuflects quickly before a steel cabinet full of warm pastries. A lovely gesture.

"Of course. He asked me to his villa near Cogolin." For her, it is a stepping stone. "What would he mean by a dress code? What could that be?" She looks helpless.

I shrug. "Very informal, what would you imagine, some form of nudity?"

Kiwi looks puzzled then busy. It doesn't matter, nudity or not, she will go to Villa Roseau. It could make the difference. Her need saddens me. I carry a tray with coffee croissants and sweet butter to my seat. Anna reappears suddenly. She is magic. She makes me breathless; she sucks the air out of the cabin. In the east, the sun. God lives in Europe.

"You were asleep when I left." She bends down and kisses me. "Sit."

"No. I can only stay a minute, I've brought food, see?" It is a tray; strawberries, a mushroom omelette. I unroll the napkin, there is nothing colder than a fork at 20,000 feet.

"Meet me in Paris, Anna."

"No." Her eyes are on the omelette. "It is not well-cooked."

"In two days, after Cairo and Rome, meet me in Paris on your way to the south." I try my French, "*Une caprice.*" She answers in French and translates. "Every fiasco I've ever made has been on caprice."

"You can meet that fop from first class."

"What does 'fop' mean?"

"A dandy, an Eduard de Haen."

"A visit is nothing serious."

"Did he mention a dress code?"

"It's only an invitation. Pitou is harmless and it would be funny. If it isn't, 'Ta-ta!' and I drive away to Antibes. It's so simple."

"And I'm not so simple."

"No, you're not." For an instant I see regret in her eyes, regret over this entire flight. Me.

Soft *poongs* continue around the plane. The long cabin has

become a bed-and-breakfast. It has been a grueling night. A baby screams nearby, its shrillness is stunning.

"Why are we only able to make that scream when we're babies?"

"Or in Brazilian prisons." Her child's eyes brighten.

"My God, look at you. You shaved."

"You said, 'I wonder what you look like.'"

"You used much too much cologne."

"It was there."

"You look nice."

"Meet me in Paris. Meet me in two days."

She looks down, sighs grandly. "But I won't stay."

"We'll have tea in a public place."

"Yes." She says it emphatically.

"Do you know of an out-of-the-way hotel for me?"

"An old friend of my mother's owns one on Rue les Deux Eglises, I think you would like it. It's the Paris version of Mrs. Connors's on John Jay Street."

I write the address in my notebook. It is named after the street.

"Here's another idea. When you borrow the car from your friend, why don't we drive down to Eduard's together?"

"But he hasn't invited you."

"He will."

"Are you really the mythic Simon Lister, this felon, the lunatic who has burned his paintings and tried to kill his wife, who is running from the gendarmes, who is famous but somehow invisible and has avoided the world of magazines? Aren't you afraid?"

"I'll take care."

"But you are afraid?"

"Of course, I'm a fugitive. But don't ever say my name. And speaking of names, I still don't know yours."

"My middle name is 'Savoia.' My father named me and only called me that."

"May I?"

"Only if we have a love affair, and not a minute before."

"When we meet in Paris, do not make the mistake of driving

away to Villa Roseau without me."

"On one condition."

"Which is?"

"Throw that dreadful coat away. Kiwi told me about it."

"My coat?"

"When she first spotted you, she brought me coffee in the pilot's cabin. She said, 'Oh my God, you don't know what a strange man came on board.' And she described your floor-length coat that looked like seaweed and goat hairs, and strings dangling from your Noxzema carton, a beard, metal-rim glasses. Kiwi couldn't imagine what language you would speak, but she was intrigued. You weren't what she was used to seeing. Outside of her range."

"I got rid of my beard, is my coat next?"

"Yes. They have stores in Paris that sell coats."

She stands, smooths her lap.

"Now, I've got to go. My apprentice can cover only so much. Now what are we going to do about you? We have almost ninety minutes."

"The question is what's he going to do." He nods toward First Class.

"Pitou. Why don't I just go up see if he wants breakfast and sit with him for a second and see what he says? If you want me to."

"Don't be careless, Anna. Not the right thing to say."

"I'll come back as soon as I can."

She leaves me with my doubts. Nothing is resolved. Out the window gauzes of morning are dissolving, lowering for the sunrise. I want the sunlight to crash full into my face when it cuts above the horizon.

Kingdom come! Villa Roseau. A trip. Anything can happen. We'll be together. I'm close to hysterical laughter. I cannot lose her now. Do I love her? I love her in fragments, and what the hell is love? To be real, isn't it painful, changeable, mindless and without rules? I can't stop myself. Why? She makes me free, she raises hope, her ideas are lighter than erections. My tired words are wet goats toddling through her temple.

She comes back in two minutes. It's all wrong, I can tell. She whispers, "Simon, you have to go up and talk to him." She seems distraught, resigned. The skin of her cheeks pale.

"You need to be serious with him," she whispers. She seems changed, she seems to care. She is afraid. I want to involve her in my life, to do something dangerous with her, it is the strongest bond I can imagine between us. She stands.

"Sit down, one minute."

"I'm not leaving the plane, Simon, just going up front. I work here, you know." She looks toward the first class cabin.

"I'll talk to him," I say.

"Don't you be careless."

She leaves. In a minute so do I. As I go through the curtain to first class, immediately I see the blond head from behind. Eduard de Haen has little-boy hair, the kind you see on dolls, a loose blond bouffant. It has given him much success.

"May I join you for a moment?"

"Well, hello again." He half-stands as before, waves his hand as if the plane were his study. I take the seat beside him.

"Hello, Eduard." I'm too vivacious.

"Please call me Pitou, all my friends do."

"Why don't we wait a while longer?"

"*Bon.*" He accepts the rudeness with a small pout. "I am just coming from New York where I have seen all the plays and ballet, even the movies and dreadful art." At that moment, the right wing tips down, sunrise floods the cabin. "A sunrise is so much more brilliant when one flies above the clouds, no?" Eduard de Haen has the face of a man accustomed to good news, who expects it. He has arranged his life to be so.

"From Anna, I understand that you believe I am Simon Lister. I am amazed."

He twinkles.

"And you know I'm not."

"But I believe you are." It is a cute French accent.

"No, I am Samuel Lasker. This name confusion has become very boring."

"In New York they are still talking about Lister, it is the only news, the topic at parties. The latest affront. The reward as you know is one-hundred-thousand dollars."

"I heard fifty, put up by Anasor Gallery."

"No, my friend, the Tokyo gallery Ueda has now matched Anasor's."

"It's absurd."

"Of course it is. *Incroyable!*" Eduard smiles, he is delighted.

"Is the money important to you?"

"Surprisingly, yes." He is glowing. "One would not think it. But now that it has become one-hundred-thousand dollars it does concern me more. I feel better about wanting it. One hundred thousand American dollars, after all."

"Even if Simon Lister was me, and he isn't, I would be honored by such a sum, but of course he's someone else."

"So you have said."

"But if you insist, Eduard, as a game, let's for the moment say that I am him."

"I'll play. Is it my move?"

"Yes."

"Then you won't mind showing me your passport?"

"No, no, of course not."

I have no choice. Walking on grapes, I go back to my seat for my passport. I'm quickly tiring of his bluff. Under my seat, I untie the string on the Noxzema carton. I bring out a sheaf of five-thousand dollar bills, to match the reward. Twenty bills bound by a strip of orange paper with the number **$100,000** printed in black. It looks impossible. I stuff it in my pocket. My bluff has outlived its usefulness.

Eduard half-stands. Breeding will tell.

I hand him my passport. Eduard opens it, scans my photograph, holds the third page up against the window into the sun. He hands it back. The game is in full swing. He is purring.

"Do you still believe that I am Simon Lister?"

"Now more than ever." He smiles. He has me. His manners are impeccable. "But it is up to you, sir, are you willing to take a chance?"

"Are you?"

"Of course. I have nothing to lose." But Eduard is nervous. He has walked too close to his prey.

"What chance are you going to take, Eduard?"

"D'accord." He looks into the sunrise then back to me. "I have several avenues."

"So have I."

"For example, you would not mind if I were to mention your name to Interpol? Only to say that I shared a café-croissant with you en route to Paris and that your passport seemed to be an exquisite work of art."

I look at him as if he were a stain. I whisper clearly. "I can kill you before you open your mouth again."

Eduard looks damaged. "Are you threatening me?"

"It seems appropriate."

"But let's be serious."

"May I join you?"

Anna. Without looking up, I can only see her hips and waist.

"Oh, please." Eduard half-stands. "I was just receiving a death threat."

"Oh, then I am interrupting." A joke. She tries to say it casually, but she, too, is nervous.

Eduard cackles, he is not afraid. He knows he will win a prize.

"We are only gossiping, Anna, I am telling Mr. Lasker just now that he is a guest in my country traveling under a mythical passport."

Anna looks aghast. Eduard smiles at us both. He seems charged.

"Don't you feel vulnerable?" he says to me.

"No. Thanks for your concern."

"You know what I can do. It is on the highest level of deceit. Yours is a fascinating story. If told nicely, it would make me a reputation in New York. I could open a restaurant based on my findings tonight."

I reach into my pocket. Ten bills. It is a thin packet. Eduard stops mid-gesture. He pales. He has never seen a picture of Woodrow

Wilson. And has certainly never seen a ten thousand dollar bill. Nor has Anna, who perches on the arm rest. Flicking his eyes, Eduard counts ten bills. Our talk ascends to a second level.

"And now I extend an invitation for you to join us at my villa in the south."

He hands me his card, it is the size of a joker, engraved, the title "Baron" has been slashed with a single wide stroke of a fountain pen. Capri blue ink.

"It is a lovely gesture. The money. I accept."

"What is it you accept, Pitou?" Anna looks directly at him. "Are you accepting this money instead of the reward money?"

"Yes, it is perfectly simple."

"But what is to keep you from turning him in for the New York and Tokyo rewards?"

"I would never do such a thing."

"Maybe not," she says.

I am overwhelmed.

"Anna, do you remember the leather box I showed you? In the sack under seat? Would you bring that to us please?"

She hesitates.

"Please, Anna. Let's do this."

"Alright." She leaves us alone.

"Eduard, if I am apprehended in France or even picked up for smoking, you will have a very unpleasant visit. You are easy to find, Eduard de Haen. Your small quartered figure will fit snugly into a standard Louis Vuitton suitcase."

Anna brings the box. I snap the lock open, hand it to Eduard.

"In this box is a painting."

Eduard regards the dark red Florentine box.

"It will be too small."

"Maybe not," I say.

He opens the box, lifts the velvet guard.

"It is no bigger than an Advent calendar," he says. He glances at the house, the desert, the moon, the palm, the black moon shadows. He looks away. The painting is lyric to him. He says, "Pleasant *enough, but little more."*

"Pitou, look at the painting," Anna says. Her voice is grave. He does as she says. It takes him a few moments to enter the painting. It happens quickly—after a few moments, he looks as though he may vomit. He recovers, glances away from it, away from us, then comes back to the painting. For a long time he cannot take his eyes from it.

"Mon amour mon amour mon amour ..." He is crooning softly in a voice we haven't heard, crooning in a child's voice, only for himself to hear, over and over. He is crying. He closes the box carefully and closes the catch with reverence.

"Merci," he says. He is in tears. He looks directly at me, his face is wet, gaunt, naked of plot. "I saw a dead boy. Paul. We were in school together. I loved Paul very much. He died at school when we were so young, not more than children. It is the only time I have ever loved, truly loved, I miss him so. I must have this painting."

"You may not have it."

"Here." He holds out the ten bills I have just given him. Even Anna smiles.

"Don't make the chickens laugh, Pitou," she says, you know it's worth ten times that amount."

"Then what? I will give you ten times this."

I shake my head. He looks defeated. "I would kill someone to own this painting."

"So would I," I say, "including you. I'll say this once to you and I will ask Anna to translate it into French."

"I speak perfect English."

"To avoid confusion; if I encounter any difficulties protecting this painting while I am a guest in your country, I will make an assumption. I will destroy this painting in the time it takes you to say, 'Stop!' In the time it takes for a bomb to go off at Villa Roseau. And you will never see it again. You know my history."

"I do indeed."

"It is shaky."

Eduard sighs, sits back.

"Yet I cannot agree. I find myself wavering terribly. In spite of your history, even though you may be deranged, I must risk my life to tell you that I cannot be without this painting. Kill me, go on. There are so few reasons worth living for and here, in this box, is one of them. You must forgive me but I insist."

"You would turn him in?"

"I will, as they say in cinema, 'stop at nothing!'"

"You would do that?"

"At Orly, of course, immediately. It would be simple for me. I will inform your pilot to alert Interpol."

"Then consider the painting yours."

Anna looks ill. Eduard slumps, his head falls back, his bouffant drops over his forehead, his hands cover his eyes, tears run down his cheeks. When he can, he grips my forearm. He whispers words of thanks I do not understand.

"You have my word, Eduard. But for my safety I will keep the painting until we see one another at Villa Roseau."

Eduard doesn't answer, his hand covers his eyes.

"It has to be yes, or no painting."

Eduard clears his throat. "For my peace of mind I must write down your passport number."

"Of course."

"The other number."

I open my passport to page three. "Just make the eights threes."

Eduard finds a pen and in his flat billfold, writes the nine-digit number, changing the eights to threes.

"I agree. I will not see the painting until you arrive safely. But I must insist it be carried by Anna to insure its safe arrival. And yours."

"And yours, by the way. If anything nasty happens to me, you'll never see it again."

"I can't, she says."

I hand her the box. "Go on, take it."

When we are alone, back in tourist class, Anna gives me her navy blue scarf with its white border. It smells of her.

"I'll see you in two days, Sunday at midday I'll call from the terminal, at that hotel, she says. "The car is in a garage in Neuilly, I have written the address. His name is Jean Batard and he will expect you, no need to telephone, he always leaves the key for me under the front seat."

As I'm re-tying the Noxzema carton with string. She asks how much money there is in it. I tell her, between two and three million dollars.

"Should I ask where you got this money?"

"Of course. I put it aside. It is for paintings bought with cash. Part of my cut."

"Two or three million in a Noxzema carton? Who would think of it?"

"Apparently no one."

She is delighted. Suddenly, it all made sense. He is also practical.

The coast of Ireland lies just ahead of the wing, its cliffs rising through mist.

"My first day of freedom on land."

"My first baguette."

"I'll miss you, Anna."

She kisses me several times on the cheek and stands.

"I'll see you Sunday. Don't forget."

"What'll you be wearing?"

"Dark blue."

The soft *poongs* continue.

During the final approach to Orly our wheels punch out of their holes. I hear the wind screaming through them.

We have landed. The flight is over. As I walk off the plane festooned with boxes and bags, I pass Eduard. He has been waiting.

"One thing," Pitou says.

"Yes?"

"Will you please call me Pitou, as a kindness?"

"Alright, Pitou, and you can call me John.

... Flight One. It was where I fell in love. And all without crashing into the Atlantic Ocean. Paris at last ...

CHAPTER 9

Paris: January 18, 1964

There are streets in Paris where it is always winter. The sun never touches their sidewalks. Even if there were a sun. Today is another day of cold rain. The hotel leans out above the narrow street. One house doesn't look any different from the others. My room is Numero Huit, a large key. I drop my bag on the floor, throw the Noxzema carton on the bed and flop. The elaborate sound of bedsprings makes me smile.

Salvation? Friday morning in Paris. I wouldn't have known it was a hotel unless Anna had told me. Rue les Deux Eglises. Later today I'll pick up the car, from her friend, buy a new coat, sit in a café nearby, and wait for Anna. Anna makes me well. Waiting for her gives me something to live for—we will cure each other. We will be safe. But isn't her profession a problem to be considered? I will ask her to quit the airline, she has flown too many years. How many flights can you take without dying?

A weak rain that doesn't stop, not as cold as New York. I hear it dripping on the tiles. I open the veiled drapes, revealing tall window, there is a balcony large enough for milk bottles and a plant.

The room key is medieval. The door to the small armoire will not close. The wallpaper is never-ending—it continues from the walls to the eaves, around the tall window and across the ceiling. It is blue and white. I am engulfed in its patterns—scenes of country people rolling and falling, doing odd things to each other. I am surrounded by their actions which go on overhead. It is easy to imagine madness breeding in this room.

The bathtub is puzzling, as if it were personal. It gives up ice cold water then suddenly it is so hot it steams. The hotel is an invalid that must be understood. After my first bath in months, I am exhausted, exhilarated. I undress the bed. The sheets are chilly, as if they had not been slept between for years, dank as the weather. Anna. She will not be here tomorrow. She will not be here until the day after tomorrow. I will wait here for her in this room.

Everything I do until then will be fake. Even my appetite.

On my way out to the street, I see the plaque, HOTEL. The people who stay here probably know its name. A resilient woman in house slippers tells me it is named after the street. The Street of the Two Churches; but where are the churches? She tells me that one burned in the Great War. The other was never built. I walk a block, then another, sure to look behind me like an explorer so that I can find my way back. A pale, cold day. My Russian hat, my drab flowing coat. I am unnoticed. In New York people stare, but not here. Paris is part of a continent. There is a glassed-in café with fogged windows where four small streets converge. My first café in France. Le Café Pas Mal. I order a café-au-lait, a bun. The butter is sweet, the bun has many layers. I won't stay long. I have too much to do today. I must find Neuilly and the car that belongs to Anna's friend. I have an address. A note will be waiting on the car.

"Where is Neuilly?" I cannot say it. I write it.

"*A-a-ah, Neuilly!*" The rail-thin waiter reads.

I feel retarded.

"*Neuilly. Non. Ce n'est pas loin, dans les environs de Paris.*" The faultless pronunciation. But what is he saying? A lady speaks from the next table.

"He says, 'It is not far, in the environs of Paris.'"

"Taxi?" I say.

"*Mais non. Prends le metro,*" The waiter insists.

"*Non,*" from the table, "*Ce n'est pas possible!*"

"*Mais le taxi est trop cher,*" comes the response from the waiter.

The two argue briefly on my behalf, taxi or the impossible subway. It is decided I will first take a taxi, then the metro, and for the privilege, I will pay dearly. I say goodbye.

Behind ornate iron gates, the house is formal, brick and stone, the vertical look of austerity from a time when Paris had contempt for Ravel's music and Monet's painting. Tall windows. The trees are black. There is dead ivy. I push open the iron gate, walk across the courtyard to a garage that was once a stable for carriages.

Inside it smells of motor oil. The ancient Citroën is parked alongside a maroon Façel Vega Six, clean as a perfume bottle. There it is a note under the windshield wiper, a handwritten note on graph paper, that could be about anything—oil, gasoline, air for the tires, love. It is signed 'Jean'. The key is under the seat as Anna said it would be. Beside the Façel Vega, the Citroën looks distressed, complicated. An orange direction finder protrudes behind the front door like a puppet's leg. I open the door on the driver's side. Wizened old leather. I hear muzzy sounds as a desperate mouse disappears down a hole in the floor by the accelerator. In a moment, another mouse follows. The car wants to be driven, warmed up, rid of mice. It seems to be an emotional thing.

Heading back toward the hotel, I drive through tunnels of leafless trees—Le Bois. Couples walk arm-in-arm. Paris is not romantic. It is the masonry, the monumental past that makes people feel helpless here, pale beside the stones of their ancestors. Near the Café Pas Mal there are alleys that smell sweetly of seasoned garbage. A rancid-smelling man soaked in his own urine, asks me for a franc. He has forgotten that in his hand are yellow pencils to sell. I give him a new note, probably a hundred francs probably enough for a meal with wine. It is more than he can bear. I ask him for a pencil.

I return to Le Café Pas Mal; it will be an excellent place to get tired enough to sleep. I try to sit at a table outdoors, the optimistic tourist, but the rain forces me inside. There are these three noisy women at a table laughing in German. There is a small case of medals on the wall, won by the café owner, maybe by his father? Probably won fairly for war service or soccer, displayed for those who have no medals. I nod to The waiter who gave me directions before. He is young, his face pink with acne. His waiter's jacket is several sizes too large. He takes my order—ham omelette, red wine, bread. He sits nearby, waiting.

I'd rather not think about Anna. I play with the beggar's soft lead pencil, trying to make it jump into a glass, but she will not exit my mind. I have too much time on my hands. She will not even be here tomorrow, but noon the following day. I sit waiting for my omelette. Waiting for Anna. She walks into my mind. She is wearing blue. She is everything. I attribute all powers to her. I am too excited. I have hardened under the table. The erotic is so close to fear that it overlaps.

At the next table the three German women look at street maps, with nothing on their minds except the next charge toward a monument. Speech bubbles that sound German come out of their mouths. I don't care to know. The waiter is watching me instead of the television news. I am worth watching. I am a curiosity. My eyes are tragic. My overcoat is too large. My new pencil suddenly lands in the glass.

The waiter smiles, *"Voilà!"* In pantomime asking me if I would like the pencil sharpened. He is calm, too friendly. Is it a sign that he is impaired like me? I watch him sharpening my pencil over the sink. Every man in France carries a penknife, ready to sharpen pencils, cut cheese, bread, fruit. It is an obscure mandate. The omelette arrives. It is irreproachable—sienna, ochre, umber tones, the eggs yellow as sunrises. The dark smell of wine from the carafe, a brioche with sweet butter, a sliver of paper that is to be my napkin. Are there no trees in France? I taste the omelette, I trace the first ounce of wine in my mouth, down my throat, into my stomach. I am in France. When I have eaten, instead of worrying about Anna, without thinking, I begin a sketch on the paper place mat. In cafés, my forebears did so. Dali, especially Dali, famous for paying his bill with a sketch. Picasso, the Picasso without a sou. Roualt. I avoid drawing Anna. I draw no one familiar. It is a crude sketch of a young woman, heavily shaded, a woman with a distracted look, just about to speak. Her light hair lies flat on both sides of her face. The waiter studies me, watches the sketch develop into a face. When I put it aside, he says something I cannot understand. Our eyes meet, there is an uneasy look in the waiter's eyes. He is nervous, he tries to say something to me, pointing at my sketch then to my eyes. Naturally, I cannot understand. The three women stop talking and turn, facing me. They watch, fascinated.

One of them comes over, smiling. She points to the pencil sketch. In a thick accent she says, "You must excuse my saying it, sir, but the young man is saying about your drawing that …" She stops, unable to find the next word.

I stand. "Excuse me?"

"This young man says for you to understand that this is a girl he very much admires."

I turn to the waiter. *"Voici,"* I say, it is yours. I can do no more.

"Mais non!" The waiter says to her.

More mumbling. French into German into English.

"You must tell him where she is." The woman continues.

"Excuse me?"

"This girl, say to him where she is."

"She is not real," I explain.

"Mais, oui!" The waiter insists.

"Where is she?" from the woman.

"She is not real, Madame. She is only here, on the paper," I say. Pointing to the sketch.

"He only wonders where last you saw her."

"Tell him never," I shake my head. "She is nobody. Tell him she's nobody."

The woman turns to the waiter. *"Non, elle n'existe pas."*

The young man listens as though it hurt his face. *"C'est une image de Claire. Incroyable."* He says it is incredible, it is a picture of Claire. He hasn't seen her for a year, she is in the Midi, he thinks, with another man, but he still loves her anyway.

"Vous l'avez vu oui?"

I shake my head.

The German woman translates again, "You have seen her, yes?"

"No. I told you, she does not exist."

"How do you know how she looks like?"

"It is from my imagination. Would he like to have the picture?" I ask.

I am still on my feet. The other women watch; the man behind the bar has turned down the television. Two red-faced men drinking *Pastis* have stopped talking. "Of course he would like to keep the picture. *Est-ce possible?*"

"I am offering it to him."

The woman explains this to the waiter. His expression softens. He reaches for the check from Simon's table and tears it up with a smile. The German women don't understand what has just happened.

I feel good that my senses have survived the crossing. The waiter motions me to sit. "Are you famous?" he asks in his thick accent. Everybody in the café thinks I am somebody, a celebrity, well known. Suddenly, it is my café. I am famous, not as Simon Lister of course, but as somebody who has done something bizarre. I tell the waiter, who does not understand, that my paintings have been shown for years in France, owned by museums and exhibited, but never sold privately.

"Are you famous?" He must know.

Outside, passing couples are holding gloved hands. I imagine myself and Anna among them. I duck into a bank just before it closes, ask the teller to change a thousand dollar bill. The teller becomes angry at me. It is my appearance, my tourist status.

"*C'est impossible Monsieur.*"

I insist, pushing the bill back to the teller.

"You are a tourist on vacation?" The teller asks in broken English, smiling.

I reach forward with my index finger, touch him on the chest. "Yes," I say. "I am indeed, a tourist on vacation, here to visit my father who lies buried at Normandy." The manager comes over. The money is changed. Parisians only need to be touched.

Back at the café, I will attempt to get drunk. I have bought the American newspaper, *The Paris Herald*. A new star in a new galaxy has been discovered. They have named it "Levy," after the astronomer. I laugh much too loudly. The waiter sees me, asks what's wrong? I try to explain that they have discovered something vast but that they're too late because it's been dead for 100 million years. The waiter watches me laugh and tries to understand.

Even though my face is unknown in Paris, I must take care. Things can go very wrong very quickly. I have committed a major crime. In Paris there is anger over the loss of my paintings. Six were lost, they were on loan, I understand that. There will be half-a-million francs paid to anyone who discovers me here. I will become more famous, again for the wrong reason, not as creator but as destroyer.

I have made a friend. The waiter stares at my hands as if they were magic, I've had several Cognacs, several *bierès*. I try to stand, falter. The waiter wants me to be safe.

"Hotel?" The waiter asks.

"*Les Deux Eglises,*" I tell him.

"Walk?"

I shake my head indicate a car by holding an imaginary steering wheel. The waiter nods. We go to the window. I point to the Citroen parked across the street. "*Voilà.*"

"*C'est ancien, mais c'est beau,*" The waiter smiles, old but beautiful. The waiter twists his finger in the air indicating car keys. I hand him the keys. Suddenly, I trust him.

Outside, the rain is everywhere. A taxi is called. I am taken back to my hotel.

I flop on the bed. Its old noises make me smile again. Anna and I will make this bed sing. I lie like a marble knight on a tomb gripping my sword. My head is reeling. I can't possibly sleep.

Madame Janneau showed me this room, the only one available. I counted fifty-eight steps up from the street, almost as many as my room on John Jay Street. I can hear the rain above me striking the gutters. The ceiling slants following the roof line. A lower room would have cost more, of course, but only a bit, she tells me and shows me just enough gold in her smile to make me smile. "*Peut-être demain,*" she says in her rich singsong voice. I can hear her sing along with Edith Piaf, "*Padam!*"

Alone, lying back on the iron bed, I stare up at the shape of the roof, the gable window, casement and all. I am close to the ceiling in this part of the room. The street sounds chant up to me, voices and songs, the tensions of Rue les Deux Eglises are subtler than the steel-hammer din of John Jay Street. A corner of winter light, chilly as sorbet, frames the dormer window. The room has aged nicely—so many travelers' nights since the last century. The rain is slowing. One afternoon is gone, the first. I cannot stay in the room. My massive overcoat is sodden, heavy. Below me, on the third floor landing, a white-goateed man in a scurries from his room holding a sauté pan of sizzling onions and sardines in a gloved hand, down one flight to a door on the second floor that opens magically at his approach and closes behind him, leaving me in a wreathed bouquet of onions, fish and olive oil to savor on my way to the street.

On the sidewalk, I turn left then left again at Rue Colonel Pim to a junction of four small streets opening to a *rond point*. I spot a bistro, Alfred, glassed-in fogged windows, where I order my own plate of fried sardines in onions, *pommes frites, salade tomates,* and a carafe of red wine.

Sitting with the nearly finished wine, my elbows on the paper tablecloth, I can see Anna's aura as a source of beauty I cannot imagine growing tired of.

On my way back to the hotel, I pass more monuments, scattered little tributes, to France's victories so long ago, Napoleon's last tattoo.

I wonder if I can get up to the roof of the hotel. I creak down the hallway to a door marked '*Toit Defendu*', then up a thin wooden staircase, steep as a ladder toward the roof, and push open a door. I am out on the roof. There it is. Paris at night. The drizzle. I can see everything, there are no tall buildings, none more than six storeys. Paris can admire Paris. It makes the city quaint.

I enter my room. There is nothing here. I look for Anna's scarf, her blue and white uniform scarf. I need it around my neck. Where is it? Its perfume, her scent. Did she untie it and take it off her neck just before they landed? I open the Noxzema carton on the bed. I take out the money in its slim colored wrappers. Orange, blue and gray. There it is at the bottom of the carton, Anna's scarf, wrapped around something. The painting. She was afraid of keeping it after all. She carried it down the aisle. How did she manage to slip it in without my noticing?

I know I shouldn't look but there it is, the painting. Its elements are simple—the desert, a plain adobe house, four windows without glass, the half moon, a palm tree, black shadows stronger than their sources. I see nothing. Did a bird fly past the house? A black bird? A crooked bird with dark eyes? Without a breath, I am standing before the front door of the house. I raise the doorknocker, drop it. It echoes within the house. I turn the doorknob.

The door swings open. I am inside. The room is high, barren of furniture. Two or three candles make shadows on the walls. On the raised area at one end of the room, is it Anna seated on a wooden chair? She is wearing her blue uniform. Her fingers are too white. They are clasped over her head holding it down between her knees. Her hair has fallen forward, revealing the pale nape of her neck. Anna? She raises her head. She is startled. She looks up at me. Her face is wide with terror. She opens her mouth but I can hear nothing. She is too white. Anna! A flapping of wings outside the window. The candles flicker, then it is black. Anna? Anna? Something has gone wrong.

I am standing on the sand outside the house. The door is closed. I have heard it lock. It is a calm night. The half-moon hangs above the desert, the palm tree stands in deep shadow, shadows from the deep-set windows. Something has gone very wrong. I need to know what it is.

The rain has stopped; the streets of Paris are glistening. I pass the Café Pas Mal with its misted windows. I have no direction. Anna? I keep walking. I see a gendarme, ask him, "*Champs Élysées?*" and point to the left. The gendarme points in the opposite direction. I walk a dozen blocks. From the Rue Jean Mermoz I enter the Champs Élysées. It opens up, a vast river of lights, lit for a mile. The conception! Whose was it, King Charles or Marie de Medici? Long before the string Louis improved it, it was there, laid out—this incredible idea that you could stroll the mile from the Élysées Palace to the Etôile. It is whiter than I imagined it to be, brighter. Its whiteness calms me. The buildings on either side are low. There are no high-rises against the sky. Cars seem tiny, moving without direction, so many of them brushing each other. So many people on foot, surging. Cafés gleaming. Paris is all focused down on itself. Only a monarch could hold onto this conception. The widest boulevard in Europe—from the obelisk at Place de la Concorde to the Arc de Triompe, sparkling in the light rainfall. Beneath the great arch, shielded from the rain, the flame of the Unknown Soldier flickers. A great display case for a past that usurps the present, a bravery that has become outré I walk a long block. Where am I going?

It is after midnight. I pass a news kiosk bright as a fruit stand, selling newspapers, magazines, its newsdealer trapped in its center surrounded by newspapers in dozens of languages draped over wire racks—appetizers that will spoil by tomorrow night and will need to be replaced by fresh ones. In *British Life,* a pictorial weekly, the headline, "Simon Lister: WHY? WHERE?—ALIVE or DEAD?" Beneath it the photograph, the only existing one, the one that I saw in Maurice's room on John Jay Street.

I shudder and walk away, slipping through milling people, adrift, tempted to sit on one of the wicker chairs of the Simplex Café. But I can't. I need to wander, to think, to walk, to try and understand Anna's look to me inside the house in the painting. Ahead of me, still a block away, another brilliant kiosk with stacks of magazines, newspapers. A three foot poster clipped to a sandwich board stands in front of it on the sidewalk. In fat black letters it proclaims:

AIR FRANCE VOL NUMERO UN:
NEW YORK–PARIS–ROME–CAIRO.
S'ÉCRASE EN MER!

Mer means mother doesn't it? I stare at the poster. The newsdealer sits engulfed in drab scarves inside his kiosk.

AIR FRANCE VOL NUMERO UN:
NEW YORK–PARIS–ROME–CAIRO.
S'ÉCRASE EN MER!

I grab a paper, translate the words *Vol Un* and *Mer.* I need to know more. What is *écrase?* I need to know *écrase.* There are no pictures. I am half-alert.

"Read it to me! Read it! Read it!" I yell at the news-dealer, a dark Algerian.

The man regards me warily. It is past midnight; it is tomorrow. The news-dealer will be here for the white sunrise. Something is buzzing in my ears. Seconds are passing. I am holding the paper. Something in the words catches me, stops me dead. The buzzing is louder. The news-dealer says, *"Cinq francs, Monsieur,"* without looking up at me.

I turn away, I need to know more. A woman in a carpet coat approaches the kiosk.

"Read it to me!" I beg her.

She shrugs.

"Read it to me please," I say. "Help me, someone!"

The woman looks at me, then glances at the headline. The word *accident* is clear, so is *grave.*

"Grave accident?"

"Zere has been grave accident," she explains in bad English.

"Grave accident in zee ocean."

My legs tingle, I feel lighter than helium. I see a map of France and Italy below the headline. A dotted line from Paris ends in a black Maltese Cross just west of Italy, near an Italian coastal city called *Civitavecchia. Accident* is clear so is *grave.*

I am dizzy. I reach for the side of the nearest building. My legs go, I am sliding down, down onto the wet pavement, grasping the newspaper I cannot read. Someone steps over me; someone walks around me; someone drops a coin at my feet.

"Ecoutez bièn, Monsieur, cinq francs!" the newsdealer calls out to me.

I am lost, alone on the wet stone pavement, rocking back and forth, sobbing, drooling. Even in my misery I understand, want to pay him. I reach into my coat pocket, pull out several coins. Struggling for balance I lunge forward dropping the coins on the kiosk's narrow counter. Several of them roll off on to the papers stacked below. The newsdealer gives me a disgusted shrug.

I fall back. I cannot see through my tears. I am a blind man slumped on the pavement clutching a paper I cannot read.

The woman shakes her head, *"C'est tragique, une tragédie très grande!"* Now she is crying as well. I try to stand but fall backwards against the building wall. The woman wants to help me but she is afraid of me.

I feel the rain splash against my face. I am at sea floating on an aluminum wing that is slick, impossible to hold. I am losing my grip, the wing is sinking. Human voices cry out. There is no sky, only black sea. My shoes, my coat are pulling me down under the wing. I am drowning.

"Anna! Anna! Where are you? Anna, please find me, Anna. Don't leave now!"

I have her by the arm. She is calm, resigned. But I cannot hold her, and she slips away, just beneath the surface. Her eyes are watching me. Her face is beautiful.

"Anna!"

Hands grip my shoulder. I am being rescued.

"Monsieur, Monsieur, levez vous! Levez vous! Je vous en prie!"

It is a voice I know. I open my eyes. I am breathing air not sea water. It is the waiter, the pink-faced waiter. The only person I know in Europe. Why is he here?

"Monsieur," he is saying, *"levez vous!"*

The rain is louder than ever. I feel it down my neck, chilling my spine. A young woman holding an umbrella is looking down at me, *"Mais, il est soûl. Et sans abri."* He's a drunk beggar, she says.

"Non Madame, pas soûl," The waiter says. *"Je le connais, il est Americain."*

"Ce n'est pas mieux." She says, that is no better. She walks away.

"Attends! attends!" The waiter shouts. He has rotten breath. He is trying to heave me to my feet but he cannot without help. *"En voiture,"* he says, into the car. I feel the helplessness of a child. Nausea overcomes me in waves. Then I remember. Anna!

"My friend," I stammer. *"Terrible accident."* I point to the news-stand.

The waiter sees the poster. He has been following me, watching, waiting.

I am on my feet. The waiter guides me to the ancient Citroën parked nearby. It is idling in small, childlike coughs. I collapse onto the passenger seat. I will not face what I fear. I am feeling quite fine, as if I would like to go for a drink with my new friend.

"Pourquoi?," I ask. I can do one word at a time.

The waiter turns and shrugs. He says the name "Claire." I know the name; it is the girl in my pencil sketch. She, too, is lost in another way. Does he think that I was on my way to meet her, this girl he cannot find?

Suddenly, I feel bright but I know there is something dreadfully wrong, that I am in the car, that my new friend wants to help me.

"Vôtre amie, est-elle sur l'avion?" he begins, but sees I cannot fathom what he is saying. I am shivering. The waiter turns on the heater.

"Quel nom?"

I look blank.

"La femme? Quel nom?"

It takes a moment, "Anna … Savoia."

The night breaks in two. I am alive. The newspaper says Anna is not alive. We drive up the Champs Élysées toward L'Arc de Triompe. The letters AIR FRANCE are glowing in the distance, but the building is dark. I am huddled against the passenger door. There is a telephone booth just ahead. The waiter pulls to the curb, jumps out. There is a choice of six languages, first, French. He listens to a woman's voice—calm, recorded: "The search for survivors of Flight One, New York-Paris-Rome-Cairo has been discontinued and will resume at the first light … no fatalities have been confirmed as yet."

I lean out the window; I vomit on the curb. The cold air revives me. There is nothing to do.

"A vôtre hotel?" the waiter asks. He is keeping it simple.

We are in the car again. The odor of old, worn leather still alive, the sound of the tires sizzling on the wet skin of the streets. There are few cars. On a side street we pass a church, a notice taped to its door. In French it says: A requiem mass for the passengers and crew of Flight One is to be said at eight o'clock this morning.

We arrive at the hotel. The waiter escorts me up the stairs, ready to break my fall. But I don't fall. I find the large key in my pocket, unlock the door. In the slanted room, I sit on the bed. The wallpaper overwhelms me. I point to two glasses. The waiter pours us each a dram of Cognac. There won't be enough Cognac to take me through this night's lifetime.

"Regarde," my new friend points to the floor. *"La carte postale."*

Someone has slid a postcard under the door. I see my name above the address of the hotel. A mistake; no one knows I am here. But yes, it is a card from Anna sent *Poste Rapide* from Orly this morning. Her soft handwriting fills every millimeter of the card.

My darling S,
I am still at Orly. You have just left me. I have another
twenty minutes before my flight leaves for Rome. I couldn't
tell you what I felt for you when I was with you but now I
can, isn't that strange? You make me shy. You are a very
perfect man. Please be safe. I promise we will sleep together
when I return. I can barely wait. Have you found our car?
Is it well? Suddenly, I understand you! I have never given
myself to anyone or loved anyone so completely as I do now,
this very instant, and I want it to last the rest of my life.
Je t'embrasse très trés fort.
Savoia.
P.S. I will be wearing blue.

I fall back on the bed, the postcard pressed against my chest.
"Savoia, Savoia, Savoia," I whisper. I want that final hour back,
the last hour of our flight before landing in Paris. I knew then
that I wanted to yank Anna off the plane and drive away with
her, drive south, start our lives again, change everything we had
known as if it were not too late. If I had forced her to come with
me … after so many thousands of air miles, after so many miles
it is impossible to imagine a divine safety-net. No, she would be
with me now, not in soaked newsprint on the sidewalk in the
freezing rain, but curled against me in this bed, asleep.

I turn suddenly, imagine her seated beside me on the park bench
when she first laid her head against me and confessed—because I
was a stranger and would not tell—that when her married lover
died in her apartment, a martini in his hand, he had not died of
natural causes but was poisoned by his own drink. He had
poured himself a martini with a drop of imported vermouth, a
green olive, and a large dose of Nembutal—shaken not stirred.
He had told her the day before that he had decided to leave his
wife, but Anna had told him it was too late, after a year of his
promises. She loved his brain and his body, but could no longer
love his soul and certainly not his character. And so he had killed
himself at cocktails before the theater. Sitting in front of her,
showing off, he simply went away.

I give The waiter a handful of francs and ask him to go out and
find a bottle of Cognac somewhere. The waiter leaves.

Alone in the room, I face the small painting. The sand, the desert, the palm tree, bright under the moon, the gaunt house, the deep shadows. The moon glows brighter. Soon I am inside. It is cold. I strike a match. At one end of the room there is a step up to a slightly higher level; on a table there are candles. I light several. There is no sign it has ever been lived in. Then I see in the glow that the walls are covered with script. It is Savoia's clear handwriting, the same script as on her postcard, but the words are huge, painted gray on white, pale, each letter bigger than my hand. The words are barely legible by candlelight.

> *Simon,*
>
> *I have never felt the way I feel now. I long to be led by you down all our days. I will return to you Simon. All journeys end in bed and there our ports will be found.*

Jesus, that's all it is! Who is she, really? Who is she outside the Navigator's uniform? I will wait for her here in the house until morning. I am drowsy; I lie down to sleep on the bare floor, my head on my arm. I close my eyes. I can hear the sound of the Constellation crashing into the black choppy sea. The fuselage, fractured, breached, screaming, the agony of wings bent to the breaking point, the torque of propellers in the sea. I hear each hidden singular sound that creates the din of a crash, from the smallest sound in that searing, screaming place, to the dreadful silence of a neck being severed clean through. I see Anna without her head and arms, but no blood on her uniform. I don't sleep so much as disappear into a dirty sleep from which I wake corroded.

When I wake, I am no longer in the house. I am on the floor of the hotel room in Paris, a blanket covering me. But I will never wake from the dream, never as long as I live. I have given away too much, I cannot rise from its depth, not without Anna. I see the house in the painting, it is small, remote, closed. I am in agony. I never heard the waiter come back to the room and pull the blanket over me. On the bureau beside the painting is an unopened bottle of Hine Cognac. The waiter is slumped against the wall half-asleep. I wonder what he would do with a half-million francs? I don't know who the waiter is, nor does the waiter know who I am. We like it that way. One is The Waiter, the other, *L'Artiste.*

It is still night, The Waiter helps me down to the street. In pre-dawn Paris we drive away from the hotel. It is Sunday; the Champs Élysées is ours. The ancient Citroën moves up the middle of the grand boulevard in a dream of the 1930's, toward the Air France building. It is unlit except for the giant letters spelling out AIR FRANCE, along its façade, as if it had nothing else to explain. A crowd has gathered. There is no news. It is becoming light. The doors open. Tea and coffee are being served inside. Bulletins are posted; they are not hopeful. Now food is brought in. Paper cartons are opened on long tables in the art deco lobby. Is it a procedure from the crash manual? There is cold food, sandwiches. There is a muddy soup. There is fruit, pieces of melon wrapped in prosciutto, croissants. An hour passes.

The bulletins have become less and less optimistic. Finally, it is light enough outside of Rome. A televised picture appears in black and white on several screens in the lobby of the Air France Building. The wide sunrise along the Italian coast at Fiumicino reveals a grubby, pebbled beach, where men and women stare out over the black sea, some wading up to their knees in the freezing water. It is all so familiar—floating seats, hats, overnight bags. Whatever does not belong in the water bobs on the surface. I have been expecting this. Its disarray is familiar.

Inside the Air France Building there is no sound. A small group stands holding onto each other in disbelief, staring at one of the monitors on which a helicopter hovers over the spot where the plane is presumed to have gone down, as if their prayers could cause their loved ones to rise from the sea and swim ashore.

Inside the Air France Building are faces, mine and The Waiter's among them. We are the living. At the far end of the lobby, behind makeshift sandwich and buffet tables, two men are striking each other with their fists, landing blows on each other's arms and shoulders. A guard pushes between them. *"Messieurs, messieurs, soyez calme, je vous en prie, soyez calme."* The men turn away, their faces marked with tears. There is nothing for me in here.

Outside the building we join a crowd of people willing to do anything to save their loved ones.

I stand knee deep in imagined sea water, hoping that Anna will wade ashore, whisking her dripping hair from her eyes, the look on her face lifting suddenly from horror to joy. Why didn't I drag her off the flight, why didn't I know?

"Is it possible?" I ask myself.

No. Air tragedy can never be undone; that is its hallmark. There is black magic in flying—we nod to its luxurious impossibility, pay the alchemist not to remind us that we do not belong in the sky. The imagined sea retreats from around my legs. I am aware of eyes. Pedestrians stop and stare. Grief without explanation can become entertainment. I am not alone on the boulevard, of course—a lone Arab is wailing the name 'Danielle' again and again. Two French women, in the midst of their grief, have given up all pretense of being chic and cry without abatement. Arms around each other they seem to be dancing. An old man sits on the curb wrapped in a camel hair coat, head in hands.

A few feet away The Waiter watches me, hesitant to approach. He stands by the aged Citroën hurriedly parked on the sidewalk, its doors open.

Suddenly, I feel fabulous, full, my flesh tingling. I am sunny, everything is fine, I'm laughing. It is all ridiculous. The Waiter is at my side, takes me under the arm once again. He helps me stand, walks me to the car. The motor will not turn over. Pedestrians who have not been able to take their eyes off me gather and push the Citroën to a rolling start.

The Waiter drives me back to the hotel, helps me upstairs to the slanted room. Gently, he eases me on to the bed and covers me with a blanket.

The Waiter has been given bright blue pills by an airline representative—sedatives to knock me out. He opens the box, gives me two pills with a glass of water. In a few minutes my eyes close and my breathing slows down.

When I awaken I am on the floor in a beggar's knot of supplication. I crawl up on to bed. I don't remember The Waiter being there when I fell asleep. I feel nothing, I'm alone. Overhead, above the dormer window, the rampant wallpaper surges with passengers caught in the roiling waves. Anna and I are entwined beneath the surface of the water. She clings to me as we swim through the blown exit door. From a rescue boat a voice calls out my name. *"Monsieur Lasker! Monsieur Lasker!"*

I am back in my room. Someone is at the door.

"Entrez!"

The door opens and a small woman wearing an apron and house slippers appears carrying a tray. She is rosy, lovely, homely. From the bed, I half-bow to her. She sets the tray on the chair near the bed. Black coffee, hot milk, warm, fresh bread and butter.

"Merci," I say.

"Pas du tout, pas du tout," she clucks. *"Merci Monsieur,"* and she is gone before I can ask her if it is morning.

Where is my watch?

I am wearing it. Its pallid face full of dials soothes me. Four-ten, it says, but it has stopped. I wind it without setting it. On the bureau Anna's Hermés scarf is draped over the painting. I pull it off and stare at the small landscape. I feel nothing. I cannot enter it. My stomach is still on the floor, but my mind is at sea. I drape the scarf back over the painting.

The black coffee, bitter, hot, makes me nauseous. In the bathroom I vomit richly into the toilet, twitching and jerking, then splash icy water on my face. I step out of my clothes and stand in the iron tub, letting the warm dribbles from the shower-head run through my hair and down my body. Wrapped in my towel moments later, I shave carefully.

Now in the dim room, the curtains drawn, I sit naked on the edge of the bed in front of the painting, my stomach convulsing, eyes focused on the plain adobe house, the palm tree, the deep black shadows on the desert, the moon.

A minute passes, then a bird flies behind the house. My focus sharpens. I hear a wider silence. Now I am walking toward the door, my bare feet cooled by the night sand. The face of the house is blank; the windows are dark, without glass. I stand at the door. It is open the width of my hand. I raise the door knocker, drop it. Its hammer echoes through the house.

Silence.

I wait. I push the door open. The room is as I remember it— long, high. Moonlight cuts harsh patterns across the wooden floor. I see the table at the far end of the room, one step up on the raised platform. The candles are still, unlit. The wooden chair on which Anna was seated is gone.

I feel lost. Is there nothing left for me in this house? Maybe I no longer belong here. I must see Anna. I must see her as she is now. Outside a breeze rises, I hear the swords of the palm tree scrape against each other. I see the bird fly past the window again. There is movement upstairs, the sound of heels on bare wood. Anna comes down. She carries an overnight bag, a raincoat slung over arm. She stops halfway down the stairs. I cannot move. By moonlight I can see that her child's eyes are bright. On her face there is no expression of death. She smiles directly at me, takes a step down, then another. How can she be so calm? Where is the horror I saw in her face when she was seated here in this room?

Back in my hotel room it could be morning, it doesn't matter. I stand, begin to dress. I walk down the stairs to the street feeling nothing, not wanting to be seen. I leave the hotel without hope. The cold air burns my face; I don't hurry.

A woman in furs glides past me, two tiny dogs flitting behind her like dustballs. As she passes, she chirps something unpleasant to me in French. I half-turn and collide with a dwarf in a jumpsuit carrying a tray of bread rolls, though none spill. I am veering badly; the sidewalk is narrow. My vision is cloudy from lack of sleep. I try to focus. I leave the sidewalk and walk down the street among the jittery cars. I want it to be over but it never will be. If I could get to a high place, really high—The Arc de Triompe? I follow the Champs Élysées. There it is, in the distance, The Arc de Triompe, no bigger than a table lighter. A souvenir. Once more I will pass the Air France Building on my way. My course is clear, I have a vision. Why defy oblivion?

The Algerian newsdealer, buried deep in his kiosk of magazines and newspapers, does not look up as I pass. The fat, black head-line stapled to the board reads:

TOUS SONT PERDUS

As I pass the Air France Building, a lean woman in a dark uni-form pushes her way out through the door, hurries across the wide sidewalk, weaving in and out, through the flow of walkers.

She is carrying a small overnight bag, a raincoat across her arm.
She stands at the curb, signals for a taxi. A taxi speeding down the
boulevard does not stop. Appearing and disappearing between the
rush of pedestrians, she is there. I fix my eyes on her, still two
hundred strides way—a tenth of a mile. Now I look toward where
I saw her. She's gone! Eye mischief, I'm too good at that. It is true,
I can see what I want to see. I plunge ahead as if it doesn't matter,
as if she is there. A jackhammer punching through the pavement
raises the tempo.

I am a city block away when I see her again. She has moved. She
is standing by a tall leafless boulevard elm planted half a century
ago. Standing on the curb now, she waves to another taxi that
does not stop. But there are cabs parked in the center of the
boulevard, a brace of riderless vehicles lined up in the order of
their arrival. She might take any one of them.

"Don't hail a cab, Anna, please, not now! Don't hail a cab and
drive away!"

She doesn't. She stands at the base of the tree waiting for something, somebody. A hundred steps between us now, I try to run
to her, but my legs force me into a shuffling jog.

For an instant she stands there, decides, then turns and walks in
my direction. She moves quickly. She seems to be looking toward
me. I stop, I try to focus. Is she looking at me? Her stride lengthens, she is walking faster, She drops her bag, her coat. She is running. She calls out my name. She is almost to me; she is shouting
my name.

Now she is holding me, kissing my neck, my face. Her face is
damp. We stand feeling each other's heat, we are alone in the
universe.

My arms move. With my hands I feel her back, up and down her
spine, my fingers dig deep into her body—her hips, her waist,
her muscles, tight as a cougar's. I hunch over her, leaning on her,
supporting her. We are swaying. I cannot speak. There is nothing
I want to say. I'm afraid to speak her name.

A boy taps me on the back. He has brought her overnight bag
and her coat and places them at her feet. I thank him.

Now I pull away from her; I must see her face. Her child's are eyes sad, her mouth, serious, unsmiling. She is speaking. What is she saying? The moments are smeared; we are both crying.

There is a crack in the sky as the gray burden of winter clouds separates. I can feel the sun enter me with its radiant heat, its current. We stand, gripping each other, swaying on the sidewalk. We are breathing quickly, breathing each other's breaths. Anna is the only sharp image in these smeared moments. I am shaking. I had condemned myself to die and now I am free. I feel our bodies hemorrhaging in unison. I yank her closer, dismissing the impulse of suicide. Her flesh gives in; I feel her moan. I try to take her into me even more. She gives way. We kiss. It is the kiss of our night-crossing of the Atlantic, the kiss of her death in the Mediterranean, the kiss of her return from Rome, the kiss of our days ahead together, driving south. It is the deepest kiss the world has ever known.

We stand, sucking our lives back into one another, stand, like a sculpture on the sidewalk. There is no time, nothing is exact. We are open to the world. Walkers passing by stare without stopping, glaring at an eternity they cannot reach.

It is a long way to the hotel. There are no taxis so we must walk the distance. We walk back toward the kiosk. Once again the thick black headline pulses from the board:

TOUS SONT PERDUS

She reads the words, ALL ARE LOST. I see her absorb them. I squeeze her incredible hand, tighten my grip around her incredible waist, and as we walk, I watch her incredible face.

Passing the kiosk, I flip my middle finger at the newsdealer.

"Translate this!"

CHAPTER 10

Salve De Dios: Canary Islands, May 10, 2001

The rooster wakes me again. I see the third journal on the table beside me. It is closed, read, done. This is the journal that confuses me, the last twenty pages are filled with unfinished pencil sketches of a woman's face from all angles. They are superb. She has slightly sunken eyes, eyes that seem to shine. Her nose and jaw are strong, well formed. Her hair is fine, in various rigs. In several sketches her mouth is grave, her eyes, downcast. In others, her eyes brim or smile. She seems smart, light, I can see humor in her face. Even though these are pencil sketches, she seems quite wonderful, and from the many angles I am able to bring her to life. Of course, she is Anna.

I write Simon a note inviting him to supper, take it up to his house, and leave it with Señora Natti. I have discovered that there is a restaurant near my lodgings. I did not know it was there, but written in chalk over the door it says, *Restaurante*.

Simon has accepted my invitation. The restaurant is a single room with an overhead light, stone-tiled floor, of course, and is extremely clean. The owner, a heavyset woman, is delighted to see us, especially him. She brings out a selection of local fish on a wooden platter and we choose our dinner. We both order grouper, a Caribbean fish that has been swept into these waters by the Atlantic Current.

I cannot bring it up at dinner; I cannot ask him. I only tell him that the sketches are superb. He changes the subject.

"There is a guitarist from Spain on the island who is giving one performance and it is tonight." Then he hands me the fourth journal. "I can't believe you're finding these worthy of all the attention you're giving them, but at least you'll get my side of the story."

I tell him again how much I appreciate his trust. I think he knows by now that I am on his side and am hooked.

After dinner we walk to a cave entrance. There is a packed dirt floor gradually descending, winding down. We pass small pools that have never felt wind or seen the sun, with tiny crustaceans living below the surface, white as ivory. The tunnel entrance opens finally into a whale's stomach, a large ovoid room, wide and long, completely rounded except for a flat floor. A raised stage, wide enough for several musicians, is set against one wall. A hundred folding chairs with comfortable canvas seats are set up in rows of ten. The lighting is eerie. There are lanterns as well as oil torches. Just before the concert begins, two dozen robed monks enter and sit in the back. Simon goes over to the eldest and greets him warmly, then returns.

"He's the abbot; would you like to meet him?"

"Of course."

"Tomorrow, then. We will go to the Monastery for supper. The food isn't bad."

He tells me that the old abbot, who died fifteen years ago, saved his life and made it possible for him to live here on a dispensation from the Monastery.

"How did that happen?"

"He believed my story. It was a religious thing. He was the only one who understood." After a moment he adds, "We had many conversations."

The evening is remarkable. A Spanish guitarist sings flamenco over his mournful strumming. It is the best theater space I have ever been in.

The Fourth Journal
Paris: January 19, 1964

୨⸺ଓ

We came back to the hotel. She liked the room. Midmorning, and we were ready for bed.

"Simon, don't ask me about the crash, not yet, not today."

She has lost friends. Certainly, Kiwi is gone, but I don't mention her. They were not close friends.

We undress each other carefully, I unfasten each button of her blouse as if it might break. We are in no hurry. In the good gloom, with the curtains drawn, the happy village folk on the ceiling are only patterns. Anna's nudeness is so sudden, so vibrant, it makes me smile. Her skin is translucent. My body is oyster white, underfed, without muscle tone. I am brittle the way a grasshopper is, my arms strung like a bird's wings. We engulf each other. There is not enough of me for her, nor enough of her for me. She has lustrous, pale skin, without tan lines. Her breasts … her thighs … her back … her buttocks. She is around me, her limbs, her extremities are everywhere. She is all motion; she has no center.

The healer in her stirs. She wants me to grow with her beneath me, she wants me at her nipples, she wants me to nurse high between her legs, the loving aggression of my tongue poking toward her womb. She has inspired a fire-hardened billy club of lignum vitae for her personal use. I cannot see her; my fingertips read everything. I hear her sighs, her breaths, her sobs; I smell her scents. She cannot have enough of me, or me of her—there is nothing else to have in the world. She cannot stop; there is no air in the room. We cannot do enough for each other.

There is harmonious violence to sex, a positive anger—two people arguing the same cause. It is better than anything else. There is no food, no drink, no drug, no vision that comes close to this, no other natural phenomenon. These spasms are everything. I feel that no one has ever done what we have just done, that we have created something that has never happened before in the history of the world. We are unique. We have broken the bounds, found solace where the legends thrive, consorted with the gods, the few able to understand our love. There is a totality in our scourings; no love, not ever, has been like ours. We are alone in this wildly spinning room. There is a wondrous thing about making love—you can feel that you have actually *made love*. It is what women's magazines are constantly urging men to feel.

The images that guided me through the night, horrible images of her dying over and over, smeared against the ceiling of this cheerless room, come back to me now. I stay inside her a long time after we stop moving. We lie together in wait, my bony flanks between hers, my arms flaccid, draped along hers. Though she is lean, she absorbs my weight.

We peel apart.

Water! I need water! The heater has not stopped heating, it ticks like an old clock—the room is an oven. I cannot will myself to cross the room and turn it off. I reach under the bed for the bottle of burgundy; it is dry. It is like uprooting a plant. I fall asleep without a claim, falling through blackness.

When I wake again, the day has gone. It is night. I reach for Anna. Miraculously, she is there for me to touch. I cover her shoulders with the bedspread, slip out of bed, my knees on the floor. Pressing my palm onto the bureau, I am able to stand. I turn the heater off. Anna stays asleep, framed in the light from the bathroom. She is askew, vulnerable, breathing like tides.

I crave food. I envision omelettes. I see bread and butter, hot juicy hamburgers, french fries, hot pizzas, beer. She has given me my first appetite in years. A feeling of great luck sweeps over me as I watch her sleep. It is so simple. For me, she is hope, knowledge that what I knew to be lost forever is not, and that my life with her can begin from this drab room tonight, exactly where it should have begun. She is here. I will not let her go. I will possess Anna. It is my helplessness, a human invention. Anna is exact, an exact memory I cannot do without. Nothing about her is vague. I will possess every breath that she ever breathes again. I will possess every moment that she is awake.

I become aware of steps on the stairs, talking in the hallway.

Knock-knock-knock.

Anna wakes, looks surprised. I whisper that I know only one person in France other than Pitou, and it is probably not Pitou, so it must be my new friend, The Waiter. She covers herself with the bedspread, darts into the bathroom and closes the door. Draped in a sheet, I open the door.

It is The Waiter. His overcoat is soaked and too large, but everything he wears is too large. His face is even redder than before, and blade thin. He resembles a ferret. His hair drips rain; his face is a tragedy. He holds a covered, wrapped tray. His appearance makes me smile. He is relieved.

"L'omelette jambon avec un bouteille de rouge. Et du bon pain."

I'm thrilled by what he has brought—a ham omelet, good bread, and an unmarked bottle of red table wine.

"A vôtre sante," The Waiter says. He sets the tray on the bureau. *"Mangez, mangez!"* He is determined to save my life. He hears the sound of the dribbling shower and points to the bathroom. *"Elle n'est pas morte?"*

"No, not dead!" I beam, recognizing the word I have feared most until now.

Immediately, tears run down the young man's cheeks.

"Ah Monsieur, je suis ravis." He hugs me, sobbing on my bare shoulder.

The Waiter is so French. He'd rather eat cheese than chocolate, bread than doughnuts, drink warm red wine, rather than icy beer. And so very generous. It is winter; he is alone. He is young but seems middle-aged, beaten. He loves only Claire and she has disappeared. He will work at the café until summer. My impulse is to give him money—a year's wages to free him to search for Claire. But then, what would be the result? I would become his patron. Maybe I could hire him as our driver, to drive us at least part way to the south?

After The Waiter is gone, I have made the bed, I have put my soft leather bag against the headboard and propped the pillows against it. Anna comes out of the bathroom draped in the bedspread, a small towel knotted over her hair.

"Lie down, Anna. Eat, drink."

"Please call me 'Savoia', remember? My father named me that and he loved that name. Please, I want you to call me 'Savoia'."

"Will you tell me something, Savoia?"

"No, not yet."

"The only worthwhile questions are the ones you don't want to answer."

"I will, I will, Simon, please give me time."

"Just tell me why you didn't call?"

"I tried, of course, but between Rome and here, the circuits were awful. I hadn't slept, either. I'm sorry."

"Me, too. I'm glad I didn't kill myself."

"Don't joke."

"I'm not. You would have come to see me in Paris and found a note instead of me."

"Seriously?"

"Yes, of course."

Savoia is leaning against the bathroom door barely draped in the thin bedspread. Except for the bathroom light behind her, the room is dark. I'm still on the bed, my joints pressed into the mattress. She is smiling at me lying there wearing only the sheet. Suddenly, she sobs.

"What is it, Savoia? Please?"

"I can't believe I'm really here with you, Simon."

"I know, I feel the same thing."

"But what if I'm not here?"

"What are you talking about? You are here, and there's nothing to cry about. Let's eat, look what my young friend brought us."

"But I don't feel that I'm really here."

"Why not, what is it?"

I wonder why she doesn't show any signs of the crash? It was a major disaster. What has happened to her? I need to know. I'll let it come from her. The room is rich with silence. A wave of emotion passes through her and then, a gentler wave, as if she's seen my thoughts. She opens her mouth to take in air, then sobs again.

I press her against me again. "What we don't have now we'll never have." I say.

"What do you mean?" She is choking on her sobs.

"You and I, Savoia, we have everything. At this exact moment in our lives, we have everything."

"I know, I know. That's why I came back. She begins to cry more solidly than before, leaning against me, shaking, gasping.

"But what if I'm not here?"

"But you are!"

I cannot say any more. I cannot speak. She doesn't say anything either. Still sobbing, she drops the bedspread. Her knees are together, a dot of light at the top of her thighs. She runs her fingers down my back, down over my bare buttocks. Then she grasps me firmly in her hands, holds me as if I were the gearshift on the old Citroën.

We fall back onto the bed. I know she will tell me about the crash but it will have to wait a while longer. She does not stop sobbing until I am inside her again. Then she is exquisite, her tears wet on her breasts. She lets me choke off her sobs from the inside.

Afterwards, when we separate, when I withdraw, spongy, when she is faint, drifting, I bring her back.

"Tell me."

She closes her eyes.

"Tell me about it now, I don't want to wait any longer"

"I will, I will." She sits up. "There's not much to tell. Do you remember my apprentice?"

"Yes."

"His name is ... his name was ..." She hesitates a moment, "Claude Ravier. I let him go on instead of me."

I interrupt. "What do you mean, 'let him go on'?"

"Let me finish!" she snaps at me. "I let him go on from Rome to Cairo. Instead of me. He was qualified, but not on Trans-Atlantic flights. So if I had gone on to Cairo, I would only have been deadheading."

"Deadheading?"

"Yes. Flying off-duty as a passenger."

"I don't like the word."

"Nor I, anymore."

"So Claude flew on to Cairo."

"Yes, Claude flew on to Cairo, that's right."

She speaks carefully, "I got off the plane at Rome." She says it as if it needed to be memorized. Because the apprentice, Claude, is now dead, she will always believe that she killed him.

"Of course! Now I understand."

"I needed to come back here to you, to be with you, Simon. Something might have happened to you."

"Like what?"

She is whispering; I can barely hear her. "I don't know. Any number of things. I didn't want to take that chance and find out. I couldn't just sit in Cairo and wait two days wondering what was true about us and what wasn't. It happened so fast between us on the flight across. I knew I loved you, but I didn't realize how deeply. My flight would have been coming up from Cairo the day after tomorrow and it seemed a horrid test of time, when we could have the day and night together, here. I'd already left the airport terminal, and was killing time until my flight was sched-uled to depart for Paris. Then the news about the crash broke loose and everything was cancelled."

So that's the answer! We were both so unhappy at being apart. We'd fallen in love and then separated. The first twenty-four hours were an eternity. I thought about nothing else. She felt the same. So she got off the plane at Rome, that's how it went. Before leaving Rome, before the plane went down in the Mediterranean at Fiumicino, after it took off from Rome. She got off the plane and saved her life. My life.

I had assumed, I don't know why, that the Constellation had crashed on its approach to Rome, not on its departure. I was wrong, thank God! I'll always be grateful for that. But didn't the diagram on the front page of *Paris Soir* show a dotted line run-ning from Paris to the Italian coast? Obviously, it couldn't have. Or was it a misprint? Had the newspaper reported an uncon-firmed bulletin?

"Try not to be sad anymore tonight, Savoia."

"The others? Isn't that sad?"

"We're not the International Red Cross and I can't pretend to care about the others."

"What about Kiwi?"

"Yes, poor Kiwi."

I kiss her face. How is she able to hide all that she must be feeling? So much sadness for the passengers, so much happiness for her luck?

"How can only one of us be so happy?"

"I'm happy, I'm ecstatic. Forgive me, Simon."

She is sad-eyed, smiling, still in shock.

"Anyhow that's what happened."

"Thank God you're here!"

She smiles, her lips flat across her teeth, the smile of a survivor. But what if I am alone, what if she is not with me now?

Her eyes go bright with a burnt glow as though she has seen too much. Her pupils widen, darken to me—no longer blue. Her mouth turns down. She is through crying.

"Let's eat!" she exclaims. It is the first time she has mentioned food.

"Is it too late?"

"Never."

I watch her bare arms disappear into a sweater, her bare legs, one at a time, into dark cotton stockings. She snatches her Hermès scarf from the bureau, suddenly, revealing the small painting. It leans against the mirror, no longer hidden by the scarf. She is startled. It seems to be calling to her. I, too, feel its presence in the room as strongly as if someone were standing there watching me.

"I have the box," she says.

"I know. Can you get it?"

She digs in her bag for the red leather box, empties it of her panties and bras. I lay the painting in the box, cover it with the velvet cloth. We will not go there tonight.

Outside the air is thin as blades. Savoia and I walk without a plan. The narrow sidewalks are dark between street lamps hanging from the fronts of the buildings. The shops are dark, cats sleep in their display windows. The night is raw as ice. At the end of a cul-de-sac we see two lit windows, a door, and a boxed hedge framing a painted sign lit by a naked bulb: *Le Chat Pas Chat*.

"What does that mean?" I ask her.

"It sort of means, 'the cat that is not a cat'."

It is a bistro, of course. Inside it is French, not Parisian, there are no plates wired to the walls, no posters; it has a rawness that might discourage tourists. We are alone in a room of six tables. An old woman is seated by the kitchen door, a cat sleeping on a newspaper beside her. The woman wears spectacles, but it is too dim to read. A dog lies asleep under the table warming her slippered feet.

I ask, "Is it too late?"

She looks up and nods, points to a table. We sit.

I light the stubby candle on the table and look at the menu. It has been written in cursive lettering, the perfect penmanship of a French schoolgirl. The old woman is watching. She pushes herself up, comes over and stands between us, arms folded. Her hair is wiry, fierce. She is wearing a black apron and seems weary, but in the candlelight I see her bright, watchful eyes.

"*Monsieur?*" she says, with a practiced smile.

I reach for Savoia's hand across the table. The woman turns to her as if she hadn't seen her.

"*Madame,*" she says.

"*Madame,*" Savoia answers without smiling. The two women are immediately connected by the word.

"*Avez-vous faim?*" She speaks roughly, too loud.

"*Oui.*"

"*Bon. Attendez-moi.*"

She takes our menu. She has large, useful hands.

"*Monsieur, Madame, laissez ça va.*"

She leaves. The kitchen door closes behind her.

"She will take charge," Savoia smiles raising her eyebrows.

In a few moments she returns with a bulbous carafe of dark wine, and two small glasses without stems. We hold hands and Savoia begins to speak. She talks beautifully about her life before we met at Captain Padewicz Park, and what led her to John Jay Street. She is achingly honest. She tells me that after her lover's suicide, she no longer believed any man would want her, not any man whom she could possibly want. Until the night before last, she feared that she would become an old spinster.

Savoia's face was made for candlelight; it is luminous. She talks directly to me, sipping wine. She has poise, she reads, she's been through storms and has saved lives. She has beautiful legs. She says that there are predictable men who show you everything at once—wallpaper men, decorative men, brick-and-mortar men. She is a woman of taste who has opinions and is comfortable being alone. She is more interesting than the men she meets, funnier, deeper. Other than Max, there were no men she wanted, no men who mattered. A few months ago she began to understand that she might always be alone—a woman with movie and luncheon girlfriends, who might one day succumb to loving someone, without a choice, out of desperation.

The wine carafe is empty.

Without being asked, Madame brings another. She sets down a small plate between us, a terrine—a country paté of wild game—and a baguette, crusted hard as shellfish.

I remind Savoia that everything she feared is over. I ask her what she wants now.

"To leave Paris."

"But what else?"

"Just you, and a room without even a view."

"Nothing more?"

"You. Every morning and every night. It's a shopgirl's dream. I have lived my lives. I think I only want to survive."

"That's all I want, too."

"Could you survive a lifetime without any expression of creativity?"

"I can try. Each day. There is an old Noxzema carton tied with string, remember?"

"Yes, your fortune. I don't like to say this, Simon, it's a cliché, but there simply is no wealth without time or love. And all I want is this."

Madame brings us small bowls of fish soup, and later, what Savoia says is a *navarin* of lamb—a stew with garlic, onions potatoes and carrots. There is a salad of tomatoes in olive oil and vinegar, and a dessert of crêpes. It is very simple, and in the end, the best meal I have ever had.

Savoia laughs. "I can make this for you every night."

"Then you shall," I say.

When we are finished, I blow out the candle. We stand and get into our coats. Savoia winks at me and takes the candle. Without asking for the bill, I put money on the table. Madame emerges from the kitchen. She does not count the money, and bids us goodnight.

On the wall by the entrance I see a black-and-white photograph taken outside a church. Several young men, some without neckties, wear black suits. I assume it was taken at a wedding, maybe a funeral. One of the young men, as thin as a letter-opener, wears a suit that is too large. Of course his suit is too large. He is The Waiter!

I point to him, and with Savoia's help, ask who he is. Madame sighs, she tells us he is her grandson and that it was taken on his wedding day.

"He was going to marry Claire, wasn't he?"

Madame nods without surprise, as if everyone in the world knew that her grandson was to be married to a girl who disappeared.

Later, on our way back to the hotel, Savoia says, "Simon I want to go away now. Let's leave Paris tonight."

Damp cold has chilled our room. The heater is off. Savoia lights the candle she took from the café and sets it in a soap dish on the bureau, beside the Florentine box with the painting. It is the only light in the room.

When we are in bed, we curl like foxes, conserving our heat. Shadows tremble on the ceiling in the slight draft. Before Savoia falls asleep, she insists on looking at the painting. I open the box and pull back the cover, leaning the painting against the lid.

"When I first saw it on the plane, I remember that I felt like crying."

"Do you feel that now?"

"Yes, a little. The feeling is still there."

I don't want to say this to her because of what it will begin, but I cannot stop myself.

"Savoia, when I painted it, I was crying."

"What?"

I don't say any more. The painting stands in the flickering candle-light, small and distinct, all of its elements enlivened by the pigments I mixed. Every detail in the painting is real, the adobe of the house, the wood frames of the windows, the surface of the moon, the bark of the tree, the grains of sand in the desert. The painting is as solid as the scene itself.

"What did you mean, you were crying when you painted it?"

We are both exhausted; we have had too much wine, a long day.

"I don't want to get into it right now."

"Please."

"I will tell you, I'll tell you everything. Just not now."

"Why?"

"It's complicated. There's so much to it."

"What's the worst part of it?"

"That you'll stay awake all night."

"I don't mind."

"Or that you'll say I'm insane and disappear from my life forever."

"You mustn't be afraid of that, not now, not ever!"

"But I am afraid. You did it once before at Captain Padewicz Park. Look, I've been institutionalized."

"And I should have been. I'm recovering from a breakdown."

"And very nicely, but this is different, I promise I'll tell you sometime, not now."

"Tell me now, you've got me excited."

I roll over and reach out, pulling the velvet guard over the face of the painting. I roll back, draw her to me. She jams her elbow against my chest, her arm locked between us.

"Is our making love contingent on my telling you?"

"It is."

"Then you leave me no choice; I'm forced to seduce you."

Her legs become rigid.

"Don't."

"'Don't' is the key word. Without the word 'don't', there can be no seduction."

"And if I say, 'yes'?"

"You lose again. No seduction, only sex."

She relaxes her legs.

"I can see our life ahead as a series of little games," she says.

"God, I hope so."

"Me, too."

She smiles, releases her arm. Her fingers move like pickpockets down my sides, my hips.

"Then I will seduce you."

Later, her eyes close, her breathing softens and becomes sound-less. Nearing sleep, she whispers, "Poor Kiwi is gone. Poor, silly Kiwi." A minute passes, her arm drops from my shoulder. She is asleep.

It is over. The longest day I have ever lived. By the lone candle's light I watch her sleeping. I imagine that to feel the love for her as I do now, one must wait. But one can wait a whole lifetime. I know I did. By morning I will know more; I will know what to do. But I know now I must go into the painting. I sit on the edge of the bed, careful not to wake her, and slowly lift the velvet cover. I move the candle closer to the painting, fix on it. It is small, tidy, simple, sophisticated. I stare into it a long time before I am able to enter it.

Walking toward the door of the adobe house, I feel my feet shuf-fling in the sand. I push the door open and listen. The house is still, dark. I enter, stand in the main room. Formless moonwash rises from the wooden floor.

I sense movement.

I'm back in the hotel room. I turn and look behind me. Savoia is awake; she has been watching me.

"I want to know, Simon. I want to know now." The candlelight is luminous on her face. "Tell me." Her eyes are wide, deeper blue than ever.

"All right. Since you insist. We each live in our cognitive mind, our *noesis*, as the ancient Greeks would have it. We comprehend the world through our intellect."

"Okay …"

"I don't live in my *noesis*. Not the way other people do. I have lived outside of it as long as I can remember. So, whatever is not in my *noesis* is out there, right?"

"I suppose, yes."

"That's what I've been trying to achieve in my art, in all my paintings—to bring the 'out there' onto the canvas without it being interfered with by my cognitive mind. This little canvas here is my last painting—the only one left. It is as much from you, the viewer, as it is from me, the artist. It is as if you create it yourself every time you look at it, because it never passed through my *noesis*."

"Then what did it pass through?"

"Would you understand if I said, my being?"

"How were you able to do it?"

"I'm different from other people."

"What do you mean?"

"I can't explain it, Savoia. Not tonight, not at this moment. I'd only confuse you."

"Please try, Simon. All we really have is this moment, now!"

"I began differently. I understood from a very early age that we are a kind of formula—hydrogen plus a few billion years of evolution equals consciousness. What we are, we were from the beginning, except in a different form, and yet most of us, the vast majority, don't know it. I'm losing you, aren't I?"

"A little."

"I'm trying to explain what the doctors and the critics and my wife and probably almost everyone else who knows me want to label as my madness, my affliction. But I know it's not an affliction. It is my reality, my—I won't call it 'genius'—but maybe it's my gift. A few others, past and future, have had or will have it. And every effort has been and will be made to have it expunged, because of the power it carries. Does that make any sense?"

"I know you aren't mad, Simon. And if you are, then so am I. You are truly gifted and I believe in you. That's all that matters to me. I'm not sure I understand, but I thank you for telling me this." She kisses me and we hold each other for a long moment.

Before I fall asleep, I reassure myself that she believes me. That means everything. And I believe her. I have to believe her. She got off the plane in Rome, before it crashed on its ascent to Cairo. I misunderstood—my French is rotten! The Constellation couldn't have crashed on its approach to Rome or she wouldn't be here now. I can see that would have been impossible. Savoia is here beside me. We are lying in the bed together in the hotel on Rue les Deux Eglises.

CHAPTER 11

Manhattan: January 20, 1964

❧

Martin Anasor places his left foot on the quarried black granite floor of his penthouse bedroom, exiting his bed and officially entering the Manhattan winter morning. He is alone. From this vantage point in his twelfth-floor Park-side apartment, he rules his tiny republic. It has recently been fatally attacked by Simon Lister's act of betrayal, followed by his disappearance, leaving a hole of devastation worth tens of millions of dollars.

He reaches for a black object no larger than a cake of soap, on which are buttons. He presses a button and the ceiling parts. Suddenly, it is day, announced by the cerulean sky overhead. He gazes upward with pleasure through the skylit bedroom on Manhattan's upper East Side. He presses another button again and again, until he hears the opening chords of Sibelius' Fifth Symphony. Another button alerts Mann, his long-time butler. Then he sets the control box down and unknots the tie on his silk pajama bottoms, allowing them drop to the floor. He steps out of them, leaving them as they fell, and walks into the bathroom. He is not a tall man. But his legs are shapely and graceful. He considers their reflection in the wall-to-wall mirrors.

Anasor has passed through life with one eyebrow raised, as if waiting for someone to say or do the wrong thing. Though he is a collector, he has curbed his impulses and allowed only a few select pieces to decorate the large room. A massive table of roughed slate stands before tall windows hidden by winter drapes hung floor to ceiling. The table was created by Isamu Noguchi and is modern as only a few rare works of art can ever be. It will forever be modern. Anasor is caught between the past and the future.

Steaming water gushes into his yellow marble bathtub—a timeless sarcophagus. The door to the bedroom opens and Mann enters, carrying a lacquered tray bearing English tea in a Denby teapot, a silver box of toast, a quarter slice of cantaloupe, and a covered bowl of Irish oatmeal. There are two newspapers, a lone telephone message clipped to the topmost one.

The message is from Émile Galante in Nice. Normally, Anasor would let Galante and other people in his employ call several times before acknowledging them. But it is different now. This message says "Important," and is followed by one word, not to be confused with any other, *Eisenstein*. It is the only code word Galante could have used to secure Anasor's immediate attention. Wrapped in his monogrammed bath robe and before touching his breakfast, Anasor places a call to Nice and instructs Mann to tell him when the return call comes through.

A framed photograph of Henri Matisse is tipped onto a thank-you note written to Anasor on a small crayon sketch by the great Impressionist himself during his final illness.

A gaping space mocks Anasor on the wall where one of Simon Lister's paintings hung. It was Anasor's favorite, the one he loaned to the Whitney, which was destroyed by Lister along with all the others. Whatever rage Anasor felt toward Simon has not been quelled. He feels it is justified. He had treated Simon as his son from the time he discovered him ten years before, squatting on 14th Street under the blistering summer sun, painting a wall.

It is noon when the call from Émile Galante comes through. Anasor is at his desk, shaved and bathed. Galante tells him that someone has spoken to someone and that Eisenstein is most certainly on the continent, probably somewhere in France. As he listens, Anasor feels his hands tremble. Death by disappearance has an uncomfortable vagueness about it. Better to have him alive. He thanks Galante and for a moment they speak of other things before Anasor returns the gilded receiver to its cradle.

"Will you take lunch at home today, sir?" Mann asks.

Anasor does not answer. Mann waits in the doorway the allotted time for an unanswered question, then turns, and closes the door quietly.

Alone again, Anasor can hardly contain himself, "He's alive!" He has rehearsed this moment a hundred times, just as he has rehearsed the other moment—when the telephone call comes through in the middle of the night requesting that he identify the body of Simon Lister. Anasor, Lister's mentor, the only one who really knows him. Engulfed by emotion, he repeats, "He's alive!"

He opens the door to the hedge-rimmed balcony that wreaths his penthouse. Up comes the muffled roar of traffic from Fifth Avenue, and with it, the sharp sound of competition for position on the streets below, telling him all's well with the world. The air is thin as paper, the sky cerulean. It is that one New York winter day of days that helps explain why anyone would thrill to live here.

"I knew it," he consoles himself, "Simon would never take his own life." Anasor knows that any artist of Simon's complexity is capable of anything, but one who insists on such depth of beauty would never kill himself. He can understand the suicide of abstract expressionists, even of Van Gogh, but never of Simon Lister.

Maybe once, if he is fortunate, an archaeologist will enter a cave and discover a bone, a rock, a fragment, a drawing, and realize that this object is what he has been seeking for his entire life. For what remains of his lifetime, he will constantly look back, remembering that moment of discovery as the supreme incident of his life.

So it was with Anasor on that blinding summer day when he first beheld Simon Lister kneeling on the pavement, facing a wall. It was what he was painting that caught Anasor's eye—an exact replica of a brick wall that existed somewhere else, in an alley around the corner on 13th Street. The two walls were so similar that later, when Anasor had them professionally photographed, no one could tell them apart. It was not a trick; it was something else. What Anasor saw in Simon Lister that day was enough for him to know everything he needed to know. Over the next few days, they met at Simon's favorite diner, when it had emptied after lunch and was quiet. Lister was obviously a savant. But what sort? He had never encountered anything like the young artist's extrasensory perception before. Simon described his method as something he never thought about—a driving impulse generated by light, such that nothing else seemed to matter to him. Anasor would remember that moment for the rest of his life. Finding Simon Lister was the culmination of his life's endeavors. His ability to understand who Lister was, to see him as no one else had ever seen him in his lifetime—which, granted, was only twenty-four years. It established him as the premier art dealer in New York and not just another impresario. He understood that he and Simon were entirely different men. To him, who read the entire *Wall Street Journal* each morning, time equaled money. To Simon, who lost himself in his art each morning, money equaled time. And that was what Anasor decided to give him … time.

Anasor had always been surrounded by people who didn't matter. Suddenly, someone mattered. So he drafted a letter of agreement that he and Simon signed before a Notary Public, assuring Simon the eccentricities of an artist's life—his own studio, materials, food, expenses. Most of all it paid for solitude. It was agreed that Anasor would be an unwelcome visitor unless he made a request in advance and Simon agreed.

It was a unique offer that Simon could revoke at any time. There were no other promises made in it. Simon would not owe Anasor any debt—no paintings, only the right for Anasor to see them before anyone else did and make an offer if he felt like it. He had never committed to anything in his lifetime approaching this unprecedented generosity. It was not a familiar template to anyone who knew art or Anasor. Thanks to him, Simon Lister rose from obscurity to the status of an acclaimed artist within a matter of months. Without realizing it, or perhaps by doing this, Anasor had created an imitation of life—a son. There are few highly successful men who do not in their later years yearn for an heir.

Simon's exceptional act of betrayal was overwhelming. Not only was it the destruction of everything he had ever painted, estimates running as high as a billion dollars, it was his dismissal of the man who had given him permission to succeed in the first place.

Anasor has struggled to understand why he was able to foresee what Simon would do when he found out about the upcoming exhibition of his paintings. One critic called Simon's act, "psychopathic pyromania, executed with the petulance of a spoiled adolescent." But Anasor realized too late that putting all of Lister's works in two spaces—the Whitney and the Anasor Gallery, both within easy walking distance of each other, was too much of a temptation for someone as clever as Simon to pass up.

It is too cold on the terrace. Anasor slips inside the heated bedroom, his face and ears burning from the chill. He is bewildered. He is depressed. He is elated. Can he assume the rumor from Émile Galante to be true? Should Galante continue searching for Simon? Neither men mentioned the reward, now doubled. Should he fly to Paris tomorrow? It has been five weeks, but in the time since Simon vanished, Anasor has continued his normal life as the owner of the most successful art gallery in New York.

The original Simon Lister paintings are gone forever. All fifty-one—his lifetime output. Anasor wants him dead for what he has done. But it is not his "son" he wants dead; it is Simon, the extraordinary artist, who could destroy his own priceless work in an act of petulance. If he could only speak with him, there might be hope. Of course, Simon would have to face trial in New York. And there is the matter of restitution. But if he could be persuaded to begin painting again, in Europe, under a different name, different circumstances, Anasor might re-discover him as a new painter, whose talent is strong enough to erase the memory of Simon Lister.

He places another call to Nice and leaves a message for Galante. "Fly to Paris ... do whatever you can to follow up your rumor ... report to me daily. Interpol must never be involved. If you locate Eisenstein do not give him away. I will come immediately. I will guarantee you both of the rewards. Imperative I speak with him!"

Mann brings in lunch—a tray of oysters and a small tomato salad, with a chilled glass of Vouvray. Anasor surveys the meal, then asks for lamb.

CHAPTER 12

Paris: January 21, 1964

ও৺ঙ

Early morning. Paris is still dark. In our room at the Hotel les Deux Eglises, I consider the possibility of getting out of bed, turning on the heater. In the dim gray light I can make out shapes—the furniture, as still as forest animals, our bags standing like rocks, our clothes strewn everywhere.

Savoia climbs out of bed and stands by the heater. In this light she has great beauty. She wears only a brassiere. She doesn't know I'm awake. I watch her strike a wooden match, then squat as she inserts it in the heater. With a soft implosion the row of jets ignite. She blows out the match, drops it on the heater grating, then stoops over her bag, reaching in and pulling out several items of underwear. She chooses a pair of panties, holds them open, curves her body downward and raises one knee to her chin as she slips her foot through one hole, then the other. Balanced like a gymnast, she draws them up taut over her buttocks, settles them into the familiar level across her waist. I am a voyeur. I watch her comb her hair in front of the mirror. Beauty can never be explained. I slip out of bed without her noticing and move behind her, undress her. It is always early enough, there is still time.

I grip her shoulders lightly, and turn her toward me. Her face flashes the look of fear she had when she was inside the painting, bent over on the wooden chair.

Her eyes darken and glare into mine.

"What? Savoia, tell me?"

Her lips are pressed together; she lowers her face and presses it against my chest.

"Is it the crash?"

She doesn't answer.I feel her tears on my skin. After a minute, as if a brilliant idea has come over her, she says, "I need to wash my hair."

CHAPTER 13

Manhattan: January 21, 1964

୬∽ଚ

It is midnight. Anasor is still at home. He has not been able to go out, regretted a dinner party down the block at Prince Faisal's. He cannot think clearly, he has made two or three telephone calls to Mrs. Inez at Anasor Galleries. He has been paralyzed by the news of Simon's possible discovery, his re-emergence, in France. He has thought about little else since Simon's disappearance. He has dreamed about him the way one dreams of a son missing in action, a brother lost at sea, an abandoning father. Neither alive nor dead. He wants him punished for his crimes. He wants him alive, to be able to create again. He wants him dead. He wants him to sell. Every hour of every day since the fires, Anasor has faced a vision of himself walking into the galleries at the Whitney Museum, when he first beheld the burnt paintings, their smoke still clinging to the high corners. The scorched cadavers of paintings he had once loved and sold, created by the artist he had found and nurtured and also loved. Their residue, the gasses and oils smeared upward into smoky impressions on every wall, narrowing toward the ceilings. In these unique, ruined shapes, Anasor knows that Simon would have admired their beauty. Had he stayed to see them burn out, their inflamed oils dying, he would have seen them as his vision of his paintings—his ultimate exhibition. But he fled while they were still aflame.

Anasor waits. There is nothing else to do. It is lag tide. The hour when calculations of disillusion are made. He hears a telephone ring. Mann brings it in.

"A call from Nice, sir."

He reaches for the receiver without raising his eyes.

"Anasor," he says.

"Mr. Anasor? It's Émile."

"Yes, Émile, I'm here." He catches his breath. "Have you news of Eisenstein?"

"Yes. Of course you have heard of the crash of Air France Flight One on its way from Paris to Rome the day before yesterday?"

"Apparently, there were no survivors."

"Not one."

"I see." Anasor can feel his heart pounding in his chest. "You aren't going to tell me now that Eisenstein was on that flight?"

"Not exactly. I am calling because a friend in Rome, a contact at the airline, has given me some news. A person with a name very similar to the one you are looking for was listed aboard Flight One out of New York. But he was not listed on the continuing flight to Rome. Most likely he disembarked at Orly."

Anasor's heartbeat feathers.

"And there was something else, sir. A piece of paper was recovered in the pocket of one of the flight crew's uniforms. It may mean nothing."

"Why is this important?"

"Because it listed the name of a street in Paris, "Rue les Deux Eglises, the street of the two churches."

"I don't know that street."

"I have found it, sir. There is such a street in Paris."

"Then I urge you to fly there."

"I am flying there immediately."

Anasor sees that his left hand is trembling. He is exhilarated, close to crying. He falls back into his leather chair, eyes closed. He wanted Simon to be alive, but he had no idea until this moment how much he did not want him to be dead.

"Do they know the identity of the person in whose pocket the address was found?"

"It seems to have been a member of the crew, sir, a woman, her identity is still uncertain."

"Why is that?"

"She has been … decapitated."

Anasor is surprised by the word. "Please repeat that."

"Her body was found floating without its head." After a moment he says, "It is in the nature of plane crashes."

"Yes, of course. Thank you."

"I will call you from Paris."

"Yes, of course."

Anasor hands Mann the telephone receiver, speaking as if to himself.

"Decapitated, he says, she was decapitated."

"Yes sir." Mann answers dutifully.

"We come to expect that from plane crashes."

"Yes sir."

There is nothing to do now. He must wait.

He feels a surge of appetite. There is hope.

He moves to the sofa, in front of the meal that Mann had set on the Noguchi table hours earlier. Mann unfolds the starched napkin, places it across Anasor's lap. The lamb has cooled, but it is quite good with pepper.

Chapter 14

Paris: January 22, 1964

༺๛

Savoia has washed her hair and gone back to bed. The look of terror has left her face; only traces remain. I tell her how lovely she looks. The room is dark, cold; we have no matches for the heater. There is a knock on the door. I open it and climb back into bed. The Waiter enters carrying a covered tray. Savoia lies concealed, her firm outline inanimate. The Waiter clears the wooden chair and sets his tray down. I point to the heater, miming a match striking.

The Waiter nods, pulls a small lighter from his pocket and ignites the heater. No clothes seem to fit him. He is exactly who I want to see now. I try to explain that we met his grandmother by chance last night at the Chat Pas Chat, but I am not sure if I have succeeded.

The Waiter smiles and nods, "*Elle est bien aimable.*" He pulls the cover away from the tray. There are two brioches, two cups, two napkins, two halves of grapefruit, and a pot of coffee. Savoia peeps her head out and smiles at him. The Waiter is delighted to see her emerge.

"*Bonjour,*" she says.

"*Bonjour, Mademoiselle, je suis Le Garçon. Ça va bien ce matin?*"

"*Merci, oui, et vous?*"

"*Bien, merci.*"

"*Je m'apelle, Savoia, je vous en prie.*"

"*Très bien, Savoia.*"

"Who is this?" she whispers.

"The Waiter, my new friend."

"What's his name?"

"He told you. He's 'The Waiter', that's his name."

"You actually call him '*The Waiter?*' "

"And he actually calls me '*L'Artiste.*' "

"Isn't that rude?"

"These are our professions, there's nothing rude about it. We don't know each other's names."

"Why don't you find out?"

"We hadn't thought of that. Maybe we will, we could, I suppose. He's looking after your Citroën."

"How did you order *café complet?* There is no telephone here."

"He likes to do this."

"But he knew we were here."

"He is the one you saw in the wedding photograph at the Chat Pas Chat."

"Whose wife disappeared the day of the wedding in the Midi? The groom with the broken heart? He's so thin."

The Waiter tells them that he's seen a man in the hotel lobby, speaking with the concierge, and asking her questions. About an American.

"Do you think someone's after you, Simon?"

"It's possible." I say, pouring myself a cup of coffee.

"Well why don't we get the car and leave. That's what it's for. Isn't that our plan after all?"

"Coffee comes first. It's the only brain food I know and I need it. Can you ask him to describe the man?"

Savoia translates. The Waiter answers that he is a small, finely cut, gray-haired man.

"Does he remember what he was asking the concierge?" She asks him.

The Waiter shakes his head.

"Ask him if he can find out."

She does. The Waiter leaves.

I pour her a cup of coffee. We eat in haste.

The Waiter returns, explains that he man is from Nice. His name is Émile Galante. It is true he was asking if there was an American registered here.

"Vais je avoir la voiture?" The Waiter asks.

"What's he saying?"

"He's reading your mind," Savoia says.

I turn to The Waiter. "We escape from Paris now!"

The Waiter drops his eyes. He tells Savoia that he would be pleased to procure the Old Gentleman for them, but that it is in distress at the moment, in need of certain repairs, and that he has taken it to the garage.

Savoia explains. "It's either the Citroën or we catch a taxi to the station and take a train away from here."

"Where to, Spain?"

The Waiter senses what they're saying. He reaches in the pocket of his loose jacket and pulls out the sketch that Simon drew on the paper tablecloth. Savoia asks who it is. The Waiter tells her that it is Claire, his bride.

"Elle est vraiment jolie." She is truly pretty.

He nods sadly.

Savoia whispers, "What does he do?"

"He is a waiter at that café down the street."

"He looks so sad but he makes me smile."

"He sees no end to his life. He will work at the café until the summer when he has the money to go to Lyon, looking for his wife."

"I think he will miss you."

"He'll miss our bedroom farce."

We hear footsteps climbing the stairs, a knock on a door down the hall. We stop talking. We hear the voices of two men. Another knock on another door, more voices.

I turn to The Waiter, "Get into bed!"

"Pardon, Monsieur?"

Savoia yanks the blanket back. She is naked. *"Vite! Dormez!"* she prods him. *"Ici. Vite!"*

Confused and red-faced, he obeys. I throw her the robe, then slip into the bathroom and stand in the tub with the curtain drawn around me.

When the knock comes, Savoia jumps out of the bed and opens the door, leaving the robe slightly open. She faces two men in rumpled suits, white shirts, neckties, overcoats. She is fuming. The Waiter lies on his side in bed, eyes closed, pretending to sleep, the upper part of his face protruding just above the sheets.

He has far too much hair, all of it black. The two men explain that they are looking for a man, older and American.

"Would I keep a second lover hiding under the bed?" She insists angrily in French.

It is not logical, the men agree. This is obviously a married woman who is having an indiscretion with what appears to be no more than a teenage boy.

Savoia retains her anger, but stands aside to allow the men the opportunity to enter and search. They decline.

"*Pardonnez-nous Madame.*" They touch their hat brims and leave.

I come out of the bathroom. "Were either of them the man you saw?"

"*Non, Monsieur,*" he shakes his head. Blushing, he slides out of bed.

"Tell him we must have the car immediately."

"I will, but by his proper name."

"Then do."

"*Comment vous appelez vous?*"

He looks to me then back to Savoia "I ham 'de waiter'."

"*Non, non, Monsieur, vôtre vrais nom.*"

"*En francais? Je m'appelle 'Le Garçon'.*"

She nods, smiles. "*Garçon, je vous en prie, nous avons besoin d'une Citroën ce matin.*"

"*Ce n'est toujours pas possible, je suis désolè.*"

She translates, "It will still not be possible."

"Ask him exactly what he thinks is wrong with it."

She does. "It is a question of the irrigation not marching," she translates.

"He must mean the ignition."

"No, no," Savoia insists. "He says it is the irrigation. The Old Gentleman does not make water."

"If he's talking about the water pump, I re-connected it earlier. I know a water pump from an ignition switch! Anyway, I don't think he's telling the truth, but I can't for the life of me figure out why not."

"Maybe you should look at it," she says, "maybe it really doesn't make water."

"There's nothing wrong with the water pump."

"Could the water be frozen?"

"I filled the radiator with water and alcohol."

"Maybe he doesn't want the car to run. That if it runs it means we disappear from his life."

"Clearly, he doesn't want me to go."

"Why would he cling to you?"

"He honestly believes I can help him find his wife."

"Why?"

"That pencil sketch of the girl? I drew it on the paper tablecloth at the Café Pas Mal while he was standing beside me. I was just sketching from my imagination. The sketch is her, exactly. It could not be anyone else. Her name is Claire. You saw the photograph in the café. Now he believes I know where she is. Or that I can find her somehow."

"Can you?"

"No! I mean how should I know?"

She smiles. "Why doesn't he come with us?"

"With us?"

"As our driver, why not? He'll drive and we'll sit in the back and we'll sing. I'll teach you French country songs."

"Do you think he'd want to?"

"Of course."

"Shall I put the question to him?"

"Why not?"

When The Waiter hears that he's been put on the payroll as chauffeur, he's overjoyed. It will be difficult for him to leave his job so suddenly, he says, but after all, if he is to be a chauffeur, it is a good job. It is decided we will part company at Lyon. Once they have done their best to find Claire. He will need to make his excuses to his boss at the café and to his grandmother.

"Can you bring the car to the Chat Pas Chat."

The Waiter nods. He will try.

"Okay, he'll take us only as far as Lyon, where we will try to find Claire, but not to Villa Roseau."

"Must we go there?" she asks.

"I promised my painting to de Haen. And anyway, he has my passport number. He can sound the alarm; he can call the police; he can contact Anasor. If we don't go, he'll claim the reward. So, we need to visit Villa Roseau."

I close the Florentine leather box with the painting inside, and pack it in the Noxzema carton on top of the bundles of cash. I knot the string again.

Savoia takes her clothes into the bathroom to change. When she emerges a few minutes later, she is wearing a wool suit and dark wool stockings.

Bags packed and in hand, we leave the room, The Waiter going ahead of us down the stairs. We wait in the hallway above. In a few moments The Waiter signals us to come down quickly.

As we descend to the floor below, a man steps in front of us.

"*Pardonnez moi,*" the man says impolitely. "My name is Émile Galante and you are the American I have been looking for."

Savoia is at my elbow. I bend suddenly, feigning illness. She responds to Galante in bad English.

"I haim so sorry but he does not speak."

"*Mais Mademoiselle me dit qu'il est un Americain.*"

"*Non, non, non, pas Americain, Il est Canadien.*"

"Yes, he may well be, but his name is Simon Lister, *n'est ce pas?*"

"He is Jonathan Boot. He does not make French words. It is not in his power."

Galante will not be put off.

"Monsieur you are Simon Lister, aren't you?"

"He is Jonathan Boot! Anyone who knows him will tell you that, and he is now late for an appointment with his doctor thanks to you."

I've been making rough sounds, indicating illness.

"Pardon, I must disagree entirely. My employer in the United States wishes to talk with him on the telephone. Now."

"I will tell you only once more, he does not speak. If you continue, I will call a gendarme."

"Do you understand what she's saying you pompous French asshole?" I stiff-finger Galante in the solar plexus sending him backward, down the last flight of stairs. Galante strikes the lobby floor head first. We hurry past him and out of doors.

The Waiter smiles broadly as we enter Le Chat Pas Chat, breathless. He has packed a duffel bag with his things and has set out a carafe of wine for them. We drink hastily. The Waiter has packed a wooden crate with wine, cheese, and bread.

"Où est la Citroën?" Savoia says.

The Waiter points to the alley behind the bistro. The Old Gentleman is idling, its headlights bulging like frogs eyes. Vapor rises from its vents as Simon pushes the door handle down. A spare tire is secured behind the trunk.

"She is splendid," Savoia smiles.

"It is not a she," I say, "it is an old general with a walking stick, retired on a pension, jangling his medals." I laugh.

I begin loading our bags. The trunk is too small for anything but the wine crate and The Waiter's duffel bag. A luggage rack folds out above the spare tire. My leather bag will ride on it, outside in the weather, Savoia's on the back seat. The Noxzema carton will rest on the floor, covering the hole.

"En voiture!" I point to the back seat.

The Waiter climbs in. Savoia settles into the passenger seat as I take the wheel and release the brake. I turn the key and the dashboard needles snap, quiver. There is a quick clicking sound. I pull out the choke, punch the gas pedal. The gears wheeze but mesh nicely. We are moving.

"Bravo!" Savoia cheers.

Carefully, I guide the old car backwards and turn. We round the corner and are off.

Émile Galante has watched us from across the alley, the back of his head pulsing and bleeding from his fall. He presses his handkerchief to the wound, his teeth clenched against the pain. His left elbow is badly bruised. Our license plate has many numbers, white on black. He memorizes them. He will describe me exactly to Anasor. He will tell him how I pushed him down the stairs, and that I was carrying a paper carton marked Noxzema.

Driving in the Old Gentleman cheers Savoia. At last, we are on our way out of Paris. She sings a French song, then whatever comes to her mind. She sings in an uncertain, thready voice, managing Jacques Brel, Aznavour, Puccini and Bizet, singing for herself, not for The Waiter or me. She has the voice of a child, a ten-year-old, the voice I heard through the wall on John Jay Street.

CHAPTER 15

Manhattan: January 22, 1964

໔ൟ

The morning has changed and the sky has turned to white silk. The sun is a luminous disk. Now the early afternoon has become hollow. In the distance, New Jersey. Anasor has just been handed the telephone.

"I have seen him, sir, he is driving south."

"Are you convinced it is him?"

"I am certain. It is him without doubt."

It is over—two weeks of doubt, worry.

"Please describe him."

"He resembles a *clochard,* a vagrant. He is very thin. I am certain it is Eisenstein."

"Did you speak with him?"

"I spoke with her."

"Her?"

"He is with a woman. She told me he has no French. He calls her, 'Savoia'."

"That is a wine."

"Yes, and it is also her."

"Did you have any contact with him?"

"Yes, he pushed me down the stairs of the hotel."

"Other than that?"

"None."

"Where is he now?"

"He drove away with her and a young friend. I did not contact the police as you advised me. It is a simple vehicle to apprehend, a 1952 Citroën. There are few like it anymore, one sees almost none. It is black, of course. I have the license number."

"And the woman who had the paper with his name on it?"

"Only the dark blue skirt and the white blouse, I'm afraid. However, her identity is now somewhat more certain. My friend with the airline has offered a possibility on her identity. She might have been the navigator."

"A woman navigator?"

"Yes, surprisingly so. She had been on Flight One from New York and was continuing the circuit to Rome and then to Cairo. Her body was found washed ashore near Fiumicino. There was a marriage ring on her finger."

"Why are they uncertain?"

"The airlines believes her to be Anna Savoia Paulus. But it is still uncertain of course."

CHAPTER 16

France: January 22, 1964

❧

I cannot remember ever having seen the sun, the sky is too thick, we are too far from the sea, the trees seem to lose their balance. Driving. After an hour, The Waiter takes over the wheel and hums along with Savoia in a pleasant tenor voice. I doze in the front seat, my feet numb from the cold. The slaps of the windshield wipers wake me. We are passing through a tunnel of fierce, dead trees. I cannot remember who we are, nor in what country. Rain splatters hard against the flat windshield; one wiper does nothing but comb it, the other wiper jerks erratically.

Savoia is balled up on the back seat. Tomorrow morning, The Waiter says he will try to repair the heater. Savoia is holding a map showing the cities of Marne and Seine-et-Oise. She says we are 30 kilometres south of Paris. The Waiter is certain we will be able to sleep at a farm near Montereau owned by his cousins. Savoia assures us that without driving the Old Gentleman too hard, we will arrive there tonight. I reach back and touch her thigh. I yawn. Savoia says it is the first time she has ever seen me yawn.

Something made me turn away from her. Then something flashed behind my eyes, dark red. That's all. When I turned back she was gone. The rear seat where she had curled up was empty. Could I have dozed off again? Could she have gotten out? The car hasn't stopped moving. "What is happening?"

The Waiter is leaning forward, his face close to the windshield. He can barely make out the road ahead in this rain. He makes low, cursing sounds in French. I think what he's saying is that he hopes the roads don't freeze before nightfall. But Savoia is no longer in the car. I don't know what to do. Hoping is pathetic, praying doesn't count. I am dizzy; I feel a scream welling inside me. What has happened?

I sense that Savoia's disappearance has nothing to do with her. What has happened is more direct, from somewhere within me.

Headlights have been turned on and cars swish by on the glazed roads. There is nothing to do. I can only wait. I squeeze my head between my palms. The Waiter asks if I am *malade*. I squint and shakes my head. I need sun. I need time. I need her. I must go into the painting.

I touch The Waiter's shoulder. The car slows down.

"Non, non." I say. I don't want him to stop driving. I cannot speak. I reach behind the driver's seat for the carton and pull it by the string on to my lap. My fingers are not working; the knot is tight, too small. I cannot break the string with my fingers; I cannot slip it off. I turn to The Waiter *"Canif?"* I ask gesturing with my right hand. I need his penknife. *"Vôtre canif, s'il vous plaît."*

The blade is sharp and the string pops. I open the carton. We are approaching a village. The evening light is dim. I need to see. I ask The Waiter to drive very slowly. I need the light from the street lamps. I lift the Florentine box from the carton and set it on the floor beside my feet. I unsnap the bronze clasp, lift the velvet guard. There it is. The painting. I need to enter it. It seems fresh, small, exact. Its shadows are grave, the desert is still, the half-moon has clarity, radiance. The windows are open to the desert night.

I must enter calmly. There is no light inside the house, no candles lit. I stare at it. After awhile I walk toward the house, my stomach churning. The door is slightly open. I enter, close it. The long room reverberates. Inside there is nothing but moonlight streaming through the windows onto the floor. A minute passes. I go up a step on to the raised platform at the far end, light several candles. They flicker on the table. I wait. Footsteps echo upstairs, high-heeled shoes on wood flooring. At the head of the stairs stands Savoia. She seems to be adjusting her clothes, pulling her jacket on, knotting the blue and white scarf.

"I need you, Savoia."

"Yes, you do." She speaks with sweetness.

"Are you coming with me?"

"Yes. You go on out. I'll be along."

I cannot make out the expression on her face.

"Go, Simon. It's alright."

I blow the candles out, leaving the house dark, barren as I found it.

Outside of the painting again, in the Citroën, I put the velvet guard over its face, close the box. Without looking, I feel her arrive, sense her presence. She refills the emptiness she left in the back seat of the car. I touch her knee. There are things that even my imagination cannot do. I ask The Waiter for the time and he holds up six fingers. Savoia has been absent for a long time. It seemed to be a matter of minutes, but in more pertinent time, it was longer.

CHAPTER 17

The Fifth Journal
Montereau: January 23, 1964

ა৯

Maybe it is the sun; our eyes open together. It is morning. Savoia and I are in a farmhouse belonging to The Waiter's cousin. The sheets husky cotton, the walls plaster, no wallpaper. Branches from a tree scrape at the window. Across the frozen fields I hear a rifle shot. Another. Then, lazy echoes of gunshots that arrive after the bullets have struck.

"Hunters!"

"Are they coming for you, Simon?" she whispers.

I try to pinch her bottom but she squirms away. Beyond the farmhouse the fields are wide, open, brittle, lifeless, discouraging. Three or four ducks fly past our window, one of them faltering, wounded by the hunters, lost, deranged, not going anywhere, just getting away, trying not to fall from the safety of sky, looking for the best place to die.

Another shot.

Savoia sits up erect, tries to see out the window. Her breasts are firm this morning, heavy, her tide is full, she is in line with the Moon. I cannot keep from touching them. It is her time. She feels her own heat. Her skin is on fire.

"Hand me my shirt." I point to the floor. She unbends and reaches out with one hand on the floor, her fingertips tugging a shirt from my valise. We cannot make love on the farmer's sheets; we must lie on something that is ours.

We come together softly, as if we are long familiar with one another, then lie locked, looking up at the grayness through the window. Outside, the unpleasant day, a long-fingered day of farm chores, a day of thick soups. I stay inside her a long time, as long as possible. I roll on my back, somehow keeping her with me. I will not surrender her so soon. We lie upside down looking through the window at the whiteness, the absence of day, the sticks of the black tree slapping the wall close to the window pane. In the winter sun, the tree glints with ice. Savoia wakes me with the tips of her hair, barely grazing my forehead. I twitch. Sleep is so dangerous at this time. When I feel her under my hands again, I come back, I kiss her lower lip, and feel a wavelet pass over her, then another even gentler wave, and I hold her so she won't be swept away. Wrapping herself in the blanket, she scurries out of bed into an open doorway. I go to the tiny hearth. The stone fireplace is cold, the gridiron swept clean, not a speck of ash. No coal, no wood. She returns, climbs back into bed. We warm each other again, breathing each other's breaths, smelling each others smells rising from the nether regions of the bed. I whisper to her, "You were never dead."

She whispers, "No, darling, never dead. Never, never, never, never, never, never, never dead."

"Swear to me you will never be dead again, not as long as we live."

"I've never felt further from dying than in this instant. You're kind and you're brilliant and you're everything."

I hear solid footsteps register on the stairs. It is late, almost eight o'clock! This is a farm not a resort. The Waiter's cousin stamps up the stairs, knocks on our door as if with brass knuckles. *"Bonjour tous le monde, levez vous, pour le petit déjeuner. A vôtre service."*

"What's that all that about?"

"Breakfast is served."

Savoia calls through the door. *"Oui Madame. Merci, deux minutes, nous vous attendons."* Savoia sits looking into a mirror. She will never get old. "Will it snow today?" she asks.

"It looks like snow."

"Should we leave soon?"

"You're the navigator."

"No hurry." She crawls over me, kisses my lips.

Downstairs the kitchen fire is blazing. The brothers are out across the fields in the crackling cold. The Waiter is in the stone barn working on the Citroën, trying to cut a vent hose from an old tractor and connect it to the heater. In the corner a very old woman in black, wearing wooden shoes is washing entrails in a porcelain bucket. We nod, she smiles. We are from the city. We sit. The woman who called us down for breakfast is stronger, younger, a wife and mother. She smiles a wonderful broken smile, pours coffee for us into bowls. There is scalded milk in a pitcher, half a baguette of bread, white butter. A pan of blackened chestnuts. No one speaks. It is not rude. There is nothing to say. It is a morning in winter. The younger woman returns to her work, skinning a rabbit on the stone table. There are two rabbits, victims of the shots we heard in bed. In the frozen fields the two brothers work toward a midday dinner of rabbit stew.

On the floor in front of the fire, a silent child licks an icicle. There is a crude bandage wrapped around his left arm.

We smile at each other. We have a secret. We hold our bowls of coffee in our hands like prayers. We pry open roasted chestnuts, peel away the black husks. Inside the fruit is white, scored, and has the look of tiny brains. Our bags are by the door. It is a motor trip. We are not on vacation; this is something else. It will go on until it cannot go on. We will drive until we come to the sea, or stop somewhere to live ever after. It is what we are doing.

Later, in the car, The Waiter tells us that the boy by the fire was bitten by a wild pig, and that he is lucky to be alive. The boars in France are descended from myth. Savoia sings a boar-hunting song in her thready voice, then another longer song about a legendary boar who frightens a village until a little girl comes out one morning and kisses the boar on the nose.

CHAPTER 18

Manhattan: January 23, 1964

৩৵ৎ

Émile Galante is calling Anasor from Paris. Anasor is lying in bed, his ear to the telephone.

"You must decide, sir, what it is you want me to do. Up to what point. You are being generous with me but I would like you to tell me exactly. It is in an old classic car. I have the license number. The car is a Citroën, one does not see that many aged Citroëns anymore. The police will be able to find it instantly, but you do not want their interference. I mentioned a young man to you earlier?"

"Yes?"

"By chance I have found his grandmother and spoken with her. She tells me that they will be driving to Lyon to search for the boy's wife who disappeared last year. I will be in contact with the grandmother. She will tell me where they are staying. She does not suspect anything of course. You will certainly be able to find Eisenstein once he arrives in Lyon."

"Good."

"Please, sir, tell me what it is you want me to do. You must hire local private detectives. If we lose our man in Lyon, there will not be a way to apprehend him without the help of Interpol. His crime is international and if we are forced to ask Interpol's help, they will arrest him and bring him to trial in France."

"I see. Do you feel it might be possible to involve only the local police?"

"And the possibility of keeping the arrest quiet?"

"We might make the effort but there would be no guarantee. With the international flavor and the reward so high, as well as the famous client … for now there is simply too much notice in magazines to let it alone. So I feel a rendezvous in Lyon is of extreme urgency."

"Of course. I will make a deposit in your account this morning."

"Thank you, sir."

In the past two weeks Anasor has been interviewed, not only by *Art News,* but for various other magazines as well. Simon has managed to leap the gallery stile into international news and just yesterday, after a long lunch, Anasor was contacted by somebody from *Vogue.*

"Mr. Anasor," she had asked, "If you had one single choice, what would you have taken from the Whitney fire?"

"The fire," Anasor had answered.

CHAPTER 19

The Burning of the Moths: January 23, 1964

❧

Morning, winter is in full swing. The region shudders. We drive away from the cousin's farmhouse waving to its walls. The Waiter has successfully connected the scrap of hose to the heater, and now the Old Gentleman is toasty, our legs are warm. The light is changing, the sky clearing; there will be sun after all. We drive a few miles and I ask The Waiter to stop. Savoia and I climb out so we can feel the sun's heat, I need sun more than she does. We lean against the car, eyes closed, facing the sun, letting it warm our faces.

Savoia says. "It's a luxury to have both winter sun and winter cold."

The Waiter stands off by himself, shifting his legs like a horse. We climb back into the car. At midday we stop at a large brick building rising alone, stark, in the hayfield just off the road. There is a sign:

INSTITUTE DES BEAUX SEJOURS

I ask Savoia what it means?

"Well, literally, it means 'The Institute of Lovely Vacations'."

"I don't like institutes."

We enter the building. Two women come forward, one sails by us into another room, the other smiles revealing gaps in her teeth. She greets us as if we had made reservations and shows us to a table. She is buxom, squat, I feel that she wants to embrace us. We sit. She unfolds our napkins ceremoniously. We are alone in the dining room. Everything in the room is simple. The tiny flower pattern on the oilcloth has faded. No one comes here.

We are served soup with members of the vegetable world half drowned, pleasantly undercooked, as if it had been hastily boiled. There are huge aluminum spoons and too much bread. How good it must be to serve strangers the same bowls of food you have been preparing your entire lifetime, as if these strangers were your absent children. We have been given an unmarked bottle of red wine. Savoia and I talk in whispers about the old people living here, their lives, what they do each day, each month. *Institute Les Beaux Sejours* is too many miles from anything of significance. There is no television, perhaps a radio. The residents will never leave; they have only themselves. There are walks that can be taken. If there is love here, it is a love of sureness.

Outside, the cold blanches our faces. I don't know where we are. Our guidebook, an outdated edition, has been useless. Savoia gets behind the wheel. The Old Gentleman starts on the first try. The Waiter climbs into the back seat and falls asleep immediately. Savoia and I take turns driving. Under her wool skirt her thighs are bare; they warm the antique leather seat. Thinking about her thighs makes me dissolve, weaken, harden. I touch her to confirm any doubt, to find my being. She is chatty, maybe from the bitter wine. She tells me she has been married.

"We make the best wives, by the way, those of us who have been married before. We know what we don't want and what you do want."

I tell her I've been married, and that she doesn't want to know about my marriage.

"Oh, yes, I do. Everything. Give me details, details."

"Full disclosure, tonight. I'll tell you the story of Angelique. Can't you drive faster?"

"Let's go only as fast as one can gallop on horseback."

"They might be following us."

"Not on this road. Anyhow this is exactly where we are supposed to be, on this road, driving in this car, isn't it?"

"We need a destination, Savoia."

"We need to be aimless, too. It is a great relief for a navigator not to know where she's going. Does that scare you?"

"Yes."

"Not me. It's like everything I cherish. Knowing where you are going is nothing. My greatest luxury now is aimlessness."

"Not mine."

"Don't be frightened, Simon. This whole trip—The Waiter, everything else—is truer for our not knowing it completely."

"Our love has trouble with those elements, too."

"Why do you talk about love so much? Not knowing, even being lost is everything. You don't want to talk too much about love. It's bad luck; it weakens it. I want a life away from talk, from intellect. Animals never think about love or dream about death. We think of death every single day. All I want is a room of my own in the country, and a window. Nothing more. I want a room, Simon. It's very ordinary to you, but in all these years I've never have had one I can call my own."

"That's all I want, too."

"This is our bond, then, solitude."

We drive past miles of wide, sad fields, quaked from frost. In a while I fall asleep—a dangerous, deep sleep, a 'what-if-I-never-wake-up' sleep. Bottomless, black.

When I open my eyes it is late afternoon, and we are in a country without houses. Haystacks big as churches, barren fields hunched down for the frozen months sweep past our windows.

After driving through a village numbed by winter, the Old Gentleman coughs, then quits. We are stuck. I rouse The Waiter. Nothing he can do seems to work. Approaching us, a pair of plow horses is being walked along the field by the road. They stop at the farmer's command. The horses gaze at The Waiter cursing the engine under the hood. Savoia speaks to the farmer.

"Combien de kilometres jusqu'au village, s'il vous plait?"

"Pas trop loin."

"Mais combien, cinq, dix? Quoi?"

"Oui, presque."

The farmer releases his reins and walks over to them. He wears a *casquet* on his head, laced boots and a well-worn coat. His face has been cracked by the cold, a complex of tributary veins ornament his cheekbones.

It is decided. He will help us back to the village we just passed. The Citroën's bumper is roped to the horses' yolk. The farmer likes standing on the front seat with his upper body poked out through the sun roof. He shouts *"Ga! Ga!"* to his team, reaching down for the brake handle to slow the car when we come to a slope. Savoia, The Waiter, and I walk alongside the car in the breathless cold, I keep one hand resting on its roof, the other holding Savoia's.

We parade into the village just before evening darkens it, leave the Old Gentleman locked in front of the town's single gas station, which has closed for the night. I insists on paying the farmer and buying him a pastis at the café. He refuses politely and nudges his horses on toward his farm. We find rooms at the Grande Hotel, which is not particularly grand. It is on a canted square and there are stone benches and walls maybe a thousand years old, an iron monument to war—either to celebrate it or regret it. The trees in the square have no leaves on their black bones.

From our hotel window Savoia and I watch hundreds of people gathering in the square. The maître d'hôtel has told us that the people are gathering there for this unique night. The winter moths will arrive tonight. Of course, we are curious; we watch from our second floor window. It is too early for dinner. After awhile we bundle up and go outside to stand in the square with the villagers.

By now it is dark, though there is a good moon rising. We are two of maybe three hundred people—the entire village has gathered here. The clock on the church tower reads seven. Most of the people are holding short, stocky tree branches, with a wad of cloth tied to one end smelling of kerosene. Savoia asks a woman what they are doing.

"We are waiting for the moths, of course."

Across the square, standing in the watchtower of the medieval church, we can see a white-haired man wearing a béret. He shouts down to the crowd from time to time. Each time he does, we all stop talking and whisper. We wait. At seven-thirty he signals for the church bells to be rung, *"Sonnez! Sonnez!"* It is the signal for each of the villagers to lights his torch. It is a wondrous sight, hundreds of torches burning in the village square. The ancient church flickers in the glow. The bells ring; they do not stop ringing.

Suddenly, the moths are here. They swarm out from behind the moon, down the black sky—thousands of white moths, all of them huge, the size of sparrows, flying toward the torches' light in the square. Silent in flight, softly flying downward, toward the torches, then into them, the moths rise on fire like cinders, flying away, higher and higher, wings aflame, back toward the moon. Hissing, crackling, popping, flapping away. They fly as best as they can on flaming wings, then fall, each one a fist of orange flame, becoming tiny lines of gray smoke. Flying, flapping, falling, hundreds and hundreds of them each offering a tiny pageant of its death. Some fly higher than others, nearly to the top of the church tower, causing the villagers to cheer, *"Ah! Ooo! Ah! Ooo!"* before each moth stops for an instant at the apex of its flight and then falls hissing into their midst.

When it is over, the bells fall silent. There are no more moths, nothing left but sweet smelling smoke and dust on all our clothes, our hair, and at our feet. The men retire to the café for drinks leaning their charred sticks against the wall outside. The old man from the watchtower comes down and talks about how this night was better than most in his memory. He has stained, ruined teeth, and I can't help wondering if they pain him. I invite him to join us in the hotel restaurant for dinner. Our young friend, The Waiter, is tired but we press him to join us. Inside the restaurant there is an upright piano covered with a tablecloth. The wine is dark and filling, the food, common, good French food. We suck meat off bones, savoring every morsel.

The old man from the watchtower struggles to chew his food. He accepts a glass of *Marc,* then pours one more for himself. Through Savoia, I ask him if standing in the watchtower is an honor? He shakes his head and answers surprisingly in English, "No. Not at all. I would rather stand in the square with a torch." I ask if he can explain the burning of the winter moths. He shakes his head again. "There is no explanation. It is something that we do each year because we have been doing it each year."

It is late when we stand up. I leave the hotel waiter a full American tip that he will probably resent. We say goodnight to the old man and walk upstairs to our rooms. The Waiter is exhausted and can barely make it to his door. Inside our room it is brittle with cold. We can see our breaths. It is a room not worth heating tonight, and we dive into bed drunk, unwashed. We pull the blanket over our heads. The bulb strung from the ceiling glows amber through the walls of our makeshift tent.

I touch her face. A rim of moonlight along the low windowsill. How perfectly Savoia sleeps, so much a part of the night. The room glows with moonwash from the village square. I watch my breath cloud like a dream above her, I can see it enter her. I'm so very much alive, I ache from my severe mortality. She lies so still. I feel afraid of the distance between us. It is the greatest distance I can think of. I cannot resist. I kiss her hair. I must own an image of her. I must keep her with me forever. By the time I doze off, I have made up my mind—I will paint her portrait. I will paint her asleep as she is, in the moon, awake in the sun, alone in the dark, in a field, by candlelight, alive. Wherever we stop, maybe Lyon, I will find materials. I will paint again. No matter how slowly we drive without direction, defying oblivion, even if we become lost, our trip must end somewhere.

The thin curtains, a white morning. I wake grateful to be alive. Savoia stirs, warm, full of her night. The air is wintry. She whispers in a voice from another land, telling me that I kissed her in her sleep. I kiss her again. She turns, rolls over, swimming away in her sheets, tells me goodnight. I sit on the edge of the bed. The room's air is cold on my face. Images of the night haunt me. My head burns. I shuffle barefooted into the bathroom to identify myself in the mirror. It is possible I have grown antlers in the night. There is no evidence. The village square is still part of me, my head is full of burning moths. The white winter moths big as birds flying toward us from behind the moon, down into the torches, rising aflame, the bells in the tower tolling while the moths rise upward from the heat of their own flames, then at each apex, no longer able to rise, spiraling downward toward their torches again. I cannot rid myself of these images. What were they doing?

I leave Savoia to rouse herself. She'll pack our bags from memory hardly knowing she's doing it. She's become so deft at packing from her years with the airline. I walk downstairs and out into the quiet village. It is Sunday morning. The stillness is overwhelming. Two men with long twig brooms are sweeping the village square. I can hear their brooms whisper, 'shweet shweet' in the thin air. They are sweeping moth ash toward the base of the trees. Something is wrong. I don't like it here in this village.

I visit the garage, The Waiter is attending to the Old Gentleman. The garage owner remembers this particular model, admires its weary illusion of grandeur. He says its headlights remind him of silver egg cups. It first came out at a time of the *Delage,* the *Hispano Suiza,* the *Delahaye*—cars fit for kings. But the Citroën was fit for middle class families motoring to picnic spots, racing each other to catch trains, parked by row houses. A classic of bourgeois elegance, the design hasn't changed since the 1930's. Certain older people are startled by it, regard it as if they'd seen a ghost.

Shops have come alive. Fat white chickens with their blue feet tied, are caged in front of a market, waiting to be chosen. Bread has been baked early this morning. Gaping fish, from the Sâone River, expressions of surprise on their faces lie on crushed ice. I tour the streets until the cold pushes me into a humid café. Seated at the nickel bar a man with short-cropped, blond hair, is snapping through the pages of *Paris Match.* I catch a glimpse of the cover—an aerial photograph of the Air France crash site dotted with floating seat cushions. The man snaps the pages, flips past photographs of floating debris, under the black words *TRAGEDIE. MORTALITE.* There are vague snapshots of passengers.

"S'il vous plait," I ask him tentatively. The man looks at me, eyebrows raised, mouth open. He sees the urgency in my face, shrugs, slides the open magazine toward me. More photographs—floating seats, shrouded corpses on picnic tables in a gymnasium.

A row of not-too-recent airline portraits—all crew members, four of them women. I scan them—three air hostesses, all of them pretty, among them Kiwi with darker hair. Wrecked, destroyed. Their ferocious deaths seem masculine, not intended for such pretty women. All of these portraits are printed below the single word, *MORTES!* There are comments from divers complaining of murky water while searching the midwinter Mediterranean. So many victims cannot been recovered. Death by disappearance has a vagueness that leads to speculation.

A headless body has been found, washed ashore at Fiumicino—

a woman in uniform. A crew member? She has lain unidentified in the temporary morgue. The lack of privacy as a result of dying badly. Sensationally, the heading pleads, *QUI ÊTES VOUS?* It asks her, it asks them, it asks us. There is no clue. Who knows her? I feel her disgrace, whoever she is. There is no dignity to this sort of dying. The French adore their dead, *Paris Match* shows fluey photographs of corpses. It is their métier. It is required of them.

Here is a picture of the Air France navigator. Her name is spelled out, Anna Savoia Paulus. A dreadful flash portrait, her hair is longer, darker, parted like a schoolgirl's, pupils reddened. I grip the bar. The name *Anna Savoia Paulus* glares up at me from the page. It causes the floor to slide away from me. It is her. The café is in motion, its walls moving. I tear the page out of the magazine. The magazine's owner watches me. He seems aware that I am somehow involved with these dead. He shrugs.

"She's alive," I tell him, "Look at her well, my friend, she is alive, she was here last night just over there, outside, we were at the burning of the moths, you must have seen her."

The man is confused; it is his magazine after all. I put a bill on the counter—fifty francs.

"Where did you get this thing?"

The proprietor translates. *"Où avez vous acheté ce journal?"*

"Dans le magasin de tabac," the man says defensively, *"naturelement."*

"They are wrong! I will call *Paris Match* and tell them so. I will attack them in court," I threaten.

He looks at me, says, *"Bonne chance,"* and leaves.

The proprietor is intrigued. I give him another bill, maybe a hundred francs, and asks him for telephone *jetons*. The telephone is in the back by the toilet. The proprietor gives me a stack of *jetons*, helps me dial the number. The number listed in the front of the magazine. The process is not quick. It is Saturday. Just then, I see Savoia passing outside the café. She stops, looks in, scans the room. I wave, but cannot catch her eye. She is gone. I wait. Someone must be there at the magazine. I stand for several minutes. Finally, an operator connects me to a news editor who speaks some English but has not spoken it recently.

"*Importante!*" I shout into the phone. "I have with me a survivor from the Mediterranean plane crash you listed in your article as being dead."

"Would you repeat this again, please?" he says in a formal bird-like voice, "I am not certain that I comprehend you correctly."

I try to speak clearly. "She is not dead. On page 12, you listed Anna Savoia Paulus as dead, but she is not dead, she is here with me, alive!"

The news editor must be able to hear the tremor in my voice. There is a pause.

"Please, repeat the name."

"Anna Savoia Paulus."

"No, your name, sir."

"My name is not important."

"I think it is important, sir, as well as your telephone number."

Another pause.

"My name is Jonathan Boot."

"You are *Americain?*"

"Look, this is not a joke. You made a mistake. My telephone is 36 17 44 48 22, I am at the *Tabac* in the village of St. Lis-sur-Sâone."

"Can you confirm what you are telling me sir?"

"I certainly can. If you would like to speak with her, I'll get her. Would you like to interview her? You may, right now, if you like."

"Sir, Monsieur Boot, before you do that I would like you to speak with a special editor. Do not quit the telephone please."

I hold on. A minute passes. A deeper voice comes on with better English. I explain myself again.

"You can confirm the presence of this survivor?"

"I most certainly can."

"You are at present with this survivor from Flight One?"

"She is here. And she is not a survivor. She is a member of the crew that you mistakenly listed as dead. But she was not onboard Flight One. She got off the plane in Rome. Before the crash."

"Her name, please?"

"Anna Savoia Paulus. You made a mistake, see?"

"What may I do for you?"

I am stumped, it's too obvious. "What do I want? Correct your stupid mistake!" I say.

"I would be pleased to do this but how can I know you are being true?"

"You may speak with her now."

"I have her photograph in front of me. This same person is there with you now?"

"Yes, sir, she is standing just outside the café."

"You are not in Paris?"

"No, no, I told you. I am in St. Lis-sur-Saône!"

"This woman can speak French?"

"She is French! I'll get her. Please don't quit the telephone!"

Something good is happening at last. My stomach is slipping back into its basket. I set the phone on the shelf, beside my *jetons*. I run out the door, Savoia is not outside the café, she is not next door in the market, or in the bookstore. Nor at the hotel. She is gone; she is nowhere. I return to the phone.

"I cannot find her."

"I see."

"But she's here, I swear." I try not to sound like a crackpot.

"Please understand, sir, that these mistakes are very rare. The list of fatalities has come to us directly from Air France, but we have also done our own investigating. We are assured that Mademoiselle Paulus could not possibly have abandonned the flight in Rome, because Flight One crashed on its approach to Rome, not after departing Rome. Please understand, I am in sympathy with you, but the mistake has not been made by us. Please excuse me."

"I can find her, I'm trying to tell you, she's not far away."

"Yes sir, I understand."

"No, no, no, pay attention, you can talk to her, you can hear her voice!"

"Thank you sir, I am sorry for your loss.

"I'll have her call you back."

"I wish we could help you, sir …"

CHAPTER 20

The String Quartet: January 24, 1964

੭~ⴺ

We must stay away from small cities. We don't want Dijon, Dampiere-sur-Saône, or the back roads—the Citroën killing roads. I don't care if we never reach Lyon, except for my promise to The Waiter to find his runaway bride, I would skip Lyon and drive to Johannesburg.

The car is aged, a vagabond. It has seen maybe too many dusty roads and is dark from travel but it is working nicely again. The Waiter is a good mechanic. He has taken over the driving while I watch the countryside pass from the back seat. We climb a long hill. When we reach the top, along the horizon fifty miles to the east, the Alps stand like a storm at sea. Here the road is treacherous. At one steep turning, where the alternative route would have resulted in death by rolling, the Old Gentleman refuses, kneels in pain. He cannot go on another step. His little fuel line has been jogged loose. Savoia says he shook it loose on purpose. At one point, the road disappears. The bald bones of the hills poke through the road marked only by cairns of stone.

Savoia tells The Waiter to stop the car, she needs to go into a frozen field to pee.

"Will you pee, too?" she asks.

"I'm sorry, I can't pee," I tell her. "I may piss."

"Men can't pee?"

"No, men piss. Ladies pee. It is a difference between them, however fine."

"I'm not so sure I'll make it," she says.

The engine is knocking the wispy scent of rusted steam through seams in the dashboard.

"Yes I will," Savoia vows, running her shoe along the car's small, battered dashboard, "He'll be fine," she says.

And by her prophecy, the road levels, the motor calms and then, rounding a green slope, we come into a wide plateau of stone

houses and stone walls. A blue-bordered sign reads L'AUBERGE
D'AUGUSTINE. There are two dogs and a small auberge but no
people. We decide to stop the car, rest it, down the road from the
auberge, along rows of deep-sighing pines combing the breeze,
Savoia decides this is her place. I stop the car.

"Well, then, I will pee, you may piss."

"*Vive la difference.*"

When we get out of the car, Savoia thinks she hears music on the
wind, a violin or a cello, a faint melody that grows on the wind
then fades without the wind. Is it possible? There is only a wall, a
barn, a row of brush. I will follow her. The Waiter will stay with
the car. She walks a short distance to where the grass is higher
along the stone wall. She squats like a nesting bird. It is very
pretty. Her panties are white.

"Do you mind if I watch you?"

"No, no of course not."

She glazes, briefly staring at the sky, then at me. It is the same
glazed look as in the airline portrait. She taps herself with a tis-
sue, drops it as a marker. She stands, whisks her panties up under
her skirt.

We walk between the stone walls of the auberge and a field where
the walls narrow and open up, we come to a scene of exquisite
beauty. A quartet of old men is playing music on violins and a
cello in the high grass, on the rounding of a green hill, above
lower green hills, not far from a wide stand of pines that sometimes seems to join their music, with the gleaming Alps off behind them, but not that far off. I wave back to The Waiter to
come along, too. Two dozen people have gathered, probably of
another town. It is Saturday. They sit on the low wall at the edge
of a natural green terrace, by a good stone house not far from the
road. The quartet sits in a half-circle on wooden chairs, wearing
their good suits, black city hats for warmth, white shirts. One
man wears a tie. I imagine them to be friends.

The slope drops steeply away behind them, leaving them outlined
in clarity against the distant line of Alps. The men play their
music from memory; it seems from another era. Wind seen in
high grass. We three walk down closer to the quartet, careful not

254

to enter badly and disturb anyone. We sit near the people but a bit away because we are the outsiders and the only ones. The grass is wind-dried and we don't feel the snow-chill when we're down in it; we can let the sun warm us. Savoia sits in front of me wrapped in my old coat. There is no road in sight, nothing but wind and sky, the distance across the valley, the white Alps far off, and close to us, the connection of these people. We listen, I watch, sometimes through her hair blown onto my face. The Waiter, silent as always, keeps time with the tempo with his head and shoulders.

One of the musicians stands. He cannot continue; his fingers have cramped—arthritis? Another musician is required. By any chance, is there someone among them familiar with this music able to read these scores? The violin. The Waiter raises his hand, walks forward head down through the grass, nods and bows, accepts the violin, sits in the vacant chair. Suddenly, he is among them, playing the violin superbly, his hair blowing wildly above his bow. He is part of their music. He is of army age, with a long, crooked nose and a red face. His nose is running and he plays watching the sheet music, eyes nearly closed in his privacy. It is so unlikely. They play on. Though they don't need the shelter of the wall, they move into its lee side to be among the people. Some are smoking and talking while they are listening, using the music for themselves. A dozen children are fooling around beyond, at the edge of the slope, bored with the idea of having to sit to see music played. Sometimes they laugh but their laughter doesn't interrupt the musicians. I watch the children tussle around the legs of the musicians. The music seems to have been scored with the sound of the children in mind, the wind sounds, blowing through the grass, the pines. They pause. They are finished. The Waiter turns the page to the next score, speaks to the three who nod to him with respect. Quietly, they begin to play the "Canon in D" by Johann Pachelbel. I have never seen musicians who look so much like the music they are playing, I sense that each of them cannot hear what he is doing with the music, but each is inside it instead, and happy to be there. No quartet that I have ever heard has fulfilled the score of the "Canon in D," simply the way it is, the way it can be. The Germans play it as a dirge, the

Swedish as a march, the Americans as background music. The French play it as dinner music. Everyone else plays it as a hymn and now I can hear it, such a short piece, just a few minutes, yet there it is, birth, lifetime, death, resurrection. It is over. The musicians stand and bow to each other, not to the audience. The Waiter's eyes are running. No one claps; it is not that kind of thing. The people are there, that is enough. I get the feeling the quartet will come there to play on Saturdays whether anyone listens to them or not, and that the local farmers have gotten into the habit of sitting on the wall to rest as well as listen and watch them play.

The Waiter shakes hands with the four musicians. They hug him, Savoia kisses him, he reddens. It is impossible. He has never even mentioned music. But Savoia says that neither has she mentioned celestial navigation nor have I ever brought up the subject of painting.

"*Merci, mon fils,*" one of the farmers smiles at The Waiter, giving him a paper bag full of radishes, thanks him again for playing. The Waiter shares them with us. The first radish is exciting, the second just tastes hot.

CHAPTER 21

L'Auberge D'Augustine: January 24, 1964

୬ঔ৬

… We walk away from the hilltop, back to the car. Savoia holds onto my forefinger, the grip of a child afraid to let go. The way she clings. reminds me of lines written by Stephen Spender, now I try to remember them, and what few I can, I say to her.

> *Bright clasp of her whole hand around my finger*
> *… as we walk together now."*
> *All my life I'll feel a ring invisibly.*
> *Circle this bone with shining …*
> *far from today as her eyes are far already …*

"Did you just make that up?"

"Some other guy did. I just remembered it, is all."

She asks me to say it again and I do less hesitantly We walk past L'Auberge D'Augustine then turn back and go in. The auberge is warm; entering it is like being tucked into bed. A dark, generous main room. The Waiter is talking with a deer-like girl he has met outside who admired his music. After Savoia and I have gotten glasses of Calvados for our chill, she says, "Why don't we stay here, wherever here is, if they'll have us?" But it is still early, I want us to get on the road to Les Ombrages before nightfall. I'm running. My fear has spread, tightening my anus, moving up my spine. It is irrational for the moment, Savoia tells me.

It is decided. We will stay at l'Auberge d'Augustine. It is a farm, really. The large room, once a stable is now a kitchen with a wide fireplace, a large table with chairs, and a small bar, a cabinet with bottles. The farmer and his wife take in guests but only in the summer. They are surprised by us, fascinated, and set about pleasing us because The Waiter has played the violin superbly, because of Savoia lightness and sense of being, and because of my sadness, as if I were grieving. It is a summer inn, yet with a pine log fire growing in the huge hearth, and the Calvados in the glasses we carry up the stairs, it has become a winter inn. And that is how we came to sleep here. The farmer's wife warms the two best rooms for us by lighting pine logs in their small fireplaces, she turns down our feathered comforter on the high posted bed. She is very sorry she tells us, but there will be no food for dinner, only cheese, bread, chestnuts, paté campagne, their own red wine.

I come out of a deep cavern of sleep ravenous. A single stroke of light between the shutters shows that it must be morning. The smoothed plaster walls painted white, various planes, cemented cracks left unpainted, framed life-sized portraits, the faces of astonished, grave men and women with hand-tinted rosy cheeks. Farm sounds—a rooster, iron wheels scraping on rock, a dog barking a horse away. Savoia feels my new five-day beard between her chin and neck, says that it is no longer pleasant.

Downstairs, we three drink from our bowls of café-au-lait, the bluish milk fresh from the barn. We are offered rolls which the woman calls *boules*, gruyère cheese warmed at the fire. The Waiter is smiling. After he has gone out to warm up the car, Savoia says that he has had a success with the *jeune biche*.

Later, we go to the barn, the girl is watching The Waiter as he tunes the wheezing, spitting old man.

"Why'd you call her a bitch?"

"I called her a *biche*, a young female deer."

I never mention the photograph I saw of her in *Paris Match* or my telephone conversation with the news editor. I will wait. Nothing must change between us. We will talk about it soon. Until we do, until I know what she answers, I will live without certainty.

The Waiter kisses his new friend goodbye and drives us back down the hills, away from the auberge, coasting most of the miles we had climbed yesterday.

"Let's visit my mother," Savoia says.

Why did I think her mother had disappeared or died?

"I didn't know you had a mother."

"I don't speak to her."

"Why not?"

"I can't remember."

"Shall I turn in here?" We are passing a farm. "Is this her house?"

"No, no, she lives miles and miles east, at Plon. You can hide there forever if you like."

"Can we drive there today?"

"Yes, yes, I think so."

"But we have to be fair to The Waiter. After all, he's being very nice about our leisurely approach to Lyon. Can't we visit her after Lyon?"

"But we're so close."

"You planned this."

"Well, of course, a little. One always knows where one is."

She points to the folded Michelin map. "Let me see that please."

The Waiter passes it back to her. She opens it, moves her finger across the colored lines. She is a navigator after all.

"Here we are and here is my mother, we could stay at her house tonight. She's my mother, after all."

"Ask The Waiter what he thinks."

She does; she calls him *Patron,* he nods, makes a brief smile, *"D'Accord."*

Savoia says, "I never brought any of my husbands home to meet Mama."

"So, it will be like a state visit," I smile.

"That's exactly what it will be."

"Is it a nice place?"

"Well, she doesn't live in a garret. I remember the house as being very beautiful. She's lived there since I was a tiny little girl."

I'm glad. For what? For Savoia taking me further into her life. We stop in a village near Plon for lunch and wine. Inside the café it smells of coffee and roasting duck and sausages. When we sit, we speak only French, The Waiter is silent as always. Savoia watches him across the metal and plastic table. *"Q'uest-ce que vous pensez, Patron?"* she asks him what he's thinking.

He says in French that he wants me to draw another picture of Claire. He misses her. It's the least I can do. I don't have the right pencil, I tell him, but I'll try. In a couple of minutes The Waiter looks over my shoulder and says, *"Incroyable."* It seems to be her.

"She's lovely, so young." Savoia says.

"Is there hope?" he asks me.

"Oui," I answer him in my broken French. We will find her the first day without doubt so he should not concern himself further.

Two young girls at a table nearby are puzzled by my French. They are speaking naturally and keep glancing at me, laughing discreetly, amused that I cannot speak their language as well as they can. I am so old compared to them. It is something they can do better than me, an adult.

Our coffee is old, the omelet is strange.

Savoia tells The Waiter, we are going to visit her mother. He wants to stay with the girls. We should only be gone for an hour, maybe a little more. Savoia tells him.

Plon, the village where Savoia's mother lives on, is not beautiful, as she has described it. Not anymore. It was once, of course, all villages were when they were created, she explains to me. We drive slowly down the main street while she tells me how pretty this part of Plon used to be. Each new building reminds her of the old building torn away to make room for it. The village has grown and she can no longer see the low hills beyond it. When we do see the hills, houses have spread over them like lichen. The houses on her street are shabbier than they used to be, she says. Her mother's house is strong and old, not large, built just before the Great War. Its bricks are still red. The neighbors' houses are closer to it than she remembers them being when she was a child.

No one is at home. Her mother lives with a companion, a woman. Savoia takes me around behind the house where a long, narrow field slopes down, away from it toward the river. Tall grass, stung by frost, is bent, above the stone walls and higher than the neighbor's grass.

"My father would never have let grass grow this high. He would come back here with his scythe when it grew up to his knees and slice it back down. He understood grass. I would always watch him scything it so very well with his long strokes, such a beautiful gesture."

She walks away through the crackling sallow grass then turns back to me. "We had cats and they really loved him. They followed him like sheep. They stayed so close, I was afraid that one day his scythe would cut one in two. A cat would be missing from time to time and I would believe my father had cut it in two and wasn't telling me. But the cat always came back in the morning. Well, one day in the summer, when he was out swinging his scythe where the grass was very deep, there, just in front of him lay Maja surrounded by the kittens she had just delivered. They were all there in front of her. She had not run away, of course, but just lay there nursing her kittens, glaring up at him."

I look at her, waiting.

"The End."

"I love your stories, Savoia. Nothing ever really happens in them."

"Or goes wrong. I make sure of that."

By the wall, she shows me the head stones of her dogs' graves. "One was called 'Gulliver', the other 'Ralphe-Ralphe', for his bark," she says.

"Why don't dogs have last names?" I ask her.

"Don't they take ours?"

"It is a presumption to have more than one name."

We enter the kitchen using a key that is still under a flower pot after all these years.

I want to see her baby room, I tell her, the room where she first examined herself in a mirror. We go upstairs behind the kitchen. It is a room, not large, grown gray with absence. An empty room. No trace of a little girl waiting for her breasts to arrive, who stared at herself in the mirror wondering if her head was too small, if her eye-nose-mouth proportions, the balance that separates beauty from un-marriageable loss, was correct. There is only a bed without a mattress, with a thousand rusted springs. A palm from Palm Sunday is tacked to a wall, and oddly, on the floor, a horse's harness.

"Really, Simon. All I ever want is for us to have a small room with a bed."

"Nothing more?"

"No. Not today."

"Is that the dream of a frightened person?"

'Yes, it certainly is."

"Well, OK, I'll grant you your one wish but only because you are an honest person who is not afraid to be afraid. And because I love to make love to you."

"I didn't say anything about that, did I?"

But we do. In her bedroom. On the floor.

In her mother's bedroom. There is a photograph of Savoia on the bureau, age ten, so unconfident, that serious look.

"I was much too serious."

Serious little girls are forced to be serious if they're too ugly; they have no choice. Her stick legs were always elegant.

On mornings after her father had left, she remembers standing in the doorway to her mother's bedroom. "I stood here listening to her lectures on life while she sat up in bed after I brought her her breakfast tray."

Waiting in the house for her mother, Savoia becomes sad. And so it is, she can return to her earlier life, and even lie in her own bed, but she is no longer the same Anna and the country is no longer the country she remembers.

"I can speak to my Mama now. It's no longer impossible, but let's leave. I'll write her a note. I can telephone her tonight."

She writes, "Hello, Mama I am completely happy for the first time in my life." She tells me to write something, too, and I say almost the same thing. She slides the note under the front door to pretend that we have not been in the house. A cat is waiting for us. It wants to know what we are going to do next. There is always a cat waiting for us in France.

CHAPTER 22

Paris: January 24, 1964

On both of his two evenings in Paris, Émile Galante has dined at *Le Chat Pas Chat*, the six-table bistro. The Waiter's grandmother recommends the *Poulet Grand-Mère*. After dinner Galante sits with a Cognac and they talk. She is in daily contact with her grandson, she says, and he is finally happy. He tells her that he knows he will find Claire, that his new friends are wonderful, that he feels safe and that the three of them will arrive in Lyon at the latest in two days, not later than Tuesday.

Galante telephones Anasor.

"It will be a simple matter to find them," he says. "Madame's brother owns a café in Lyon."

When Anasor hangs up the telephone, he makes reservations on Flight One, the New York to Paris Constellation, then a connecting flight to Lyon. He will be waiting with two men recommended by Galante when Simon arrives at the café.

Le Trompe L'Oeil de Trion: January 25, 1964

At dark we drive into Trion, a poor village. We visit a stone church, its inside colder than outside. I cast a prayer to the rafters, drop coins loudly into the alms box, light a candle for the three of us and a weeping woman on the steps. There is a café, of course. The Waiter says he must leave us, the car needs to rest. He will replenish its fluids, water, gas, oil. Pump the tires.

Savoia has bought a book in a stationery store—a novel with a white paper cover, an ordinary book, not Joyce or Stendhal. For the first time I watch her read a book. I stay close to her, feel I cannot go away from her for long. I never know anymore what I will find when I return. She will never grow old.

The hotel restaurant is closed by the time The Waiter comes back, so we walk along the river embankment until we see the lit doorway, windows and boxed hedges; an open bistro. Inside are a dozen tables, all empty but one. A man wearing a *casquet* sits with coffee and liqueur talking to the maitre d'hotel, a short well-fed person in an apron who has the veins of a leaf spread across his face.

"Bonsoir, Messieurs Dame," he stands, seems delighted to be interrupted by the three of us, *"Dîner?"*

"Bonsoir, Monsieur," I manage in my most serious French, *"Oui, dîner, merci."*

"Trés bon," he nods to me as if I were a borderline countryman, maybe Dutch, then turns to the kitchen, *"Claudine!"*

Claudine comes out, a downtrodden woman who looks as though she fights each night for sleep. She puts her head to one side, and with a smile we cannot help joining, she leads us to a small room, warmer, with two long-used tables and wooden chairs. The walls are painted garden green and seem closer together at the ceiling than the floor. There is one piece of art in the room, a trompe l'oeil. Nothing else. The trompe l'oeil depicts a series of concentric trellises and entirely covers the third wall. A latticed border frames another border of finer lattice-work, inside of which are trellises cut even more finely, set more closely together, and inside them, are more trellises cut at steeper angles so that the closer we approach, the finer they appear. They are cut so precisely, so meticulously, that we are forced to gaze through arcades of diminishing arbors, passing through imaginary gardens and startling imaginary birds archway after archway, until, in the final garden, there is a perfect fountain the size of my thumbnail.

It is as if we have been led toward that one garden, invited to enter, but are denied; we can only imagine the tranquility that awaits us there, if it were possible to enter. The trompe l'oeil looks old, older than the tables and chairs of the restaurant. Its colors have faded from it rendering its whites now to yellow-beige. But the deception is perfect, the feeling of mystery, strong. We sit facing it. Strangely, I have never seen a lattice trompe l'oeil, never any trompe l'oeil with the perfection of this one. Here we don't need to cooperate with it by squinting to make it real. It is real. We are there in a dark room surrounded by stained walls, looking down a covered walkway that we want to walk down but know we never can. A walkway that does not exist, that leads to an inconceivable fountain, as if that is where we were meant to be, and not here. Savoia asks Claudine if it is painted by someone from Trion. She replies that it was made by her son.

Savoia asks where her son is living.

The woman answers, making a French face, mouth down, eyes up, an expression that can mean almost anything. Her son may either have been be-headed for unspeakable crimes or elected prime minister of France. I ask Savoia to tell her I would really like to talk with him.

"So would I," she smiles. *"C'est un vrai trompe l'oeil, n'est ce pas?"*

Savoia says, "I feel such an urge to walk through the arcade, to the garden, isn't it amazing? I could walk all the way down by the fountain and sit, and if I did, I know I'd hear birds. I can hear the splashing water in the fountain. It's warm in there isn't it?"

"It is always summer in there with my son," the woman says in French, setting bread and butter on our table, "regardless of the winter here."

I ask Savoia to tell her that her son is a wonderful artist, that his painting is certainly the truest of all trompe l'oeils I have ever seen. I do not mention that I too, once created trompe l'oeils for a living but never as well as her son.

Claudine laughs, not rudely and says, *"Vous êtes Anglais?"*

I nod. She says no English person has ever said trompe l'oeil with a good accent, and then with another hopelessly beautiful smile, she tells us that our dinner tonight will be potage a l'ail, ragout d'agneau, et du bon Camembert.

We smile and make a fuss of appreciation. It is late. When she is gone, Savoia whispers to me, "He is dead."

"Yes."

After dinner I ask the woman how her son died. She is surprised for an instant, her secret has been uncovered. "He was killed in a battle," she says.

We walk back to the hotel, it is a narrow hotel with uneven floors. Our room is on the second floor. The glow of a street lamp illuminates our ceiling. Just before sleep, we hear the Nachtmusik of bedsprings in the next room. The scherzo of lovemaking is so offensive when it is not your own—the iron squeaks of joy, and in the final movement, the adagio, the humming while lighting up, fumes of Gauloise have somehow wafted into our room. Then to the toilet, allegro, the man's urination inches from my head, as though it were entering my ear, the plummeting flush of water and sleep.

It is getting light outside. Something causes me to open my eyes, Savoia is awake. She slips out of the bed naked, crosses to the window, yanks the curtains apart. Outside the window it is gray. There are stubby fragments of a dormant tree. I study her. I don't move once I set my elbow and post my jaw on my palm. I'm waiting for the courage to speak to her. She stands above the heater combing her hair, gazing out the window. The day is colorless. Of the few lights I have ever seen her nude in—after we've made love in the glow of a single candle against a wall, in the bright cut of sun muscling through an opening between drapes, in the white blade from a nearly closed bathroom door—it is in this morning's light, subtle in our small room, a pale sculpture, the light I see her in now, framed in its bizarre arrangements of dark spiny beams and brace-beams, that I'll remember her by, in this winter morning light, the tall window, the white marbled sky. It is a bold, stark light, that gives her a look of beauty I've seen only once when I snuck past a locked gate and wandered through the underground storage rooms below the Metropolitan Museum of Art, where the sunlight fell from highly placed side-walk prisms and barely lit the vast mausoleum, full of unused armored knights and abandoned statues. There I saw, suddenly, reclining on her hip, a young woman in the pallor of marble, maybe Greek—her breasts, her hip, her stomach, shoulder, arm, buttocks, her saddened face—I was too young to know what I was looking at or why I felt what I felt about her, or why I stayed so long with her. She seemed to glow from a source of light not given to the knights or the statues of emperors or the heroes, light that came neither from outside of her nor from within her. A light that was her, and so, too, is Savoia.

"You are so very nude," I tell her, "so free, so luminous, so tall, so nicely formed, please put something on." She smiles openly and slips into my robe.

I must ask her now. The photograph. The conversation. Now it is time. In my ears an awful sound, a rushing wind. I lie in bed, warm, silent, bundled, not wanting to know. Why should I know? She has stopped combing her hair. She stands. She is star-ing out, waiting for me to speak; she senses what I'm going to say. I stare at her so long my eyes water. Without asking her, I say, "When your plane went down, it was approaching Rome."

My voice hangs in the air like smut. She seems not to hear. After a few moments I speak again.

"Was it leaving Rome?"

The silence between us takes on vast proportions. I begin to tremble, I feel the widest gap between us.

"No." I can barely hear her.

"You were still on board when it …?" I snare the filthy word 'crashed'.

"Yes, my darling."

I look at her as if from memory, I hear my voice say; "Did you survive?"

She does not take her eyes from the window. She moves her head sideways, twice. There is nowhere for me to look, I close my eyes. What has been impossible is now true. The dreadful wind is screaming in my ears, hollow, wide, deafening me. My mind goes blank. Black, tumbling, my head apart from my body, down through a building without floors.

I open my eyes. How long have I been gone? Back in the room, Savoia is standing there, at the window. I have stopped thinking. I hear my own voice.

"Savoia. Tell me. Say, 'I was killed'. Say it to me."

I need to hear her say the words.

"Say it!"

She turns her head to one side. She looks at me directly, her eyes back into my own. "Yes, Simon, I was killed. On the approach to Rome, aboard Flight One in the Mediterranean Sea."

It can only happen once. Nor is it meant to happen at all or ever again. It may be in my power to allow others to deny reality, to imbue them with whatever I want them to see. To delay reason. The strength of my power I can see in them by her presence. I'm awed by this will. What I succeeded in doing over the years, my ability to draw people fully into my work, made me the great painter I became, and now the power of my ultimate trompe l'oeil has become my *trompe de vie, my trompe de reves, my trompe de corps.* The genius of it!

What a creatively insane person I must be, if that's what I should call it, to be able to do this. The closest thing to truth is insanity; what else is new? I've known that for a while. But in spite of this power and as deeply as I love Savoia, I must accept that she is dead. This person I love more than any man has ever loved any woman in the history of the world. I must acknowledge it. She is dead ...

CHAPTER 23

Salve De Dios: Canary Islands, May 12, 2001

৵৵

The fifth journal ends with these words, 'She is dead.' I close the book. I am asleep moments after I blow out the candles. When I awake I read the last words again. Simon has spoken to me. It is the key that no one has ever discovered, explained by Simon himself. I leave the journal open to the last page and lay it on the bed in a square of sunlight from the window, and photograph it as carefully as I can. This is a book jacket if I've ever seen one. Euphoric, I make notes from the journal transcribing selected passages. The battery has died on my laptop computer, so I continue by hand, writing in ink on paper, in the grand tradition of writers.

"No more journals," he tells me that evening. I expected this sooner. I am sitting with him as I have most every evening since I've been on his island, watching the sun go down through the open window. As usual, he's in his good chair in the front room I'm in the wooden chair. We watch the sun lowering over the Atlantic. We are a mile inland. Tonight the wind is blowing the seas high. As he does every evening, Simon stares the sun into the sea without blinking, as if he were defeating a rival or maybe wishing safe journey home to an ally.

Late each day I have walked the road up the hill with the journal I have finished reading. Even though I bring a bottle of rum or wine, or leave a fish on the kitchen table, I wait for him to ask me to stay for supper. He allows me to sit with him for the sunset whether he's grown tired of my company or not. At the end of the evening, dizzy, sober, or drunk as a hoot owl, he opens the metal chest and I take the next journal back to my room. If I can, I start reading it by candle light and finish it in the morning. His handwriting is fine and varies in its quality.

He has not yet asked me why I am here, what my motive was in searching for him, and what I will do with my discovery now that I have found him. He has taken a chance. He may believe in me. I have spent most my money figuring this puzzle out, trailing him here to Salve de Dios, 37 years after he came here. My motive is to write his biography, of course, I'm a writer. That's why I'm here. He hasn't asked. My working title is *Simon Lister, the Lost Years.* His life since his disappearance. Most people assumed him to be dead. It has been a great mystery, a guaranteed best-seller. My first, *Ravel in Paris* sold well but was by no means a best-seller. *Simon Lister: the Lost Years* will more than make up for that. It will come as a complete shock to the people who assumed he died years ago. It will be a publishing triumph. I have told no one of this, I have not even contacted a publisher. Publishers will bid for the rights.

It'll be dark soon. He hasn't mentioned the word 'supper.' He will; he does each evening but it's getting late. I'd ask him to the restaurant down the hill but Señora Natti's in the kitchen, cooking. He swirls the rum in the thick glass which he tips it toward the sun, "Fuck you. Amigo."

He has a fine head, he could use a shave. His face is lean, dark, his teeth stained with age, his eyes hooded. I can see his mind in his eyes. he speaks very little, always in a quiet voice, sometimes even a whisper.

"Some nights I can smell Africa," he says to himself. Activated by the sound of his own voice, he glances around at me. The visitor.

"Why no more journals Simon?" I ask.

"The rum's not as strong as it could be, is it?" he says instead of answering, "And it's so sweet you must crush up a lime in it, if you have a lime. Do you require ice?"

"You know I don't need ice Simon, I understand about the rum we've been drinking, for God's sake!"

"Please tell me why you don't want me to read any more journals?"

He refuses to hear me, he's having a private moment with the solar system. He smiles, sips. The room has filled with crude smells, elegant odors, powerful arrangements of aged recipes from this deprived island, fiery smells coming from the other room, the hot room. I will ask him again. These notebooks, thousands of words in each, some clear, some unreadable. His handwriting is fine, no words crossed out when the love affair with Savoia was going right, when he was calm, sure, passionate. Then, in his despair, the words become larger, dashed off without caring if they'd ever be read by anyone but himself, written to protect him from what he was seeing happen around him. He knew he was going to lose Savoia, that he had made her up and that she would last only as long as his madness. That's how I understood it— the variations in the strength of his belief, his love never wavering. Then it did and so did her presence. Thinking about the book I will write gives me a rush that keeps me awake at night.

We are both watching the sun; it is almost gone, bleeding over the horizon. "You see that boat out there?" he points with his glass. I go to the window, peer out. I tell him I don't see a boat.

"Look harder, to the left of the sun."

"I don't see it."

"Try. Small fishing boat, one mast, net hung down to dry. There, just there."

I see it. There it is, a fishing boat, rigged just as he described, coming out of the sun between swells. I tell him I see it.

His voice becomes gentle, tired. "There's no fishing boat out there."

"But I did see a boat, I can describe it."

"Of course you can, but there was no boat, why would there be a boat out there? No one fishes that side in this weather, this time of day. Coming from where, going where?"

"I swear I saw one!" I squeeze my glass, embarrassed.

"I believe you did."

Silence.

Suddenly, I realize that I saw what he wanted me to see, not what was there. He created a boat, and I saw it, just as he had created Savoia. I am numbed. Was this just a trick of his psychosomatic power?

"Would you call this psychosynthesis?" I ask him.

"Christ, no, I would not!" he stands up. I am about to be ejected. "Greek. That's all they used at the Eisenstein. They didn't have a glimmer. Doctor Ellie called it my 'perfect psychosis' and it would always get her spanked. But she liked getting spanked, so she kept it up. If you got to have a name for it, call it '*a trompe de bateau*'."

I can hear the radio in the kitchen bringing the news to Señora Natti but fading in and out.

"Can you understand the news?" he asks me.

"Can you?" I say automatically.

"I can understand it or not, whatever I feel like."

Señora Natti enters now, carrying an oval china platter. The *mero* split wide, cooked honey brown with dark garlic cloves clinging to it, and small cilantro leaves tucked inside. The fish is ringed with potatoes wrinkled as prunes, flecks of sea salt on them. Tiny tomatoes blackened by cooked olive oil. It is the same dish served on that first day when he presented me to la Señora Natti. She speaks to me in a lilting, musical voice, the way so many island women speak here.

"I can never understand what anyone's saying here," I confess.

"More Greek."

"*Gracias, Señora,*" I nod.

We sit.

After a moment of forced silence, I ask, "Did Anasor ever give Émile Galante the reward for finding you?"

He nods. "He was very philanthropic. I wouldn't be surprised if he also gave him the Japanese reward out of his own pocket."

"Did Anasor try to have you arrested?"

He nods. Over these past several days he's been generous with me. But he's been slow to answer my questions or he's left them hanging. But the journals, he has given me those words. And tonight I sense that he wants to say something before letting me read another journal. He wants to explain, he wants me to listen.

The sun has set. He puts his fork down, stares at me until I look away. "Tell me, do you think of these journals as the journals of a madman?"

"At first I did," I admit. "But not now. Now I tend to believe every word. Late last night, as I read the final words, in the fifth journal I was stunned. Through all the five journals I've read there was this single strand. Yes, I have felt waves of disbelief, a curious fear, but there was always a strong inkling that everything I was reading was true. Why would he write such a fine daily account of something that wasn't happening?"

We've finished the bottle dark honey rum which I brought with me. We have been sipping, not gulping it, but the bottle is empty anyway. So is the day. A liter bottle no matter how slowly you drink it is no match for a long evening. Señora Natti clears the table of dishes. From the kitchen radio, Spanish singers sing of the torments of love. Then, rather shyly, he says, "It makes me want to dance."

"You dance?" I ask.

"Of course I dance, don't you? I dance. Why not? I dance with La Señora Natti. She taught me *la jota*. I dance with girls at the *Nocturno*, and in Teguisa, with old men, I dance alone; I dance with anyone who'll dance with me." He turns to the kitchen, *"Señora Natti! El radiofusion de Tenerife, por favor."*

I can hear small eruptions from the radio then, in a moment, there is a different sound The rhythm changes to an exotic beat.

"Bueno! We can't always get that station from Tenerife. When we do, we dance right here." He gets up and stands, neck straight, like a rooster, and begins. Step by step. He dances with a musty finesse, a soft step, a fine dragging of the feet, a solemn shuffling—a dance I find more pleasing to watch than the hectic punctuation of *flamenco.* In the spill of a single lantern he looms gigantically on the walls and ceiling. He holds his glass away from him and balancing with his other arm outstretched, turns slowly. He fills the room with grace. He is much younger at this moment than I am.

"You think I'm *uno antiguo*? Come on, what are you afraid of?" He is smiling at me, challenging.

"Nothing." I stand. But I am embarrassed. An American male on foreign ground. Then I follow what he does, step for step. Slowly his movements come to me, naturally, the canted room, the feel of my bare toes on the stone floor. Soon I am moving alone with the music and I don't want to stop. When the song ends, he sits. I feel elated he doesn't comment on my great performance.

"We need women, you and I." He grins, showing some bad teeth but more good ones than bad. Then he hands me the next journal. Señora Natti is standing by the door. She has cleaned the kitchen; is there anything left for her to do? She does not want to be asked to dance with either one of these unusual gentlemen. She is going home to her father. She wonders if she can bring some leftover fish to him. When she has closed the door behind her, Simon strikes a wooden match on the floor and lights a small lamp on the table. Out the window the island is black and the sea is gone. There are no lights on the north end of *Salve de Dios.*

CHAPTER 24

The Sixth Journal
Lyon: January 25, 1964

᠕᠊ᖾ

The meadows give way as we approach the city of Lyon, which drains the countryside of color, straight highways shoot into it, arrows point; it is a serious city. We will dine in Lyon tonight. The Waiter is singing, *"Tomorrow We Will Be Lucky"* in French. Slowly, on small narrow roads, we have driven three hundred miles in three days.

Still, here the sky seems brighter. The air is thinner with the smell of high snow—the Alps are close. The Waiter wears a jersey he says will bring him luck in finding Claire. Madame, his grandmother, had just finished knitting it the day before we left. It is bright red; it makes him look wide but thinner than ever. I have promised him again it will be a simple thing finding Claire; there will be no problem.

All the signs point toward Lyon. It is France's second city, the widest city in the country. The city begins. It is smaller than Chicago set just about in the middle of France. Unbelievably, the Romans used to sail all the way up the River Rhône and use Lyon as a port, but it will never be a port city again, only more and more of what it is.

Everything I know has changed. I am afraid at times even to touch Savoia. There is a sense of danger, always. At the old hotel in Paris Savoia threw the banknotes on the bed. It was very funny to her. They weigh nothing, yet they can mean so much. Packets formally marked in the hundred thousands take up no room and represent villas, chateaux, a lifetime of food, years and years of simple comfort.

Looking at my banknotes on the bed, she imagined our villa. She liked to pick them up and toss them around. Now she won't touch them. There is no reason to. Amazingly, I feel anger toward her for what's happened to her. There is no room left in my life for spontaneity. We seem to breathe at each other more than we talk.

A headlight flashes behind us. A signal? Has it been there all along? Naturally, Savoia isn't aware of it. One rarely knows when one is being followed. It is a common car. It passes us, pulls in front of us, and cuts us off. A discreet light is flashing inside the back window. Savoia slows and stops. She knows the sign, turns the motor off, waits. What has she done? Two men get out. They wear coats, no hats, and have short haircuts. They look like gendarmes in plain clothes. They ask to see her license. They won't answer questions. She has an international licence. and explains the car, the friends in Paris, all of that. One goes back to the car, verifies the number on the licence plate. They seem satisfied that the Old Gentleman hasn't been stolen. They are not impolite. Still, they seem restless. One peers in. The Waiter is in the back. They ask him to step out of the car. He might be Algerian. Standing outside, he looks French. He is constantly blushing. One of them asks if I am English. I tell him, *"Je suis Americain."* He asks for my passport. The light is dimming. The passport should be acceptable. The altered numbers are ignored. He looks at the photo, at me, hands it back.

"Êtes-vous en voyage d'affaires?" Are you here on business?

Savoia answers, *"Non, pas du tout. Nous sommes de passage."* We are just passing through.

"Bon." One does not see cars such as this every day. He salutes. It is about the car.

We go. The second man forgets to salute. Savoia makes a hissing sound.

"What is it?"

"Those men weren't with the police."

"No?"

"Lyon is the head office of Interpol, you know."

"So you think they were with Interpol."

"They didn't seem to be with anybody. I was afraid to say anything of course."

I feel nothing. I am no longer hungry. I wonder if it is Anasor doing this, and from then on will we be watched 24-hours a day? There is a warrant out on my life in France I suppose, just as there is in America.

There is ice at the edge of the roads, the car skids through the city. Its tires are smooth.

The city brightens. Savoia says it is a city of cuisine, the robust specialties—sausages, fish dumplings, pike and trout from the rivers. There is a topless girl on a billboard promoting health. "It is not sexist at all," Savoia says. *"C'est beau, c'est normal."*

Finally, we pass blocks of medieval streets, close houses standing for centuries shoulder to shoulder in the old section of town. Dogs stand in doorways like relatives; a love-locked couple embrasses on a stone bench. There is time before supper.

Prostitutes are dressed for warmth. Sleeping with strangers for money is legal. There is no wariness, no need for pimps.

It is eight, all lights are lit. The city sits down to eat.

Outside a restaurant I give a smart looking beggar 500 francs. In a few minutes, he follows us in, takes a table, orders oysters, paté de foie gras, duck, a red wine that is nearly black. The Waiter tells us it is a local wine. We order the same. It is excellent. A Rhône valley red without a name.

We order pike, The Waiter excuses himself, returns with a bottle—a local dry white wine with what he says is good authority. He turns the label to us, It is from the Savoie, a plain label. He says, "Take care that the label is not too pretty, bad wines hide behind chic labels."

The wine is fine. The Waiter is tired and excuses himself.

Savoia says that her father loved the Savoie district and that's why he named her after the countryside east of here. When the waitress removes my plate, I see that Savoia has written on the tablecloth:

I love to travel with you
you are so able to travel with me

"Is it a poem?"

"I suppose," she says.

Certain words, hers, certain gestures, they enter me. She cannot make a clumsy gesture.

We walk to a nightclub three blocks away, ancient streets tunnel under buildings. When we walk into Jany's Retro Club, we hear a tango, the smoky outline of a singer. I order Cognac. When she sings Jaques Brel's songs we dance as if nothing mattered.

We sit and watch dancers tango, then stand up and try it our-selves. We manage it, gripping each other's body with our thighs. It is a clandestine dance, as if a shade were drawn, designed for whores, a dirty dance. We sit down ready to walk back to our room. I am desperate for her. Climbing to our room, the conci-erge ahead of us because the lights are out, we aren't able to keep our hands from touching each other. When we close the door, we make *'le sport'* as one says. We make it toward the bed and partly against the bed, the wall, wearing some of our clothes, never quite attaining the bed. By the time we slide away into a black spinning sleep, she has gotten out of her raincoat. Her cashmere sweater is unbuttoned, her plaid wool skirt flung uselessly above her waist. My pants are bunched around my ankles as if we were fools in an erotic comedy.

I cannot sleep. In the night something leads me out of the hotel. I must read words written by others about her. I walk to the rail-road station to find the *Herald Tribune*. A man is walking across the street. He walks my way to the station. When I leave the sta-tion he walks his way back to the hotel. Have I imagined this?

January 26, 1964

I am better this morning. The cold stabs in my stomach are gone. Yesterday, I was sick. Today, I feel the absence of pain. What strengthens me? Adversity? Not always. What I fear most is soli-tude. Once I required it. Complete solitude. Now I fear solitude as I fear death. I cannot be alone. I have not yet learned how to be alone. Is she beautiful to me because she conforms to me? She has given me a way to help me stand, a place for my mind to bleed into. Do I see only what I need of her? What she has become, the wonders of her being. She is so sure.

The curtains are drawn but I can see lines of grayness on either side of them, it must be morning. Her thoughts come to me. I love to travel with you. Of course we don't know where. It's al-ways the present and the past, never just the present is it? I want her to open her eyes. She does.

"Savoia. Do you ever want to see the desert?"

"I've seen the pyramids. The tombs."

"What about the sand?"

"Maybe we can go there by car, I suggest."

"Probably not, with Israel and Beirut standing in the road."

"We'll fly."

"Maybe one day, yes."

But it's the future I'm speaking of, isn't it? Can I be forgiven for conjuring up the future even if there will be no future?

The streets are snarling this morning, motorbikes everywhere, screeching small car horns. There is nothing here to trap the clamor. It is cold; there is no escaping the city.

We have been in the country, we have been waking up to roosters. Alone at the café this morning, I dread the French newspapers, their stories, as if they were serialized adventure fiction. There is no mention of Flight One, only Algeria, Israel, the assassination of JFK, Russia. There is a strong Communist Party in Lyon. I have left Savoia in the room. Every time I see her now it seems to be a fake miracle, something I do not deserve.

After a modest breakfast of pain chocolat and café au lait I begin to search for Claire at The Waiter's cousin's café. I find it easily and show the cousin my pencil sketch of Claire. There are no photographs. In a rage, The Waiter had burned them all the day after she left him at the altar. The cousin makes suggestions, says that she looks so familiar. She is a waitress here he thinks. He gives me streets and cafés. Someone recognizes my sketch but says her name is not Claire. I feel I have found the right café. She is not there, she has an obligation, she will come back after lunch. Stores close at noon; cafés stay open. Everyone comes back to work at three.

I sit and write in my journal. When she enters, I know it is her. She is young. If I were someone else I would call her "Baby." Her face emanates from her mouth, she has luscious lips, lazy, cat eyes. It is her lips that her face depends on. She is skinny, just as tall as I am. I slip away to find The Waiter in the park.

Back at the café we see her before she sees us. I tell The Waiter to sit. She will be our waitress. He is trembling.

"Be still," I say, "Let her come over to us."

The Waiter lies crumpled like a sock in the corner of the booth. It is minutes before she comes to our table and asks our order. He looks up suddenly and says her name.

She drops her pad onto the table, closes her eyes, blushes, hides her face in her hands. He stands, holds her, their eyes are wet. She has much to tell him, she says. She is crying. She has been waiting to be rescued. She remains a victim. It is so simple. In a few minutes he brings her back to our table and introduces her. His eyes are pink from crying. She continues working. She told him that she ran away on the day of the wedding last year because she was pregnant. It was not his baby. Who knew? No one. Not even his grandmother, she was so ashamed, it was to be an Algerian baby. He doesn't know much more, he doesn't ask any more questions. In time, she will tell him what she wants him to know. She could not marry The Waiter, of course, so she ran away. She could never tell him. There was no father. She had no possibilities as a young mother in Paris, so she simply ran away. Eventually, when she was ready to deliver her baby, she became frightened. She contacted cousins in Lyon and swore them to secrecy. When she first arrived in Lyon last year, she wanted more than anything to become a shopgirl at a large department store, but there was more money as a waitress. She needed to earn tips.

In the kitchen of the café there are signs of a baby, a portable crib, a tiny blanket with friendly predators in bright cloth, stuffed reptiles. She will take him to see her daughter after work. I will wait at the café.

When they return to the café the baby is in his arms. *"Le bebe,"* he says, *"C'est un ange."* It is an angel. Claire will marry him, she agrees. He still carries the gold ring in his pocket on a string. He has telephoned his grandmother; she will arrive by train in two days. "We will have a baby too. She promises me a son, a brother for the angel."

He is crying, of course. So is she. Customers are crying. Everyone is crying.

Claire has a roommate. It is a confession. A man, he is good to her and the baby. He pays most of the rent, he has given her a motorbike. He has asked her to marry him so that she will be respectable. So far, she has refused. It is not a good arrangement.

He comes by the café. She introduces him. Jaqui, he sells factory products. He is a mushroom-headed man, unlike Claire in every way, far more than her opposite. He says he is delighted to meet The Waiter, he has heard all about him, only good things. He was only doing his duty. He will defer, one can tell. He has a mouth like a *boutonniere*.

When I get up to go to the bathroom, a man in another booth gets up, walks after me to the back of the café behind me. By the toilet there is a door to the alley. When I come out I see the man at the telephone, he pretends to be talking but there is no light on. I am being watched.

I sit again, look around the café. Two men at another booth. The two men who flashed their light at us yesterday and cut us off on the road entering the city. They have newspapers and coffee and are smoking. They are not crying about the broken marriage, the illegitimate baby, they are watching me. It is why they are in the café, it is their job. They have seen my passport. They know the license plate. They know Savoia's name.

I have seen the music stores with trumpets displayed in their windows, Lyon is a city of culture, after all. After lunch at the café, I buy The Waiter a violin as a wedding present. Savoia and I must leave soon. We cannot stay for the wedding.

We leave them at the café. We will see them tomorrow, make our plans. Now, in the street outside, walking we have an argument. She walks away. What was it about? I don't know what started it. Who knows? Maybe about the whole thing. Maybe I'm not supposed to know. Why should we quarrel? Why shouldn't we? It is all so delicate. Aren't we immune? No. Just because I can lose her at any time doesn't mean we cannot quarrel. It is part of life I suppose, the least brilliant part. Anyhow, she's gone.

Salve de Dios: Canary Islands, May 14, 2001

৩৵৽

Simon has never asked me my name. He has given me several of his journals. He has accepted my presence. He may realize how creative it must have been of me, finding him, but he doesn't seem to care how I did it. He warns me never to use the prefix "psych" in his presence. There are other levels, he says, unknown to the American Psychiatric Association.

Until this morning, no one has ever unravelled the mystery of Simon Lister. It had long been assumed that he had died. The statute of limitations has run out on his crimes. The insurance companies have long since paid off all claims to museums, collectors, galleries, and in turn, they sued the Whitney Museum for negligence and won. The Whitney was forced to close. The building was sold to Neiman-Marcus which is doing well. I read that on today's art market, the paintings he burned would easily have surpassed the billion dollar mark. He has given me another journal, number seven.

Chapter 25

The Seventh Journal
Lyon: January 26, 1964

Savoia has disappeared. She's had a nervous letdown. The tension of her week has burst and now she is the oppressed one. She has come all the way back here and I am being selfish. I want to be alone with my thoughts, for the love of God. She makes a great effort. She lives with massive suppression for my stability, not hers thank you very much. It stops just short of "Well, I didn't ask you to bring me back, did I?" It's a quarrel in name only but one of fantastic implications and dimensions, if you happen to be sitting in the next row, which Mr. & Mrs. Len Kramm of Los Angeles happened to have been, accompanying their daughter, an art student at the American School of the Arts in Lyon, who will later report that someone she overheard is Simon Lister, and he was arguing with a beautiful woman who claimed to have come all the way back from the dead just to please him and shouldn't have bothered!

I suppose that on the night she died, I reached into the transmigration, to touch her. Then afterward, I refused to believe her death, my refusal, and her need to save me from my own demise brought her back. We must have met in the middle distance, both holding the balance. I am her perpetrator as much as she is. If she is supernatural, I am her co-creator …

I am approached by the two men from the café. They will not answer my questions. Am I under arrest? Of course. They drive me into the huge courtyard of a Renaissance mansion. I walk between them as we climb a spiral marble staircase. Our steps ring out. One of the men knocks on a carved double door at the top of the stairs.

"*Entrez!*" The voice is familiar. The door is swung open. Neither man follows me into the suite.

Anasor. He is sitting at an Empire table at the far end of a large room. There are tall windows. He is gray; he seems to have aged. He is calm, confident that his men are nearby. There is an unfinished lunch on the table, remnants of a duck. He doesn't stand; he glances up at me without speaking, without blinking. His eyes are crystal. He is a man like any other, capable of great kindness or murderous rage. He can have great charm, of course, he has spent much of his lifetime explaining theories he does not believe to his clients. I cannot tell if he wants to weep or have me killed or both. He doesn't speak. I am a wanted felon. He has lost everything. I have the same chance a cigarette butt does swimming to safety in a swirling toilet. If Anasor sends me to prison, it will take me less than a month to die. I have a thing about barred windows and doors.

"Come here, Simon," he orders me evenly.

I stand before his table—Anasor the benefactor, Simon the betrayer. He reaches his hand across the table to be shook. It is a friendly gesture. His handshake is like a bag of marbles.

"I knew I'd find you." He says it without energy—as though it no longer matters. "Did you think I wouldn't?" His hair is worn out; he might be anyone. He coughs. I shrug. The air is heavy with justice. "From the first day I knew you were alright." His voice is uneven, he will not look at me, instead he stares out the window at the wide 17th century courtyard. Still without looking at me, he sits and resumes eating. I watch him pick the last bits of flesh off the duck's wing. He chews his food as if he were angry at it. I look away, out the window, Anasor's eating is lewd.

There is a discreet tap on the door. A soundless waiter enters soundlessly, wheels in a gleaming gurney full of desserts, iced wine, silver coffee service. We are in a Renaissance mansion, now a deluxe hotel. The waiter leaves.

"Why, Simon?" He has rehearsed this question many nights. There it is, of course. I have betrayed him. I have broken the primal bond and have run away. I have betrayed my benefactor. Worse, our bond was based upon my art, an exhausting art that changed both of our lives, that made him millions of dollars. That made him enemies in the bastions of contemporary art whose members are easily disturbed. Their delicate bastion is balanced on enormous investments. Piles of money. My crime against French businessmen alone is enormous. Anasor sold six of my paintings here, six that are gone. If it were known that I was here, I would face trial in France even before my extradition to face trial in New York. I must try not to hate what I fear. I must dance. Anasor can end my life with a nod. How angry is he?

"I was a father to you, Simon."

"Then why didn't you act like a father? You never took me to ball games, you never gave me a train, nothing."

"You are being rude."

"I always spoke to you any way I wanted. I thought you respected that."

"But you are making a fool of yourself. I gave you everything. I gave you life."

"And the life you gave me cost me my life, Anasor."

"I named a school of art after you."

"I burned the schoolhouse down."

"We had a great friendship."

"It was the friendship a bird has with a tree."

"What do you think I am saying?"

"That if you can control your rage, you probably want to give me another chance."

There is no loyalty in art; there should be none, none other than the artist's loyalty to his canvas. Anasor won't say that to me; his ears are still ringing from lost revenues.

The world of gallery art is not a democracy, no one votes. Kings and fascists rule. All I say is, "The destructive impulse will always triumph over the creative impulse." There it is of course. I have tried to destroy it, I have run amok.

"Are you still psychotic, Simon?"

"That's a question a moron might ask."

"Answer me."

"No, I got over it."

"What would it take to straighten you out?"

"Why would I want to straighten out?"

The project of my sanity.

"Answer me, this is not the best time to test me."

"Thanks for your concern, Anasor, but straightening me out, as you put it, would be like straightening out those bones in front of you and re-assembling those pieces of duck meat into something that could fly out that window."

"I will take that as a no."

"Take it up your ass."

"I expect better manners from you, Simon."

"Manners are necessary in your business. They don't exist in art."

Without a sound, the door opens, Pierre, the smart one who has been listening, looks in, Anasor has been badly affronted. It may lead to worse. Pierre observes our tableau—a man eating a duck, a man watching him eat a duck. All is well. Wordlessly, he closes the door.

"What do you want, Anasor?"

He has been talking to himself, since I vanished four weeks ago. There is my personal debt to him, of course, then to his galleries. There are museums, nice people, a great museum of modern art that may go bankrupt. Even the insurance companies.

Pity them? My feelings of guilt are non-existent. The reasons are why I did it. This is the curious part he doesn't mention—that burning millions of dollars worth of art was only the caprice of a delusional paranoiac. He never asks what my reason was to do what I did. He has the advantage. It is the duck.

He picks up the duck's body in his fingers. His fingers are shiny from its grease. Now the duck enters Anasor's system. He gulps wine to wash its fragments down. He wipes his hands and face with a huge linen napkin, sucks his teeth. He picks up the duck again. Suddenly, the room is too hot, I feel my head swelling. The duck is flapping, struggling to free itself from his fingers, making that busted duck squawk, I feel sick, my time is limited.

"Either go down on your duck or fuck it, Anasor! Make it feel that it did not die in vain, that it lived for some worthwhile cause—to voyage through your large intestine."

My face is drained, my toes prickle. Anasor ignores me, puts another wad of duck meat in his mouth. My stomach turns. I reach across the table, pick up the plate and throw it over Anasor's head, out the window into the courtyard below. The duck's carcass bails out in mid-flight and joins the drapes. Anasor is stunned. Pierre has re-entered the room and stands like a Doberman at the door waiting to bark. Dimly, I grasp that I'm more valuable alive than dead.

"I can see that you are still psychotic," Anasor nods at me.

"Don't use that word again or I'll throw you out the window."

"It would take that kind of person to do what you did because no artist has ever caused such diabolic desecration. Never in the history of art has one willfully hurt so many people at once."

"What about Jasper Johns? What about de Kooning, Pollock, Rauschenberg and all the others you love. What about Norman Rockwell? Are you putting me up there with your gods?"

"How can you be so flippant?"

"How can I be so flippant? Because I have fuck-all to lose. What's the price, Anasor?"

"God, you make it hard for me. I am giving you a choice."

"During the Inquisition it was either chop your head off or burn you alive. What's mine? I deserve better than that. You realize your art collection is famous for one thing, being meaningless. You know that my paintings were not meaningless and you'll do anything to get it back."

"Not anything." He is not amused. "Shall I call Jean-Paul in here? He is a magician, he has assured me he can make people disappear without a trace."

"What have you got?"

"I don't know why I want to give you this second chance."

"I know why, Anasor. It is because you can't throw me away. You're a frugal man."

"Where do you get your arrogance?"

"From the same well you draw yours."

"Alright. We understand each other. I need you. You need me. I can give you a new life, Simon. Free you of persecution. I can give you everything you had once again. It can be done."

"On what conditions?"

"Leave us," he says to Pierre. Pierre exits. Anasor whispers, "in secret, it would be possible." He tells me there will be a story, my body found, death by fire, I will be declared officially dead. I will live in hiding, in a studio in Morocco on a private estate near the foothills of the Atlas Mountains. A place I will be able to work and live. I will have whatever I want. I may bring my friend. There will be a pool. After one year, a painting will suddenly appear on the scene in New York City, its canvas seasoned long enough to varnish and roll onto a spool. It will be stretched again and framed in New York.

Another will come, then another …

Hallelujah! Pandemonium! Foul, discord. The appearance of paintings as powerful as the dead Simon Lister's. I must be alive. It will be a most elegant mystery, a black-tie dinner crime; hostesses will make guests imagine possibilities. It will be an enlightened game. The chic magazines will engender clues to the mystery that they cannot unravel. It will never die. Critics will be suspicious, of course. When the first painting appears in the Anasor Gallery, pulses will race; the drooling chimpanzees will buy. Some of them will suspect, but no one will cry, 'Fake!' There will always be doubt whether Simon Lister is alive or not, maybe somewhere in the world painting huge canvases. Anasor will be called a magician. The hunt will begin in Manhattan. For The Anasor Galleries, it will be a coup. If the paintings were expensive before, their value will multiply and multiply.

"They'll call it 'The Resurrection Of Simon Lister'."

"Every hour of every day I thought about you, Simon, I dreamt about you the way one dreams of a son missing in action, a brother lost at sea. And you are always alive."

"It sounds good, Anasor, to begin my life again, this time in a country where you can't trust anybody, or drink the water, where sex is with little boys and the main industry is sand, the national dish is couscous served with flies on it."

"Dream on, you cultured pimp. You Park Avenue madam. You fight manager to the smart set. You dream of promoting a Muhammed Ali—Rocky Marciano match that will never happen. You had a world champion, me, a heavyweight with a 42-inch reach. But I'll never fight again, not for you, not for myself."

"Are you refusing my offer?"

"I can't eat couscous without gagging."

"I am being very generous."

"I'm being very undecided."

"I am losing my temper. You are standing now within five-hundred meters of Interpol's French Headquarters. Pierre!"

Pierre appears. Anasor motions him in, he takes up his post by the door.

Anasor goes toward the bathroom. He looks truly sad.

"When I come out, if you do not agree, I am going to give you up to Interpol."

He leaves me alone with Pierre.

It is a hotel room of great opulence. The curtains are heavy, there are vases. One aspires to this sort of luxury, it is all yours until midday. The air has thickened, the walls are close.

"Turn the heat down," I say to Pierre. Pierre does not understand.

Anasor is an art expert, not about art, but about what makes it sell. He sees property, not horizons. It must be framed. He still does not understand what I do, or that during the act of painting I hallucinate. That it is the origin of my gift. Anasor is not a continuum. I am.

The toilet flushes. The door opens.

"Well?"

I shrug, *"Comme tu veut."*

"Good." Anasor smiles. And let me say, Simon, you have made an excellent choice.

"You sound like a headwaiter."

I smile when I shake Anasor's hand.

I've made a deal with the devil this afternoon. I had no choice. Did I?

What about Anasor? He looked tired. He isn't an old man and he's not through fidgeting. He made me an offer I couldn't refuse. He has a plan. He wants me to move to Morocco. He says it is one of the countries without an extradition agreement with the

U.S., so that if I am ever discovered living there, I will not be charged with a crime. It would mean living in luxury but without a passport, probably under house arrest. I am to continue painting. The paintings are to emanate from Morocco. Not signed by me but they would be Listers to anyone who knows. They would have what I have. It would shock a few people. Not a complicated plan. For him it's a generous offer. I suppose it is. It's not that he's greedy. He is a man who has been wronged and he wants restitution.

CHAPTER 26

Leaving Lyon: January 26, 1964

૭–ન

When I climb the stairs of our hotel, the concierge stops me. A man has asked for my room number. Later I saw the man on my floor perhaps trying to enter our room. I give the concierge a few thousand francs.

Inside nothing has been touched. The bed is empty. There is no note. I need to find Savoia. She may no longer be mine. I go looking for her. In the cold drizzle by the monuments, I sit on a wood bench, deciding where to begin. I feel a gray emptiness. A crucial scraping. Stone facades, skies that turn purple-black at the horizon. I feel the skin leaving my face. I will tell her everything. It doesn't matter.

There she is! She is wearing the blue skirt I like her to wear, the one that flaps easily in the wind. She walks slow-legged as if she were imagining the rain. She is walking on the winter dead green. She hasn't noticed me. Now she is walking on the pavement between pedestals. I catch her from behind a statue, surprising her. I hug her. I never ask her where she is walking or why.

I tell her where I've been, tell her about my meeting with Anasor, and the agreement I have made with him, that tomorrow we are expected to be driven to Marseille and then continue by yacht to Morocco. I point out one of the men, Pierre, who is standing a distance away watching us.

"It's impossible," she says. "I can't go to Morocco with you, Simon."

"I know."

Back at the hotel in our room we lie down wearing our clothes. There is the chill of a crypt. I feel her loss even when I think about touching her in bed, only to take her hand and put it on my cock. Her fingers know me better than my own. They heal. I can tell her anything now, nothing matters. I hope for tomorrow, that there will be one, but I dread the day after.

I tell her about the night I passed through a large canvas in my

West Village studio. My first experience. I lay behind it breathing too quickly, I didn't know what had happened to me. I saw the stretcher bar behind the painting running down its middle, shattered. Yet the painting was unmarked not a thread torn. I can't expect her to believe me yet she does. I don't mention that I have never told this to anyone except the examining psychiatrist at the Eisenstein who put a check mark in front of the word 'delusional.'

"We should think about leaving ahead of them," I tell her.

"I'm already packed."

"Good. Tonight."

The Waiter is lying under the Citroën in the alley behind the café looking up into its grizzled entrails. He is trying to attach something that dangles. I open the door and sit on the front seat and speak to him though the floor.

"*Patron*. Do not move. It is urgent that I speak with you, do you understand?"

"Yes," he says, "Where will it be?"

"It will be right here," I say. "If you cannot understand what I am telling you, stop me."

"*D'accord.*"

"First. I would like to make you a gift, a wedding gift that if you are careful, will last you for the rest of your lifetime."

"But why?"

"Because you are getting married and because I need you to do something for me. One more thing."

"*Merci, merci infiniment.*"

"*Patron,* at the moment I am being watched by a man who is standing across the street, understand?"

"I do."

"He only sees me sitting in the car reading the newspaper. He does not see me talking. He does not see you."

"So I must not move."

"Correct."

"What may I do."

"I will leave money on the seat. You must go to the Agency Renault down the street and buy an ordinary car, not a new one, not a white one, and when you do, park here and leave the key inside. You must go the moment I leave."

"I understand."

Simon hears a hissing sound under the car.

"What was that?"

The Waiter's voice comes up through the floor.

"I have lost the oil pressure."

"Do not move. Listen. After dinner, I want you to enter the hotel. It will be ten o'clock. Walk to the top floor. There you will find one suitcase. In it will be my coat my hat, my astrakhan."

"Pardon?"

"My Russian hat. The one I always wear."

"Yes, of course."

"Please listen carefully. On the sixth floor is also a closet for brooms. Go inside and wait there until they turn the lights out in the foyer. Put my clothes on and go downstairs. You must pretend to be me. You will carry the small bag and you must hurry as if you were running away on a secret errand. It will be dark, you must try to make the man across the street who is watching me believe that you are me and make him follow you."

"Do you understand everything?"

"It is all clear except why."

"I am only running away. You are making it possible for me to do so."

"Without Mademoiselle?"

"No, of course not without Mademoiselle. Do you understand everything?"

"Yes."

"Then repeat it to me."

He does, word for word.

"Perfect. Now the gift I want you to accept may shock you, so please do not bump yourself on the head."

"You have already given me my violin."

"And take good care of it. But this is a gift of a different nature. When I leave the car I will put an envelope on the seat. In it is three million francs."

There is silence from below the car.

"Do you understand what I said, Patron?"

"I understand. I do not believe."

"That is how important it is then. Let me make it clear. There is very little time. Three million francs. It is enough for you and Claire to buy a house, to begin your lives, to provide for your children, even enough for you to study at the music conservatoire instead of working as a waiter. Of course, you may spend the money any way you want. I am only giving you one example of the enormity of the gift. Do you understand so far?"

"I cannot speak."

"Good. Please listen. Can you do what I ask? The car, the hotel?"

"Exactly."

"You have only one hour before the Agence Renault closes. Do not get a white Renault."

"I know of such a car. It is a simple Renault camion."

"I am familiar with the car, one sees them everywhere. This one is not young. It has been used for deliveries. There must a million of them, but they are all white."

"Yes, sadly, it will be white. The key will be on the floor as you say."

"Good. This is our secret and must always be."

"I swear. I will do my best, he says. When the man discovers that it is me and not you what will I say?"

"You will be surprised, of course. You will tell him of course you are not me. I am asleep at the hotel. You simply borrowed the car to drive to your cousin's house. He will go away."

At ten forty, just after The Waiter, wearing my hat and coat, left the hotel and drove away to his cousin's house in the country, I slipped downstairs and walked to the alley behind the café. There it was. A four-year-old Renault camion, white, parked in the alley. The key was on the floor. A letter of thanks was on the seat. I drove back to the hotel, Savoia was waiting for me with our bags and my Noxzema carton. I hid the Florentine leather box inside the spare tire that rides under the car. We drove away. No one saw us. We have no identity.

CHAPTER 27

Salve de Dios: Canary Islands, May 15, 2001

❧

I bring the seventh journal back with me. I lay it on the table as usual. Tonight we are going to Teguise to dance with the girls. It is planned. Saturday night in Teguise. The woman has laid a meal for us. It is a melange he calls scordalia. He taught her how to make it. It is fish stock of salt cod, many potatoes, the usual amounts of garlic, limes, olive oil, sea salt gathered by the monks, and a few greens chopped up fine. It is one of his favorite recipes from Spain and now mine though I can only guess at the amount of each ingredient. While we are eating, he says indifferently; "How did you do it?"

Find him. I swallow what I am chewing, recover. At last. I begin not at the beginning but toward the end.

"By chance I met the owner of a café in Lyon and we fell to talking. When I mentioned your name I noticed him change, he reddened. I asked him why. He wouldn't tell me, but he was very emotional. I went back the next morning. He said he was sworn to silence. We had it out. Go to Venice he said."

"What did he look like?"

"Thin, tall, bony."

"Red-faced?"

"No pale, gray-haired."

"Already?"

"If I find you I am to tell you, you gave him his life."

"The Waiter."

"Yes. I recognize him in the journals."

"Is he well?"

"He's been sick, he's alright."

"Good. Does he have children?"

"Yes. He has three children he put through college."

"Did you meet his wife?"

"Yes."

"Is her name Claire?"

"It is."

He smiles brownly, food in his teeth, "Not bad."

"He mentioned a boat called the Ave Maria."

"I wrote him a picture postcard with the boat on it."

"No name, just told him I was okay. He's my friend. Maybe now I can see him again."

"Maybe I can carry a message."

"You'll come to that boat," he says.

He indicates the trunk under the heels of his feet.

"Not too many left."

The Eighth Journal
The Hunters: January 27, 1964

꿍ᴥ

The deer is swimming up the middle of the stream far below us. We are in the National Forest several miles inland from the Mediterranean. We have parked the Renault on a sinuous round-about road, lost, watching the deer swim below us. A beautiful sight.

"I could live in the forest, could you?"

"Yes," she says, "as long as I can come out from time to time and shop and walk along the sea."

We watch two hunters, way below walking just out of the forest along the stream's bank walking with guns behind the deer.

"The way a hunter walks and the way a deer swims," Savoia says.

We stand together and watch the hunters and the deer, a thumb-nail apart. The hunters cannot see the deer but are walking after it, not walking right. We cannot tell if the deer knows it is being hunted or if the hunters just happen to be walking in the same direction as the deer. It is impossible to track an animal in the water.

Savoia picks up several rocks from the road bed and hurls one out over the steep mountainside to warn the deer. But it is lost in the air long before it enters the trees below us. She throws another rock and another one and the hunters never know about the rocks nor does the deer.

Villa Roseau: January 27, 1964

The Brazilian kite flies like a great-winged bird. The long bowed, kite string leads downward on its wide arc, it begins among tiled rooftops among pines and palm trees. We are in a National Forest, maybe a dozen or so miles from the coast.

We arrive. Without realizing it, we have found it. On the winding road, we have climbed a few hundred feet to a small plateau and here it is, Villa Roseau, in perfect isolation. The name is glazed on an ornate tile set high on a white wall.

The sun! The day is suddenly blazing, not a trace of January. Villa Roseau, all of it white. It is painted stone—wide low, Arabic. We walk up hot stone steps between white walls. There are several villas built over the ruins of a medieval watchtower, a lookout where farmers once peered out to the distant sea for the sails of invading Saracens. I am sweating and yank my jersey over my head. Savoia pulls a chain, and a tinny bell jingles. *Tink tink tink.* In moments, Eduard de Haen bounds down the white stone steps wearing a white galabea. He is browner than he was on Flight One. He looks edible. He seems delighted to see me. He does not seem to recognize Savoia from Flight One. Anna is dead. He is polite to Savoia, bows slightly, pantomimes a kiss on her hand.

"I am Eduard de Haen. Welcome to my small villa."

"Savoia Paulus."

She is so changed. She is pale, she has cut her hair off in Paris. She is wearing pale loose clothes.

"I am delighted that you both could visit, but hello!, where are your bags? Come, come! You will die of heat prostration standing here. How long can you stay?"

I mention that our bags are in the car and open the door.

"No-no. Coco will bring them."

He holds the gate open for us then, to show off his attire, turns in a swirl of robes, leads us up white stone steps. He is in white, one

of Faisal's men. Gold attachments hang from him, bracelets
buckles, figas on chains, all in gold. His hair is yellow with traces
of smokier tones. He wears it in a hairdo that seems to be in a
high wind blowing in his eyes like a little boy's hair, though there
is no wind. He lets Savoia go up the steps ahead of us. He turns
and faces me, whispers.

"Tell me."

"You know what I'm going to say."

"Tell me anyway."

"It went down with the plane."

Eduard turns away, covers his face.

"I knew it!"

He beats his arms against the sides of his galabea, a mad butterfly.

"I'm sorry, Eduard."

"What a stupid, stupid, stupid stupid, thing to give it to her to
carry."

"She's dead, Eduard."

"*Quel cauchemar!* What a nightmare."

"It was your idea, Eduard."

"No-no, it was yours! I only agreed. You were the one afraid, not
I. You were the one that needed safe passage. It was a collateral.
You could not even trust me."

"I trust now."

"Of course you do. Why not?" He is deeply hurt.

"And now look."

"Either way, Eduard, I cannot bring it back."

"But you can make me another. You will make me another, there
is no question of that. If we talk about safe passage and I do, you
must present me with an original Simon Lister."

"Agreed?"

I have no choice. "I will make you an original."

"And then I will not betray you."

Savoia is waiting for us on the top step. Suddenly Eduard runs
ahead and hugs her.

"Villa Roseau is not a good place to come if you do not like the
sun," he says.

He is right, the walls seem to catch and hold the sun while the forest was gray.

At the top step we are at an iron gate open to a wide glaring area, a *clos* and just beyond, a radiant swimming pool that is too blue. A dozen sun-blinded figures sit or lie in stages of torpor. The women, several nude, sleek as smelts, lie around the borders of the pool in open shade.

Others peer out at us from under straw hats to identify us as arrivals, nothing more than their colors, shapes, ages. All are dark. There is a fat man, another man small, lean, limp. One smiles at them. A woman lies stony as a lizard across a mound that rises forming an island in the middle of the pool. The blue water surrounding it seems more daring than nature. A huge person in a black hanky lies reading on a chaise. "That is Treblett." He is a hull rather than a body, a galleon in dry-dock. Treblett nods. I recognize the name.

"Eh, bain," Treblett says or what sounds like it. When he sits up he reveals lying behind him, as if he had excreted her, the curving shape of a blonde girl face down, nude, apparently asleep. She is on another scale, hardly of the same species as Treblett. He opens his book, folds its pages way back, slips it under his arm, squeezes it to dry his armpit onto the dry pages, then goes back to reading it.

It is all white. White, walking up the steps after the meandering drive. The nudity seems neither erotic nor clinical, only descriptive of beauty and its opposite.

Eduard claps his hands twice. *"Coco, écoutez, leurs baggages s'il vous plait."*

Eduard makes much of Savoia.

"You remind me so much of that poor girl, Anna, who died on our flight. Wasn't that dreadful. It is a miracle you were not with her."

"She is very much like her," he says. "It is a miracle she is not her."

"Very."

"Everyone was lost. I'm sure I saw her name in the newspaper."

"She is too thin, even for the dead girl."

"Tu plaisantes," he says. "But she is so like her."

"Elle est mon trompe l'oeil."

Eduard laughs, it is funny again. He changes the subject. He speaks to Savoia in French, "You must change your clothes immediately. You are gray, both of you, like goats."

"You probably means ghosts," Savoia says.

"Ghosts." He says it carefully. "There is food here from the lunch." And in the shade of umbrellas, I see a buffet, sweating ice buckets, platters of pink seafood. Large silverware. "But first you must change."

He leads us away to a plastered changing room to put us into sun clothes. I ask for the striped robe I see on a peg. I'm afraid I'll burn. I give Savoia a bright scarf to make into a bottom. We choose Sisal hats that are from Guadeloupe on pegs. A small Corot landscape hangs on the uneven plastered wall.

The houses are long, descending. There are several. Ours is cool, shaded. Everything is stone. The furniture is old, simple. Mats on the floors, a long bathtub from another age. There are framed prints of birds caught in flight.

We come out from our room dressed like strangers. In my striped galabea, I feel white as a spy. Savoia looks ripe, slim, normal. She wears the silk scarf between her legs, tight on each hip. Her breasts look fine in the sun and make breast shadows on her stomach. No one notices us, except Eduard from across the pool who smiles. He pulls his robe wide at the top and lets it drop from his shoulders. He is oiled, more or less naked. His penis is tan. He wears a cartridge belt with many leather pockets. "Nepalese army belt, full with herbs," he says.

In a teak chest in the shade of fronds are icing bottles of Barsac and on the tablecloth, crystal tumblers without stems. I take two glasses out. The wine is sweet, in keeping with the villa, the early afternoon, our vicinity. I taste ceviche from a platter on the table. Savoia walks with her wine over to Eduard. She lies down on the wide tiles in the shade, leans against a wall. I sit eating crab meat with various sauces, drinking chilly Barsac, watching them.

"May I give you one of my herbs?" He speaks to me from across the pool hardly raising his voice.

Savoia says to him quietly, "he'd better not have any herbs, he's not too well yet, Eduard. He's unstable."

"Yes, she's absolutely right," I add, "I am insane."

"As a matter of fact," she nods agreeably, "he is."

"Then you have found the right address." Eduard answers.

From a leather pocket on his belt, he takes out a lettuce leaf green cigarette the size of his thumb and with a girl's fling, throws it high over the island with the sleeping girl on it, across the pool to me. I trap it against my chest. A perfect throw. "It is specially because you are insane it will be better for you." I wonder if he's right but in the end I don't light it, I put it in my pocket. I must remember to keep my guard up here.

He doesn't even remember her! Is it because he can't? That he knows Anna died? That it would be impossible? Or is it simply precluded by Savoia's presence. But she does look different I suppose. What I am putting her through tells on her face which is sometimes gaunt. Her clothes are baggy. Her hair is shorn off. She's china-white and her name is Savoia.

I asked her two questions, Where are we? And why are we here? She said she didn't know where we were, and that she felt safe here for the moment. And that I had to be here, because I promised Eduard I would give him the small painting.

CHAPTER 28

Salve de Dios: Canary Islands–May 16, 2001

It is windy and wet. It is just after dark when I knock on the door. "Come in!" he calls out. I do.

"Windy," he says. "Get yourself a glass." I do. I pour myself two inches of rum. "I sent Señora Natti home." He is staring at me, he has been drinking. "This is the only weather I can't …" He doesn't finish.

I open the trunk and put the eighth journal inside. I don't take the ninth. I have so many questions to ask. He stares at me too long. When he is ready, he breaks the silence.

"They say I was born dreaming of the sun."

He has read my mind.

"Who said?"

"The doctor who delivered me, and then, later on his staff. I was never born dreaming of the sun; I was born wide awake. I remember the bloody curtain parting, it was maroon, as a matter of detail. I saw the first rays of white light oozing in. Florescent, a light I still have a low opinion of. Of course, I would have preferred seeing sunlight instead, or even moonlight, or the fake light of any planet. But of course I had no choice. Everyone in the room was talking. I didn't know what language but it sounded awkward and I remember thinking I didn't especially want to learn it. Anyway, I had nothing to say, I'd just been born and it was all very new compared to what I'd been used to so I kept my mouth shut and just watched what was going on around me."

"Which was?"

"Not a lot, really. Activity, people running around grinning, gesturing. They slapped me on the ass, dried me off. My first contact with humanity. Not a good first impression."

"What would you have preferred?"

"At the time, I didn't know, but something else. Now I realize I would have liked to have been licked dry by my own mother."

"Yes, of course."

"It was very pleasant being at the epicenter of attention, natural enough, but after one day I felt vulnerable."

"To what?"

"Don't know. Maybe predators."

"In a hospital?"

"I know. It wasn't for a long time, more than a year that it was announced I was to be called, a 'savant'."

"Why?"

"Attitude maybe. I felt like a guest on earth. I would tell anyone who'd listen that I'd been invited to stay here temporarily. That my visit here was by invitation and that it was a privilege to attend the world, to spend my lifetime here. I was in a town where they thought what I said was cute."

There is a second bottle. He keeps it in the small shrine built into the stone wall at the time the house was built. I open its carved, deal-wood door and there it is, a nearly full bottle of *Ron Miel* standing among santos and an aged burnt-out candle. I hand him the bottle. He uncorks it, pours it into his glass and swirls it with the lime. He sets the bottle on the table for me, motions with an open hand for me to pour another drink for myself. The woman has gone. The house roars with wind.

"My life was uneventful until a young doctor showed up. I was two. And Doctor Sachs was determined to find out everything there was to know about me. He'd heard I was some sort of prodigy. He would give me tests. He was trying to isolate my power. He gave me a five-thousand piece jigsaw puzzle. Do you know how long it took me to put it together?"

"How long?"

"About a year, I never really finished it. I was worse at arithmetic. I was definitely not a savant, idiot or otherwise. But I could run through a crowded room blindfolded and not hit anyone. How could I do that? It fascinated him. He ordered x-rays of my skull because he believed that I might have sensors behind each eye similar to the ventricles in pit vipers that enable them to sense warmth. Tiny mutated vents?" Simon chuckles at that notion so I agree.

"He sounds nuts."

"Well, he wasn't, he just didn't know what he had on his hands. He told my mother and father that I had another sort of power he didn't understand yet. Then he happened to notice that I always slept turned toward the window, always facing the sun. I had never let go of my primary magnetic field, he said, or was never released from it. It was rather enlarged. He told my parents he'd never seen this before, he said no one else had either. He wrote a paper on the Solar Baby. In it, Dr. Sachs suggested that I had a fully developed sixth sense and hinted that I might have a seventh sense, something he didn't know anything about. I was a freak of nature of course. He chuckles again. Now my father was really embarrassed. He regarded me as an alien being. He was barely hanging on anyway, being an unemployed alcoholic and all. He had one of those jobs in radio that had become obsolete. He had never adjusted to television. He couldn't find work. He was getting very edgy. Even at two I felt sorry for him. My father didn't want anything to do with his solar baby. It was as though I had come from another source. It turned out I had. Blood tests showed that Mr. Eugene Lister was not actually my biological father. When he heard that, he nearly killed my mother and took off. At the time, we lived in a town called Great Falls but all the falls had dried up in the 1930s when a dam had been built in North Dakota. As a baby I thought that was funny. One morning, Dr. Sachs found me in a daze, staring out the window, drawing without looking at the paper, unconsciously. He tested me, blindfolded. The results impressed him. So he encouraged me to draw every day. He stayed in contact with my mother. He was from the University of Chicago then. When I was two, something he visited us again. He said that my art had exceeded art, that it was involved with another energy he didn't understand yet, but suspected was cosmic. My mother couldn't stop laughing. She called my ex-father and told him what Dr. Sachs had said. He came right home. The divorce wasn't final so he moved in with my poor guilt-ridden mother.

He had a vision; he saw his way clear, through me. I was to demonstrate clairvoyant drawing, as my father described it. In a theater. He would sell tickets, he would advertise. Everyone would pay ten dollars. He rented the huge old opera house down in Arcola, Illinois. Some people contributed even more than the minimum ten dollars. He called it a fund for my research. All the tickets would be put into a wire basket onstage. When one was chosen, the number would be called out and that person would come up and I would draw them blindfolded. I would do this clairvoyant drawing in front of a paying audience. It could not be faked, not with twelve hundred tickets in an open wire basket.

The night arrived. The theater was full. There I was, standing alone onstage blindfolded, two-and-a-half years old wearing a diaper, crayons in my fist, a huge pad of paper on an easel. The audience would see a miracle alright, my father had guaranteed it in his advertisements. To make it legitimate, he introduced the Mayor of Arcola who came up onstage and chose the first ticket. The Mayor called out the number and a woman came up. She held out a photograph of her deceased mother for the audience to see. Naturally, I couldn't see it. When the mayor turned my drawing around and held it up for everyone to see, the audience burst out laughing. I had drawn a beautiful picture of a rhinoceros I'd seen at the zoo the year before. The woman burst into tears. But the mayor tried to laugh it off and just told me to settle down. He said, 'Let's try it again, youngster.' I did. The next person he called onstage was a man who described his wife, she was in the audience. I drew a perfect likeness of the neighbor's cat whom I was really fond of. Behind my blindfold, I could hear the audience getting restless, I could hear them talking, whistling, the rumbling sound an angry audience makes, like city traffic. It happened a third time, I made a good drawing of my dog."

"Why did you do that?"

"Ask a psychiatrist, to get rid of my stepfather. I think I knew then that the only power we have is the power to reject, to quit."

"And to vanish."

"Yes."

"But wasn't anybody impressed that a blindfolded baby could draw animals so well?"

"Not for ten bucks they weren't. That was a lot of money then. My stepfather had to refund everyone's tickets, and the following week he ran away from home again, this time for good."

"After that rather long night onstage I never drew for years. I never drew pictures for anyone except my mother. Not for twenty years. I think she understood. She tried to. It was hard on my mother. She worked, and I was always demanding answers for everything from her."

"Like what?"

"Like how old is the world. I was overwhelmed when she said

billions of years. I asked her why we couldn't control time better." He laughs suddenly. "I asked her, which creature was the first creature on Earth to laugh? To cry? And which came first? She told me it was the dinosaur so I fell in love with dinosaurs and I told her exactly where the last one had lain down on its side and died, the very last one."

"Were you right?"

"Pretty close. It was endless. Dr. Sachs stayed in contact with her. Every few months he would call her from Chicago to ask how I was doing. He visited us when I was six, and we three went to Chicago where he put me through two days of tests. He told my mother that as far as he could determine I had a sort of power he could not yet get a handle on, that an invisible world seemed to be flowing through me like a river—images without opinion flowing from a source, he didn't know where. My domain was out there. But whatever it was I had, my isolation proved to him what we all had; a deeper neural base."

"At the time I didn't realize how hard all this was on my mother." He pauses. "I really loved her." Past tense.

"Did she die?"

"Yes. She did, pretty suddenly when I was nine. After that I was sent to my aunt's outside St. Paul. I had no function there. I constantly tried to behave like everyone else around me but my childhood was spent driving people away. The winters were alright but the summer sun made me too different. I had to find a place where my preoccupations were acceptable. When I was sixteen, I looked older, I was able to enlist in the navy. Nuclear submarines seemed a perfect answer. A numbing atmosphere always in motion, just the right amount of isolation, never at rest. And the sun. The sun meant everything to me. According to Dr. Sachs, it was my source of power. There's no sun on a sub. Away from the sun I seemed almost normal. Volunteers only, the irony was that they paid us extra for the danger. So I disappeared underwater for four years in the navy and when I got out, that's the year Anasor found me on a New York sidewalk. Once again lost and found." He chuckles.

Simon seems exhausted by what he's telling me. I'm trying to remember every word. He doesn't say it but I feel he's never told this to anyone outside the Eisenstein. He turns the lamp up and shaves the wick with a small sharp blade. We pour the last of the rum into our glasses. He empties his glass and pours half a glass of the local wine, pigeon blood dark, and pushes the bottle my way.

"Are you spiritual?" I say.

"Do I believe in God?"

"Yes."

"Then say it."

"I think you know I'm spiritual. God is only one of many spirits. He and I made a deal a while ago: If He could stand me I could stand Him. I have my senses, my eyes, ears, nose, luckily a sixth and, as Dr. Sachs said, a seventh."

"Which is what?"

"According to him, the seventh sense was the power to alter visions in others simply by using my mind."

"How do you know you can do that?"

"I can make people see fishing boats that aren't there." He stops talking for a while.

"What was she like?"

"You've read how many journals?"

"Eight."

"And you still need to know?"

"Can you say it?

He takes a last wet sip holds it in his mouth pursing his lips as if a La Perouse waiter were poised, waiting for his judgment. When he swallows he says, "I believe that woman is the greatest invention known to man, don't you?"

I nod. He knows it is not what I wanted to hear.

"The snag is, the eternal snag in the absolute world, is that there's only one-per-man. That's if the man's damned, damned lucky. There are no practice great love stories, it's never a drill. If you find yours, that's it. I found mine. You don't look again. You never look for another."

When he stops, he lifts his bare feet from the trunk, opens it, pulls out a journal, and hands it to me. Another book with a black cover different than the others, a square of tape with a number written in ink that has softened: *9*. He closes the trunk. "Nine," he says. I stand up, take the book, half-bow to him.

"I wonder what secrets you'll discover in nine."

I feel very much like embracing him but I don't, of course. I am who I am, I cannot help that. I go to the door and open it. The moon is settling over the black island. It is very late or very early, that impossible time between night and morning, the invisible line that legends need to cross, before they pass into being.

"Goodnight," I say to him. I love you, is what I don't say.

CHAPTER 29

The Ninth Journal
Dinner at Roseau: January 27, 1964

ᵍ~ᵍ

It is dark. We have been in our room for hours, managed to fall asleep and overslept. Now we are late for dinner. Savoia is fiery from the sun, stunning in an evening dress she has fashioned from silk scarves. I wear an Arabic robe I have found in the armoire that seems to fit me, Savoia has made me a headdress, a bright *kaffiyeh*.

Eduard is seated at the head of the table. He gleams under the glow of the candles. He is wearing a tight, black-striped vest and a series of black accoutrements around his neck and wrists, probably onyx, black against his yellow-wheat hair parted and oiled, black against his exquisite teeth.

He half-rises when we enter. We sit beside him in the empty chairs to his right. The room is candlelit and subdued. No one seems to notice us. There are no introductions. We have agreed to dine together and will learn more in the course of the evening. Where we came from is not important to anyone now. Decanters of near-black wine and icy white wine are being served down the table by a pair of strong-looking farm girls in simple uniforms. When they have poured the wines, they serve *pulpes vinaigre,* platters of rice and shellfish.

I see that several of the women have left their shoulders and breasts, free of clothing. Only their jewelry is displayed. Their nipples shine from oil or wax.

The walls are of stone, finished in a distemper the color of chicken blood. I admire the scale of the room. The table is long, dark, narrow and sits in it as a bucket sits in a well, and I wonder if the room was built around the table, which is mottled and hewn from a single plank of black walnut. But even though the table looks very old, it is centuries younger than the walls of the room or the medieval tower, where ancient farmers once stood watch for the headsails of invading Saracens.

Between his thumb and forefinger, Eduard suddenly snaps a triangle of glass from the globe of his eggshell wine goblet. His wine doesn't spill. What does it prove?

It seems normal that the women have left their breasts and shoulders bare, adorned only by jewelry and their scents.

Beside me sits a woman from the world of birds—the neck of a cygnet, the beak of a seagull, ravenblack hair, and self-supporting breasts so symmetrical they might have been turned on a wheel. She leans toward Eduard, pressing her breasts against the black walnut tabletop.

"Your new guests are so obviously in love," she says to him in a salon accent of mixed origins.

Eduard takes his small, triangular shard of glass between his thumb and forefinger, holding it as a lorgnette, and peers through it inspecting Savoia and me.

"Are you really in love?" he asks, rich-voiced. Is it possible that he is jealous? I wonder.

Savoia's toe touches my knee under the table. Turning her head she makes a *moué* at Eduard. "Can't you tell?" she smiles, still fiery from her brief visit to the sun, flushed from our day, our love making.

With the triangle of glass, Eduard scratches 'S L' on the table-top. Is it a symbol? The breaking of his word to me? Is he commemorating our presence here at Villa Roseau? The table-top has taken well to being abused over the years. Under my fingers I feel dozens of scorings. I wonder if symbolic acts are important to Eduard. Will he now rise and introduce me as Simon Lister, the celebrity fugitive? Eduard is good at this.

He touches Savoia's chin with his fingertips, toasts us privately. We drink our black Medoc. He fills our goblets again from a decanter and I'm not sure of a damned thing.

"What does any of this mean?" I whisper to Savoia's profile. "What the hell are we doing here?"

"We have to be here You promised him you'd come." She sips from her glass.

"She's right," Eduard says. He has the hearing of a deer. "You owe me too much."

"Do they know?" I ask in a whisper.

Eduard smiles, shakes his head. "Do you think they'd be ignoring you if they did? No. They'd be straining to hear every word you uttered. You are being ignored on your own merit."

"Who are we then?"

"You are nobodies. You are my funny friends from New York, *commedia dell'arte* American friends."

"But everyone knows you detest Americans."

Then, turning to Savoia, he laughs his pointed laugh. "I must say you greatly resemble the dead woman form the plane."

"Thank you, I hear that all the time," she smiles.

"Tragic loss, I so enjoyed her company. But the greater tragedy is that my painting perished with her."

"I imagine it did," I say.

Simultaneously, Savoia and I notice the night sky above the walls. There is no ceiling. We arrived late and only saw the people and candles, unaware of the ceiling's absence. A remarkable room. The table chatter drifts upward and out, leaving below a pleasing quietude, no laughter to echo against the stars. Now through the candle-shine above our heads, we can see stars. The moon is better cut than it was at Plon.

Whatever else there is in the room beside the table—our steel plates, wine goblets—are in strict, useful style. Nothing is priceless. The large, white, metal knives, forks and spoons, are oversized, uncomplicated by designs. The impression is of purity rising from the nearly-black table, scarcely touching, lit by bristling candles. Along the distempered walls, the ensconced candles drip their wax onto the stone floor, forming abstract patterns on the stone floor.

"What an amazing looking man," Savoia says.

A servant wearing a white jacket is standing against the wall in the shadow made by a sconce, supervising the farm girls serving us platters of mussels, crab and rice. He is a thin person, ageless, lean, bent. He might once have had an oriental face. His eyes are black olive pits. So far, I have been unable to look at him for more than a side-long instant, but as I drink my wine I look at him for longer moments. Whenever we make eye contact he yanks his eyes away, then eventually looks back. He doesn't seem to have a face; what he has instead is a visage without complications; no lips, no nose, no ears, no hair. A visage swept upward, molded to one side, the look of a man swept away in a thousand-mile-an-hour wind.

"Coco is from Hiroshima," Eduard says, he has noticed me trying not to stare. "He was a tiny boy going on a picnic one morning when there was this bright flash ... well, you probably know the story. A delightful little boy who suddenly knew the sun very well. Now a delightful little man."

"Like yourself," I say.

"Well, I would never presume."

A dark woman with Moroccan pendants is seated across from us. "Coco understands everything he sees, he rarely speaks, and he is a subtle cook. I have asked him several times to marry me," she smiles, not in a cruel way. "There are no mirrors in his room."

"Have I seen him before?" Savoia whispers to me. "He gives me quite a chill."

"He's a subject from Hieronymus Bosch. And you've only seen them in museums, none ever come on the market."

The bird lady beside me begins speaking a form of Russian with the huge man I'd seen earlier in the day drying his armpits by the pool.

"That is Treblett," Eduard says. "He is huge, isn't he?"

"Fundamentally, he is only fat, but he doesn't know it. Beside him is his woman, *Bébéfruit*. You may call her 'Babyfruit'."

She has luscious cheeks, alert wide eyes and when she smiles, her face widens into a pan and spreads her puffy lips, revealing baby teeth.

"But she is smarter than he is," Eduard says. "She runs his galleries in Rome and Paris."

Another guest, a tall, silver-haired man with light eyes, the color of a crocodile's, a long, generous, handsome face, who has a name I don't quite catch, which sounds to me like *Regard*. He reminds me of a elegant fountain pen. He has said almost nothing throughout the evening, but has been watching, listening in unbroken silence, smiling. He watches the others with a thorough concern. He watches me. He sits across from a woman he calls *Silence*. She seems to be his wife. She has not spoken. She is a deeply black, beautiful layered woman her skin appears as if it had been lacquered. Her nipples are highlighted in sky blue hue. Her breasts remind me of fruit I've never seen before but have imagined.

"Before you leave Villa Roseau," Eduard says, "I want something from you, Jonathan. I want what you promised me as we descended into Paris?"

I nod, but say nothing.

"You're always falling in love," someone says to Mathilde, the lean-boned woman who had been asleep on the island in the swimming pool.

"With Fugasse, I must," she answers. She is a long-nosed Iberian beauty, with small breasts and nipples the hue of Burgundy grapes. She can only smile darkly, implying an open life style.

Fugasse is ringlet-haired, and seems clear headed, with an easy, conscience-free smile that doesn't depend on anything but his pleasure at the last remark. He toasts Savoia and me. Gold items dangle from all parts of his upper body, which is shirtless. He is sweet, open, laughs easily, uncomplicated, tanned, handsome, healthy, muscular, but not tall, and I wonder what he's doing here.

"I am always in love," he smiles, as if in answer to my question, looking across the table at a large woman twice his age. He calls her *Lady Bountiful*, and takes her hand. She seems to be comfortable within her size.

"Love! Love is being able to pass gas in your sleep and then make a joke about it to your partner," Fugasse says with a smile.

"I wasn't discussing marriage," Lady Bountiful says, "only love."

"I was discussing gas." Fugasse retorts.

"My gas is made by Chanel," Babyfruit says.

A *fugasse* is an anti-personnel land mine, Eduard informs us. It is not a compliment to be named *Fugasse*."

"Love's a narcotic," Babyfruit says, raising her glass to Treblett.

She is a passenger on his hull.

"Is this a comedy?" I ask Eduard.

"I'm always in search of comedy," he answers.

"Do you always find it?"

Our host has an ability to allow his control to slip down the table, letting his guests carry the night along any way they want, and they have, gossiping without shape, in other languages, up and down the length of the table. I sense that the chatter is on the brink of something darker, that might or might not be turned against me.

Savoia has suddenly vanished. I'm spinning now, storm-at-sea-drunk. The table is rising and falling, like a life boat in choppy seas. I reach for my glass of Cognac. The worthy Cognac. Where has Savoia gone?

The men are old friends. I am new among them. I have been accepted by them as Jonathan Boot, and talk with them as I would with passengers on a ferry boat during a rough crossing. Bracing my hands on the table as on the rail of a ship, I have the feeling that I've passed through this channel, that it will be over by morning, that the best pose I can adopt for tonight is to be entirely candid, as Jonathan Boot, of course. I don't really give a damn what they think of me.

Michel Treblett, sweaty, an ovoid fetus with painted black hair sits opposite Babyfruit his polar opposite, a fabulous connection between them. Treblett, Babyfruit. Which is the courtesan, which is the master?

"What fruit are you, Babyfruit?"

"She is so many," Treblett answers with a dreadful grin. She doesn't look at him.

"Tonight I am lemon," she says. Treblett shakes his head. "Tonight you are cantaloupe. And too ripe."

Jarred suddenly by the image of their copulation, I fear for her safety. I see them wearing masks, harnesses, chains. Babyfruit pinches Treblett by the ear. "Tell Mr. Boot how old you are. He can see how fat you are."

Treblett loves this. She makes him feel small. "I am forty-two," he announces to set the record straight. Babyfruit toys with Treblett's fib, still pinching his ear.

"Quarante-deux?" she says, *"Oo-o-o, blageur!"*

Treblett turns to her, *"Mais non, Bébé ... dites."*

I hear myself interrupt. "But how old are you Babyfruit?"

"How old am I, Mr. Boot?"

This is an entirely different question. She looks directly at me, coy to the tips of her nipples, holding onto Treblett's porcine ear as if he might trot off. "Screw you! That's how old I am." She catches my blurred vision with an intimate flash of beauty, releasing his ear. His head drops. She likes saying it to me so much she says it again, "Screw you, that's exactly how old I am, Mr. Jonathan Boot," delighted with her discovery, smiling for the others, especially Treblett.

Strangely, I feel no meanness from her, only the fun of her saying it. She knows more than Treblett, Fugasse, Regard, possibly not Eduard. She knows how to make any man helpless, and that is her strength.

Paul Regard, the entirely silver man, pale-skin, silver-haired, is never without his two women—Lady Bountiful and Mathilde. They are his memory bank, his opinion, taste, conversation, his game. There is no jealousy between them. They are as fond of each other as they are of him. The two are well-born and well-traveled. Regard is married to them both.

"Art, all art, is a trial," he asserts unexpectedly. "I am a victim of my own attitude. I put not only art but everything in life on trial —wine, food, you, the Moon, art. I look for reasons to dismiss, not embrace. By doing so, I eliminate and continue searching instead of contemplating."

He should be searching for a blood transfusion. He seems to have aged without fluids, calmly.

Fugasse is propped at my elbow or I am at his. He has kept me from falling onto the stone floor.

"I give a nice impression quickly," he says to me. "I sell, I buy, I order impeccably, immediately or not at all. I am, in fact, an impressionist."

He is, in fact, a moron, but like the others, a very successful one.

"I have perfect pronunciation in every language. I can express abstraction of faith in any language, you see."

"Your art is a lie, of course," I say with a wobbly wave of my glass. "Isn't it?"

There is a long pause.

"Yes, of course, it's a lie." Regard smiles. "But only when there are curator and collectors in the room." He laughs his metal alloy laugh.

Cigars are passed around by Coco. Cognac is served again, this time not by Coco but by one of his helpers, one of the farm girls, the most graceful woman in the room. She dazzles me. She wears an ill-fitting, one-piece frock. She's barefooted, elegantly supple. Her name is *Nans*. She stands poised, her legs balanced evenly as she moves. She is young, not Babyfruit young, but still learning young, she does what she does with a calm face and purpose. Without having known it, I realize I've been watching her all evening. So has Babyfruit, who sits with her left heel on her chair, her knee high. She signals Nans and accepts a cigar from her, she lights it, by placing her knee on the edge of the table and stretching up to light it from the flame of the tall candle. She is marvelous, her lines taut, the underside of her breasts catching the glow of the candlelight. The men enjoy her exhibition quietly.

With his crocodile eyes, Paul Regard, fixes his gaze on me.

"Eduard tells me you once knew Simon Lister."

There it is. My name. I sober just a notch, turn to Eduard, and find him watching me, waiting for a reaction. He smiles, waves his chipped goblet. So perverse, so flagrant, so Parisian.

"Of course," he challenges me. "You must have an amusing story, Jonathan. You grew up with him, if I'm not mistaken. Don't be shy, tell us."

"Yes," I answer, playing along with him. "We were little boys together in Illinois. I remember, that he could see perfectly in the dark."

"I once read that he had sensory membranes like a snake or frog." He points a pale finger behind his ear.

"No, I don't think so. I would have known. But it was a popular rumor about him." I turn to Regard. "By the way, what do you do? As a profession."

"I am in charge of Eduard's galleries in Paris, Munich and Amsterdam," he answers.

Treblett is losing his grip. "Eduard tells me your paintings remind him of Simon Lister's."

"You're still having fun with me. I, too, am good with fun," I answer in bad French.

"Eduard tells us you know where Simon Lister is hiding at this very moment," Treblett presses.

I feel a chill run through my guts. This is too playful. *En garde.* Treblett narrows his gaze at me implying that if his words fail, he may attack me. I laugh, not bothering to look at him.

Eduard draws his right hand back and hurls his chipped goblet across the table and onto the wall.

"Jesus Christ, Michel!" He slumps down in his chair, the petulant duke.

"For Heaven's sake, why can't I even say that?" Treblett moans.

Nans swoops to the floor to gather the fragments of glass and collect them in her apron. I feel the night veering toward catastrophe. Babyfruit leans toward me and whispers for only me to hear. "I would gladly submit to Simon Lister. If you could arrange it I would be grateful." She makes much of my name. She is very close, her eyelashes flutter against my cheek. "His paintings, I know them all, I have wandered through so many of them—*The Field, The House, The Room, The Bed, The Lake*—all devoid of people. At the Tate in London last year, we were all warned in sixteen languages. One painting, *The Door*, I fainted in front of it. Others did too. We were told where to stand and not to stare directly at the painting, but to find a spot within the frame and let the painting draw us in. After a time I found myself inside the painting entwined in the arms of the man who was responsible for my de-pluming when I was still a girl. I was on the floor in front of the painting experiencing my first orgasm. The guard watched, along with several of other visitors. I will never forget that moment." All this whispered inches from my face. "He is amazing, his painting spoke to me through all of time, through the cosmos. He must be alive. I must touch him. If you know where he is, you must tell me, I will give you anything to be with him." I want her to say the words, *Simon Lister*, again and again. Her sibilance excites me.

She pulls away from me and turns back to Treblett. For the first time this evening, I'm aware of who owns the table, this tiny empire. It is I. The guests stop nattering and turn their eyes on me. No sophistication, just childish wonder. They know. A line of flickering faces, waiting for me to say 'Yes, I am Simon Lister.' They all know and they have all been sworn to silence.

"What is he like?" Treblett calls out. Down the table, I see his face, drunk in the viscous light. Of course they know.

"Yes, what is he really like, Jonathan?" Eduard says. I glare at him. He stares richly back at me, shrugs cute, as if to say, 'what did you expect?' Too late, he sees what he has done. He has betrayed me. He must die. I am capable of killing him.

I stand, reeling, walk to Eduard holding my goblet in one hand, a silver and crystal decanter in the other.

"You are truly an imbecile, aren't you?" I say to him. In a quick arc I raise the decanter and smash it on the tabletop, in front of Eduard. The fragments fly onto him like diamonds. He withstands it all without defense. He sits motionless. With a gentle flick, I empty my glass of Cognac in his face. Eyes closed, Eduard allows it to run down his face and drip onto his silk robe. His hair glitters; his face shimmers. He leans close to me and in a voice just below a whisper he says, "You may think I have no character, Simon, but you are a crazy, paranoiac drunk. I have not told them! Anything! Ever!"

The mood is charged, silent. These are Parisians, after all. Eduard's American friend is clearly drunk, maybe berserk, but regardless, it was a truly spectacular gesture. I am aware of solitary applause, from Babyfruit.

"*Quel beau geste, Monsieur.*" The comic book action has excited her; her opinion of me has soared. I swallow another Cognac. It is entering me as easily as my breath. The room is reeling, the talk is reeling. The men sit around, the candles flickering above them, aiming the evening at me.

"What does he look like?" It is Treblett's turn to talk and the subject isn't changing.

"It's been years," I say. "He would have changed."

"What was his method of painting, do you think?"

"His painting was instinctual. There was no hesitance in his brush."

I look at Eduard, nod at him. In my blur I see my downfall—my arrest early in the morning by plainclothes men from Interpol. I must not sleep naked. Will Eduard betray me? I cannot think. I cannot think why or why not. I see Regard's women stand and slip away. Babyfruit is the last woman remaining at the table. She is dozing prettily in her chair now. She might not yet be a woman, still just a girl, although bedding down with Treblett qualifies her for full womanhood with plumes.

Cognac is passed around again. Babyfruit wakes abruptly and stands. "Bébéfruit bye-bye now, *messieurs*," she says to the table. She rounds the chairs kissing her host on the forehead, kissing me, letting her naked breasts graze my ear. Then she sits on Treblett, with no more than a flick of her buttocks, kisses him gently on the mouth, then slides to her feet. He tugs the hem of her cotton skirt as she pulls away. And then she is gone. There are no women left. The room has been cleared for action.

The men shift their attention to me. I accept another Cigar from Coco, light it and take its fumes through my nostrils. The room is spinning; the conversation is wheeling. Not just 'I would like to see you again' sort of thing. Treblett cannot take his eyes off me. More is coming. I can see decisions being made inside his huge dybbuk head.

"Are you staring at me?" I ask him.

"Who are you that I should stare?" Treblett responds. "Are you somebody?"

"You fat fruit!" Is all I can think to say.

"Pardon?" He does not understand.

"You fucking French pervert! Can you understand that?"

Treblett, pink as pork, the pedophillic driven gallery owner from Paris and Rome, rises and surges across the table toward me, a hopeless gesture, yet he would only need to roll on me to snuff out my life. One of the painted altar candlestick topples, candle splashing wax across the table.

"How did you get this way, sir?"

I cannot tell if he is truly angry, amused, or in heat. Simultaneously we brandish our cigars as daggers. We will duel with them. "They tell me I was rolled on by a hippo when I was a baby." Eduard bursts out laughing, Treblett laughs, the table laughs, I laugh.

Savoia enters, she has come to retrieve me. Only Regard rises.

I can tell by the furniture that I am back in our room, but I cannot tell how I got here. I suspect Coco had something to do with it. I recognize the large carved objects, the small high windows, stairs, a bannister along one wall, paperback books, heavy wall and ceiling beams painted yellow. I hear water dribbling into the bathtub, the huge laundry washtub carved from stone centuries ago. Savoia sits up to her shoulders in pale, soap-water. Beside her, on the edge of the tub, a lone candle flickers. Two bottles of Barsac icing in a bucket. It is a sweet wine, in its way, ideal for the end of the night. Its chrome-yellow liquid glints in the candlelight. Savoia accepts the wine I pour gently from the bottle into her open mouth. She shivers and ducks below the water.

"You missed the best of the party," I say as she resurfaces.

"Did I?"

"Eduard was outrageous. I think he's told them."

"No!"

"I think so. Things ended close to a duel."

On the bed table, I see a plate of mashed potatoes still warm, in its center a large dollop of caviar. Surrounding it are shaved crescents of onion, slivers of lemon and small triangles of toast. I sit in the pine armchair. "Doesn't anyone sleep at Villa Roseau? I don't get the feeling this plate has been here more than a few minutes."

"What plate?" Savoia calls from the tub.

I'm famished. I take spoonfuls of mashed potatoes. "You want to know what a moron is?" I call out to her, "Someone who eats the potatoes and leaves the caviar."

"That's a snob. Bring me some caviar please, Moron."

The caviar eggs are gray-gold, big as capers. With a spoon, I pile caviar and onions onto triangles of toast and bring them to her.

She takes one in each hand, nibbles.

"Yummmmmm, I respect his caviar," she says. "Beluga, is the best."

I drop my shirt and trousers on the floor and lower my body into the tub.

"I also respect his bathtub," she says.

"I respect his crabmeat," I say, "his potatoes. I respect his moules, his wine, his sense of color."

We are both slippery from the cube of local olive oil soap. We soak, her back to me, her soapy blades amber in the candlelight. We lather each other into foaming people, then drown ourselves until the water runs over the tub.

"I respect his keeping his word," Savoia says. "I'm sure he did. If he told them, he would lose you for himself, but now you are all his."

"I will have to give him a painting."

"How can you?"

"I don't know yet."

"Simon, you can't."

"I swore."

"It could bring everything down on you again. It's not worth what it will do to you."

"Tell me my choice?"

We emerge from the tub chilled. I am nearly sober. The Cognac from the armoire sears me nicely. We engulf ourselves in heroic-sized toweling robes, thick enough to bed down in, which is what Savoia does on the floor.

"I feel completely out of time and place," she says.

"That's because you are. Come to bed."

She nods once, yawns deeply and gives in to sleep. The shadows flicker on the misshapen pyramidal ceiling, on the yellow beams, on the white walls, lit by the lone remaining candle. I lift Savoia onto the bed and draw the sheet and blanket over her. She half wakes. I draw back the sheet and stare at her. She lies like a runner at the finish line. She is my illusion. My *trompe l'amour*. But is that all? Am I capable of this? Villa Roseau, in itself, is a *trompe l'oeil?* Am I on a *trompe voyage?* "As long as I live, I will measure everything against you," I say aloud to her. But she is asleep.

There are no lights outside the room. I close the door behind me. I am in a covered stone walkway, a narrow passage. I hold the lantern ahead of me, shielded by my hand. Is this a servant's passageway? A medieval redoubt from the watchtower? The stones are head-sized, whitewashed. At the end of the stone walkway, I turn left. Soon I am outside, under the stars. There is a small house ahead of me, with stone steps. I open and close a door. Inside is a timeworn room, then another, then the smell of sleep. I see a form curled up on one side of a bed. The sheet rumpled like dunes. I move closer and see it is Nans, fast asleep. I must be in the servants' quarters. I lift the hem of the sheet above her shoulder, without touching her and carefully, slowly, I draw it back revealing her nude body. I am a thief of visions. Nans, full-bodied and beautiful in her young woman's sleep—solid breasts, chocked buttocks thrust out, hands half open, knee forward, a rampant swatch of hair between her legs. She lies like someone cycling to the Moon. Her only adornments are the silver rosary around her neck, and a glint of gold on a finger. She sleeps on under the glare of my wavering lantern. Asleep, she seems more alive than Savoia. Her contours are voluptuous. I cannot stop staring. There are two pillows, side-by-side. She has not been alone tonight; someone has been sleeping with her. I lower the sheet over her and raise the lantern. Seated across the room from me, sitting in a straight-backed chair, hands folded in his lap, Coco wears a white sleeping robe. He is watching me, his black, olive pit eyes glint, watching me with the remains of his face, skin taut, no expression, only ancient calm.

"Ma femme est très sympathique, n'est ce pas?" His voice comes second hand, a slight echo. *Ma femme*—his wife!

"Pardonez moi." I apologize.

"No, no, no, pas besoin. Elle est jolie, non?"

"Oui, oui. Sûrement." I say.

Coco stands, reaches his hand to me, palm out, angled toward me. As he stands he half bows. We have both paid his wife a compliment. He understands a visitor admiring his wife's beauty.

Nans stirs in her sleep.

"A demain, Monsieur Lister."

"You know my name."

Coco nods.

"Who else knows?"

"I believe we all know your name, sir," he says.

"I see. Treblett? Babyfruit?"

He nods. I feel cold.

"Baron de Haen will make a gala the night after tomorrow. Monsieur Anasor has been invited."

"Will de Haen betray me?"

"Of course."

"At the gala?"

"Oui."

I don't speak. I hear my voice as if it is coming from behind me.

"Keep your promise to him, Monsieur. Make him your painting. It will free you."

"May I take your hand?" I ask.

Coco, extends his sere hand toward me. I take it delicately as if it were glass.

He sits on the edge of the bed and lies back, his head on the other pillow beside Nans. She turns, reaches for him with an armful of sleep.

Back in our room, I blow out the guttered candle by the tub, then the lantern. Standing by the open window I become aware of the unfathomable beauty of a new day forming. I lean out the window. I try to see the hills. The day is still dark. I lie down beside Savoia still afraid to close my eyes. Her fingers move across my chest. Tomorrow I will keep my promise to Eduard.

CHAPTER 30

The Phantom Painting: January 28, 1964

❦

It all begins with the morning. Savoia's breath has a private, animal scent. The deep white of the walls, the burnished stone floors, the silence made by trees. Our room is above the sea, miles inland, the highest point in the National Forest. You would not know there was another world beyond this room. Coco brings us our tray. There is coffee in heated bowls, warm bread with the crust of lobster shells, sweet butter, raspberries, tangerines on a bed of lavender sprigs from the hillside. There is an envelope marked *'Villa Roseau'*. Inside, a stiff card. Savoia reads:

> *"Kindly do me the Honour to*
> *attend my Birthday Gala*
> *Saturday evening at nine in the Grand Salon."*

It is signed, *Baron Eduard de Haen*. As before, the word *Baron* has been slashed with a single pen stroke, indicating abject humility. Savoia has gone into the bathroom and is bathing in the stone tub. I call to her from the bed.

"Savoia listen to me."

"I can hear you."

"No. Listen." The splashing stops. I come to the door.

"They know."

"No."

"Yes, all of them."

"What makes you say that?"

"I visited Coco last night. I went to his room. He told me."

"All of them know?"

"Everyone. He told me."

"Why would he do that?"

"He feels a connection I suppose."

"Why didn't anyone say anything?"

"They won't until the gala tomorrow night. Anasor will be there."

"Tres diabolique, isn't it?"

"A party."

"A surprise execution!"

"How very Parisian. What'll we do?"

"Well, we have to leave."

"Of course."

"Quietly."

"When?"

"We'll play it straight tonight. They're all so delighted with their secret position. After you left Eduard smashed his glass against the wall. I wondered why when he did it. Now I realize it was because Treblett had given away their secret."

By the time we arrive at the pool it is nearly ten. We will have safe passage all day long. The blue of the pool is lurid against the low white walls, unpainted doors, black-shadowed awnings. The buffet is set where it was set yesterday. A bucket of wine, maybe champagne, steams in the sun. The food is iced on silver platters. The Modigliani women, nearly nude, lie on chaises sipping drinks. Babyfruit sits wrapped in muslin under an umbrella, head down, reading. Treblett lies beached nearby. Eduard is absent. Others snooze. Paul Regard, wrapped in a burnoose, waves feebly.

"I dreamt of Van Gogh last night." He says this to be funny. Lady Bountiful looks over, nods once.

"I did too," I say. "He came to dinner with us. Looking great. Both ears. He did a little clog dance on the table. Then made a scene with you." I look at Lady Bountiful. "Treblett, you represented him and had made him a fortune. He was painting more or less the same stuff but working on a bigger scale, and now into acrylics."

No one is amused. Treblett watches me the way a scientist watches a rat with sores. Treblett, Regard, Fugasse, Babyfruit, half-listening, sun-stroked—they all know who I am and what is going to happen tomorrow night. I'm too alert. It is a reaction to fear. Mathilde mentions the gala. One of the few ruling ex-monarchs is expected. Anasor's name is not mentioned.

I go to find Coco. I enter the two-room cottage. He is napping.

He naps most of the day, a cotton veil over his face. Nans curtsies and slips away into the other room. Coco sits up slowly, doesn't speak. He bows his head once.

"I'm sorry to disturb you."

Coco stands, walks to his chair. He leaves the veil over his face. He wears white clothes, maybe muslin.

"Thank you for talking with me last night."

He nods. I know his fine eyes are watching me.

"I understand everything you told me."

Coco says nothing.

"Can you tell me what will happen at the gala?"

Coco nods.

"C'est deja fait." It is already done.

"I know that I am asking you to betray the Baron."

"Sir, at the gala there will be a toast to you. You will be revealed as this person you pretend not to be."

"And then what?"

"You will be honored and praised, there will follow a celebration."

"But the day after tomorrow, what will happen then?"

"Nothing more. I have heard the intention is for you stay at Villa Roseau. To live here."

"But not able to leave."

Coco shakes his head.

"And I paint for the Baron and Mr. Anasor."

"As I have heard it, that is the assumption, sir. There has been made an agreement between the Baron and Mr. Anasor."

I find Eduard half-asleep, lying in a rooftop cabana with the black choreographer, he calls 'La Negresse.' It is cool. A rising breeze passes through from the forest below.

"You startled me," he says sitting up.

"I didn't mean to. I just came by to tell you that I am going to make you the painting I promised you."

"But that's marvelous, marvelous. Will I see some progress today?"

"Savoia will find you and tell you where to come."

I follow Eduard down to the pool. He offers a prize—10,000 francs for whomever can hold his breath the longest under water. No one stirs. Then Savoia slips underwater in the shallow end wearing only her silk scarves and moves along the floor of the pool. She seems to be at ease, a Pucci bottom fish. After four minutes, I reach in for her hand and pull her to the surface. She is not even breathless. She refuses the prize.

The beach near Ville de Vent isn't as white as the others along the south coast of Provence, but it is wide and flat, surrounded by bluffs with a gentle descent to the sea. Emerging rocks break the surface of the sand here and there. No houses can be built along the bluffs. There is a wooden staircase, some two-hundred steps, with a wood bannister, leading down to the beach. And because of the cove's remoteness and dangerous descent, it has become a rare place for people to visit. I walk the margins of the cove along the U-shaped base of the cliffs. I scan the great bosses of raw stone, the cliff above, the great eminence gored by dozens of cave openings. Walking the dimensions, mindful of my materials, I take in everything. It is surrounded by bluffs a hundred feet high and the beach is wide, with a gentle descent to the sea. It lengthens to a quarter mile when the tide is fully out.

I have brought with me a knife, a serving spoon, a broom, a rake, a spade, four wooden stakes and a long white line. I pace off my dimensions. Then with a rock, I pound in the stakes and tie off my lines forming a rectangle thirty feet across and fifty feet long.

It now is late afternoon. There has been little sun all day, no visitors. The tide has ebbed leaving the beige sand stiff with salt, drying and hardening. Clouds have lain in rolls of fat above the horizon and now that it is afternoon, the sun is making a small show, flashing out across the water and onto the beach. I have been working without a stop since noon and I have before me, under me, a vast sand painting of *Villa Roseau*.

I take my tools and clean them in the sea. The tide is out. The waves break in small flops. I walk to the wall of the bluff and sit, wait.

Savoia appears. "Tell them to come," I yell up to her.

The sun is radiant now, a flamboyant apricot yellow glinting across the sea and highlighting the sand painting closer to reality. I wait.

Treblett appears first at the head of the bluff, a bulbous figure in a gray beach robe. Below, I stretch my arms. He half waves back to me. The sand painting faces the bluff. He sees it immediately. He clambers down the steps clinging to the lean wood bannister, his suede slippers flapping on each step down to the hard surface of the sand. He is panting, awed by what he surveys. He is blushing, wheezing, gesturing. "This is marvelous!" He staggers over loose sand, a portion left above the high tide mark. Now Fugasse is down. Paul Regard is at the head of the bluff looking down, an inch-high figure wearing a Panama hat, a pale suit, a tie, observing, maybe understanding everything. He descends gradually, carrying a stick with a silver head that catches the sunlight. "Magnificent!" he shouts to no one, not to me. He does have an eye. He does know.

Eduard is the last to appear—the blond head, the youthful hair blowing—a small, robed figure standing at the head of the steps. Eduard de Haen. Golden sandals. I watch him descend.

"That's my end of the bargain," I say.

"Yes, I can see that. It is considerably larger than I expected."

It doesn't seem to bother him that it is made of sand.

"This beach is hard as rock," Treblett observes.

"That's the salt. It's very salty here," Eduard explains.

"It can easily be moved," Treblett is saying, "section by section.

"It is a work of great genius," Fugasse says, "I am overwhelmed."

"It can be cut into, what, eighty-eight sections?" Treblett suggests.

"Pour plaster, and lift them out."

It sounds insane.

"How can that be possible?" Fugasse asks.

"The fine texture of the sand, for one thing." Treblett explains.

They don't seem to understand the idea of tide, that it is out, not in. It is turning now, a lag tide about to return and cover the beach. Within an hour what Fugasse called, "a work of great genius" will be gone.

Eduard has not spoken. He gets it, he knows about the tide, what is about to happen. I see it all in his poisonous glance.

"It is magnificent, Simon," he whispers, "You devious bastard! You beat me. You disgust me. But I want to kiss you as well. Do you have a title for this?"

"*Villa Roseau*. Tentatively titled of course."

"Tentative, indeed. It won't be here in an hour."

"Fine with me. It's your painting."

"It is my painting!" Eduard hisses.

Treblett is wandering around the picture, circling it, enjoying it, careful not to cross its surface, making marks in his notebook.

"This is a priceless work. Anyone can see that. *Le Pavilion d'Alliance* in Paris would pay that. They have already commissioned me to find something." He's talking to himself, smacking his lips, making odd gestures, stopping, starting and stopping again.

Without smiling, Regard repeats himself, "It's magnificent!"

"It's priceless, isn't it, Paul?"

Neither of them has mentioned my name, but they know.

"Of course," Regard stands detached, as if he wants to feel the last heat of the sun on his face.

"It will be gone in an hour." Eduard mumbles.

"What do you mean? It's perfectly protected here." Treblett barely looks up from his journal.

"The sea is out there," Eduard explains impatiently. "The tide comes in quickly, along these flats. A hundred meters is nothing."

"What are you talking about?" Treblett's mouth hangs slack. He looks at the sea that is not far away and then at Regard.

"It won't be here long Michel. We have to see it now and remember it." Regard says.

I catch the exact moment when Treblett sees the edge of the tide moving in. "Why would he do this?" He asks in disbelief.

"It's going to go away, Michel. You must get used to the fact." Regard seems to have passed through disbelief into a more enlightened stage. But not Treblett. In these moments, he is insane. Seagulls that were attracted by the activity, nettle him like flies. He is smacking at them with one of his sandal. "How can you let it disappear? Do something!"

"Do what," Fugasse says. "Build a wall?"

"Maybe, A wall, yes!"

"There is to be no money changing hands today, Michel." Regard says. "Let it go."

A mournful silence follows.

Eduard's eyes are are bright with tears.

In a soft voice, Fugasse says, "We five will be the only people in the world who will ever have seen it."

I scan the top of the cliff and see Savoia. "Six," I say.

Suddenly, Treblett stares at us, gaping, his robe open revealing his belly roll of tanned pork, its pink jockstrap showing its pink mounds of Edam cheese. "No!" He shouts, "No! I won't let it go! I'll get my camera anyway!"

In a burst of comedic energy he starts churning toward the two-hundred steps. Then, just as suddenly, he stops and crumples into the sand, kneeling, staring up at the bluff, "I could never get back in time!" Treblett moans.

The waves are barely waves at all, but everyone can see them now. The wide, rounded edge of the foam is swarming a few dozen yards from the upper edge of my sand painting.

Savoia watches from above. She does not descend. Regard has hardly spoken, sighed a few times, moaned, not said a word nor shown any feelings.

"I am afraid he's a genius," is all Fugasse says to Eduard. And Eduard, by far the calmest, watches him with something like fear.

Treblett will not surrender; he continues moaning, confused, incensed, full of gall for me. He has no resources, no recourse, only anger.

"You're such a prick!" he shouts at me, holding his chest to keep his heart from beating its way out of its rib cage.

I ignore him. I go to pick up my tools. I don't want to lose them to the rising sea.

"It's over," Eduard says simply. "It wasn't here this morning and it won't be here tonight."

"That's the sea out there, Michel. The tide comes in and goes out. It is an old idea."

Eduard walks away from us toward the water.

Savoia has descended the stairs now carrying a wicker picnic hamper and sets it down at our feet. Inside are glasses and a bottle of chilled champagne.

Resigned, Eduard walks back and joins us. He reaches for the bottle, presses the cork until it pops onto the beach, and pours it into our glasses.

"I toast Jonathan Boot, who has kept his pledge to me and presented me with a marvelous painting."

"You're insane, Pitou! You've lost your mind!" Treblett is enraged. "He's fucked you! He wins the game!"

Eduard smiles at him, speaks quietly, "It won't be here very long, my friends. We must enjoy it now, while we can, and remember it."

Regard looks directly at me as the first flat sheet of water covers his espadrilles and slides back to sea.

"Maybe you're right, what you said last night. Maybe the nearest thing we have to truth is insanity. If so, it'll have to do, won't it?

I see Savoia climbing the stairs a hundred feet above us, caught in the dying rays of the sun. The wind billows her dress, messes the short strands of her hair. She brings her hand up and waves to me, once, twice, three times. I stoop to pick up the last of my tools, turn, and start to walk toward the bottom of the bluff carrying them, When I look again, she isn't there. I start for the stairs. I say nothing more to the four men, I don't have to. I've done enough for one afternoon.

"You pig! You are the most selfish man I have ever known," Treblett shouts after me.

As I climb, I look back down. Regard is standing at the base of the sand painting watching it being erased by the sea. The water has now covered his espadrilles and soaked his trousers, now narrow as riding breeches clinging to his calves.

"It's going, it's going!" Treblett is calling to nobody, a funereal call, calling to the sea to stop its destruction of the painting. He is willing the water not to rise by the sheer volume of his voice, interposing his girth between the sea and the sand painting, but another wave sweeps in, hissing smoothly across its face, rounding it, wiping more away, leaving smooth dents and soft ridges, little more. Now he is churning in a strange weave, splashing in the film-thin rise of water. Another wave covers the roof of the villa, smoothing away its details, not quite erasing them, leaving it halfway gone as the sea advances, in a lovely display of gradual restraint. Another wave, then and another. The simplicity of the event Treblett is watching stuns him.

And then it is gone.

"I cannot tell you what a gaffe you have made with this … thing of yours!" Treblett shouts at me.

"I keep my word," I answer, before I can stop myself.

"There's nothing less significant than an artist with a tongue," he sputters back at me.

I turn and climb the remaining steps. At the top I look back down again at the beach, the men. Regard, the furthest out, still hasn't moved, the water advancing, drowning his knees, letting the sea have him, too, it seems. He gives the impression he might stand there as a landmark. Treblett is inconsolable, volleying around the open beach, robe blown open, displaying his full body, raging against the rising tide. Fugasse leans against the base of the cliff and smokes.

Eduard in his pale robe, the calmest, standing, waving up to me, glowing nicely, golden, making sure to catch my eye before I leave. He has lost the afternoon to me. He has not found it necessary to mention that during his gala tomorrow night he will win triumphantly.

Back in our room, I slump onto the bed exhausted. Savoia, is sitting on the sill of the casement window staring out at the sunset. I have never watched her for this long without her knowing it, and now I see sadness engraved in her face. The yellow-green aura has left her. She is tinted by the setting sun now but as she looks toward it with dead-eyed intensity, her child's eyes bright but vacant, I feel helpless to do anything about her grief. There are no tears. The grave pallor I saw before was a sadness that tears could disqualify. Now I feel I cannot intrude on her. Though I love her as I love her now; I feel I don't know her well enough anymore to comfort her. I stare away, up to the ceiling.

"I was sitting here missing you," she says. I feel the chill of her lie.

She drops her eyes. Then she slips out of the window seat and closes the door to the bathroom behind her. In a few minutes, she emerges, surprises me wearing only ribbons from the night before. Her chic breasts, her pale pubis.

Later, after making love, I wake from my nap. I see her sitting again in the deep window seat staring into the glow that the sun sometimes leaves after it has set, to mill around high corners and be remembered a few moments longer. I go to her and sit, knowing we will slip away from Villa Roseau in the middle of the night.

Chapter 31

Leaving Roseau: January 28, 1964

శ్రీ

At twilight, Coco knocks on our door. What aperitifs will he bring us? I ask for a chilled bottle of the local Muscadet and a plate of cheeses. Savoia asks for grapes. He brings us caviar with our Muscadet, cheeses, grapes. "We will avoid the buffet tonight," I tell Coco. "We will stay in our rooms."

"Le Baron de Haen will be very sorry," Coco responds.

"So will we, of course. Please tell him we certainly look forward to his gala tomorrow night."

Coco barely nods.

"Comme diner pour Madame et Monsieur que désirez vous?"

"Surprise us, Coco, a cold supper will be fine."

"Le Baron will insist that you attend dinner."

"Tell him I have rabies and am having a fit. But that I am excited and looking forward to my demise tomorrow night."

"Mais, non, Monsieur." Coco shakes his head, turns, closes the door behind him.

"He knows we're leaving tonight," Savoia says. Her flight bag is lying open, half-packed, spilling clothes onto the floor.

When Coco returns with our cold supper, I tell him we're leaving.

Coco nods.

"I will miss you, Coco. You have been an amazing friend to me. How can I thank you?"

Coco shakes his head and leaves us with our supper. On the tray is an assortment he has selected from the buffet downstairs— moules Provençal, blinis, saumon fumé, shrimp ceviche, a pepper soup, a terrine of foie gras, a pear tart, an apple. There is a vial of vodka in a small bucket of ice.

"After a while, caviar tastes like sardines," Savoia observes.

"That's what it becomes if it's lucky."

It is still early, not even ten. We bathe. Savoia tucks her hair under a bath towel, making her head tower above her bird-boned neck and shoulders. We cannot stop soaping each other. Eventually we fall asleep. I'm the first to wake up in the bathtub. The water has cooled. I touch Savoia, she shivers.

"We must finish packing."

She sits on the bed and dresses too slowly. I know she'd rather pull the sheets over her, curl on her side, sleep through the night. "I'm tired of running. Aren't you?" She asks.

I agree. But of course, we can't. Our lives are at stake. I wait for the lights at Villa Roseau to go out, the outlying rooms to go dark. She seems exhausted, dangerously close to a breakdown. She touches me, tries to pull me down. We've got to get away from Villa Roseau long before anyone wakes. We need as many extra hours as possible. I pack the rest of her things in her flight bag, folding them as neatly as I can. She has so few. Whatever clothes has brought are wispy, plain. I cannot imagine her ever following fashion. I pack her toothbrush, plastic bottelets of oils, an amber flaçon of perfume. In my bag, I pack two bottles of Barsac, a bottle of Cognac from the armoire, the open Muscadet that is standing on the floor by the stone bathtub.

It is after midnight when I put our bags by the door. I tell her to wait in the room for a few minutes, then to follow me. I want to see if the route to the main gate is open to us.

Outside, I walk by touch on the gradual tile steps up toward the pool, toward the main entrance, my bag in hand. The night is clear. Full moon, low to the west, with a robust breeze. The main rooms are dark now. I pass shuttered windows of suites within the compound. The night is much too quiet. I stop. Suddenly, the air shifts places with me. I feel a presence. What is it? Something has just passed close over my head, a whirring sound, a blurred, rushing sound as of something large. Then, silence. Savoia is behind me now carrying her flight bag.

There it is again! Rattling low over us again and again. It passes over our heads, back and forth, whirring loud, then it is gone.

The front gate is locked, of course. It cannot be opened. The walls are high. I cannot see the ground, maybe fifteen feet below. There must be another way out.

Carefully, carefully, each step an enterprise, I walk the perimeter of the entire compound. I find a cleft in the rock wall. It is covered with shards of broken glass set into the stone over a drop of ten feet. We are imprisoned within a fortress.

The whirring again. Now I can see a form against the moon. It is a kite, the same kite we saw welcoming us when we first came to Villa Roseau. Looking upwind into the starred sky, I see the outline of a man standing on the roof of the villa. A lean figure, one hand held high, holding a string I cannot see. It is Coco. The kite drops, hangs in the air, floats closer, stands in the air by my face. Dangling on its tail is a weight—a small package wrapped in paper and string. I take hold of it and break the string to free it. Inside is a fossil-like key and a car's distributor cap. It is the key to the gate!

Once outside we climb into our little Renault and let it coast forward down the hill. After about a mile I stop the car. I open the hood and reattach the distributor cap. After a few turns the engine starts. We drive away. "Bless you Coco!"

Savoia lies crouched in the front seat, balled like a fox conserving its heat. She looks up at me without moving, as if she may bite. I senses her fires are fading.

I'm exhausted. The long day is behind me—the sand painting on the beach, watching it disappear under the rising tide, the wine, Coco, our escape—it has run me down. I cannot concentrate on the road. There are no lines along the median. I am constantly veering, gripping the steering wheel. Our little car seems to want to crash through the forest which drops down on either side of us.

Eventually, we are out of the forest, approaching the coastline. "Can we stop?" Savoia asks.

"No, you can pee when we get to Italy."

"I don't have to pee."

"What, then?"

Suddenly, she engulfs me with her fingers, her arms. I veer off the road into the dirt and stop the car. She pulls my hands away from the steering wheel. She so clearly needs me now, here, before I can drive another foot. The tension of her needs overpowers her, then me. We will make love, or whatever it is called, jammed in the cockpit of a dwarf panel truck. She cannot wait, she needs more than the space allotted by the manufacturer of Renault camions, a car without a history of success in sexual matters. Behind us, the grimy steel-encased cavity designed for poultry not lovers. We tumble out onto the chilled ground fully clothed. Tumbling, fumbling out onto the road, Savoia wearing a loose, cotton dress she's found among others in the armoire at Villa Roseau. I anticipate headlights, death. Our escape has been too simple. Despite the more dignified shelter of the trees just beyond us, I lift her and press her against the hood of the car, picking her up by the hips. She lies back against the warmth of the metal, raising the hem of her dress to her mouth biting down on it. I stand with my feet apart, my trousers at my ankles, churning into her, feeling her need for my complete being. I am saving her life; I am the tool for Savoia's survival on earth. My giving comes back into me from her. I feel a wide sense of excitement; every part of me is involved now inside her. From her there emanates a sudden world of pure exclamations. To fuck her here, without regard for passing cars, as fully and for as long as I can—with it comes a surprising gentleness from my urgency—the power of what I'm doing to her by fucking her, the rush of saving her life, of bringing her back with me, maybe, the risk of it as if, without fucking her as soundly as I can, she will vanish. If this is her salvation, it is a good bargain. She makes no girlish whimpers, only the sounds a lioness can make. Her impulses quake as her full woman's needs expire. Is this making love? Is it less than love and more transfusion from my body into Savoia's? Against the hood of the Renault turned off the road, in the black in sight of the ocean, the swarming sea far below us. That's making love, I suppose and all it is, what else could it be called?

I collapse across the hood, my head below my body. Savoia lies askew, open, under the roof of stars. No cars have passed us; we are alone. There are moments that sum up whatever you can have here on earth. When they pass, you see there is nothing higher. My head is nearly touching the ground; I pull myself up. Savoia's child's eyes gaze in wonder at the stars. I am learning, as I balance my mind, I am beginning to see what I never would have seen before. I straighten myself against the hood of the car, my trousers still bunched at my feet. Is this how I will keep her with me? The rush of tides is stronger than I have ever felt from her, from any woman.

Back on the road, driving through the night. I sip Villa Roseau Cognac as we drive through the night and into the morning. I tell her about Coco and about watching Nans sleep.

"I wish you'd seen her," I say.

"I did see her," Savoia says. "She is lovely."

Just after sunrise we park the car at a high turning point in the road. We climb out and I stand in the sun holding Savoia. The hills glisten in the first light, the water below us still gray with night, the stark sun caught at the horizon performing its rite, lifting the world from darkness. A fine moment, and grabbing the Muscadet and the bread wasn't a bad choice at all. Driving further off the road behind a wild hedgerow, we stop for breakfast. We cut our bread, pour our wine, eat, drink, and I fall asleep on Savoia's lap. When I awake the sun is high sun, the air, thin, cool, blue, clear.

By mid-afternoon we find that the road to Ventavon, our chosen destination for the night, is not a good winter road. We are driving uphill, mile after mile. The engine is knocking again, the familiar scent of rusted steam coming through seams in the dashboard. I say that I'm not so sure we'll make it.

"Yes we will."

"Can you do your shoe thing."

She runs her shoe along the car's battered dashboard as she did before. "It'll be fine," she says. And by her witchcraft, the road levels once again, the motor calms and rounding a green slope, we come into a wide plateau of stone houses and stone walls and a fork in the road.

"You're magic still works." I assure her.

In a while, the slopes turn green and we see a farmer prising something from his broken furrows. We stop and ask him the way to the Mediterranean. His face breaks into a beautiful, yellow-toothed smile, *"En descente"* he says. Simply downhill. Now I want to get to any village before dark, hide our car, find a room, and talk all night.

CHAPTER 32

Vent les Pins: January 29, 1964

৯৵৯

A blue-bordered sign reads *Vent les Pins,* the name of the auberge, our destination for the night. It is twenty kilometers from the nearest village. I pull the car to a stop along rows of deep-sighing pines combing the breeze. I see an open barn with a tractor and, without asking permission, I drive the Renault behind the barn, hiding it. In the auberge we are given a room with a dark wooden bed, and an old mattress stuffed with duck feathers. We fall asleep without supper.

In the morning Savoia is gone. None of the staff knows where. Anxiously, I eat breakfast upstairs in our room—trout with almonds along with bread and coffee. After the meal I drive the car in search of her, wandering, getting lost among the cutback roads, some no wider than footpaths.

In the nearest village, twenty kilometers away, there are horses standing outside a church; they have winter coats. None of the locals in the café has seen Savoia. I drive back to the auberge, return to our room. No Savoia. I sit on the bed. I am terrified.

Finally, I open the dark leather box. I stare at the adobe house in the painting without entering. Savoia is there! She is alive, her face is calm. I fall back on the bed. I try to rouse myself. Try as I may, I cannot. I lose consciousness. I cannot dream of anyone but her. In my dreams she is never in motion, always still, in colorless images, posed, staring at the lens, as if she knows. What? That I am her creator?

When I wake up, it is afternoon. I drive to the village again, park behind the church. The horses are gone. It is market day. I buy her a dress for twelve francs, a bar of lavender soap, a packet of black Italian cigars for myself. I have nothing to do. I cannot go to the gendarmes. I can only stay here in the village and wait for her to reappear. But can't she reappear anywhere? I climb the stone steps to another café perched above the uneven granite square and below a rough-hewn 19th century church. I sit and think of reasons, clues. Recently, I have been more afraid than ever of losing her. I sit like a terrier watching doors she may have entered, waiting for her to reappear. I buy a newspaper, *Paris Soir*. On page seven, I see a picture of myself, not a photograph but a sketch as I appear now, quickly placed by Anasoi, probably from Lyon. Beneath it is a small advertisement promoting the half-million franc reward and a telephone number.

I put off returning to the auberge. There is a cinema nearby, but I cannot enter another hectic world. I go back to the car, my heart racing. I drive to the auberge; I have no choice. I go to our room. Savoia is in the bed, lying on her side, asleep.

I am crazy with fear. Did I drive her away? I looked for her for seven hours and now she is asleep in our bed. Time is slipping by. I haven't faced it for so many days. Now it faces me. How many days are left to us? What distance can we travel in that time? Where will we end?

The Bell: January 30, 1964

৯৵৶

Savoia puts on the cotton dress I bought for a few francs at the open street market. She ties it tight around her waist. It flares loosely about her. She looks lovely in anything. In the kitchen of the auberge, we dine on lamb stew. There are large potatoes, crisp haricots verts, oily greens.

Upstairs alone, we are our own best entertainment. We play. The world is off-limits; we have each other for our amusement. We are better than films. Tonight in bed, we talk of permanent ways of disabling the other, of confining our world to a simpler more intense sexual cycle. There are effortless new positions, inventions tried in the dark. It excites us telling hectic tales of confinement to small rooms, binding one another into the freedom of help-lessness, a lifetime of casual suggestion that become strictly-followed orders before sex or during the spiraling, unmargined time afterward. After making love, we tell these stories. She has her stories; I have mine.

"Where do they come from?" I ask.

"From nowhere, absolutely the best place I know."

"Mine, too."

But in the open-curtained morning they seem crude, *jejune*, clearly traceable to a problemed male ego and competitive fe-male. It is fun. We only have each other.

The days are shaping themselves just right, curving down toward the end, so what we did we did and we did it because of clocks. But there are no clocks for us anymore after Villa Roseau, no days that seem so urgent.

We cling to each other; awake or asleep, we touch. In the morn-ing, she recites her dreams to me verbatim. This morning, she tells me her dream of having had two children with me and for-getting their names. I know that whatever plans we create now will never come true, the strain of my subconscious forces me to continue. She cries, not in front of me, but later. I hear her in the bathroom.

Tonight in our room we invent olive races. We fill our tumblers with champagne and set them side by side. We drop one black olive in each glass. Tiny white bubbles form on them, and when there are enough bubbles, the olives rise to the surface where the bubbles burst in the air, causing the olives to sink to the bottom again. White bubbles form on them again, and the olives rise. We smother our laughter in our hands. This is a working farm, not a retreat for giggling lovers. I win seven out of twelve races and for my prize, I can have anything I want. Savoia will willingly submit.

"What do you want me to do?"

"I won't tell you now. Tomorrow."

I want to be married to her, my pathetic means of holding her to me. How many days are left to us? We laugh at our dreams but when will she fade for the last time?

We feel the deep silence of the barren fields surrounding us, the animals sleeping in the barn.

In the morning I wake, slick from my dream in a rush of remembrances—who we are, our room. Laid out on the table are Savoia's necklace of local spices and herbs which she has collected from the countryside, a handful of dark olives, and the empty glasses from the olive races. The thick curtain lets in two bright bars of light which cross the floor. It is not yet seven. I ease myself out of bed with the stealth of a thief, trying not to make the bed squeak. I don't want to talk to her now; I don't want to face her. I have a surprise.

Our wedding day.

My bride-to-be sleeps naked, her face scrubbed clean. I want to tell her, but I don't. The handsome sight of a rumpled bed with a naked woman askew in it. There is no mess more beautiful. I dress in silence, slip out the door without waking her. Downstairs, I sit in the kitchen enjoying my bread and coffee, then I hurry across the road to the barn.

The sun's raw today, open and coarse. Just how I like it—rude, mean, deadly dry, a winter morning. The cold pinches my ears. I drive into the village to find a priest. I will take me a wife.

Driving down the unshaded stone streets, I look for the church. In the bare branches overhead the amber possibilities of spring await, the anatomy of miracles. It is the day I am to be married.

There he is, a priest in a black cassock, light gray socks showing above his shoes, toting a basket with bread and a few eggs. His face is wintry, unshaven, the hard features of a farmer—strong, wind-bitten, harsh angles.

I speak to him in my bad French. *"Pardonnez moi*? I am looking for the church."

The priest regards me, then, smiling, says, "You would be welcome to walk along with me."

"May I drive you?"

"But it is not far."

The priest has cheery, turned-up eyes, rosy cheeks, and a single expression wherein everything he says is expressed as if he were smiling about it, or about to smile. I wonder how those optimistic eyes cry, how he delivers a funeral sermon? He tells me his name is *Pere Clair*. Later, in the small vestry of the church, with the benison of good coffee in a cup between my palms, I ask him, "Would it be difficult for you to marry my fiancée and me in the church today?"

"Very difficult." he says, "In fact, impossible. Strangers cannot marry here." His eyes remain cheery.

It is my desperate need to marry Savoia, as if by gripping her with ceremonial words, she will stay on. We both know that it is only her death and my life that are true. Together, Pere Clair and I watch the loud-ticking clock above the armoire. It is nearly 8:00 a.m..

He smiles at me. "Would you like to ring the bell to summon the people for *matins?"* I accept the honor. He leads me through a black stone hall into a room with a narrow window and a high ceiling. He uncleats two thin ropes and hands them to me, nods his head several times so that I can follow his tempo. I pull on one of the ropes, and from high above I can hear a thin *tink tink tink,* light as bird's call. The church has a tin bell.

"I will come back to stop you. I have no acolyte today. He has a toothache."

Pere Clair leaves and I continue the rhythmic pulling of the bell rope. A toilet flushes nearby, an explosion of water from an overhead tank. When he returns, he grins, then signals me to stop.

"Our bell is illogical," he says, "a goat's bell." The Nazis stole our good bell. They stole all the bells in the countryside, all the bells in France, to make guns during the Occupation. We have never been able to raise the money to replace ours."

He invites me to take communion; I agree to kneel before his God.

After mass, he asks me, "You are English, no?"

"American," I answer.

"Then, your marriage here is truly impossible. To be married, you must live here, but even then it would still be difficult. It would be better if you had been born here, but not much."

After a moment I ask him, "Would you like to have a real bell, like the one that used to ring here before the War?"

"Of course, I would delight to see this goat bell replaced. My congregation would welcome it as well. Everyone would be able to hear it then."

"Why are you asking me this question?"

"I will give you a bell."

Pere Clair stares at me. I look especially indigent this morning. He stares at me while he is trying to decide if I have been drinking this early or if I have been up all night, and if I am dangerous. He speaks with caution.

"May I know who you are, sir?"

"I am an artist." I say it with hope, gentleness, mystery, as if my manner of describing my profession were a disguise, as if there were the possibility of an angel standing in the room before him.

He gets it, I can tell. He sighs, looks at me oddly. "Who are you, sir?"

"I will tell you who I am only if you accept my gift of the bell and agree to marry my fiancée and me this evening. If you find that our marriage is possible, of course. Then you will own a bell fit for this church, a bell that can be heard for miles across the fields surrounding your village." I say this with clarity so that there will be no confusion. "Then I will tell you who I am."

"Such a bell will cost in the thousands of francs, perhaps even more next year."

Pere Clair seems to know the price of bells. We are standing by the 14th century baptismal font. I reach into my overcoat pocket and remove a sheaf of bills, count them out on the worn stone surface. So many babies' bottoms have slid across this ledge into this faith, babies grown and now long dead. Pere Clair watches my hands fan open the stack of bills. I count out 100,000 francs, on the stone font—bell money and more. His mouth hangs open in a disbelieving smile.

"Tell me now what you think about the possibility of my wedding, Pere Clair?"

I roll up the bills up and put them back in my pocket. His face has brightened; he has closed his mouth.

"I will pray for guidance, my son. Please come back in an hour."

An hour in a strange village. I cannot sit at the café. I explore all manner of alleys and yards. When I return to the church, Pere Clair is weary from praying.

"I have spoken not only with God, but with our mayor. It will be possible to marry you, after all."

He grasps my hand in both of his, his upturned eyes welling with tears. When I free my hand from his grip, I place the roll of bills on the altar beside a silver-plated chalice. With a small gesture of the cross he blesses the money. He suggests a quiet ceremony this evening viewed only by the eyes of the participants, two witnesses, and the Lord. I make a request that he include the words, "To love, honour, obey, and cherish, 'til death do us part."

He agrees. I assure him that we will never live within his parish or the district surrounding it. He fixes a time, seven this evening, following vespers.

Driving back through the village, I see a girl, ten or twelve years old, leaving the bakery. She is wearing a brightly colored ring. I pull the car to a stop beside her.

"Bonjour, Mademoiselle," I say. "You have such a pretty ring."

Run child, run! Don't you know you should run away from

unshaven men in long coats who make conversation?

"Thank you, Monsieur, it is my birthstone." It is a silver-plated ring with a milky blue stone.

"I am being married today and my wife does not have a ring. Perhaps …"

Of course I offer her too much money.

"*C'est trop, Monsieur, c'est trop,*" she says. A thousand francs is too much money. She is so naive.

"Your mother will not agree with you, I assure you, young lady. Accept it all, please." She pulls the ring off her finger.

Now I must buy my bride flowers. There is still time, but it is winter in a small village and the only flowers I can find are dried ones at the bakery.

At the auberge, on the way upstairs, I stop by the kitchen. Monique is mopping the back stairs with boiling water. I ask her if she and her husband, Marc, would act as witnesses for our marriage this evening. She is thrilled. When I climb the stairs to our room, it is not yet midday. I am carrying a box of pastries and the dried flowers from the bakery. Savoia is still in the position she was in when I left her, her face smiling in its dream. How can she sleep so calmly? The room is as it was, with our clothes strewn on the floor and bed, wild. But why is the air fragrant? The answer lies on the table. She has been out gathering in the fields and gardens, gathering and gone back to bed. She has made an arrangement of her findings—sprigs of thyme, and rosemary and assorted twigs in the crown of her hat.

I set my things on a small octagonal table near the bed. She hears me but doesn't move, feigning sleep. "Breakfast time," I whisper in her ear. She vanishes under the sheet, leaving her toes as evidence. I bend down on one knee, and kiss each one. Her toes twitch; she twitches, all of her. I crawl onto the bed and lie beside her. Her scent reminds me of where we've been the night before, and I can't keep myself from wanting to return there. I whisper that I envy her serenity.

She props herself up, letting her breasts dangle forward, pointing with her slight shifts. "Isn't there anywhere you want to travel to besides bed?"

"Where do you want to travel?"

"I've been there, I've made things right with my father and I settled up with my mother. That's all I wanted to do."

"What about you and me, where do we go now?"

She doesn't answer.

"Look. I've brought you something," I hold out the little girl's ring. I hope it fits. I sit on the bed and push it onto her finger.

"It's beautiful." she says.

"You're lying."

"Of course. It's cute, Simon, and I love it." She kisses me coyly. I move my fingers across her breasts. "I had one exactly like this once when I was around ten. I never knew what became of it."

"A little French girl found it in her village."

"I think she must have gotten the better of you, Simon. Is there an occasion?"

"Does there need to be?"

"Usually, yes, with a ring."

"Then I may as well mention it. Today is your wedding day."

"To become your wife?"

"'Wife', that's the word. We have an appointment at seven o'clock this evening with Pere Clair at the local church I am giving him a bell in return."

"Seriously?"

"A wonderful bell. One that will ring across this countryside. He is a very happy priest."

"Are you being serious?"

"About the bell?"

"About our wedding."

"Tonight at seven."

"But you didn't ask me."

I get on my knees and hold her hands. "Will you marry me?"

She slaps me solidly across the cheek. It is too quick. Behind my eyes I see a maroon flash, a dull light inside a cave.

"What if I'd woken you up with a ring and said, 'I have a priest waiting in the kitchen. Put on a robe let's go downstairs and get married?'"

"I see your point."

"Did Romeo marry Juliet?" she says.

"It was illegal for twelve-year-olds to marry then. Anyway, she died."

It is the wrong thing to say.

"Were Tristan and Isolde married?"

"Not as far as I know."

"What about Daphnis and Chloe?"

"No. What are you doing?"

"Great lovers don't marry."

"Can two play?" I ask. "What about Elizabeth Barrett Browning? She married Robert."

Savoia tosses her new ring high and catches with skill.

"Okay. Napoleon and Josephine. They married."

"What about Adolph Hitler and Eva Braun?"

"They just barely married."

She tosses the ring up again and catches it.

"Antony and Cleopatra."

"Eloise and Abelard?"

"Queen Elizabeth the First never married."

"Neither did Gertrude Stein."

"Neither did J. Edgar Hoover."

"Hmm, Euridice, of course."

"Euripides."

"Him, too."

"Scott and Zelda did."

"Big mistake."

"Irina and Karl," Savoia says.

"Who?"

"My cousin, Irina, never married Karl."

"'Great lovers', you said, Savoia."

"Elvira Madigan wasn't married."

"All of your people killed themselves."

"For love. Katherine Hepburn never married Spencer Tracy."

"What are you doing, Savoia?"

"All I'm saying is that great lovers don't marry."

"So you won't marry me because Gertrude Stein didn't marry Alice B. Toklas. Samson and Delilah had a beautiful marriage!"

"No they didn't, it was hell."

"They didn't have Hell then."

"In the movie they did."

In an instant she's crying.

"I came back for you," she sobs. "I came back for you, Simon. I'm not meant to be here. You're meant to be here, not me. I'm borrowed, an expired library book. I can't marry you, Simon. It's a lousy idea anyway. Do you want to do it for me because you feel it's something one does when someone is leaving?"

"No. It's what I need to do."

"I love you, darling Simon, but I can't marry you. Some people aren't meant to be married."

"Why not?"

Savoia is pale; the sadness in her face is overwhelming. She speaks slowly. "I can't carry anything away with me." She is whispering now, "I must be the way I was the day I returned to you."

I can't look at her. I stare out the window.

"Please keep the ring."

Later, I drive to the church. Pere Clair is waiting, I'm late. He is startled to see me alone.

"Where is your bride?"

"There will be no wedding."

His expression darkens. Then there can be no bell. Wretched American. He has lost a bell he never had. He didn't ever truly believe there could exist an American angel.

"You will have the bell anyway."

"Pardon?"

"The bell is yours, and please buy the finest one you can." I place the roll of bills in his hand. "I never liked the Nazis."

"In the name of God, I thank you."

We walk out into the chill dark. I tell him that I desperately need to paint a picture tomorrow and I do not have paints or canvas or know where to obtain them. I ask him if he knows an artist who lives in the environs of the village.

"You must meet my brother, Camille. He is a painter. He will detest you, of course."

"Because I am American? I am used to that."

"No. He will detest you because you have two arms. He only has one. He dislikes any man with two."

"How did he lose it?"

"He didn't. One simply doesn't work and he has never come to terms with that fact."

"When may I meet him?"

"I am on my way to his house for supper. Perhaps you would like to join us. I have told him the news of the bell."

"He will still detest me."

"Yes, of course. He is a painter who detests painting."

It is not a large house, built in the early part of the century. Camille's wife, Sophie, is at the door watching us between the lace curtains.

Once inside, she takes our coats.

"Madame Clair, I am Jonathan Boot."

"Yes, I have heard you are an angel in disguise. Thank you for your generosity." She is rosy, dimples on her cheeks and elbows, full of pudding. "I am Sophie."

I am introduced to Camille. He is younger than his brother, shorter, darker, grimmer. He does not mention the bell. When I ask to see his work he walks me outside into an unused stable, cold as the night. Camille turns on a bright overhead bulb.

"I do not paint at night," he says. His paintings are not hung, but stacked, leaning against the wall, turned away. One at a time, he stands them on an easel, as if I were a buyer of art. It is what painters do. And, after all, the bell. The overhead light is remorseless. Small paintings, the largest, two feet across. One at a time I see that his paintings have been painted in revenge against the village and the countryside. They might have been painted a hundred years ago by an impressionist, by Van Gogh if Van Gogh had no love of color, no joy, no awe; if he had nothing in him but anger.

Sophie calls us in as if we were boys. Dinner is succulent—a tureen of wine-soaked meat and potatoes, onions, and a simple, nameless specialty made by Sophie's family for generations. Across the table I say to Camille, "I am a bit of a painter myself and tomorrow I must paint a portrait of my fiancée."

"Why?"

"She is going away soon."

"Yes. And so?"

"May I please borrow two of your brushes and some of your paints?"

"As you wish."

"It is only for tomorrow—the use of a very fine sable brush and a medium-bristle brush. I will certainly pay you."

After supper, we return to the stable. "Do you see what you need over there? In that milk can there are two dozen brushes."

I'm surprised to see that they have been carefully maintained. Camille has made the brushes, he tells me, and tied the bristles made from the hairs of his hog.

"And what about paints? For the portrait, of course, you will need only noir, rouge, ochre, blanc."

"Yes, and ultramarine if you have it. I may paint herbs."

"What surface will you paint on?"

"I was also hoping you might sell me a small canvas."

"Ah, Monsieur, there is no canvas here. I paint, as you can see, only on wood. These are oak panels that were saved from a rectory that was bombed a long time ago."

"I have never painted on wood."

"We have always painted on wood. It is our custom from the Middle Ages. I have such an oak panel for you. You will require burnt umber for the background."

I drive back to the auberge under the reeling stars, in the clarity of a winter night. Tomorrow, I will paint Savoia's portrait. On the seat beside me are paints, brushes, the ancient oak panel from the burnt rectory, all I need to carry Savoia with me forever. The distances left to travel in our lives are now shorter than ever.

CHAPTER 33

The Portrait: January 31, 1964

❧

In our room I clean the oak panel with mineral spirits, rub it into the wizened surface with a newspaper. They mixture is sucked into wood instantly. I open the window letting the panel dry in the cold dry air. Then I paint a gesso of rabbit skin glue and chalk into the wood. It is an old formula. I squeeze umber onto my palette, a broken piece of window glass I scavenged from the barn. I brush the umber into the wood with the stiff brush. From the bed Savoia watches me. Her eyes are bright, curious.

"How long will it take?" she asks, as if I were a dentist.

She will sit in the winter light beside the deep-set window. I have scattered the herbs and spices she has collected on the table at her elbow. "I don't know. I may not remember how."

When the rabbit skin medium is dry and I am ready to paint my underpainting, I go to the bed and lead her to the chair by the window. She drops the blanket. She is naked. We are both naked. I glimpse our naked reflections in the mirror over the bureau.

She sits obediently, good as a schoolgirl, her elbow on the small octagonal table. She is perfectly formed, her bones long as a colt's, like one of those marvelous walking creatures who wheel and pivot down the runways of the fashion world dangling raiment with a delicious rolling strut. But with one restraint, Savoia has none of the runway model's blank cockiness, arrogance, contempt. There is no emptiness, no formulaic smile. She has moved into her face. She is at home in the world, at home in herself.

Sitting beside this window at this moment, Savoia might be anywhere. There are white rooms in Monrovia, Galway, Hokkaido, Saint Kitts, and in Provence a few dozen miles from the Mediterranean. White rooms with deeply recessed windows by the sea, by the cliffs, by the frozen fields. She is anywhere. She wears my wedding ring. It will be on her finger in the painting and the painting will marry us.

When I first see her seated beside the deep stone window, the herbs at her elbow, as if to bring the life outside the window inside the room, she has created her own portrait. She stares into me, her mind in her eyes, full of love. In her face there's hope, and yet, if I succeed, the painting will be in perpetual turmoil.

She could be anywhere, this plain, small, whitish room behind her. I could paint the gardens, cliffs and lakes from the *Mona Lisa* behind her and it wouldn't matter.

Silence.

"What are you doing?"

"Preparing the wood to take oil paint."

Silence. I begin to sketch the outline of her head, neck and shoulders; line after line she emerges. I haven't lost my skill.

"What shall I do?"

"Nothing."

Silence.

I talk to her as I paint, as if I were a dentist. I will drill. I will see if I can save this tooth.

"What shall I think about?"

"Think of us sitting in a plain room in an auberge in the winter sunlight wondering what our next step will be and how far to take it."

"I'll think about last night."

I can see last night in her face. I stare at her for a full minute before she blinks, I close my eyes and open them, looking at the wood panel. Her face is on the face of the wood.

"Can I see it?"

I have only painted the underpainting. Her face, shoulders, arms are painted in umber shadow against the pale gray background.

When the underpainting is dry, I squeeze color from the five tubes onto my palette. These five colors are all I need to make any color I want.

I begin the painting. I don't so much paint her as let her emerge. I do nearly nothing, She renders herself.

Two hours later I set it aside, The portrait is finished. It is what I will carry of her for the rest of my life. Now, I must touch her. The reach of the paintbrush has held her away from me.

I watch us make love, detached, posing as subjects, painter and painted. The artist is fucking his model, a flamboyant performance that resembles bad acting. On the soft mattress we jolt against the plaster wall as the afternoon goes down into the sullen winter fields. And as we always do, we make love without an afterward. I wait for some sort of reprieve, as if what we have done weren't enough, as if it weren't the end of it, but it is the end of it. It is over. The ability to make love is the greatest right available to mankind regardless of wealth, status, intelligence, religion, beauty, race. Yet it is only an event. There is no afterward. You get up pulled by threads back into your continuum. Or you collapse.

We collapse. at the same instant, we sleep, falling, dropping away. We could be dead. It doesn't matter. All death sentences ought to be carried out at this moment. It is the only last meal worth eating.

I wake up long after we have gone to sleep.

"Do you know when I want to die?" My voice does not wake her. "With you. Doing whatever we're doing."

What I feel next is a springtime zephyr passing through both windows which have been thrown open to the sun-drenched winter day, a dream of warm wind blowing in across fields of goldenrod and mustard-seed.

CHAPTER 34

The Cat: January 31, 1964

୬∽ଚ

I painted her portrait today. Painting is an act of love. Especially painting the portrait of someone you would die in place of. All art is an act of love. That is why it creates suspicion. It is too right.

My life is a map of scars. All lives are. Only mine show as if they were outlined with a pen—each scar, in blue ink.

It is morning. Mathilde brings hot bread, coffee, milk from the farm across the road, a stone crock of sweet butter, two small loaves of bread wrapped warm in a cloth. I smile into Savoia's sandy, morning face. She smiles back into my calmness, my new calm face, my invention, grateful—a face she's never once seen.

The Renault is crouched behind the barn, trying to hide from us, trying to sleep off the day. Savoia takes the wheel. We coast down the miles we climbed to the auberge. We speak in bursts. She drives us to the village where we are to meet Camille at the café and return his paints and brushes. There are no other cars until we get to Meves. No gendarmes.

The small streets shiver against the winter chill. At the café we wait for Camille.

He is late.

Waiting, Savoia buys a pair of girlish, English shoes. We find a table in the café near an electric heater.

Through the glass front of the café, I see something lying in the street. It has the look of something dead, probably recently run over. Now I see it is a gray tiger cat, its mild, jungle look, abandoned, its position near the white center line of rue Magrin. It lies on its side near the crosswalk, as it would lie near a warm stove. Passers by pretend they do not see it. Cars deliberately avoid it. Sooner or later someones tires will finish it, accidentally or intentionally.

I go outside. I reach down to pick up the cat with both hands. It is still warm.

It is a fine cat, full and lean, with beautiful tones of ochre, taupe, gray, white, and black. It is completely open on one side, exposing its entire cat machine. When I pick up its body, the things that made the cat a cat, that made it purr and leap straight up and land softly, drop out and dangle wetly, all its reddish components slick on the pavement in the chilly afternoon. I hold it carefully, feeling its exquisite fur in both hands—the liquid machine that is a cat, that causes its specific, wondrous manners, the stiffening bravery, the languid inspection, the disdain, the wide-eyed awe, the necessary purr, the unlisted abilities, the anatomy of small miracles. This cat means everything to me. I cannot stop crying.

The traffic moves around me with respect, drivers and passengers politely sharing ownership with me now.

I carry the small carcass across to an alley behind a market. I find a small box and with simplest ceremony lay the animal to rest in it. I find a trash bin nearby and drop the box in it.

Back inside the café I wait with Savoia. She has been watching me through the misted window and sees my eyes now. She understands.

I notice two gendarmes approaching our Renault. They methodically inspect it. There is no haste.

I order a whiskey to go with my coffee. The café is humid with moisture on the windows. Camille is now more than an hour late. Is it going to end here, in this village with the gendarme dragging me away to extradition or trial, with Savoia left to die on her own?

One of the gendarme peers under the car, looking for what? The other jots down the number of the forged license plate. Then with his pen knife, he chips the number eight back into the original three.

"Did you leave anything of value in the Renault?" I try to sound conversational.

"My hat, my new shoes, and the vegetables."

"Good."

"Why?"

"We'll go shopping again."

But if her portrait was in the car, I'm not sure what I'd do. I have just lost Camille's two brushes, his paints, his medium.

"What's wrong Simon?"

"I think we've just lost the car," I try to say in a normal tone of voice. "Look outside."

She turns, looks across the street, sees the gendarmes. Then turns back to me. "It appears we have," she says solemnly.

"We should leave one at a time from the front door and turn right. Do not look back at the car."

"What about Camille? He'll help us won't he?"

"He might have turned us in. You go first."

I leave several francs on the table for the bill and stand. Savoia is at the door of the café. Suddenly I see Camille's camion parked to the left of ours, fifty feet behind it. I watch Camille climb out and start across the street toward the café.

I catch Savoia's eye, point to the back of the café by the telephone. She catches my signal and crosses back through the bar and into the toilet. Camille does not notice the gendarmes and they do not notice him. He pushes open the door in the café and sees me immediately. Noticing the money on the table.

"You were you leaving?" he asks.

"Well, yes, why not? I didn't think you were coming."

He has had a business disappointment, he explains and makes the grand pout, tosses his head. "Bastard! He would not pay my price. "But where is Madame?"

"She will be here in a minute."

"I have some bad news, Camille, I have lost your paints. Here, please." I hand him a roll of francs.

"Ah, merci." He pockets the roll, intuitively knowing that it is more than enough to buy an easel as well. I have balanced his losses. Savoia glances out of the toilet, I wave her over.

"This is Monsieur Camille Clair. And this is my fiancée, Savoia Paulus."

She looks into his eyes; she is slightly taller than Camille, he is stunned by her.

"I must see your painting. Is it possible?" Camille asks.

"I would be honored. But I have returned our car to its owners. I am afraid I must ask you to drive to *Vents les Pins.*"

It is late afternoon when we enter our room, the three of us enter our room at the auberg. The painting is there propped on the octagonal table. If Camille was stunned by Savoia, he is overwhelmed by her portrait. I am, too. It is good to be with it again, to own such a possession. It does everything but breathe.

"I cannot remove my eyes from it. If I had this skill of yours I would paint without ceasing."

"Thank you, Camille."

"I would wish to die completing a great work of art such as this."

"An excellent idea." We both laugh.

"But I have nothing to give." It is a simple announcement.

"Of course you do, Camille, everyone does."

"No, not like you."

I am being taken very seriously from the last place I expected to be. Camille is forming a question about my artistic life in America, what my successes have been.

I interrupt his thought, "Where is the nearest railroad station?"

"*Draguignon.*"

"Is it far?"

He shrugs, "Forty-five kilometers."

"Where do the trains run to from there?"

"Everywhere. Paris, Marseille, Geneva, Trieste, Venice. Barcelona."

"Would it be possible for you drive us there this evening?"

"But to go where?"

"We haven't decided. It doesn't matter, Camille. We are on our honeymoon and the world is ours for the moment."

"I understand fully. I will telephone Sophie."

We squeeze into the front of his Renault; Savoia sits on my lap. Camille drives with his right arm, his left arm is useless, and rests on his lap. He uses it to hold his cigarette. There is no radio. It is a long drive through black winter roads.

Neither of us knows what makes us decide upon Spain as our destination. It happens in the front seat, passing the countryside, the villages, the night. Why Spain? Why not Venice, closer, or Rome, further along. Trieste, a bit further down the road. No, it must be the Iberian Peninsula. The ancient cliches based on the ancient romantic beauty of Catalonia, but not Barcelona. A house of our own in a coastal village, eating paella for breakfast within sound of the sea, visiting Salvador Dali's house. To be someplace that will be beautiful for her to leave from. Without saying any of this, we agree on Spain. Would we separate there at the end? Why not die in Spain? Now that I know, I feel we are playing a tragic game of musical chairs. When the music stops, I want her to be close to a good chair, not en route to one. Our life now has its tidy destination. Onward to Spain. Draguignon, a handsome departure point.

The small city arrives in a brigade of lights. A train for Barcelona will pass through at midnight. Near the railroad station, we eat supper. Camille orders a redolent kidney stew that resembles the contents of a chamber pot and smells like it, Savoia and I order *moules mariniere*, in white wine sauce without fear of garlic. After the meal, after two carafes of red table wine pressed out of tough local grapes, we order dessert—*poire tartes tatins*. We smoke Camille's short, fat cigars. I order a half bottle of Cognac that turns out to be brandy and brutal. Finally, in the end, at eleven, I empty the open bottle into his glass.

"Will you be able to drive?"

"I am not drunk."

Camille has bought a Sunday newspaper. It is two days old. It has lain open on the table. My face in Anasor's small advertisement is on page five. At the station, after Camille sees us onto the train, he looks at me. It is the way he looks at me. He knows!

As we pull away from Draguignon, I look for him on the platform. He is not there. Then I see him outside the brick station house using a pay telephone. There is everything but a piano score.

The tracks are old, we are rising, we are passing through the night toward Marseille. I stare out the window. The villages are black, their dogs asleep. Eventually, I begin writing in my journal on my lap.

We don't speak for a long time. Savoia tries to sleep against my shoulder. I cannot forget the way Camille Clair stared at my face as we boarded the train at Draguignon. He did everything but speak my real name. An alarm must have gone off in his head. Anasor's ad, a couple on the run, an American who is an artist with no visible means of support. He knows. I am certain we will be met at the next station by the gendarmes.

"You look dreadful, Simon." She touches my forehead with her fingers. "Are you alright?"

"Did you see the way Camille looked at me at the station?"

"I did. What do you want to do?"

"Not go to Spain?"

"No?"

"We should get off at the next stop."

"Alright."

"What do you love about me, Savoia?"

"Not now."

"Yes, now."

"That you're never afraid to say the obvious."

"I was hoping you'd say that I'm decisive, alert, brave and smart."

"That, too, of course."

"Well. OK, then. I must find the conductor."

I walk through swaying cars. Compartment doors are clipped open to enhance circulation. Inside, passengers lie stacked on shelves, six to a compartment.

I find the conductor who tell me we'll stop at Aix-en-Provence in two-and-a-half hours."

"What about Trieste?"

"The name rings a bell." Savoia answers.

"James Joyce taught school there during the Great War." I explain.

Savoia looks at me and smiles. "Well then, how far is Venice? I've always wanted to see Venice."

CHAPTER 35

Venice: February 1, 1964

We catch the next eastbound train, a local that will terminate in Treviso, thirty miles north of Venice. In our new compartment we hold hands like travelers, trying to sleep against each other, afraid to let go. Finally, with the pleasant rhythm of the rails, the *kck-kck kck-kck* of the track joiners, we sleep.

My heartbeat wakes me. Morning. The false sun. Black ice along the rails. Savoia is asleep beside me. We'll run until we can't, I suppose.

The train slows nearly to a stop at Montgenévre. As we roll slowly through the station, I scan every platform. There is only one person in sight, a man in a dark blue overcoat waiting outside. He waves us on. We don't stop. We are crossing into Italy. I feel calmer.

It is late afternoon as we pull into Treviso, a small tree rich-city promoting rumors of spring. The unimaginable must happen, the stringent winter will yield, the countryside will swell and by then where will Savoia be?

There is no connecting train to Venice. I cannot sign papers to rent a car unless I want to be arrested. We are hungry. We find a café called Mario's. Inside, warm again, we eat linguini pesto and drink cheap but excellent Chianti. Mario himself brings us his family's signature Grappa, and asks if we will be here Sunday for the festival. We find a small room across the street without a view.

The next morning is skyless. In a small bookstore, we find an American murder thriller that we take turns reading aloud in our room until I throw it out the window in disgust. We have dinner again at Mario's. His brother, Roberto, is driving to Venice and will be happy to have our company. We meet Roberto at Mario's when it closes for the night. On the way, Roberto advises us to rent an apartment in Murano, an island across the bay from Venice, famous for its glass-blowing studios. He explains it is a less fashionable neighborhood than Venice, and therefore more reasonable.

After an hour, Roberto exclaimes, *"Fen-ee-chay!"*

We can see its lights coming up ahead of us; the road runs straight across the bay. It is after one in the morning. We haven't slept.

Roberto leaves us at the railroad station where I find a map. I locate the island of Murano north and east of Venice. The railroad station is unheated, windy. There is no ferry to Murano scheduled until morning. A bar is open across the canal. We cross the bridge. Three gondoliers are sitting at a table outside waiting for passengers.

"I am your gondolier," one of them says bowing to us, addressing us as if we were royalty.

"Si, si," I say, "You are indeed."

The gondola. I have never touched one before. It is finished with the lacquer of a grand piano, its markings ominous, funereal. The seahorse prow. I have seen them, black as coal, in paintings by Turner, Guardi, even Ruskin.

"San Marco?" he says. *"Salute?"*

"No. Vorrei Murano," I say in my clumsy Italian.

"No. Murano mai."

"Si, si, Murano," I insist.

The gondolier refuses again, 'without doubt, no.'

"Perche no?" I say. Why not?

The gondolier simply refuses the trip to Murano matter-of-factly. The weather for one thing. It is too far away. The Carnival is taking place everywhere but Murano. It is in the streets surrounding Piazza San Marco. Costumes masks, wine vendors. "It is quite splendid," he says. "I will take you there. You will thank me in church."

"No we must go to Murano."

"No," he offers Savoia his arm to help her across the splashing water between the gondola and the dock.

I show the gondolier two American bills. He considers them with deference. *"Murano, si,"* he nods. Months of money. But he is an unhappy gondolier.

There is a glassed-in shelter aft he calls the *felze*.

Once inside the *felze* it is damp as the canals and just as cold. With a match, he lights a candle set between the square windows.

"I am Marco," he says and closes the small door of the *felze*. Inside the *felze* we find a blanket. We are inside the *felze* when Marco drops his lines and pushes away. There is also a fur rug to cover us that reeks of use. I tap on the glass behind us. I call up to Marco. *"Che animale?"* What species of animal has issued us its skins?

"Lupo," he gives me a deranged grin, wolf. Even with the money, Marco does not seem to be entirely pleased with us. He would rather join the festivities in San Marco's Square.

Murano is in another direction. It will take him an hour to get us to Murano and an hour to get himself back.

Once away from the dock, up along a narrow canal, the steep houses dark, we feel the aged serenity of winter. The rain is sparse but it swells on the wind. A wet night in winter, late. Our nightship is a gleaming shadow. It is a Turkish slipper with a grotesque wobble, and seems to match the gloom of Venice at that hour.

We settle into a double chaise divan, lined in well-worn velvet. It is the most comfortable love seat I have ever lain in. I blow out the candle. Through the glass of the *felze* we can see the carless embankments, festivities, torches, masques, costumes. It is a scene from the 1600's.

"Bonne notte," the gondolier calls from above us as I draw the small curtain behind us closed. There is no heat in the *felze*. We make love like thieves, stealing each other, to the pendulous rocking of the gondola's imbalance.

Later, waking, Savoia's head on my lap I tap on the roof of the *felze*.

Inside the curtains are drawn. I part them and look out. If there is a sun I cannot see it. I cannot see land.

"Marco!" I call out.

There is no answer.

"Marco!" I call again.

Silence.

Savoia stirs. I open the small door, straighten my legs and pull myself up. There is no one else on the gondola! We rock un-evenly. Savoia appears, stooping in the doorway.

"Simon?"

"He's gone! Marco is gone!"

We are alone. We look around us. Day, mist, flat water. No land in sight. We scan the surrounding water for a floating lump, a hat. The motionless water is dark, untroubled, Marco has disappeared, unnoticed.

The horizon is close. A mist closes in a hundred yards away on all sides. I strain to listen for sounds from the shore—bells, dogs, children, something.

Silence. The gondola is smothered in mist now. Marco is gone, vanished in the night. But how, why?

"When we get back to Venice, we'll need to call the police," Savoia reasons.

"Where's his pole?" The long sculling pole is gone, too!

Savoia seems amused.

"You look worried Simon."

"Don't you think this is funny—drifting out to sea in a gondola in the dead of winter without a pole or a paddle?"

"I do see the humor. But ... I have no idea where we are. You're the navigator."

She laughs delightfully. "That's right, I am. Well, I suppose we're in the Adriatic Sea and that the tide's has pulled us away from Venice."

"What's so funny about that?"

"Uh oh, I think someone's worried."

"Not at all," I lie.

For the next half hour we search the gondola for something to help us move in one direction or other.

Under the gondolier's platform, Savoia finds treasure. In a pat-terned napkin that has seen use, Marco has wrapped his din-ner—sausages, peppers fried in oil, bread and two boiled eggs. She also finds Chianti in a liter bottle. There is even a glass tum-bler. Inside the *felze* we dine on Marco's last supper, speculate on his demise, his family. We approve of his wine.

CHAPTER 36

The Ave Maria: February 2, 1964

It has been a welcome meal. A blessed diversion from our grave situation. We save a little of the food knowing it may be our last source of nourishment. A sound invades our privacy, a throbbing in the water. I push the lacquered door open. Out of the mist a quarter mile ahead of us, a small steamer with one smokestack appears. Her bow is plowing directly at us. I wave, shout. No one seems to be on board. When she is a hundred yards away, I see a man gesturing from the bridge. Bells throb, water churns, engines grind.

I can read the name on her bow, *Ave Maria.* She is trying to stop. Her propellers claw at seawater in reverse, and she edges past us, a few passengers leaning over her rail to inspect us. We are a curiosity this morning—a man and woman waving for help aboard a lost gondola now bobbing wildly in the small steamer's wake. We are survivors, lost at sea overnight about to be saved by a small, rusted steamer named *Ave Maria.* She passes us by less than ten yards. Then, in a gradual arc, she turns and labors toward us again. The sea is flat as a tidal pool, but the rescue takes on emergency proportions.

A lifeboat is lowered, then, on an officer's command it is hauled back up. Finally, the *Ave Maria* drifts down on us, a crewman throws a light line, signals me to secure it to the gondola. Our two vessels are pulled together. The *Ave Maria's* engines have been cut. We drift dead in the water. A Jacobs ladder is dropped over the side of the steamer. By then most of her passengers have come out from breakfast and line the rails watching in silence. Under their weight, the steamer lists toward us. We pass our bags, the wrapped portrait and the Noxzema carton to waiting hands above us. Then we are helped onto the deck. The captain is there to embrace us. It is, after all, a rescue at sea.

We are given coffee and offered blankets, but it has not been an ordeal; it has been a marvelous experience, though not for Marco the gondolier.

But the captain must decide immediately what to do with the gondola. He must either salvage or destroy it, after all, a derelict is a navigation hazard and must be sunk. Or salvaged. It is his choice. The fog has lifted but we still cannot see land. A passenger tells us that we have drifted nearly thirty miles south of Venice. I do not think to ask the captain in what direction they will be going when they resume their voyage.

The gondola. It is his sea prize. He must now decide its fate. Which will it be—saved or scuttled? He announces to the passengers on deck that he will save the gondola. One does not scuttle a great work of art. And so it is. A cheer rises from the passengers, some applaud. Two crewmen remove a lifeboat onto the deck and push its davits out over the water, lower their lines to bind the gondola fore and aft. Once secured, the gondola is raised to the deck. She is the Byzantine slipper of Sinbad. A craftsman who can build a gondola can build anything. I am surprised at her shallow draft. She is all top, there is nothing below the waterline except a long lead keelson.

When she has been secured on the deck, attention turns away from us. The passengers return to their unfinished meal.

I ask a crewman when we will return to Venice? He smiles and shrugs. Later, inside the paneled dining room, I ask a passenger who understands English. She explains that the *Ave Maria* has just come from Venice and will not return before several weeks. Tonight we will put in at Athens. Tomorrow, our port of call will be Tunis. Then the itinerary will include Marseille, Malaga, Tangier, through the Straits of Gibraltar into the Atlantic, then down to Rabat in Morocco, then out to the Madeira Islands and on to the Canary Islands and back.

The captain assures me that we are welcome to debark in Athens in the early morning hours. If we would like to continue further, we will, of course, need to purchase passage.

It is a small vintage steamer, with a cargo hold full of wine, olives and shoes. It is carrying not many, maybe fifty or sixty passengers.

We are safe. No one can possibly find us here.

At lunch, we sit at long tables eating squid, limpets and garlic—tapas a la planche. I buy passage for two to the Canary Islands, the last stop. It is as simple as that.

After lunch, the steward takes us forward to our stateroom. It has one porthole, deep set, painted and re-painted since the 1930s. Two bunks are attached to the bulkhead, one over the other. It is the least desirable cabin, the steward explains, but there will be the possibility of changing staterooms in a day or two, after Athens. We open the porthole to the sea breeze and sleep through the afternoon lying together in the lower bunk, Savoia's arms around my neck, my arms around her waist, our legs woven like sea vines.

We wake together to the clattering of metal on the deck above our heads—a lone sailor with a ball-peen hammer is knocking rust flakes off anchor chains that have seized.

Later we have drinks in the ship's bar. I have a pair of whiskeys, Savoia drinks Vermouth. We go to our cabin to change for dinner but instead we curl up again on the bunk and fall asleep.

Sometime later, through the open porthole I see the flash of work-lights and hear the sound of cranes, grinding winches. I watch our gondola being swung out and lowered onto the dock in Athens. The *Ave Maria* will pick it up and carry it as deck cargo on the return trip to Venice.

CHAPTER 37

Count Reblochon: February 3, 1964

This morning the sea is choppy. By midday the wind from the land is brusque and warm. I can feel North Africa even before I am able to see its shores. Africa is new to me. I feel charged with freedom, even hope. Savoia and I have dropped our lines as we never could living in a mainland village in Europe. We are losing all touch with place and time.

After dinner, Savoia and I sit in the dim dining room at the long tables cleared of plates with small flaçons of ouzo in front of us. Everyone is smoking, I buy cigars for strangers. There is a Greek singer on board bound for Malaga. Her black eyes escape her face at her temples. She boarded the *Ave Maria* at Athens. From the deck we watched her and a man thin as knives screaming threats at each other on the dock leading to the gangway. The fight ended when he threw her suitcase in the water between the dock and the ship, walked to his car and drove away. The passengers were able to discuss the performance and those who understood the lyrics translated for others to savor. Recovering her suitcase was tricky and took two crew members a considerable amount of time, but she was not even slightly embarrassed, and continued cursing him from the deck in the direction he had departed. The subject of their operetta was a matter of infidelity. It was an entertainment. Her name is Melina Delius and she is easily persuaded to sing in the dining room after dinner. Her songs are a tonic, her phrasing exaggerates and beautifies a woman's loss. She sings her songs in Greek. Her voice becomes a fabulous instrument for Savoia's emotions, my thoughts. And as usual, I fear my thoughts. I am terrified of my mind. Her face is gaunt, drawn away from her teeth. When she sings I can see her skull. Savoia says she is touched though she cannot understand the lyrics.

After the gala evening, Savoia goes below to our cabin to read. A man I noticed at dinner is speaking to me. I cannot respond. I stand and walk away.

Alone on deck, I stand near the bow holding the rail. There is a slight roll tonight. It is the boat deck, the promenade deck. There is only one deck on the *Ave Maria*. For the first time since Venice, I am able to see a few bright crumbs of stars and then, the moon. But the moon is not right—a gibbous moon tinged amber like watery blood.

On deck tonight, under the few fixed stars slipping by through the mist, I try to make sense of what I've done and I can't. I can never think when there is no infinity. I need a mass of fixed stars. I only feel the dark throbbing me along. I wonder if I can go on or if I should. I must be the most selfish man on earth. What I'm doing to her, I'm doing only for myself. I know I couldn't survive her loss and that I'd be thrown back into the being I was when I lived on John Jay Street—a trembling speechless remnant of dry salvage.

It cannot be later than ten. The ship pushes stolidly through the night. A blowing mist on the quartering wind sends a chill through my coat. The man from the dinner table approaches me on the black deck.

"Good evening, Sir. A marvelous night is it not?"

"Yes, it is."

I now realize that this man stared at me off and on throughout dinner. An anecdote about Simon Lister that a woman called Bet was telling us in French, I could barely follow, but the man nodded without smiling, only watching me. My escapades were in the French newspapers brought on board at Athens. The episode at Meves with the car had been connected by the police to episodes in Meves and Toulon. So the police were connecting the dots now and the newspaper story implied that Savoia and I were continuing our run to Spain. I could understand just enough of what Bet was saying. The laughter was about Interpol, not the fugitive artist and his lady friend. Apparently, the French public is rooting for us. Anyhow, Simon Lister made a good dinner table topic, anecdotal, upbeat, current. A breaking story. A serialization with all the finesse of good fiction. But I was listening too intently.

When it got to be my turn, I told them my name was Jonathan Boot and I was on sabbatical from Ypsilanti College in Michigan where I had been teaching communications, and that Anna, as Bet called her, was a New York secretary I'd met in Rome.

"Are you debarking at Tangier?" the man from dinner asks me now. He wants to know our plans.

"Why do you ask me that, Sir?"

I remember watching him watch my face during the telling of the Simon Lister anecdote.

"That's an unusual answer, Sir. Normally one would say we are or we aren't and if we aren't, simply give their destination. Your answer indicates caution, suspicion of me, perhaps fear."

"Excuse me," I say, "but I don't remember your name."

Odd that I remember the other's names—Bet, Briggy, Melina, Mr. Queiroz, Abraham Schine and a Mrs. Hind or Mrs. Head, but I have never heard this man's name.

"If I tell you my name, or if I give you any name, what will that do? Would you tell me yours and where you are going, then? My name is, uhm, 'Gulliver'."

"No, I don't think it is."

"No, you're right. And 'Jonathan' isn't yours."

"Oh?"

"No, it isn't, I'm afraid, I spoke your name quietly when I sat behind you in the dining room for a few moments and you did not turn your head, not once."

I can see him smiling. It is all the protection he needs.

"My hearing is not exact."

"Oh, yes it is; your hearing is exact."

"Do you play chess?"

"I do."

"Then, we may debark in Tangier."

"Why are you uncertain?"

"Because the world is ours."

"It has been a great pleasure talking with you … Jonathan."

He is about to leave. He stands at the rail facing the gentle wind.

"Just one more thing. I watched your face during Bet's telling of the Simon Lister story. You did not laugh at all. In fact, you looked unwell."

"I could not understand her accent."

"I must disagree. You could understand it perfectly. Bet is my wife and she speaks to be understood. I watched your eyes. You were listening too intently."

If I walk away now, something will happen tomorrow. He takes out a cigar from a leather case and offers me one. I refuse it. He lights his with a wooden match. When it is glowing he says: "May I see your passport?"

"No."

"What are you hiding, Jonathan?"

"I'm not hiding anything. I am simply not submitting to your rudeness."

It is his rudeness that has given him acceptance everywhere. He is from a dead aristocracy.

"Do you object to my blunt manners?"

"You might say that. What is your name?"

"Santo."

"Tell me your profession."

"I have none. I am an amateur with enough money to do as I please and I please to be on the *Ave Maria* at this moment embarrassing you." He is the sort of man who does well at gunpoint.

"What else do you do?"

"I am an amateur traveler, archaeologist, psychiatrist, smuggler."

"What do you smuggle?"

"I usually smuggle ideas. From one country to the next."

"Why are you on board?"

"Bet and I have finished our Italian years and we are about to begin our Spanish years. We are sailing as far as Malaga."

"Aboard the *Ave Maria*, I mean."

"I adore this ship, she is the last of a species facing extinction—The small passenger steamer with the small bar and the atrocious cuisine. This little vessel has been at sea since the 1930's. It survived World War II as a coast guard cutter under Mussolini. Now may I know your real name?"

"I told you, 'Jonathan'."

"Not that name, your name."

He is the sort of fabulous man who provokes duels. People too close to him probably despise him and outsiders admire him, because it is they who make him fabulous.

"Jonathan Halliard Boot." I am looking at the halyard lashed to the gondola's bow. "May I know yours?"

"I beg your pardon, I am being rude, I am Santo Pietro Marie Reblochon. If that is inconvenient, I am 'Santo'. And now, Jonathan, may I see your passport?" The way he says 'Jonathan' disturbs me.

"No, you may not."

Silence.

Then he says, "You're treading on thin ice here, Jonathan, do you happen to know that? I'm afraid that I may have to discuss this with the captain over breakfast. He is a dear old friend."

I reach into my pocket and hand him my passport. He stands away from the rail leaning against the door into the light of the reading room. He regards it closely, then closes it. Smiling, says, "On your passport number, the eight was once a three. Is that right?"

I don't answer.

"Jonathan, this passport of yours is a painting. How far has this little bit of bad art taken you?"

"As far as this conversation."

"May I share this with our captain?"

"I'd rather you didn't."

"Then for God's sake tell me, what is going on with you?"

Shaking his head, he hands the passport back to me. "I suppose I'm the first to know. Now, I'd like you to tell me what you two are doing on board."

"Both Anna and I are simply looking for a place to lie down. I am world weary."

"Be serious, please, this is a grave matter."

"I am truly tired of the world and the living in it. There is only this one world and we have worn each other out, insulted, violated, disgusted and bewildered each other. I am tired of my face smiling back at me clean shaven, because it no longer cares. Every day parts of my body grind together soiling themselves, embarrassed beyond salvage for my fellow man. Why are you on board?"

"Because it amuses Bet and me. I have stocked the bar with my wines, I have brought my own coffee, cheeses, caviar. It reminds me of another era, one I cherish, my childhood. It is my pleasure."

"Welcome to our world, Jonathan."

The moon has been sheltered from us behind flocks of mist.

"Now listen to me, Sir." he says. "I will make a proposal with you, an arrangement. I'll call you 'Jonathan'."

"A deal?"

"Yes, yes, a deal, of course, how American."

"Well, Americans will talk American."

He ignores that and continues, a gentlemen's contract between us, nothing on paper, of course.

"I'm listening," I say. Humphrey Bogart would wince.

I cannot see Santo's face. Only when he draws on his cigar does his face glow.

"May I talk freely?" he says.

"Please."

"We are shy people, you and I. Yes, I am shy. You might not think it but I am, and I see that you are shy as well. And I see the world as you see it, only I am smart to see that a wise man is not a sad man. You are a creator. I am an observer. I think we both agree on one thing.—we have tried to taste the world, we do not just look at it."

He watches me. I can see, though, that his eyes are sad.

"The egotism of my own life amazes me. The flux between bliss and misery, between tedium and mystery, I float back and forth at random against my wishes. In terms of ratio, it is devastating. I need, need, need. No matter what I have, I need more. And I cannot believe my good fortune. I am standing here in complete isolation from the world on the deck of an aging steamship with someone I once admired more than any man alive."

"You are confusing me with …?"

"Simon Lister?"

I say nothing. Oh, Christ, here we go again.

"You admit that I am right."

"I have no choice."

"Do you think your escapade is over?"

"My escapade? Christ, how can you call my life an escapade?" I look away, down at the lines of foam on the waves being shoved away by the bow. Santo Pietro could be in over his head.

"I apologize. Please understand, I once despised you."

"What for?"

Santo Pietro shakes his head.

"But if you feel that I have insulted you or in any way inconvenienced you, please do not consider harming me. For example, throwing me overboard. The water is far too chilly and anyway, for your peace of mind, Bet is seated over there, can you see her?"

I look aft; the deck is black. Then I see it, the bright dot of a cigarette burning in the wind. Nothing more. It stands in the air above a teak bench against the deck house.

"Bet and I are starting our life again in Spain, a solemn land. I understand about the reward from the New York Gallery Anasor, and also from the Japanese Gallery Ueda. Clean dollars. But it's not that much, especially when it's invested. It vanishes. I have money of my own. Reward money is of no interest to me and if I may speak for her, Bet. What I am interested in is something of a more dynamic activity. Behavior. Action. Yes, thank you. Jonathan. Must I continue to call you 'Jonathan'?"

"If you want to enjoy the rest of the evening, you do."

"I think we both can learn something from this. I think we both share a secret."

"Why are we talking about these rewards?" I feel surrounded.

"What on earth would be the point of having you arrested when you will be simply be incarcerated and will no longer paint? Why not find you a safe haven, perhaps in Spain, where you may flourish undiscovered, thrive? This will give you things to think about. Talk it over with Anna. Maybe she'll provide counsel. Shall we continue this chat tomorrow morning. We have another day at sea before Marseille and I certainly would like to make an arrangement with you before then."

"You remind me of someone else."

"I am descended from Charlemagne."

"Didn't I hear someone call you 'Count' last night?"

"Yes, yes. I am 'Count' Reblochon. The title was purchased by my grandfather in 1900. Some people need it. It gives me nothing."

"My dear Count Reblochon, I can only say that I know what is so obvious, that you cannot betray me without first betraying yourself, that we are all countries that are connected that we are made of the same sun, that the sun is in us, that we have animals, reptiles, birds, in us."

"A wonderful speech."

I walk away.

"Oh, goodnight."

I wave without turning. There's nothing for me to say, I feel at an impasse. Reblochon is, after all, a French citizen, and we will be docking in France the day after tomorrow. Savoia is asleep in the upper bunk when I come in. Lying in the bottom bunk in the dark, I drink glasses of Cognac two ounces at a time until the bottle is empty. The idea of painting seriously again, deeply and with the power I once did, sickens me. Thinking about it, the excruciating voyage I would need to take to get into that world, would drive me back into what I was—more psychotic than ever and maybe this time irretrievably so. I escaped a short time ago with my life in hand and, of course, it has been Savoia's doing. Without her presence I would have been long dead, I believe that. I lie in the bunk, savoring the last of the Cognac, trying to devise a plan. Santo Pietro will not go away. He will be relentless. He has attached himself to me with tongs. This ship is as inescapable as the sea surrounding it.

By the time I fall asleep, the sky through the porthole is growing light, the sea is gray. I think I have a plan.

February 4, 1964

I wake in the late morning, alone in the tiny stateroom. Savoia is gone, but left a note, "I am somewhere reading my book." There is a metal sink with a rust-tinted mirror above it. I stoop to shave.

I am tired of my face. I shave it but I cannot look at it.

Up on the main deck, I'm alone in the dining room. I sit at a long table, empty chairs to the left and right of me. There is a pot of coffee. The steward brings a china pitcher of warm milk, rolls with feta cheese, a bowl of figs and peaches from Greece, oranges from Israel. I pour morning-aged coffee and warm, bluish milk. There is constant vibration, the teaspoon tinkles.

Santo Pietro has put his hand on the chair next to mine, "Good morning, Jonathan, is this chair occupied?"

I ignore the question. "Good morning Santo."

"May I sit for a moment?"

He sits. He is holding a drink he identifies as a breakfast drink, the old King of Spain's favorite—sherry Curacao, orange peel. "Tell me something," he says, "you were surprised that I discovered you, no?"

"Yes, I certainly was. We have been traveling here and there on planes and trains and automobiles and you're the first one to step forward and tap me on the shoulder."

"Nicely put. Well, it's a small skill I have. I am quite a clairvoyant."

"What luck." God, he wants his respect.

"My wife calls me a savant."

"Well you certainly surprised the hell out of me."

"I will guard your identity. No one else will have the opportunity to surprise you."

"You have already guarded it and I respect you for that."

He opens his leather cigar case. "May I offer you a cigar?" His first two fingers are yellowed with nicotine.

"No, thank you, and I'd rather you didn't smoke one until I've eaten my omelet."

"I should say not! Is that coffee acceptable?"

"Just."

"Please. You must have mine, I have given the kitchen a bag of my Roman espresso beans and you need only to request it."

I nod.

"Jonathan, I did not want to mention this last night. One of the paintings destroyed in the unfortunate Whitney Museum fire was mine. It was a picture of a house in a cleared field partially plowed. It had unnatural clarity. My one treasure. Within that painting I had conversations with my father that were irretrievable, irreplaceable. Within it I met many friends of mine, some of them long dead. When I first heard of this fire, I was terribly depressed. The next day I heard it was not an accident. I learned it was you who had started it. Of course, I wanted you dead. The insurance company has agreed to pay me the painting's current value, 2.4 million dollars. But of course, that's nothing to me compared to the loss I feel. I will accept the money, but I will have contempt for it. Just as I had for you. Yes, I wanted you dead, but I hadn't met you; nobody had. Of course, still, I dreamt about killing you, oddly enough. Your death involved drowning from a tiny steamer such as this one. But so much for coincidences. With you dead, there would never be another Simon Lister painting. May I see your hands?"

I'm spreading cheese on bread.

"For the love of God, Santo, leave me alone!"

"Jonathan, please don't be rude. Don't force me to make a ridiculous decision we will both regret for the rest of our lives. As far as the reward for your arrest is concerned, as I have already told you, it is not interesting. My satisfaction in your arrest would last no more than a few minutes. The loss of your work is permanent. Now tell me your thoughts about our enterprise. Have you given it any thought?"

"Jesus, I certainly have. Yes, we will debark in Malaga. Yes, I will accept a studio from you and whatever surveillance person or toy you devise to keep me in the neighborhood and, yes, I will begin to paint again and, yes, you will recover your masterpiece and it will all be yours again."

He nods.

"Malaga is a marvelous starting point for you—mountains, sea, fresh winds from the Atlantic through the Straits of Gibraltar. I think you will love it. I will ensure your namelessness, your *ausencia*, a Spanish word you will learn to cherish. I imagine that after a month or so, you might be able to find yourself a country estate, a hacienda where you can be left alone to continue your life's work. Can you agree to that?"

"Of course, Santo, I've heard nothing but good things about Spain—The Inquisition, Guernica, death in the afternoon, expelling the Jews. Nothing recent. This will be perfect. What you have told me sounds intriguing. I know Anna will agree."

It seems so simple a plan; genius, he thinks. I could not start painting again without risking a jail sentence. Such an easy way out, to this man's blurred vision, I will become his indentured artist-in-residence, as if he imagined that painting on the scale I once painted is done by merely wetting a brush, that it has no consequences, that I would simply issue a painting to him each month in exchange for his silence and half of the acquisition fees.

"While you're in Malaga that first month, it will be a great honor, of course, if you would create a small painting for Bet and me."

He has this idyllic picture of our lives intertwined in Spain. He and Bet living in an 18th century palace visiting their court jester hard at work in his studio. In exchange for his silence he feels it is his right to own me. In the afternoons, wearing white, he would visit my studio, which would also be white with high windows, be seated in an armchair near a window with white billowing curtains, and be holding a glass of sweet vermouth with ice as I paint another interesting picture for him.

"You don't want to do that," I say. "Watch me paint. When I paint things happen to me, I'm barely aware of them. I tremble, of course. I even convulse, I hurt. It's ugly. The sun is my source. I feel it enter me. It controls me. I pass through my paintings sometimes. I find myself unconscious behind a painting. On the other side of it against the wall. You understand? I've passed clean through it. So when you feel that you enter one of my paintings, I have been there first. What comes out of the painting is what has gone into it."

"That's fantastic. There were rumors, but no one ever knows, of course."

"I don't paint from ulteriors. Ideas, fashion, both are my enemies. Ideas are cheap. Fashion is what it says it is."

He is quite impressed. I can see that he feels he is seated close to genius. He says, "I am only a watcher, I do nothing but marvel at the creative ones. I am humbled."

"Artists are court jesters and humility is the hiding place of ego-maniacs."

"Please be nice. It can be a wonderful arrangement."

I've been caught. The man is just like the others—Anasor and de Haen. He wants me to paint for him, this time in Spain. House arrest. I can't, of course. This is serious. I don't know what's next. I've always found power in the inexact, the lie without edges. The strongest forces are the ones I can't or don't imagine and there is so much I don't understand, so much I don't want to understand, but the strength of faith, that's all I find to be unlimiting.

I have you, Savoia. I am infinite. If I feel something, I believe it. My feelings never lie. The scarcest thing is what was once called human nature. It all sounds like crap doesn't it, even when I hear myself say it but I believe it.

"But of course it would be impossible!" Savoia says later in our stateroom. "I know it would be, Simon. You of all people can't just pretend to paint pictures, you would need to involve yourself with your forces, regain the place you had, the excruciating wrench to your mind, and it would ruin you, my darling, just as you were ruined when I found you that day in the park."

After dinner, Santo Pietro takes me to the bar.

"Selfishness is the source of all great power. You must begin with yourself before you serve others. It is the origin of good in every-one and isn't good simply a transfer of that power?"

"In my great sedation of my art I was naturally selfish."

"Is it true that we must be bad before we are good?"

"Yes, but my loneliness was overpowering. Loneliness is a well source, too."

"True."

"As I say, Santo. I am tired of the world and me living in it. I wake up soiled from stories that have been written while I have been sleeping, written by my fellow man who never sleeps, never stops devising fresh ways to sicken me."

"Jonathan, I read somewhere that you are without resources, is that true?"

"You mean money?"

"I dislike embarrassing you."

"Money embarrasses you, not me."

"But do you have any?"

"I don't remember."

"Will you please accept an advance payment on our arrangement?"

I shrug. I perform embarrassment. "You don't have to give me any money."

"I do if I want to sleep tonight." He reaches into his inside jacket pocket, hands me a sealed envelope. This has only been an exercise. I have already been bought, or leased for the week.

Later in our stateroom, I open the envelope. Five thousand in francs, five thousand in pesetas, five thousand in dollars. A useful gift if only I had a plan. That night in bed I tell Savoia the conversation I had with Santo Pietro.

"We have to get off the ship."

"In Marseille?"

"I think he'll cover that. We'll be well-watched now that I know he knows. He'll be hanging around me, probably at bars and cafés, and Bet will be watching you."

"I'll tell him you're going to go shopping for a few delicacies and wine. Now listen, when we dock, I want you to go ashore on your own. Bet may follow you. You'll have three hours before we sail. So take all these francs that Santo just gave me and buy a canvas beach bag, a big tourist bag. Take it to a grocery store and fill it with fruits, get a baguette, get some Camembert, caviar if you see any, prosciutto, butter and be sure Bet sees you buying all this stuff. Then go to a wine merchant, buy a few bottles, whatever it takes to fill the bag. Then go and buy a hat or something. Get rid of Bet. The ship's surgeon told me there's a marine supply store on the main street, rue la Canebiere. It's called 'Jacques Cousteau's' and I hope they sell life rafts. Get one. Folded up the raft is small and should fit in your beach bag. Then leave your food and wine there. Tell them you husband will be picking it up later. We should dock there at eleven tomorrow morning and will get away by two."

February 5, 1964

We are both nervous about the plan and awake too early. On deck, I hold a cup of Santo's best coffee and think about betrayal —what it means to me? But it means nothing. It is only my reaction to his blackmail.

The day suddenly bright. Even the omelet is good. Marseille is perfect seen at a distance from the deck, the harbor with the mountains rising behind it, its small islands scattered before it. We dock easily in a heavily commercial area but just beyond, I can see the *Vieux Port,* the old harbor full of yachts and fishing boats and, for an instant, I wish we were among them, outward bound

Marseille's Old Harbor. Leafy buds have appeared overhead along rue la Canebiere, the main boulevard. As I thought he would, Santo does not let me out of his sight.

When I spot Santo across the main boulevard, watching me from a wicker chair in front of a café, I wave him over to join me at my café. I know he has been following me everywhere I've gone and, of course, I have done nothing extraordinary—a visit to the seafaring museum and picking up a bag Savoia left for me at Jacques Cousteau's.

"Protecting your investment?" I say to him when he's crossed the boulevard.

Santo looks embarrassed, he has no sense of humor. But, of course, he was protecting his investment.

"They are serving buffet lunch on deck today. A pleasant custom, isn't it, leaving a harbor during repast."

"Let us have an aperitif. We have time,"

In the box marked *Veuve Clicquot* between my feet, I'm carrying a steel bottle of compressed air. Santo sees the bag, remarks on it. "Excellent," he says, "my favorite."

"Anna's birthday," I say too quickly.

I order Vermouth, Santo orders Pernod.

"When we all get settled in Malaga," he says, "I look forward to watching you paint in the afternoons."

The idyllic picture of our lives intertwined.

"I'll see you at lunch, Santo. We're sailing at two," I say, as if he didn't know.

In the stateroom a few minutes before two, Savoia arrives with her beach bag. The life raft is folded in a 15" square and weighs ten pounds.

"No problem picking up the box I left at Cousteau's?"

"None."

"I'm proud of you."

"It's not my first time out."

I drop the box marked *Veuve Clicquot* on the bunk, another ten pounds.

"An excellent wine," she says and pulls out the steel bottle of compressed air. The instructions are written in German, *Achtung! Blah blah blah.*

"Achtung!"

"What's *achtung?*"

"It means 'look out'. I know a little German."

"We pop this at night, leaving Algiers, long before Malaga."

"Of course, darling, I know."

With three blasts of the funnel fog horn, the ship drops her dock-lines precisely at 2:00 p.m., slides away from the dock. and gets underway.

After the buffet lunch on deck, Savoia and I go below and lose the afternoon in our bunks. In our ten by twelve foot stateroom, the ship's turbines are suddenly everywhere, the bulkheads and the ceiling vibrate, the bathroom glasses trill. The effect of being drunk comes easily to me on small steamers. When we wake, there is an hour left before dinner.

After dinner, we all smoke cigars. Even Savoia tries one. We talk about our future together in Malaga, no details. Santo Pietro is loud; his life will have meaning. He is to give my life meaning. He's proud of his ability to earn a fortune simply by pointing his finger at another's creations and betting on them. He invests, cultivates. Distinguished greed, absolutely normal. Just one more member of the herd of bankers, brokers, agents, who are far more respectable than the soiled, crazy artists they do so admire.

Santo Pietro is clearly excited about our arrangement in Spain. He has no idea who I am and he will never find out what I want and don't want. He simply assumes we want the same thing.

I don't want anything. I have had such success and disguised fame. The vestiges appalled me. There is nothing I want, nothing I see for sale.

Bet smokes her cigar like a man, with finesse, her eyes lightly crossed like a Siamese cat's. She is quite beautiful in an international magazine way, her hair stuck flat as syrup to her temples, teeth wide, sullen eyes, bored eyebrows. She smiles suddenly as it suits her, she is young, old, middle aged—I cannot guess. It is all so clever.

We will arrive in Algiers the day after tomorrow. For the next fifty-two hours, we will be together at sea.

There is one class of passenger on board the *Ave Maria*, as there always is on small ships. On board are travelers who do not like to fly, who are in no hurry. She is by no means a cruise ship, there is no feigned grandeur. It is the boiled fish and chicken. After dinner, we amuse ourselves. Some play cards, backgammon, or a game known as Wari. With the help of a Greek mandolin player and an Italian saxophonist, we even dance.

For these two nights after dinner the other American passenger, a large woman who wears capes, has tap-danced for us. She boarded the ship in Marseille en route to Tangiers. She is able to tap dance to the mandolin and saxophone. After a while of this, the two musicians earnestly try to stump her. They play marches, hymns like Ave Maria. They even play their version of the American national anthem, she tap dances to that. Nothing can stop her. Her name is Celia, a smaller woman's name. If you squint, she resembles a circus animal off her chain. Then there is the man from Turino who sings opera. He is known as The Man Who Sings, but he is getting off in Algiers.

February 6, 1964

We are in Algiers. We docked this morning. This is the night. We sail at eleven. Savoia and I are on deck before dinner. It's a calm night, chilly, cloudless, a nearly full moon.

"Look around," I tell Savoia, "I want to get away as we're pulling out of the harbor at half speed. We need to be alone on deck."

But they don't let us be until midnight, all that singing, drinking Cognac, smoking cigars. Bet too. And there's that damned Celia.

"As soon after dinner as possible, we go over the side back there." I point aft under a steel weather shelter.

I locate where the rope ladder is stored. I remember seeing a crewman putting it in a locker full of gear, on deck. There it is. Locked. It is a large, bronze padlock. I cannot pick it. I can't bribe a crewman, either, this is too important. The bribed have a way of confessing later for the second payoff. I need to open it. I find a crew member. There are so few we know them by name. He is Horatio, a very deliberate thinker, a hummer of operas. "Horatio," I say to him. *"Buona notte."*

He turns with a wave, says, *"Buona notte, Signori."*

I explain to Horatio that I have a question to ask him, that it is my wife's birthday and I would like to surprise her on deck with a bottle of champagne. It is all very uncomplicated, I tell him,

"My wife and I will be standing over there by the rail at midnight. I will say to her 'Happy Birthday, darling' and then walk over here, open this locker and bring out my bottle of champagne and two glasses. After that, I will lock this lock and you have no need to worry, Horatio."

Horatio is nodding, he seems on the verge of tears.

"It is a very small romantic gesture I contemplate and here is 100,000 lira to ease your mind."

Horatio unlocks the padlock and leaves it unlocked.

I go below and bring up the box marked 'Veuve Clicquot' and the life-raft and stuff them in the locker. I close the lock without clicking it. Back in the cabin we are definitely not showing nervousness.

"We leave Algiers at eleven. We need perfect timing. It's a calm night, a big moon. The moment the deck is free of people, I'll drop the rope ladder over the stern. I'll connect the bottle to the raft then I'll climb halfway down and wait for you to lower the raft to me. I'll pop the air bottle and then tie the raft off to the ladder. You'll hand me down the two bags, the painting and the Noxzema box then climb down and get in. I'll get in last and cut them free. That's it. We'll paddle ashore and we ought to get back into Algiers and be registered at the Hotel Cadiz an hour later. Two at the most."

"They'll miss us at breakfast."

"And we'll miss them."

After dinner, we excuse ourselves from Bet and Santo, Celia, The Man Who Sings, a priest from Copenhagen who has promised us a magic show and the rest of the group that gather in the bar for four hours of drinking and smoking cigars.

It is time. At the stroke of eleven, when the captain has made three blasts and dropped the ship's lines, we are underway. We pop into the bar say goodnight to let Santo know that all's well and we're still on board.

We walk on the deck. I check the locker. All's well. We wait under the steel weather shelter aft. In five minutes there is no one left on deck. I open the locker and drag the rope ladder to the after rail.

The ship's churning wake seems too dangerous a place to drop the life-raft, but slightly forward it is quite smooth. I set the folded raft by the rail then go below to help Savoia with the bags.

"Did you go to the bathroom? You never know."

"I couldn't," she says. The first admission of nerves.

"I'm excited, too."

On deck it is calm; we are still alone. The ship is slowly pulling away not yet past the harbor lights. It seems so simple now. All we need to do is drop the raft and paddle back ashore.

In sudden fury, rain spanks the deck, the lifeboats, the railings. The moon vanishes, the deck is black, we wait sheltered, we watch the shore lights dwindle. It is too black. It is a rain squall and we cannot see its end. We cannot launch the raft in this weather.

"Not yet," I say.

In the spanking rain the invisible harbor that was so bright moments ago drops out of sight behind us. We realize we could never have made it back to shore. I stow the rope ladder back in its locker. We take our bags below again.

Back in our cabin, we are rain-soaked. I start unpacking.

"We've got a problem, Simon."

"Oh, really?"

"We've got to think. How many hours to Malaga?"

"It looks like it's about 400-miles."

"What time are we due in?"

"Tomorrow night."

"Let's find out exactly."

I read the timetable. Another 30 hours at sea crossing the Mediterranean. Due in at five a.m., Malaga, but that could be hours off.

"Hmmmmmmm," she says.

"What do you want to do, my navigator?"

"We can't launch in the middle of the Mediterranean."

"No."

"So we have to do it in sight of Malaga, when we can see the lights. If the wind direction is good and the sea's calm, we'll have an easy time of it."

"Let's not paddle ashore off Malaga. But we'll be in Spain. I don't think we're expected. Let's make up a yachting accident story."

"Too risky. Let's find out our course, find out where the captain wants to cross to Spain. You never know, we could be running along the Algerian coast all day and all night tomorrow, as far as Morocco."

"I've always wanted to see Morocco."

"Maybe we shall. Let me bring it up casually to the captain and see what he says."

CHAPTER 38

The Raft: February 7, 1964

୨ଏ୫

In the morning, we wake to the warm smell of the desert. We are running along the North African shore a mile or two out.

Savoia visits the captain on the bridge, asks him his course. She is a tourist. He tells her he will keep to the coast; he tells her everything with his hands gesturing everywhere.

The captain says the currents along North Africa are favorable. He always uses them, so we'll be in sight of land all day tomorrow. He always goes as far as Mellila, a point of land jutting off Morocco. The current turns northward there.

"It's called The Point of the Three Forks. He showed it to me on the chart. From that point, we are no longer in the Mediterranean. The waters between Morocco and Spain are called the Alboran Sea."

"Never knew that."

"Well, there you are."

All day we run along the Algerian shore feeling the new rush, squinting at villages, beached fishing boats, sometimes a car, little else. Now it is past midnight, the ship is asleep, our bags are on deck, everything is ready. We have been watching the shore lights; there are so few now. We see The Point of the Three Forks lying ahead. We are still a mile offshore. The ship is moving at its service speed, about twelves knots.

Everything is just right, the sea, the sky—clear and calm. There's a good moon. Still it will be risky.

I climb down first as far as the lowest rung, eight feet below the main deck. I cling to the ladder. It is wide. I am secure.

Savoia hands down the life-raft with the steel bottle attached. The label on the bottle is readable in the moonlight. *Achtung!* With a loud *PSSSS!* the bottle explodes its air into the raft. Once it is fully inflated, I drop the raft right side up into the wake of the *Ave Maria*. It skips along behind the ship on a line tied off to the ladder. It looks too light. "Hand me the bags," I call up to Savoia.

She hands them down one by one, then the Noxzema carton and then her portrait. I set them carefully onto the raft. Savoia climbs down and settles beside them. I drop in beside her and steady myself, then I cut the line.

With a whoosh of water from the abrupt change of speed, we are alone, bobbing in the *Ave Maria's* stern wake, her lights pulling away from us as she turns toward Spain.

In those moments, those first strange moments, we look shore-ward. We can clearly see the lights of Mellila inside the point. Morocco seems close but I know we have several miles to paddle. I hope they don't find the rope I cut too soon. If they do, they might add it all up—the stop at Marseille, the carton of cham-pagne.

We should have most of tomorrow morning before we are missed on board the *Ave Maria*. But the Reblochons, Santo Pietro and Bet, will likely begin their search for us immediately after that. We can see the lights of Mellila on the Moroccan coast. A car goes by once in a while. There are two folding wooden paddles stowed on the raft. I take one and start to paddle. The raft is round and responds by turning clockwise. I ask Savoia to paddle on the opposite side. Our progress toward the coast seems good, but after a while I realize that the lights are not growing larger. Our raft is moving past the coast and we are caught in a current. After a while, we stop paddling.

There are no more shore lights. We begin paddling again off and on for three exhausting hours, if only to stay warm. It will be dawn soon; I can see the sable haze above the North African coast. With the sun, a breeze comes up, rippling the water around us, sending us west along the coast.

Savoia is not meant to be here, nor am I. We are meant to be reg-istered in a hotel in Mellila asleep in bed now. We are so close to the water. I never realized that on deck aboard that small steamer we were eight or ten feet above the sea. Now we are on it. It is six-thirty and the clouds are hanging low in the east, becoming red. By seven, the sun reveals itself. I feel the temperature rise.

"I'd like to see a map," I say.

"What would a map do? We're at sea, Simon."

"It would give me a sense of belonging."

"Actually, it's a chart, not a map."

"It's a chart, it's a chart! I'd like to see a chart, okay? You're a professional navigator; you might contribute some ideas."

"We have no control over where we're going, Simon, we're in a current sending us west at about two miles an hour. We're heading toward Gibraltar. So theoretically, we could get pushed through the Straits of Gibraltar."

"Theoretically, we shouldn't be here; theoretically, we should be asleep in a hotel."

"Theoretically, we could be picked up by the *Ave Maria* which is heading for Tangier the day after tomorrow."

"Is that possible? If we spot her, what should we do?"

"Wave."

"How wide are the Straits?"

"Not too wide."

"How 'not too wide'? A couple of miles?"

"I think about ten miles."

"There must be a strong current there, the whole Atlantic pushing its way through."

"So what have we learned?" Savoia asks with a professorial air. "That the current is pushing us west like a rubber duck in a bathtub through a narrow opening while the Atlantic Ocean will be pushing us in the opposite direction."

I look around our raft. There are three pockets. In the first pocket I find a first aid kit, sea-sick pills, a steel signal mirror with sight, a flashlight, a silver mylar blanket, and an instruction booklet. In the second pocket are fishing line, hooks, a few lures, a small knife, glue, boat patches, six flares, and a folded, fiery red-orange Dacron bailing bucket. In the third pocket, I find food sealed in clear plastic, twenty-four heavy little cubes. There are two dozen silver envelopes of water, four ounces each. I feel a bolt of fear. Where's the toilet? Where's the stove?

The booklet is in German, titled *Überleben auf See.* It all seems very official—line drawings showing how to remove fishhooks from fingers, what fish to avoid eating, how to retrieve a man overboard, and how to right a capsized raft.

"What is *zukunft?*" I ask Savoia

"I think it means 'future'."

I hand her the book. She reads through it quickly.

"It says, 'Plan your future. Talk about when, not if, you'll be rescued. Be a survivor, not a victim. Accept your situation don't give in to it'."

"That's exactly what I'm doing, but I've made a terrible mistake forcing us into this situation."

"Malaga would have been worse, Simon." She reassures me.

"What do you think they're doing now? The Reblochons."

"They're probably still asleep. It isn't even seven. They won't see us at breakfast, but that doesn't mean anything."

"Coffee, please ... They won't start to miss us until lunch, which is six hours from now. That'll be an amazing moment; I really hate to miss it."

For breakfast, we tear the clear plastic wrapper away from two little blocks of food. They look like chocolate and taste like sawdust. Though they're only two inches square, mine takes me half-an hour to chew and swallow, and only with the help of water.

And so we spend the whole day at sea, in sight of land. We read the booklet intermittently. The sea's been calm, the sun in and out. There have been no boats, no planes. Africa is low, a dust cloud on the horizon. The shore is now probably ten miles away from us. I can't gauge our speed. Savoia says it must be two knots or slightly more. For dinner, we chew another sawdust biscuit and drink another four ounce envelope of water. Now we each have ten biscuits left. Savoia has been great. Much more of a survivor than I am. She conserves her strength, her feelings.

At sundown, the sea kicks us around for awhile. Tonight, I feel close to the night, to Savoia. We have been so rarely apart, I feel myself healing. She may be asleep, finally. I feel so sorry for her. I wonder if she's here against her wishes. Life with me will always be some form of hell. Here we are adrift at sea, and I may be putting her through the hellish business of dying all over again. But even if she's not here against her wishes, I know that the day I am well again, well enough in her mind, she will leave me. She is my creation and her presence depends upon the strength of my madness. I drew her back to me and she will stay with me until my trembling stops and my life secures itself to truths rather than ephemera.

February 9, 1964

I couldn't sleep but have been able to doze while sitting up. I wake Savoia. For breakfast, we each eat cube number three, and break out another packet of water to help wash it down.

Savoia decides that the red-orange bucket will be our toilet.

I'm careful not to watch her defecate. A fuzzy idea of romance, she says, but neither does she watch me.

Midday. Sun, cool breeze, choppy water.

"You are becoming bearded again," she says. She sounds tired.

For the past hour I have been hearing the *Carmina Burana* over and over in my mind. At first I had no idea what it was, but then I recognized the familiar chorus.

Savoia is reading the booklet again. It suggests we think of our loved ones. "You're the only one I love and you're here, Simon, so I'll think about you."

"No one else?"

"Not as far as I know. Isn't that amazing, after all these years, no one to send a funny card to? Who would you write to?"

"Mohandas Gandhi. I'd write, 'Mohandas, you aren't missing anything'."

Savoia knows I can barely afford these thoughts.

"Do you know what *streiten* is?"

"No."

"Quarrel. It says we most certainly will quarrel."

"Will we?"

"It says *vorsitch!* which means to watch out for that."

"Do you think we will?"

"Yes."

"What are you thinking now?"

"Nothing."

"Thirsty?"

"Yes."

"Drink?"

"I can't."

"It says that you will experience *der halluzination.*"

"That's all I do."

"Not right away."

"Well, just now I was riding on the Paris metro with Mohandas Gandhi."

"What were you talking about?"

"You won't believe it—parking violations."

Savoia wakes me around midnight. I stand the second watch tonight. I look for the shore, but there is nothing to see under the quarter moon.

Savoia wakes. "What's going on?" she asks grogily.

"The same ... we're moving west. I can sort of tell by that light on shore, see it?"

"I do. It could be a fire on a beach."

She's alert but exhausted.

"You want anything?" she asks.

"I better not." If I open a water envelope, I have to finish it. The entire four ounces.

"Well, I've got to lie down." We touch fingers.

I have the flashlight in one pocket to use as a signal, a flare in the other. The ocean is black, after an hour, my eyes close. I'm afraid that if I fall asleep sitting up on the side of the raft I may topple backward overboard. Covering most of the flashlight's beam with my hand, I watch Savoia in the dimness. I watch her sleeping under the mylar blanket. She is here because of me. Because I could not be without her. It is a triumph of selfishness. Her eyes are closed, of course, her mouth calm. Her hair is darker close to her head in twists and curlicues. She is serene, her features are clear, they will age well forever. I crawl under the blanket beside her. The idea of sex? What about survival? How did sex come aboard our raft? It came aboard by itself.

Savoia wakes. She smells of the sea, its dampness, of her own oils and in a few moments, of her nether world. It is a deep, thrilling smell.

Hours later, the moon has set. I cannot read my watch. I raise my head to look across the horizon. The haze of shore in the distance, a fixed light twinkles, the breath of Africa is still dry though it has crossed miles of water. I could live this way a while longer. I'm not frightened, even though I am in a life raft moving with the tide along the Moroccan coast. As long as I'm in sight of land I feel protected. We are land creatures.

Later, when she's lying awake, I ask her about the ferocity of the plane crash. She describes it fully to me. She is whispering, something from her nightmares tells it so well—the flash of sounds and lights she's felt so many times. I'm surprised. Without her telling me, I visualized the details, except for one. She describes the din in the main cabin during the final prolonged seconds when the passengers all knew they were going to die, and she describes the rising concert of moans, screams, groans, cries, words, names, prayers, curses, commands, laments, until they became a single chant. She can still clearly hear the chant sung by a choir of doomed passengers' voices.

Then the crash itself.

"Did you ever want to have a baby?" I ask her.

Silence.

We sleep.

CHAPTER 39

The Dog: February 10, 1964

The next thing I know, I'm awake. I am in a raft and a dog is barking. Land! We must be close to shore, close enough to hear the land's sounds. I sit up. Savoia stirs.

"Did you hear a dog?"

"Yes," she says, half asleep, "You really should have let it out before going to sleep, Simon."

"I'm not imagining it, Savoia."

I hear the drumbling of a diesel engine. In the distance I see a red dot. It is moving quickly just above the water line, I can just make out a shape, a dim glow. A fishing boat is passing us a quarter-mile away. The dog barks again, the soft woofing sound of a fisherman's dog that barks at strangers as it does at on land. Does the dog smells us? It is a friendly bark, not a warning bark. I try to whistle but I cannot; my lips are dry.

I dig out a flare, strike it and hold it at arm's length. It hisses, then fizzles out. I only have one flare out; the others are stowed. I reach for the flashlight, get to my feet and wave it. Savoia holds onto my legs. I could fall overboard. I can no longer see the red light, only the fishing boat's white stern light. I wave the flashlight again and call out, but the boat has passed. The fishermen must be asleep in their bunks, the helmsman staring ahead. Only the dog is aware of us out in the black ocean. I plunge into a sleepless depression.

It is the morning of the third day. Africa is no smaller.

"What is *beten?*" I ask Savoia.

"'Pray'."

"It says to pray."

"You first."

"You go ahead."

"I don't feel like it."

"What is *urin?*"

"What do you think?"

"It says here, 'don't drink your urine'."

"Did you want to?"

"Not this morning. What about mine?"

"It isn't a joke book, Simon. Why is it all so funny to you?"

"Because this is the second time you've been cast adrift on my behalf in one week. Isn't that funny?"

"Yes, sort of. You don't think it's serious?"

"But we're living out a cartoon. We've jumped into a rubber boat in an ocean we know nothing about, risking our lives to avoid certain death on shore."

Tonight, Savoia stands watch until midnight, then wakes me for the watch until dawn. She's exhausted, says only, "Goodnight."

I'm groggy, my stomach shrieks for food. I sit on the raft's side-holding onto a fishing line. Can fish see in the dark?

It is a dry summer night. Perfect. We are in a bedroom, We have come from somewhere—a party? It is a clean room, a skylight over the bed where the big moon pokes holes through webbed clouds lighting the room—strong lines, a wide-curtained bed. Savoia is kneeling on the mattress, still wearing her shoes, her dress halfway around her, blouse torn open, lips smeared. I am half-dressed. She is moving her hands up and down my body, soothing me, stroking me. "Now," she says, "now!" I obey. I come freely, fluidly, fully, well, out and up. For moments, I am blind. I reach to pull her down to me, she's not there beside me. She's not in the room.

The stars pierce my vision with their incredible complications, unimaginable ragings, and tonight they seem dreadfully real. I feel dwarfed by their unspeakable magnitude. They make me feel that death and transfiguration, though highly regarded in my neighborhood, will go unnoticed elsewhere; that death and transfiguration carry about as much mystery in the universe as the echo in my mind of the barking dog. The single being that knows we exisit.

Lights ahead. Are they real? It must be Gibraltar. We have been gone 48-hours, drifting west. We take turns standing watch.

Within an hour, the land is clearly lit on both shores. Car head-lights, street lamps. We are so close, it is so narrow, we will be seen and rescued now. It is four in the morning. I can hear a car's horn. I set off a flare and hold it high until it burns out. There is no response. Four flares left.

It takes two hours for us to pass through the Straits. We are now in the Atlantic Ocean. The open ocean. The waves have become large swells but there are no dangerous crests, no breaking waves. And now it is a different story. I am becoming very frightened, as the shore lights drop behind the horizon. We have passed through the Straits of Gibraltar unseen.

The dawn is coming; it is almost here. Preparations are being made low in the sky. From its dullness slowly comes hope. It is quite an occasion, this dawn, a beautiful ceremony even when adrift at sea in a small life raft.

February 11, 1964

Lo! The sun! We are at the source of the day, I have never seen it so. Here the day begins the way a river begins from a long way off. We are surrounded by a lightening sky. It is everywhere. When I stand, the horizon is lower than me. The day has begun below my shoulders. There is nowhere else to look, it is all day, it is all I know. Savoia sleeps on her side, curled, knees to nose.

The sea is kind this morning. It is the sea's tendencies that I dread. But this morning I feel no fear, but then, I know nothing of this life. I have never been to sea.

It will be our first day without the sight of land. For three days we have woken up to Africa a few miles away. Here there is noth-ing. It is borderless, the sea's domain. Only when the sea is near to land are there property lines, fishing rights, oil rights. Limits are landsmen's concerns.

We are still being sent west on a light breeze. We have been cut loose from the Iberian Peninsula and Africa, from Spain and Morocco. We are on the course Christopher Columbus took five hundred years ago on his first voyage west.

A calm morning, another reprieve. I do not think about death this morning; it is the night that brings me terror at sea. With day, we will be visible. It will be a bright, clear morning. Savoia's eyes are closed. She is deathly tired, or is she afraid to open them? Sailors, who for years shipped out, came to terms with dawns at sea. They knew everything there was to know about the rising of the sun in all weather. They prayed on deck. They feared the sea, its moods, but they feared the wind above the sea more, and they feared the God behind the wind who controled all. Savoia and I are not sailors. We are prisoners of the wind, without control. If there is a current moving us, I cannot feel it. We have no ability to alter this course. We go where the wind and sea take us.

We are being carried further and further out to sea, away from the mainland. I'm worried. I am being dishonest with Savoia. I have never lied to her, what would be the point? My casual bravery is a lie, my cool front, an act. I count the water envelopes again, the squares of dog biscuits. We have two days on extreme rations remaining.

With the sun comes warmth. Open sores swell on my hips and buttocks. I move continuously, but I can never be comfortable. My trousers are damp. I stand. I drop them, mooning the sun, feeling the sun's rays warming my sores. Someone is watching me. I feel eyes on my back. I turn. I'm being watched! By the shoe-button eyes of a seagull perched silently in the air, wings taut, wide, an arm's length away. He has been studying me. He has little fear. He rises slightly on the breeze, lowers himself, inspecting me. If I could catch him, I would wring his neck. This morning, I cannot imagine eating him, seeing the contents of his stomach spread out on the floor of the raft. Maybe tomorrow. Thinking about eating him makes me thirsty. The seagull has summed me up, he glides away without raising a wing. Another day at sea. He has nothing better to do. What was it? A naked man standing in a life-raft. Has he ever seen one before? In the distance, but only a mile off, a swarm of gulls hovers.

It is indeed a halcyon day, the name given to the seagulls that were fabled to nest on the sea's surface, calming its waves. And there they are, a mile away, Halcyon Gulls on the water—some floating in the air over a school of fish, some resting on the sea's surface.

I hear Ralph Vaughan Williams' Fifth Symphony and then The

Lark, last night in the dark, it was Mahler's Tenth. For years, all day, every day, I painted to symphonies—Mahler's Tenth, what there is of it, composed when he knew he was dying, leaving it unfinished. My friends in art, Mahler, Vaughan Williams. I required music. Music nurtured me. Music was my safe harbor, my empire. There are no frauds in deep music the way there are frauds thriving in art. Deep music will not tolerate fakery.

The fish-line tightens. Something pale, chartreuse, lurks just beneath the surface of the water. The fluorescent lure that I dropped over the side earlier tricked a fish into believing it was edible, and the fish struck it. I pull it aboard. It is beautiful. It struggles for life briefly, flips, then lies still. I am dazed. It dawns on me that I have caught a fish! I have never seen anything as wondrous. It is a foot long. It has reddish-pink scales, wide eyes, the lips of a movie star.

Savoia wakes.

"Fish for breakfast!" I announce.

"Simon you think of everything." She blows me a kiss.

When I'm sure the fish is dead, I cut it lengthwise into strips. I cannot separate it from its skin. I dry the strips in rows along the inflated wall of the life-raft.

The sun already feels warmer. Its heat builds. In an hour, the strips are not fully-cooked but they are no longer raw. We open a silver envelope of water. It is a scrumptious meal—chewy, powerful, filling. I do not miss parsley, lemon, capers, wine. It is superb.

"Compliments to the chef. Do we have dental floss?" she asks. She is smiling.

"No." I answer.

The only edge I can think of is a thin-edged treasury note, they are all new. I open the Noxzema carton, pull out a five-hundred dollar bill, William McKinley, grim jawed. Savoia flosses her teeth with McKinley looking on upset, as if he smelled intestinal gas. I feel privileged knowing that there are still two or three million dollars in crisp treasury notes, tied inside the carton. More than enough for our dream villa. But first we need to touch land.

We are sticky otters. Savoia's hair has tightened into tiny springs.

Her hands are red and bruised, her face scored by weather. Yet she remains beautiful.

"My hair," she says, "is in nails, I look as if I have rusted."

The salt has crusted on my hands. We seem to be aging like a pair of cheap gloves. I have sores on my buttocks. There is no way to wash, Savoia holds my belt as I lean down into the ocean to splash sea water on my face and hands. I must stand. I need to rinse my sores with fresh water. I want to open an envelope and pour the entire four ounces over my buttocks. But there are five envelopes left. Savoia asks if I would mind if she took a sip of fresh water and held it in her mouth, and, with her tongue, spread the water gently on each sore. It is an outrageous request because it will bring salt into her mouth.

I say, "No," then I say, "Yes, please."

I stand, my trousers down. With an ounce of fresh water in her mouth, Savoia licks my sores. We have the ultimate in privacy—we are surrounded by nothing but ocean. Our sea gull returns to inspect this, another unusual sight for him to absorb—a man standing half-naked in a life-raft, with a woman kneeling behind him, licking his buttocks. The seagull cannot get enough of us.

It is twilight. The sun is down. I'm not so sure about tonight, what position to sleep in? My itching went away for awhile but has now returned to wild pain. It is impossible to lie still. There is no relief. There is no water to spare for Savoia to cure my sore with her tongue. I kneel bent over the curve of the raft, my face close to the water. The sun is setting in a strange, perfect, fiery ball. I see it as a sun angry to be setting.

We say, "Goodnight." Savoia pulls the mylar blanket over us and curls beneath it trembling. I warm her with my body as best I can. When I stand again, it is late. I imagine maybe nine or ten.

After a while it comes to me that I am looking at a light. It may be a low star rising on the horizon to what must be the north. That's where the moon rises. I watch the light until my eyes blur. It disappears.

The little German survival book says, "You will see things, you will hallucinate. But you must not say to yourself, IF you are rescued; it must be WHEN you are rescued."

I don't know what direction I am looking in. The raft has turned. I may be staring west. In the glowering sky, the east has turned black. It seems to be readying for a storm. Is that the evening star?

CHAPTER 40

The Brothers Three: February 12, 1964

⋙⋘

There it is again! The light is back. Is it north or south? I say nothing. Let her sleep through this light business. It will be unfair for her to go through this again. Is it a star? The light is constant. Of course it is. A low star barely twinkling. I don't say a word to Savoia. Suddenly the light is green, there are no green stars.

"Savoia look!" She wakes. "Tell me, that green spot, is that a light?"

"Yes!" is all she whispers.

I reach into the pocket of the raft for our third flare. I hold it above my head and pull. Up it goes a fiery pink rocket, swirling high, cheap lighting, its tiny parachute opens, it drops toward the water. The pink flare hisses out a hundred feet away, then in the dark, the green light seems closer. We wait. We don't speak. We wait. The light vanishes. The light reappears. Now it is red. Now it is red and green.

"Those are running lights," Savoia says, "red and green."

It is much closer now. A white light, a sword of light, is switched on. I can see small windows. I can see a wheelhouse. Her hull. I can make out her lines, see her bow. I can make out her name, *Los Hermanos Tres.* She needs paint. She is solid, she must be easily fifty feet long. The engines are cut. In the silence, I hear calm conversation above me on the deck in Spanish. In the glow of the deck light, I can see drying nets hanging on a small crane, everywhere she smells of fresh fish. Strong crabbers' hands haul us up on board, arms tough as hemp. These are bearded men. There seem to be four all told. We have been saved by a fishing boat called *Los Hermanos Tres.* After four days, we are full of cramps. Savoia is sleepy but she seems well, better than me. My sores are livid. The men stare at Savoia as if she were a saint emerged from the water, at me as if I were her dog.

On deck, we are given water. One of the men guesses that we are

English or Canadian. I can barely understand them. Savoia is barely conscious. To bring our raft aboard, to save it, one of the men lets the air out of it. It is too valuable to cast adrift. It may be of use in setting their nets.

Inside the wheelhouse the binnacle light glows. One of the men, the captain, opens a chart. He moves his finger along the northern coastline past Morocco, through the Straits of Gibraltar, to a point further west than I imagined. Then he points south to islands I have never seen before, taps them.

"Nuestro destino," he smiles and nods.

Another man with the breath of a codfish opens a dark hardwood cabinet and unwraps a brass cross, kisses it, sets it into a slot on the binnacle. He faces the cross and kneels. With his thumb he makes a small sign on his face from his forehead to his lips, crosses himself. He brings out white ropes. Each man ties one around his waist. The fishing boat stands swaying on the sea. A candle is lit. There is no other light. The wheel is tied off. The four men kneel, one begins to hum softly then to chant. It is quite beautiful. They are radiant, shining. It is a religious moment. Are they praying for our salvation?

Savoia kneels with them, whispers to me, "They're saying Vespers."

I kneel beside her. I have no choice.

"I think these men are monks."

"The white ropes around their waists."

"We've been saved by monks. Simon."

I kneel and pray with them. It is a strange newness to me. I am an impostor. I feel defenseless, safe. We are with Benedictine monks.

"I didn't know monks fished."

"Monks do everything. They farm and isn't this farming?"

They seem lightheaded. The boat reeks of fish. They have fished Spain, Portugal and now, they are headed home. The course is toward the place where the sun has set but south of it. Anyhow, away from Spain. That's all that matters.

After prayers, when I stand, I look at the compass in the binnacle. Their course is south west. They are radiant. They have fulfilled a miracle. They have saved two Americans who sailed from Florida on a yacht that sank five days ago.

In the wheelhouse, a small table is pulled down. We eat fried anchovies and balls of bread so coarse that they must be cracked open. After dinner, I ask their destination.

"*Gomera*," one of them says, and smiles. It means nothing to me and I am too tired to find out. This monk reeks of tobacco and fish.

"Must you be bearded in your Benedictine order?" I ask him.

"No, I am Spanish," he says. He does not understand me.

Savoia touches his beard gently. He smiles.

Brother Slim clears our aluminum plates and spoons. He returns, with a specie of coffee in china mugs. One of the other brothers mixes chocolate powder in hot water.

I order a glass of Benedictine. They have heard of it. It is a joke the American is making. They laugh, nodding to each other. Savoia and I are nodding off to sleep, but there is no bunk for us. We were not expected.

Brother Capitan admires Savoia's bluestone ring, bought from the nine-year-old schoolgirl in Vent. We are man-and-wife in the eyes of the Benedictine order. Brother Chocolate brings out a box and slams it upside onto the small table we have eaten on, leaving a wall of dominoes stacked like bricks. They will play dominoes in the wheelhouse.

Savoia and I are led to the forward cabin. I can barely stand below the deck beams. There are three bunks with pipe frames. There are no sheets. The mattresses and pillows are amber and brown from use. There is a battery-powered light on the wall. We will share a bunk. We sleep in the warm bunk of whomever has gone on watch. Brother Grim shows us the toilet. Savoia has no use for it except to throw up. It is a calm sea and I open the portholes, clearing the smell of fish from the small cabin.

A splash of water wakes me. It is midnight. We are in a storm.

One of the brothers looks in on us, I don't know which one, makes sure that all is well.

The gale is on us. *Los Hermanos Tres* swivels southwest through the storm, spiraling over the waves, waddling. At times, caught

high, her hull half out of the water, I can hear her propeller fanning the wet air. We cling to our pipe bunk. Our little raft could
not have survived this night on the Atlantic. Below, in the forward cabin, two of the monks bed down close by in easy sleep,
snoring into the riding night. Brother Chocolate is standing
watch in the wheelhouse with Brother Capitan. Savoia and I hold
on to the pipes, whispering through the first hour of the storm,
among the fish-hold odors, the wet cabin odors, the mattress's
odors—odors we could not endure on land.

We are giddy to lie down together, to be alive, and like the two
sleepers close to us, we are part of a storm at sea. We do not seek
to escape from it. Every ten minutes, a wave will strike the bow
wrong, not angled, but flat, its weight measured against our
weight, making the sound of a canon. We are tossed and turned.
The brothers sleeping beside us do not stir. They have a solid hull
around them, well-founded. I feel it.

At the height of the storm, I hear the sound of voices singing
somewhere above us. Could it be a radio? There is no radio station playing music in a storm. Is it possible that the two monks
are singing in the wheelhouse? We listen. It is Latin. They are
singing a Gregorian chant, a solemn single line of melody without rhythm or counterpoint, Latin words drawn the full variety
of a single line yet nothing florid. We hear the clamor of the
storming wind, the crying of the mast, the water sluicing through
the scuppers, and Brother Chocolate and Brother Capitan in the
wheelhouse singing a Gregorian chant. On and on they go, no
subtle harmonies, but the Latin language so perfect to fit the
elongated syllables. It is not music in any sense of music that I
know, so uncomplicated it can be sung by anyone, chants set to
flight, amid the gale, medieval sounds. They are full of pleading.
There is age in them and great beauty.

"What an amazing thing it is that it is they who have saved us,"
Savoia says. "I'm so grateful."

"A miracle?" I say.

A splendor of medieval sounds carries us off to sleep, through the
roiling wind above the unfathomable sea. It is an act of inde-
scribable beauty. And so we fall asleep to dreams secured. In our
weakest night, we let ourselves feel saved.

Hunger wakes me. The storm has passed, the hull is level, the engines pound steadily. It is a clear night. The moon is reflected in a thousand images on the water. I catch flashes of Savoia sleeping beside me.

Through the porthole, I see the sky turning gray. I drop out of the bunk, climb a ladder up to the deck. Brother Capitan is in the wheelhouse. I tell him, as well as I can, how beautiful the singing was, how calming. Brother Capitan tells me that he, Brother Alejandro, and Brother Chocolate, Brother Abundio, were, indeed, rehearsing their matins and vespers. They are small men, the tallest is Brother Marco at five and a half feet. Brother Daniel, the broccoli-headed monk, who seems braindead, stands just above dwarf height.

Brother Alejandro has made a fish pudding for breakfast. It is a treat. Brother Marco says that if the sea stays the calm, and if the wind doesn't veer around, we should reach Gran Canaria in a day.

"Is that our destination?"

"No, it is where we sell our fish."

"It is a good life, isn't it?'

"Yes, he says. A good life." His eyes are deep set, magical.

On the second day, the wine. It is dark, heavy, solid, warm. It tastes marvelous and I wonder again how good it would taste in a restaurant.

I ask Brother Marco our final destination, after Gran Canaria.

"We go to our Monastery on Salve de Dios. That is where we live."

"Where is it?"

"North of Gran Canaria, not far west from Africa. An island of volcanoes. We find it quite beautiful, though no one else does."

"I believe that may be a good thing."

"Will you come as far with us?"

"If you wouldn't mind."

"Are not people somewhere worried about you?"

"No."

"Why?"

"We ran away from home. It was very romantic but a forbidden love."

Savoia stands on the deck watching the water pass the hull. This morning she is transparent as milk-glass. She is failing. Brother Marco senses something very wrong in our lives.

Later, after the evening meal, after dark, Brother Marco and I play dominoes in the wheelhouse. It is a game where the mind can wander. There is something strangely wonderful about being here at sea. It is the absence of place. The freedom of nowhere. Sailing south on a non-existent boat with four men of God. If we had died at sea if we had not been rescued, there would not have been a lone survivor left waving for help. We would have died together. Whenever she leaves me, I will follow her within the minute. I will not grow old alone, eating my plate of fish for supper. When she goes, I will go.

Brother Marco sees there are tears in my eyes. It is the great sadness of losing her that I am unable to face.

He and I go forward. We sit on the dry, fish reeking nets, in the shelter of the lifeboat. I look at him. I cannot see his shadowed eyes under his brow but I can feel them. "I have seen something," he says.

"Yes."

"What is it you need? Do you need to speak to someone?"

"I don't know what you mean, Brother Marco." I'm still clawing around, defending myself against intrusion. I have been doing it for years.

He tells me that this morning he felt the transcendency in our lives, something temporal.

"Can this be true? I do not mean impoliteness, but is the Señora gravely ill? Is something troubling you my friend?"

In that instant, I feel I can speak to him, I feel the need of it. And so I tell Brother Marco, not about me, but about Savoia, my love for her, our very brief life together, and her death in the crash of the Constellation. I say it again, that she is known to have died in the crash. It is so recent he has not heard of it. I tell him why Savoia is here and what I have done because I can do it, because I am imbued with a power. I tell him that this is the measure of my love for her, and that when she leaves me, I will leave, too. He knows what I'm saying. He listens. I feel him absorb my story. I tell him who I have been, what I have done, my real name. When I am through and it is time for him to speak, he says nothing. He looks at the moon, nods, and says goodnight. He walks back to the wheelhouse.

We are due at Gran Canaria sometime in the morning. Tonight, curled together in our pipe bunk on the bare mattress, I feel there is something wonderful about lying here in this fishing vessel run by monks. We have been saved, yes, but for how long and for what? Savoia is leaving. I cannot hold her. I cannot imagine a night without her, waking alone, yet I will not become one of those who sit in rooms, plan nothing, kill time. They are all lifers, anyway, but killing time is a felony, a death sentence.

I have always imagined monastery life to be a dystrophy of the spirit, the loss of creative force. I never thought the monastery to be a fair exchange for a man's life, and I'd always considered monks to be the donkeys in a church stable of racing thorough-breds. Imagine bishops hauling nets, cardinals plowing fields. Popes at sea? These monks are funny men. I hear their laughter day and night. They seem infinitely humble, that is, they have egos but do not need to abase themselves foolishly. They are strong men. Theirs is true humility. They have genuinely banished self-aggrandizement.

We arrive at dawn.

The low land rises gently toward extinct volcanoes. On the deck I feel the dry Sahara wind from the east, just over the horizon.

The cargo of salted fish takes four hours to off-load. We leave the island behind us at ten, bound for Salve de Dios. We reach our destination in the mid-afternoon. From a distance it looks as if the horizon has made an error, revealing a scrawny, edgy, profile. Yet closer, it spreads its volcanoes shoulder to shoulder. It is a broken island put back together in shards.

Brother Marco smiles at me. "I think from what I know of you, I think you will like our island," he says.

"I know I will."

CHAPTER 41

Arrival: February 14, 1964

ৡৣৢ৽

The ocean breathes its waves ashore onto Isla Salve de Dios, from far out to sea in long risings toward the land. I stand beside the wheelhouse with Savoia. The closer we approach the shore the uglier the land becomes. I can see no beaches, no trees, a rare patch of green, black slopes, rounded craters, white stone houses, boats with masts and cranes in a small harbor. We enter to the south, and though the village seems neat and unlived-in, and though nothing of time shows in the square white houses, each with its doors and shutters painted leaf-green, there is a feeling of age and agelessness. We have arrived after a storm has swept sand into doorways and streets.

We have arrived in time for vespers at the Monastery chapel. Savoia and I will spend the night in a cell at the Monastery; it will be arranged.

"When our Brotherhood first came here in the 1700's there were eruptions for a year. It was an act of God."

"A bad one," I say. "Didn't you take it as a sign?"

"Yes, we did. We kept tilling the land and we found that the ash that fell was good for our crops. We worked in the fields during the eruptions. There are a hundred craters on Salve de Dios. Any place can bloom. Even a black island. Do you see those craters? The last one erupted in 1752. These are young volcanoes. We laid the stones for our monastery in 1615."

"Is it still fine?"

"You will see."

"What were the islands like before your people came?"

"There were dogs here, a mystery from historic times, large hairy yellow dogs."

We arrive at the Monastery. It is a natural stone structure two storeys high. Its high arch has stood well over time. At one end there is chapel and a roof that leans. Over its door cut in stone in Spanish *Tiempo Precioso Tiempo* Time Precious Time.

And what is time to these islander monks?

The Monastery: February 14, 1964

We are taken to our cell before vespers—two wooden cots. There is no window. Inside the small room the air is damp. On one wall is a small wooden door held by a spike driven into the rock. I lift it. There is a rounded hole cut clear through the rock, no larger than my head. Brother Marco tells me that if there is a fly in the room at night I should open the hole and it will find his way out. "This room faces east, and when the dawn breaks the fly will rush toward it. We do not kill flies."

A glazed crucifix hangs on the opposite wall. Christ's eyes are open yet glazed. There is a tear in his skin above his heart with an exquisite ruby glob of what must be blood, blood on his palms and feet. It hurts just to look at these untreated wounds. Still, he is surprisingly fit, pale, for a native of the desert. His head is wreathed in a crown of thorns more symbolic than inhumane.

At vespers this evening, the brothers sing. None of them has a grand performance voice yet, combined, their music is overwhelming. In the Chapel there is a figure of the Virgin cradling her blessed son.

We dine in a bald stone room, three or four dozen of us. The quiet surprises me. There is wine with dinner, the thick red wine that is grown and bottled here, a combination of Madeira, sherry, port, even Marsala. It is fortified and I like it immediately.

Brother Marco introduces us to the Abbot. He emits beauty. He revels in his oldness. He is someone to believe in.

In the morning, Brother Marco walks me alone down the hill to the Monastery's gardens. There are potatoes, onions, tomatoes, grapes, garlic, each with recipes as old as the Monastery. The tiny, wrinkled potatoes are cooked in their skins in rock salt. The monks gather salt from the surf below the cliffs. As we walk back uphill to the Monastery, Brother Marco takes my arm gently.

"What you told me last night about your history ... I did not trust myself to respond. But I have spoken to the Abbot. He feels

that yours is an astonishing story and one that he understands."
Brother Marco's eyes are alive. He exudes love. His voice is trembling.

"The Abbot believes me?"

"It may seem unique, but it is not."

"Thank you," I say.

Savoia is waiting outside the Monastery. She nods to Brother Marco.

"Would you like to live here on the island?" Brother Marco asks us.

We haven't talked about it, but without a thought we nod.

"I will ask the Abbot if he will speak on your behalf to the Mayor of Teguise. That is the capital of this island."

"Thank you."

"There is another café in Teguise, where you must enquire about a house to live in."

It is still early. Savoia and I walk. I long to become a walker. Maybe here I will. The sky has reddened. The air is vibrant here. Two miles inland, the wind from the Atlantic blows dry as the Sahara. The scrappy black soil sucks the wet out of it.

We walk feeling the tough earth. Younger women pass us wearing cloth bonnets, linen. Older women wear long black skirts, shawls, wide-brimmed, flat straw hats. They work with hoes in the fields; they resemble mariners home from a lifetime at sea. Everyone smokes small, wrinkled cigarettes.

In Teguise at Café Domingueros, there is no sign posted for a house to buy or rent. A glass saucer and a glass thimble of bad black, Canarian coffee made with sea water knocks my head off. There are no newspapers on the island. As far as I can tell there is no news of the world here—an entertainment I will not miss. Whatever I learned in the Navy world, in the art world, the city world, is useless here. There are no outsiders.

There is a cool, sun-brightening, fibrous breeze, the air already dried by the land it flows across to get to Teguise. It is a young island sharp and black. In another million years it will all be green. Its evolution. And in a million years, what will have become of these monastery stones set in place by the Benedictine brothers 300-years ago? I assume that they will be here and that the monks will be singing Gregorian chants at matins and vespers, regardless of the world outside. But a million years is a very long time and the monks live in a permanent zone of prayer and wonder, their lives spent living in a waiting room, waiting to go to their God. Others came after the first monks, families who lived here centuries ago, a vivid history. They built simple stone houses here, in the Moorish style—white painted stone everywhere, stone floors, green shutters.

We walk. The west. The sweep of it. The dry morning air tempered by the sea, the island, the odd plants that have volunteered to grow. None of the trees and flowers I have known can grow here. There is nothing familiar about this island. It intrigues me. There are no written signs, no words, no directions, no information, no presumption, no advertisements, no lies. I have been used to lies thrown at me daily from all sides, banquets of quick cuts, tiny lies in newspapers, television and in distant billboards and signs. But here there is nothing. It is the law of the land.

We walk. Umber-dust colored slopes of tiny, jagged stones the size of lions' teeth—black, coastal lava still too jagged to walk on. Miniature Grand Canyons of decay, smoothed, scored and holed by the wind-blown sand, have been shaped into natural arcs set in stone, caves for the first settlers to shelter in. Miles of volcanic plains sweep into low dunes, with clumps of dead-looking sage brush. And in the sea, just offshore, stands a wrecked tanker, its steel funnel exposed.

The sea's a good place to start my life. Good as any, better than most. The city crucified me. The sea challenges nothing but the soul. It is a place I do not want to conquer; I simply want to live by it for awhile. This island is the cleanest place, the most mysterious, the most dangerous. In less than a week, the sea has made me feel less alone and more able to live again. The sea has begun to give a shape to my mind; to be surrounded by it comforts me.

At another café called the Parador, we find a sign advertising a house for sale. It is a short walk from the café. We walk to it. It is a classic, one-story, stone house similar to all the others—a Moorish house with three rooms, stone floors, hardwood furniture from Spain. There is no wood on the island, no trees except the ones grown by the monks. We buy it on sight from an old widow who insists that Brother Marco give us his blessing on the house. We will sleep at the Monastery tonight and then move into the house tomorrow.

We walk back up to the Monastery. Brother Marco talks more about the island. He tells us that there are no trains, no airport. No telephones here on the north end, just one on the south end and it is outdoors. There is some electricity in the south as well. Everything on the island closes on Sunday. You can do nothing but be with yourselves that day.

"Cultivating plants here is a great accomplishment, unlike growing them anywhere else," he tells us. "Every seed I plant, the dirt I shovel, the floor I clean, makes me feel euphoric. When I watch sea birds, I watch with intensity."

I buy bags of seeds from the Monastery. I know that planting will be difficult here and I want to grow potatoes, tomatoes, and lettuce—my kitchen garden. I don't know why; I've never wanted one before.

Brother Marco tells us that tomorrow is Ash Wednesday, a special day, when Lent begins forty days of fasting, when it is the custom to sacrifice something you like. He tells us he will give up swimming for Lent.

"What will you give up?" Brother Marco asks me.

"I haven't decided," I say. But I know.

"Then let us go swimming," he says.

We change in our cell in the Monastery. Outside, Savoia walks ahead of us. Brother Marco and I walk slowly, falling far behind her. She and I are separating. Our glue is wet, dissolving. Even when we talk, I feel her drifting away. I watch her in the night, as if she might vanish through the hole in the wall.

The monks are swimming, all of them pale. More than a dozen of them, black-haired, close-cropped. They wear sensible, long suits that resemble winter underwear. There is no beach here. They must approach the water from the jagged rocks, as if the approach were a test of manhood.

"We have bathed from these rocks for three centuries. We swim to cleanse ourselves, to cure ourselves, to relieve pain. Swimming is an entire use of our bodies, not just our backs or our arms," Brother Marco assures me.

For swimwear, Savoia has chosen what she has found in my bag, a long sleeved undershirt that has taken on the color of cream entering coffee. She wears slim panties. She is able to look home-less and provocative at the same time. The ocean is a deep lumi-nous green, malachite, gleaming. The surface is disturbed, unde-cided. She does not want to enter it. I watch her staring out over the water. She knows she will be going back to water. She does not cry. I ask her to talk to me. She looks away, then dives in. She emerges like a seal, her hair pressed against her head.

"Savoia!" I call to her.

She will not answer. She swims away. I dive in. The water is numbingly cold.

It dawns on me suddenly, the illusion in all that I am doing to build a stage set for our lives—buying the house, the seeds. Savoia is not in my future. She has no future of her own. Her future is over. Living an idyllic life here is only a dream. She is vanishing, maybe right now. I can feel her going. I swim a few strokes away from the rocks. She is further out now, swimming away. Waves catch my face, salt water shoots up my nose, my eyes sting. I taste salt. I gulp sea water. I swim out, further and fur-ther. Savoia continues to swim away from me. I am tiring. I swim further, straight out, away from the monks and the black rocks. Savoia stays slightly ahead of me. I am not a good swimmer. "Stop! Don't follow me!" she shouts back.

I push myself further out. She must know what she's doing.

"Turn back Simon! I mean it!"

Too late. We are too far out. We must be a hundred yards from the rocks. I swallow more salt water, cough. My legs are moving quickly, but they seem to do nothing. I have caught up to her now. I sink, my face half underwater. The first cramps cut into my legs. I grab her arm.

"No! No! Stay with me."

"Yes," she says. She is calm.

I'm gasping. I feel the first sharp fear of drowning—burning nostrils, salt-seared throat, the awful invasion of seawater. I cling to Savoia. She will come back with me now. My eyes are open. I can see her through the water. She seems translucent. It is alright now.

A familiar hand grabs me under the arm and yanks me over the side of a rowboat. Savoia helps, then pulls herself up into the boat. Brother Marco, our savior again.

"If I did not know better, Simon, I would think that you two were trying to drown yourselves."

CHAPTER 42

The Abbot: February 15, 1964

૭−⊲

In the chapel a monk is wrapping candlesticks in purple cloth. It is the beginning of Lent, a time of sadness and celebration. After dark, we follow the monks down into an underground chapel in a cavern, walking down a roped path lit by torches. We can hear medieval chanting from deep within, as we descend on the compacted dirt floor. We pass still pools that have never seen the sun. The water is shallow and clear with tiny, white crustaceans that resemble jewelry. The singing grows louder. We enter an opening thirty yards across, with natural, rounded walls curving down to a flat hard floor. The monks stand by their benches, singing Gregorian chants. We take seats along a wall behind the monks. We are in the belly of the island. The sound of chanting reverberates from the walls into our bones. The monks sing on.

Savoia and I can feel the muscle of the chanting as solidly as the island's hardness, yet it seems to have ripened. It is an amazing scene—elegiac, idyllic. I feel hugged, tangled within their mysteries. When it is over, they pray. Then the monks take the torches down from the walls and carry them, walking back up the hooded pathway. We follow them out into the moonlit night, still gripping each other's hand.

Back in our cell, we undress. I open the wind eye. The night air whooshes in. One is not meant to live in a cell of this sort for long, only for penance. It is the perfect guest room. A candle is lit, stocky as a plumber's candle. The open wind eye makes the flame waver. The figure on the cross writhes in the candlelight. Jesus looks Spanish, too pale, probably from loss of blood.

I touch Savoia. We are naked. The cots are covered by hairy blankets. The candlelight catches Jesus's eye. Is he dead or alive? He is fatally wounded, of course, and he will die, that much is certain, but is he already dead? The glint in his eye. Is it a watchful glint or is it a posthumous glint? His eyes meet mine. I decide he is still alive. If he is, will it be possible to make love under his gaze? A dying man is watching us. Or, a dead man not watching us.

Which would be better—to make love beneath a dying Christ or a dead Christ? Neither. Making love tonight is out of the question.

I cannot sleep. I open the door to our cell, walk down the hall, climb up into the bell tower. From its roof I see the island spread out before me in the moonlight. Is there enough here for me alone? I need to prepare myself. There is so much I will never know about Savoia.

Back in our cell, I lie awake on my cot. Someone knocks softly on our door.

"Simon?"

"Yes."

"Did I wake you? It is Brother Marco"

"No, it's all right. What is it?"

"The Abbot wants to speak with you."

I don't ask why. I follow him down the uneven corridor, downstairs, outside across a small courtyard, away from the wind, past a crypt with dozens of markers, under a heavy, corbelled archway. The Abbot is seated in a bald, stone room centuries old that has never been painted, lit only by a lone, squat candle that blinks between us on a dark, plank table.

"Good evening Simon."

"Good evening, Father Superior."

"Candles are dear."

"Yes."

The Abbot is gloriously old—myriad tiny veins crisscross his face.

"Sit down, Simon. Please, join me in a glass of wine."

There are thick greenish glasses without stems, a huge black bottle of wine, a Balthazar. Brother Marco pours three glasses.

"I am told you do not believe in God, is that true?"

"Yes, Father, it is."

"Yet God continues to save you."

"Yes, men of God."

"When Brother Marco found your life-raft you believed in our fishing boat but not in God."

"Yes."

"When you were in the life-raft, did you pray for rescue?"

"Almost."

"Then again, today, you nearly drowned. Brother Marco is constantly saving your life."

"It's true, Father."

"And now, Brother Marco has explained to me what you told him you have done."

"Do you resent me Father?"

"Certainly not. You are a man who possesses an astonishing gift. It is an uncommon gift and it is the essence of miracles. You have also done something that, I daresay, anyone who has lost a beloved soul has longed to do. Miracles are born of God, Simon, and you are well within His domain."

"Yes," I admit.

"I have seen your wife. She is luminous."

The candle gutters. Brother Marco lights another and sets it in the molten tallow.

"She cannot stay much longer, Father Superior."

"Will she vanish?" He seems to grasp everything.

"Yes."

"Do you know when she will go, Simon?"

"I feel she will go when I have arrived."

"What do you mean?"

"Father Superior, for a long time I have been living nowhere. Now I feel I have finally arrived somewhere."

"Your life here is not at an end and when she goes, you will go on living."

"Will I?"

"And we will continue to help you." He smiles.

"It is a question of continuous love. To love someone who has gone into the next room, or to love someone who has gone away is not the same to me."

"Yes, Simon, that is the love of God. You may continue to love her spirit after she has gone."

"But Father Superior, with respect, your God is not a fact. Savoia is. I have her with me. I make love with her. She is a fact who is about to become a memory. I have always felt that I could not love the invisible, yet tonight, in the cave, I was given reasons to."

"We live through prayer, Simon. We think by praying. I can work in a field and do it all at once—work, pray and think. Still, after all these years the work I complete here has a mysterious power over me. I want nothing from the world except what is there for me to behold. As an artist you have lived through your paintings. I imagine writers and composers do, as well. Doctors do it by healing, soldiers by killing, businessmen by harming those less shrewd. No one can take advantage of me except my God. It is our life here. It is all up to us. We do not talk about His glory. There is no need, we are all convinced. We enjoy our hunger. We wait all winter for oranges."

I sit on my cot through the last of the candleless night, feeling the Abbot's words take hold of me. Can he be right? I never thought of monks as being especially smart. Why would they need to be? Haven't they given up? Isn't it all just re-reading texts, transcribing them, laboring in the fields, praying? Quickness, the pride of society, is nothing to them, of course. And yet here the monks seem quick in slow-motion. Whatever cleverness they possess is directed toward simplicity, the elements, the ages of their lives. They understand shadows. They know that their religion is new compared with the age of animals, rocks and the vegetation that they modify. Praying and thinking to them are the same pursuits. I have always believed that God's varied outlets were built by architects who, with peculiar modesty, had claimed that it was God who built the architects.

I am seated in the dark on the cot my hand on Savoia's shoulder, feeling the slight rise and fall of her breathing slowly through the night, as if this night were one of thousands left to us. We will never be together long enough to develop into companion lovemaking, the compromise between need and the fulfillment of an old idea. I'm not waiting for morning. With morning comes day and with day existence. Fact and truth. Loss. I have no body at night.

I am preparing. Savoia cannot be replaced. Who will I wake up to each morning? Who will I admire every day? How will I live without our love-making? Self-denial. Just as the island is deprived of trees, brooks, flowers, hills, animals, beaches. It is as though the island itself is practicing self-denial.

In the morning we move our few possessions into our house. Though there is furniture, Savoia buys pots and pans and utensils at the dry goods store in Teguise to get our kitchen started. She buys a set of pillows and sheets, towels. We spend that night in our new bedroom. I wake with great clarity. I feel a prescience now, that somebody knows more than I do about what is going to happen. It is something urgent, yet unhurried. It is the inevitable.

I stand outside against the stone wall of the house letting the morning sun warm my face and hands. I feel as though I have finally arrived. But I wonder if I really have arrived. I wonder if I am able to live here without Savoia. She cannot be replaced. Is there a term to love? Can I continue to love forever? I suppose I can. What's to stop me?

On the wall behind me an iguana is basking in the sun. We regard each other, then without flinching, the iguana speaks my name.

CHAPTER 43

Salve de Dios: May 18, 2001

And so it ends here on Isla de Salve de Dios. Where it began thirty-seven years ago.

It is late afternoon, I have finished reading the last journal and am trudging up the hill to his house. Has it only been two weeks since I came? No, thirteen days. The richest days of my life. Simon Lister's story has entered my life. It is in me. I am filled with his miracles.

I enter the house without knocking. He has told me never to knock, that knocking startles him. Señora Natti is in the kitchen roasting a chicken in grapes and wine, one of her island recipes from the 1600's. Simon is in his chair where I first saw him so long ago, it seems. He looks at me without saying my name. He will ask me to stay for supper. I only need to stand up for him to say, "Sit down, dinner's on its way."

I'm sure he's guessed. I haven't told him, I pursued him for a year and came to this island to write a book, *Simon Lister: The Lost Years,* his life since his disappearance. It is what I do, of course. I condense people's lives into entities so readers can hold these lives in their busy minds. Lives that they can only imagine through my eyes. I still don't know whether I need to tell him. Does he know? He never mentioned conditions. Maybe he assumes that I will guard his privacy. He seems to trust me. Or maybe he is past caring. Either way, it will be the book of my lifetime. It will crown my career. It will be my legacy.

Today, I need to ask him a few last questions. What became of Savoia, how it ended, how she left him and why he didn't write about her departure in his last journal?

We hardly speak during supper, I cannot bring up my questions.

There is nothing left that he seems to want to say. It has grown dark. I tell him that I will be leaving the island on the weekly steamer tomorrow, and that he has been a gracious, kind host.

After supper, Señora Natti comes in and asks if we need anything more. Simon says, "No." She says goodnight and leaves.

As he has each evening, he half-fills our wine glasses with rum.

He goes to the window and stands as if he were expecting someone.

"There it is," he says, finally. He points to a nearly-waned moon rising low over the horizon. "That'll be her moon," he says. "It seems to bring her to the house." He says the moon tonight is exactly as she left it. He's been waiting for this waning, quarter moon since I came here, this frail shell, nearly gone, that she used to love. "That is her moon," he says again. This must be a monthly occurrence.

It is a perfect opening. But without my asking him, he begins to talk.

"She lived here on the island less than a week."

I wait. I know he will go on. I look around the dim room. I can feel he's lived in it with her memory from the beginning, but how?

"After she went, I came to the painting to look for her. I entered the adobe house but there was no sign of her—no bag, no clothing. She was gone. Outside there was scarcely a breeze. Night after night, I entered the painting looking for her, but the house was always empty and it stayed empty. The painting became an object of great sadness to me.

"May I see it?" I ask him tentatively.

"It's not here."

"What about the other one?"

He knows what I mean. The portrait he painted of her in Vent les Pins. He nods, pushes himself to his feet on both arms of the chair, takes the lantern, leads me through the doorway to the room behind us—the bedroom.

"This is our room," he says. A small reddish cloth covers a picture frame, not a large frame, maybe a foot-and-a-half square.

I have never seen a Simon Lister painting. None of my friends has. I feel time stopping. I stand in the moment knowing I will always remember it. And there it is above the bureau. Simon lifts the cloth.

"My … God!" I am awestruck. It is Savoia. She is in this room and has been here for all these years. Still vibrant and wonderful. I am meeting her on that winter afternoon in the auberge at Vent les Pins, when everything was safe for the moment, but when he could see the end. It is not that she is merely a beautiful woman. She is. There is the wise brow, the short hair, slightly curled, the light in her eyes, the 'child's eyes' of the journals. Savoia's smile, a small smile, her lips unparted. It is the smile he described in the journals and here he has captured it. But it is more than her beauty that touches me, her light eyes bearing so much weight. It is volatile, as if she were speaking to me on that crucial day, and she was. It is so true. I cannot remove my eyes from hers. I am light-headed. I have never actually collapsed, but I feel close to it. I sit on the bed's foot board and stare up at her. I am not only seeing a presence who has never died, I am seeing the lost nature of Simon Lister's art. He truly possesses a dangerous power. It is a masterpiece.

He keeps his eyes down. "I don't look at her very often," he says. "I try not to."

He drapes the painting gently with the reddish cloth as if to preserve her life. We leave the room, returning to the table. He is breathless. I understand. There's no one left to tell. Not around here.

"We spent almost a week together here. She didn't have to stay that long. She could have gone anytime but stayed until she knew I could go on without her." He stops as if that was all there was to it. He begins again.

"In that last week, the smallest things meant so much to her. We talked and talked. We remembered where we'd been. We reminisced, as if we'd been together all our lives. At the Monastery we listened to the Gregorian chants. There was nowhere else we wanted to be, so here we stayed, here on Salve de Dios with a hundred dead volcanoes, and we were happy. Before she went, I spoke to the Abbot and presented the Monastery with enough money to buy all the musical instruments they needed."

"The last morning, early, I was in bed, half asleep. She came out of the bedroom and was dressing in here. I caught a glimpse of her through the open door. I knew it was time. She was sitting on this chair. She had put on stockings and was pulling her navy blue skirt over her head. It was her uniform. She'd kept it rolled up in her suitcase all that time. You understand, she had to go the way she came, and at the exact time of the crash."

He is speaking with difficulty. He has never said this aloud.

"When she had dressed, she came in and bent over me. By then I knew it was over. I was paralyzed with fear, maybe that was part it. I knew what was happening. I was watching something natural happen and I could not intrude. She bent over me and kissed me. She said, "Goodbye," just as if she were going to the goods store. I couldn't say anything to her. It was as if I were held in a spell. But her tears fell on my face. She left the room, went out the door. I heard her heels crossing that little courtyard out there in front of the house. Then a small sound, very clearly, *Tink.*"

He falls silent again. He turns his head toward me. He reminds me of a great animal, a bear or a lion. He wants me to know.

"After a long time, I got up and went outside. She wasn't there, of course. Do you know what the sound was?"

I shake my head, but I do know.

"Her wedding ring, the ring with the blue stone I bought from the child in that village with the bell. She'd dropped it on the stone court-yard."

It is in his hand. He sets it on the table between us. He is not crying. He stops talking for a full minute.

"I don't have to tell you about the suspicions that followed her dis-appearance. I was visited by the local police. The Abbot spoke to them on my behalf. I think I know what he told them."

His voice trails off.

"Anyway, they left me alone after that."

He swirls his drink, looking out across the volcanic gravel, to the ocean.

I hesitate to ask, but I must know what happened to the small painting of the house in the desert.

He nods his head. "I gave it to the Monastery the day after she went away. Brother Marco wrote me a note thanking me for it. 'Such a gentle painting' he called it." Simon smiles. "He saw the house, the palm tree, the moon and the shadows all surrounded by sand. He told me it meant a lot to him but he was never able to tell me why. Maybe someday he will."

"I wish I could see it."

"You can. It's hanging in the Abbot's room."

"Is he still alive?"

"No. Brother Marco is the Abbot now. I'm sure he would enjoy talking with you. Why don't you stop by the Monastery tomorrow before you leave?"

"I will."

We don't move. We are looking away from each other. It is easily the most fascinating story I have ever heard.

Thirty-seven years ago in New York City, Simon Lister, the most potent artist in the world,destroyed his entire body of work. Some despised him for burning his paintings. Some were jealous of his gift, and some idolized him. Some still want him dead; some want him punished, but none will forget him. His story is in me. I believe every word of it. I'm not the same man who came here thirteen days ago.

His biography, *The Lost Years,* is complete, but it is clear to me now that it is not likely to be published for a very long time.

The End

Acknowledgement

სე~ჭ

Words cannot express how grateful I am to Colby Chester who tirelessly worked with me to edit this manuscript and for his amazing cover photograph. Thanks to Liza McKay Madigan for designing the cover and to David Madigan for putting it all together. To Kenna Doeringer for her guidance as I formatted the book.

I would like to express my deepest gratitude to Dura Curry for her professional expertise, and critical reading of the manuscript.

I extend special thanks to Catherine Denisiu, Deborah and Steffen Foster, Richard Fullerton, Robyn Schaefer and Bill Spear who very graciously gave their time to proofread the final manuscript, and to Jeff Ilardi who transferred all the DAT recorded tapes of Trompe L'Oeil, from *Stories on the Wind*, and put them on CD for me.

And I would like to express my eternal gratitude on behalf of Gardner to our wonderful friends who remained supportive and encouraging in my endeavors to publish Gardner's work.

Madeleine McKay

About the Author

જ~્

Gardner McKay, Author and Playwright, was born in Manhattan, 1932. His early years were spent in France, New York, Connecticut and Kentucky.

At age fifteen, He published his first story. Over the next several years he received many awards, including The Drama Critics Circle Award, the Sydney Carrington Prize, National Regional Theatre Award of Canada and three National Endowment for the Arts grants for playwriting. His plays include *Sea Marks, Masters of the Sea, Toyer, Me,* and *In Order of Appearance.*

His novel *Toyer* won critical acclaim upon its release in 1998. Gardner's "Stories on the Wind," a weekly radio show on Hawaii Public Radio ran from 1995 - 2001. He taught playwriting at UCLA and playwriting at USC. He also taught in Juneau, Alaska and at the University of Hawaii at Manoa. He had been a professional skipper, sculptor, photographer and actor, as well as a drama critic for the *Los Angeles Herald Examiner.* In addition to all that, he raised African lions.

During his final year, Gardner wrote his memoir, *Journey Without A Map,* which was published posthumously. *The Kinsman, a novel,* was published in 2012. *Ten, Bloomsbury Square,* a novella, 2015. This book, *Trompe l'Oeil,* was a work in progress from the mid 80s until he completed the novel in 2001, shortly before his death.

Made in the USA
Columbia, SC
08 September 2017